SPLINTERED

THOMAS LONDON

SPLINTERED

Illustrations by Matthew Foltz-Gray

Interior illustrations by Matthew Foltz-Gray
Cover and interior design by Coverkitchen

Library of Congress Cataloging-in-Publication Data
London, Thomas, author.

Splintered by Thomas London.
ISBN: 979-8-9932189-1-5

Printed in the United States of America
First Printing, 2015
Second Edition, 2026

This work is dedicated to those who once believed,

and those who still do.

Prologue

I'll just get this out of the way—all politicians are puppets. None would ever admit it, of course—that wouldn't be very political. Instead, politicians tell "fairy tales." They talk of being the "outsider," or the "sole voice of reason," which is why they alone are immune to the forces that have shaped the stories of their careers. But no matter what a politician may promise in his campaign, his speeches, his television interviews, or his election debates, he can't escape the fact that at some point, in some way, he will eventually be forced to do something he simply doesn't want to do.

This is the story of one such politician. Like his contemporaries, he surrendered his better judgment to the powers that kept him in power, and in doing so became a puppet to their whims. What made this man different, however, was the fact that at one time, he actually was a puppet.

His name was Pinocchio, and all he ever wanted was to *be somebody.*

* * *

When Pinocchio first began his political career, an anonymous existence seemed to be his fate. After college he had accepted a position with a notable lobbying firm, where, in his first six years he had struggled his way from the lowly position of junior analyst to the slightly less lowly position of analyst—*just* analyst. It wasn't for lack of effort, mind you. During meetings he always sat in the front row, his hand raised higher than a fourth grader asking to go potty. It fell to his manager to remind him that analysts were anonymous. "In order to have an opinion," the manager would say, "you had to make a name for yourself." Of course, that's what Pinocchio was trying to do, though the very idea confused him as he already had a name. He just wanted it to be a *well-known* name, even if it was frequently mispronounced, which was, unfortunately, quite frequently.

Pinocchio was just no good at being patient, and as a result, he looked bad: naive at best, incompetent at worst. Pinocchio always seemed to be halfway there, so much so that he had become something of a professional amateur. But everything changed one rainy Tuesday afternoon when Pinocchio ran into a man who would change his life.

That man was Congressman Frank Barnes, and Pinocchio literally ran into him with his Subaru.

Though it was debatable whether or not the accident was his fault, Pinocchio took the blame. But more importantly,

Pinocchio took the secret of just who the congressman had with him in his car. That's where I come into this story. My name is Max Wiggs; I am a reporter for the *Washington Star*, and all I ever wanted was to be Bob Woodward. I wanted to have the ultimate scoop, and even if you had told me, never in a million years would I have believed that Pinocchio would be it.

You see, Barnes was a married man, and the woman he was riding with that day was most certainly not his wife. If that had come out, there would have been a scandal, so at the urging of his boss, Pinocchio told the press that the young lady in Barnes's car was his secretary. Of course Pinocchio may well have believed it, but whether or not he did, it served his boss's purpose. Before long, Pinocchio and Barnes had become friends.

On the surface it didn't seem like much of a story, but there was something about the words Barnes used to describe the young man: "The last honest man in Washington." I ran with it. My article, "The Last Honest Man in Washington Is a Lobbyist," catapulted the unknown analyst to fame. Before he knew it, Pinocchio was on guest lists and talk shows. He was a man everybody wanted to meet. He was a man everybody wanted to like. At last, Pinocchio was *somebody*.

I'll give myself some credit—it was a catchy title, especially considering just who Pinocchio worked for. You see, Pinocchio's firm was founded by the last man to wear that label, a man who also happened to be a penniless immigrant, who also became a famous lobbyist, and, as irony would have it, also happened to be friends with Frank Barnes. That man's name was Aldous Kronos, and you can't fully appreciate Pinocchio's story unless you understand his. So let's step back from the scoop for a moment, and let me tell you the tragic story of the first "last honest man in Washington," Aldous Kronos.

CHAPTER 1

The Tragic Tale of Aldous Kronos

It was before the double-dip scandals and before the rise of the corporations that Aldous Kronos, a son of Greek immigrants and a law clerk for a once-respectable firm, decided to strike out on his own and change the world, one regulation at a time.

When Aldous first arrived in Washington, most lobbying was done by lawyers. But Aldous saw an opportunity to do something different. You see, Aldous felt that for a lobbying firm to be effective, it should be run by passionate, true believers like him—men who saw the best that could be in the government, not the reality of what was. That is why he started *The Kronos Group*, the first firm dedicated solely to lobbying the government of the United States.

Aldous Kronos was a bold, visionary man. He was also one of the twentieth century's great lunatics.

Being an idealist, Aldous could only bring himself to champion bills he actually believed in (which, coincidentally, had little chance of actually passing). As a result, The Kronos Group was almost always broke, just a bad deal or two away from extinction. The associates even joked that if you listened close, you could actually *hear* the firm going bankrupt.

Of course, Aldous could have done what so many of his competitors did and take on the causes that paid the best, whether he believed in them or not. But that would require him to actually *say* things he didn't believe, something the pure-hearted optimist could never bring himself to do. Aldous simply *could not lie*, and while that fact may have made him a decent man, it also made him a terrible politician. His contemporaries inside the Beltway even went so far as to bless him with a nom de guerre that followed him to his grave: "Aldous Kronos—The Last Honest Man in Washington."

In fact, of all the bills that crossed his desk in his years as the country's first professional lobbyist, Aldous Kronos managed to pass just one: H.R. 30110. It just so happened that H.R. 30110 was such a success that it managed to cement the reputation of the fledgling industry Aldous was creating. H.R. 30110 gave the professional paid lobby an aura of idealistic legitimacy that clung to The Kronos Group like a virus, opening doors on Capitol Hill that had previously been locked, moated, and guarded against anyone who even resembled a paid lobbyist. Only Aldous could have done this, and he could only do it with that bill, for you see, my friends, H.R. 30110 saved the speckled owls.

Kronos had a bad habit of choosing good causes, as causes rich in virtue were often poor in financing, and the owls were no exception. It fell to a rather vocal group of commune leftovers to bring the bill to Kronos's desk, and despite the pleas of his accountants, Kronos took the job. He knocked on over a hundred doors before he came to the office of an ambitious freshman from Tennessee who, despite the pleas of *his* political strategists, decided to listen.

His name was Frank Barnes, and though he may have waded through his first year in Congress posing as a pragmatist, just waiting to make his presence known, was the true believer Tennessee had actually elected—and would thereafter for fifteen consecutive terms. There was no better way to do that than by taking on H.R. 30110.

Barnes was never unrealistic about the bill's chances. The recession was on and America was ready to get back to business, even if that business was as unsexy as cutting down trees. But still, the gas crunch and the atomic meltdown had given him a rare opportunity; at that moment, the environment was ripe to champion an environmental cause. What followed was a feat of remarkable statesmanship full of late-night calls, pledged favors and poetic speeches. It was lobbying at its best, and when it was over, America sided with the raptors by a two-thirds majority. Aldous Kronos, with Frank Barnes's help, had done what people had once thought impossible—he had given voice to the voiceless.

The owls were a remarkable success, but the remainder of Kronos's career was a tragic tale—a story of middling failure that ended with his untimely death some ten years later. But before he shuffled off this mortal coil, he imparted to a young junior associate all of his wisdom and ways, though not his interest in the firm. That he left to his young widowed bride—mere pennies for a lifetime spent together.

With Aldous's passing, The Kronos Group lost not only its leader, but also the key to its reputation, and before long, both partners *and* clients were walking away. Recognizing this, as well as the ruinous financial situation that resulted from his mentor's morality, the new head of the firm quickly steered The Kronos Group in a different direction. He put compunction aside and focused on the business of business, rapidly expanding the client base beyond the noble causes of its founder to include companies with deep pockets (if shallow hearts). It was no longer the idealistic endeavor that Aldous had founded, but within a few years, The Kronos Group was better than a money-printing machine. Thanks to a former junior partner named Charles C. Stevens, the firm knew wealth beyond the dreams of Midas, and Aldous Kronos finally managed to make a decent living only a few years after his death.

Headquartered in a four-story, glass-front building on 18th and K, Kronos cast a remarkably long shadow from such a small footprint. Answering to just two partners who knew from memory the names of all the husbands, wives, children, (and lovers) of every member of the lawmaking bodies of the country, for the next thirty years, the mark of The Kronos Group would be found on almost every law that passed under the president's pen.

Stevens owed his success to one very important—and obvious—factor: He understood his business. Stevens knew that a lobby firm worked on behalf of its clients to influence the laws crafted by Congress and interpreted by the bureaucracy, which, despite its valiant efforts, still ran the government of the United States. It did so *without* passion, for unlike his mentor, Stevens knew that passion could sway both a lawmaker's judgment, and his own. Certainly there were still firms that thought the way Aldous did, but they never gained the same traction as Kronos. In the end, they were mere minnows for the sharks, and The Kronos Group never seemed to satisfy its hunger for minnows.

Stevens was ruthless. He reveled in the hunter's taste. His eyes lit up when he described to an industry trade group the wondrous weapons he held in his arsenal, and exactly how he would employ them in the advancement of a new law, or in the defense against one. He was a great salesman, just as skilled in hooking the one-shot, one-cause clients as the whales who never seemed to satisfy their appetite for favorable regulation. Of course, Kronos never let them down. Make no mistake, Stevens was successful because he was effective, and planet Washington hated him for it. He was a shark, eating everything he saw, regardless of whether or not he was hungry; and the moments he wasn't hunting new clients, he was doing his good work, bending the ears of lawmakers, and sometimes breaking them. Though never elected, for thirty years, Charles Stevens was one of the most powerful—and infamous—men in Washington. But inside the Beltway, infamy need not be a curse, as the key to influence lay in the ability to have one's voice heard, even if it were spoken by the devil himself. In Washington, the only thing worse than infamy was anonymity.

CHAPTER 2

The Manner by Which Pinocchio First Learned the Danger in a Smile

It is fair to say, dear friends, that before the article came out, young Pinocchio had not made much of an impression on his executive management; but that's not to say that he had not made an impression on anyone. For months, Pinocchio's every move had been watched by interested eyes, jealous eyes, *green* eyes—and Pinocchio, being a curious and inquisitive sort, had noticed them as well. Her name was Cassandra. She was a senior associate in Kronos's policy group, which, as fate would have it, was just down the hall from Pinocchio's cubicle. She was not an unattractive lady, though she had a dubious reputation around the office. You see, my friends, she too was a curious type, though her curiosity was not quite so innocent as Pinocchio's.

Cassandra had a tendency to turn her eyes toward men who were in a position to advocate for her, though it was not always the mere fact of their position that attracted her. Cassandra was simply fascinated with men whose belief in their own ability was their greatest strength. Washington was crawling with such men, and Cassandra's mission was to know every one of them.

One might wonder then, how it was that our dear friend, an anonymous employee who carried himself in a decidedly non-assured manner (and was most certainly not in any position to advocate for her), managed to tickle her imagination. Pinocchio would later wonder that as well, for as was so often the case in his relations with the fairer sex, he had absolutely, positively no idea what they were thinking.

Every day, Pinocchio's frequent trips to the printer took him past the ever-more-curious woman in green. Each time he passed, her eyes darted from her monitor to the smiling analyst who seemed ever so excited about a visit to the printer. Pinocchio began each and every trip by whistling a tune—some happy melody from some place in his memory—yet so often was it heard around the office that to Cassandra, it began to seem familiar. Pinocchio ended each and every trip with a smile and a wave. It didn't matter how many trips a day he made, it didn't matter if he had just done so a moment earlier; he never seemed to tire of seeing those eyes watch him each and every time he waved and shouted,

"HI-LO!"

What sort of man is this? Cassandra would wonder. He seemed so curious about her, but never made any effort to meet. True, the man wore a wedding band on his finger, but in Cassandra's experience, even the most married of men quickly forget that fact when someone in a green dress made it her business to know them. This man was different. He never introduced himself, he never stopped to pay her a compliment, and he never seemed to notice that she always smiled his way.

Until that day ...

"HI-LO!"

Cassandra looked up just in time to catch the blur racing by, a know-nothing grin on his face and a tune tooting out of his lips. That day she was not content to simply let him go by without responding, "HI-LO yourself!"

Pinocchio screeched to a halt, albeit a few steps past her desk. He crept back. His smile was still there, but it faded quickly when he saw that Cassandra's expression didn't quite match her tone. In fact, she was quite serious.

They stared at each other for what seemed like two whole minutes (it was actually four), when finally she leaned into her elbows, pushing her cleavage far in front of where it needed to be, and let her glasses slip down until those green eyes crested the rim. Pinocchio was at once both intrigued and terrified. It was a most confusing feeling, one shared by 97 percent of the male population on this planet when the attentions of a beautiful woman seem to render them helpless. Cassandra was well aware of this phenomenon, and she knew it was up to her to make the next move.

"So what's your name?" she asked. "You always say 'Hi,' but never introduce yourself. I'm Cassandra."

"And I'm Pinocchio."

"That's quite a mouthful," she said.

"No," continued Pinocchio, "that's my name."

"Well, Pinocchio, what's 'Hi-lo' all about?"

"That's how I greet people, but I only use it when I'm greeting beautiful women, because it's the easiest way to answer a big question."

"And what question would that be?" Cassandra asked.

"The question of what to say when I meet a beautiful woman. Sometimes I want to say 'Hi,' and sometimes I want to say 'Hello,' and I can't ever make up my mind by the time they pass me by. So I say both, and neither."

Cassandra had to admit, it was genius. "Well, Pinocchio," she said, "I suppose I should thank you."

"Thank *me*?" he asked.

"Sure! I mean, if you only say 'Hi-lo' to beautiful women, you must think I'm beautiful."

For a moment, it seemed Pinocchio forgot how to talk. Cassandra saved him from having to. She continued, "I accept the compliment."

"My-welcome!" Pinocchio replied. "My pleasure *and* you're welcome." Cassandra smiled as she ran her fingers through her hair. There was something to this boy. Cassandra didn't know exactly what, but she did know how to find out.

"So where are you on your way to in such a big hurry?" she asked.

"To see Mr. Stevens!" Pinocchio announced. "He says he has a big surprise for me."

"Are you busy after work?" she asked.

"Well ..." Pinocchio thought about it very hard. "I work until five thirty, but I have to be home by seven."

"Is your mama expecting you for dinner?" she asked, jokingly.

"No," replied Pinocchio, quite seriously. "My wife is."

Cassandra drew back a bit. "Oh, well, she's a lucky woman to land herself such a handsome man."

Beaming, Pinocchio started to turn when Cassandra continued, "You know, Pinocchio, you can also say, 'thank you' for that handsome comment."

He paused. "Oh, I suppose I can." Again, he turned to go ... but this time Pinocchio stopped himself. "Uh, you—you really think I'm handsome?"

Cassandra nodded and shot him a smile, but a smile unlike any of the sly grins she had drifted the boy's way earlier. This was a smile she had perfected over a lifetime spent talking to men, and it never failed to have the desired effect. This was no gift. This smile was a trap, and the image of it hung off of Pinocchio's very thoughts as he hurried off.

Like any man, Pinocchio found Cassandra to be a most attractive woman—but he was content to leave her that way. You see, my friends, Pinocchio was married, and worse still, he was in love with his wife. On the surface, it would seem Pinocchio was one of those rare men for whom Cassandra's affections would forever remain a mystery. But still, he had to admit that there was something about her smile—it warmed him. It made him remember that he was still a man, and as she pointed out, quite a handsome one at that. Cassandra's smile made Pinocchio feel perfectly safe, which was the first sign that he was in terrible danger.

* * *

Cassandra's sweet words still dancing around his head, Pinocchio was a twitterpated mess by the time the elevator hit the executive floor. He had promised himself he would be composed for this meeting, that he would stand up straight and march proudly into Charles Stevens's office, but Pinocchio was never very good at keeping promises.

As he approached the cubicle of Charles Stevens's executive assistant, Nancy DelGreco, he paused and tried to pull himself together.

Nancy looked up to find that a smirking boy was standing over her. Nancy DelGreco was known as a hard-edged woman around the office—a no-nonsense type who, on the surface, wouldn't seem to tolerate such childish antics. Part of Nancy's toughness came from thirty years of putting up with Charles Stevens's temper, but it had also come from giving birth to five children. Fortunately for Pinocchio, it was the motherly side of her that took over. She shook her head, slipped off her thick reading glasses, and asked, "It's been a good day, young man?"

"Yes, ma'am!" Pinocchio replied. "I'm here to see Charles Stevens!"

"You must be Pinocchio," she said. "Why don't you have a seat, and when Mr. Stevens is ready, I'll buzz you in."

But Pinocchio didn't take a seat. Instead, he stared at the aging secretary, his smile turning to a look of pure amazement.

"What's the matter with you?" Nancy asked.

"You're—you're the only person who's ever pronounced my name right!"

Nancy grinned. "I'm a third-generation Boston Italian, son. Now take a seat, and I'll call you in a moment."

Pinocchio sat in a short-backed leather chair and took in the surroundings. Above Nancy's desk hung a plaque—a nice one, etched in brass and fastened to a finely finished piece of oak. The words read like a prayer, though even the very Catholic Pinocchio couldn't place it:

Oh Lord, thy sea is so big and my boat is so small.

"Ma'am," he asked, "what is that plaque?"

Nancy kept typing as she glanced over her shoulder. "My grandfather gave that to me the day I got married."

"What does it mean?" he asked.

She stopped typing, peered over her glasses in that most schoolteacher-like way. "It's the 'Fisherman's Prayer.' It means you're not alone. Even in the middle of the ocean, you can always count on God to protect you."

"Do you fish?" he asked.

"No," she said as she went back to her typing, "but in this city, you're surrounded by sharks."

Nancy's phone buzzed. She nodded at Pinocchio, who made his way toward the double oak doors. As he pulled them open, Nancy added, "By the way, I read your article."

"You did?" he asked.

She nodded. "Actually, I thought it was ... quite touching."

Pinocchio smiled, and headed inside.

* * *

The only thing bigger than Charles Stevens's desk was Charles Stevens himself. At almost six foot four, he towered over his employees. He was a hefty man, but he carried his weight mostly in his shoulders, which made him a most intimidating presence in his trademarked double-breasted suits. His ice-white eyes could either stare through you or agree with you. Depending on the situation, Charles Stevens was either a terrifying monster, or a kind grandfather; and he was most skilled at using both.

He sat behind his desk and thumbed at a copy of the article. "So what do you know about this kid?" he asked.

Dominic Bayard, a well-built gentleman of about sixty was the firm's senior partner and Stevens's second-in-command. He helped himself to a cappuccino from a $3,000 machine as he replied, "He wrote a report about Aldous back in college, and one of his professors sent it to us. We gave him an interview, and he's been here ever since. I checked his performance reports; nothing too spectacular."

"What school did he go to?" Stevens asked.

"Berkeley," Dominic replied.

That caught Stevens's attention. He picked up the phone and ordered, "Send him in."

The doors swung open and Pinocchio stepped meekly inside.

"Mr. Pinocchio?" Dominic asked. Pinocchio nodded. "Please, have a seat. I'm Dominic Bayard; I'm one of the partners here. And I'm sure you know Mr. Stevens ..."

It was only then that Pinocchio saw the rather intimidating man behind the rather intimidating desk. "Pleased to meet you, Mr. Pinocchio," said Stevens as he stood and extended a hand.

"Pleased to meet YOU, Mr. Stevens. And it's just Pinocchio."

"Pinocchio ...," said Stevens, curiously. "Is that your first name or your last name?"

"I don't have a first name ... or a last name," he replied. "I'm just Pinocchio."

Stevens leaned back against his desk and began, "Well, Pinocchio, I'm sure you know why we called you in here. That article has made you quite the sensation."

"That's right," said Dominic, "we're proud of you!"

"*Pr-proud* of me?" Pinocchio asked.

"You bet!" continued Stevens. "I read that article and I said to myself, 'Wow! Now there's a man with integrity!' We need good people like you, Pinocchio."

"Well that's me!" Pinocchio exclaimed. "I am a good ... people."

Stevens chuckled. He slid an arm around Pinocchio's shoulder and asked, "So, tell me, what do you like best about our firm?"

But before Pinocchio could answer, his eyes drifted down to the glistening metal band on Stevens. Pinocchio didn't know what it was, but it was simply the most amazing thing Pinocchio had ever seen. "Your watch," he announced.

Puzzled, Stevens asked, "My watch is what you like best about our firm?"

Pinocchio shook himself back to consciousness. "No sir, that's not what I meant! I just noticed your watch; it's beautiful!"

Stevens smiled. The latch released with a metallic *clack!* as he handed the timepiece over to the young analyst. "You have good taste, young man. That's Swiss-made, very expensive. It was a gift from my mentor—Aldous Kronos."

"The man who founded the firm?" asked Pinocchio.

Stevens nodded. "Aldous taught me everything I know about lobbying, and not the least of which is to appreciate things of value. I think we have that in you, Pinocchio."

Dominic picked it up. "We need an honest man speaking for our clients."

"One with the press on his side," Stevens added.

"Pinocchio, what we're saying is—we want to offer you a promotion. We checked your records; you're always on time, and your work is impeccable. We think you're ready to move up to something a bit more visible."

"What do you say to junior partner," asked Stevens.

"Junior *partner*?" Pinocchio clarified. He could not believe his ears.

Stevens continued, "We have a very important bill we're repping right now—"

"Very important," said Dominic.

"Something that's popular with the people, but not with Congress. So we want you to go with us down to Avalon to talk about it."

"What's Avalon?" Pinocchio asked.

"Avalon is a resort casino in the Caribbean," Stevens replied. "It's a whole island."

"So pack your bags," Dominic continued, "because we leave tonight. We need you, Pinocchio. We want you to be the voice of the people."

"You want *me* to be the voice?" Pinocchio asked.

"The people need to hear an honest man," Stevens replied.

"And there'd be quite a bump in salary," Dominic added.

"What do you say, son?" Stevens asked as he slipped a grandfatherly arm around Pinocchio's shoulder. "Would you like the job?"

CHAPTER 3

Pinocchio's Family

"Centuries ago there lived—"

"A king!" little Albero said immediately.

"No, my boy, you are mistaken." Old Geppetto adjusted his glasses and scanned the book—he had lost his place again, though Albero hardly noticed. Albero was, like all grandsons, transfixed by any story his grandfather told. He listened with the sort of admiration given only by little boys, and given only to grandpas.

"Ah, there we are!" Geppetto continued. "Once upon a time there was a piece of wood. It was not an expensive piece of wood. Far from it. Just a common block of firewood, one of those thick solid logs that are put on the fire in the winter to make cold rooms cozy and warm—"

"You put *wood* on your fire, Grandpa? Why don't you just turn on the gas?"

Geppetto smiled. "Yes, things have certainly changed, haven't they? Not much use for wood anymore. But it was not this way when I was a little boy in Italy—"

"What is Italy?" Albero asked.

"It is a country very far from here—all the way in Europe! It is where your papa and I are from."

"How long does it take to drive there?"

The old man chuckled. "But, my boy, you cannot drive there; there is an ocean between us and them, the Atlantic Ocean. No, no, we must take a ship, but you know, if you do, you must be ever careful, for the ocean is where the great whale lives."

"The same one that swallowed you, Grandpa?"

"The very same, and he swallowed your papa, too! We would have stayed there the rest of our lives if not for your papa's bravery—and his wisdom. You see, Albero, your papa knew how to think like the whale, for the two of them are from the same place—the world of *growing*. That's why your papa knew just what to say to him."

"But how can a whale understand a person?"

"When you sit in the woods and stare at the clouds, you visit the world of growing, and it is here that you can talk to the animals. Everyone can do it, though they so seldom do. We hear the wind, but we don't hear her song. We walk through the woods, but don't stop to greet the trees. When we happen upon a deer, or a rabbit, or a bear, we run off, scared, not knowing that if we but took the time to make their acquaintance, we may enjoy the most delightful of conversations—that is, as long as the creature is in a good mood and doesn't decide to eat us up instead!"

He poked at the boy's belly, who giggled and rolled away—nearly falling off the tree swing.

"Do animals really talk, Grandpa?"

"Of course they do! They have lives of their own, thoughts of their own, hopes of their own, and even dreams of their own. They can be brave, and they can be scared, and sometimes they can be too proud and even become boastful. But from the most pleasant little crab who strolls along the beach to the most sour old maple who stands by the roadside—always they live in the world of growing, where each knows their place. They never venture into the world of men, the world where all grown-ups must go—the world of *counting*..."

Pinocchio was careful to keep out of sight as he watched through the window. The image of the old man reading to the boy brought him back to a time—eons ago, it seemed—when *he* was the little boy, and his father was just a little less old. The two of them swung gently back and forth, Albero's kicks a little more enthusiastic than his grandfather's. There was no denying that Geppetto's age was catching up to him. Of course, he wasn't exactly a young man when Pinocchio was born. Pinocchio could never understand what kind of woman would want to be with an old man like Geppetto—even if he were Italian. Geppetto never answered his questions about her, always rolling off some nonsensical response like, "*But, my boy, you know your mother.*" Eventually, Pinocchio stopped asking.

Still, since Geppetto had retired, Pinocchio was pleased that he had moved to be so close to the family. He came over at least once a week, and Albero was always excited, like grandchildren often are, when Grandpa stopped by.

"Hello, Pinny," said Whitney, interrupting his train of thought. "I didn't know you were home!"

Pinocchio turned, pausing for a moment to gaze at what he thought was the most beautiful image he had ever seen, his own wife. Though they had been married for years, he still found himself speechless for a moment every time she walked into the room. Finally, he broke the trance and replied, "They gave me the afternoon off." He checked his watch, a rubber-wrapped digital that was at least ten years old. "I got home maybe five minutes ago."

Whitney chuckled. "You still wear that old thing?" she asked. Pinocchio nodded, not really understanding the question. True, the watch was old—not so old it had become charming like an antique radio, but the kind of old that betrayed the owner's limited means. She had given it to him in college, a way to keep the curious young boy on time—he was often late to classes, to dates, even to his own graduation. Whenever a professor, girlfriend or dean of the college asked him why, his answer was always the same—he had followed a butterfly to see where it went. Pinocchio was curious about such things, and Whitney knew it would cost him more than a grade point average in the real world. It was just a cheap watch, but that it came from Whitney made it more valuable to him than diamonds and pearls.

"Well, I'll go finish getting supper ready," she said. "Why don't you go and call those boys to eat?"

As she wandered off to the kitchen, Pinocchio's attention was drawn to the window as Albero giggled again. A five-year-old's giggle is one of those rare sounds that can transcend glass and drywall, especially to a parent's ears, which are specially tuned to such sounds. Watching Geppetto read his story, Pinocchio realized what a fine grandfather he was, and a fine father, too. Secretly, Pinocchio knew he couldn't say the same for himself.

He never told anyone this, but sometimes it seemed as if all he could manage was to cause heartache; he put a hole in the wall trying to hang the shelf Geppetto had made for them, and it was up to the old carpenter to come and fix it; he cut the grass too short and killed it, and now Albero had to roll around in a dry, yellow patch all summer; and, of course, Whitney never let him forget the time he spent the entire week's grocery budget on cereal because that's what Albero said he wanted.

As a parent, he just couldn't seem to get things right. Pinocchio felt less than worthless; he felt meaningless—and worse, he was all alone in this feeling, for as Geppetto had often told him, a man's role is not to burden his family with troubles.

But everything would change now, he was sure of it. He couldn't wait to tell everyone the good news, and dinner seemed like the perfect time to do it.

"Do animals really talk, Grandpa?"

* * *

The conversation at the Pinocchios' table was usually boisterous. Geppetto loved to talk while he ate, so much so that he hardly got a bite in edgewise—but tonight was different; tonight it was the son who had a big announcement to make. But before he got the chance, Albero decided to share the exciting new fact that he had learned just that afternoon—

"Papa was a stick!" he announced.

Whitney and Pinocchio stopped mid-chew and traded glances. Children often said confusing things, and it fell to Whitney to clarify. "What do you mean, Albero?"

"Grandpa Geppetto told me that Papa was a stick when he was little."

Whitney laughed. "What Grandpa meant was that your father was very skinny when he was a boy. He was skinny when I met him too."

But Albero held firm. "No, he was a real stick, like a stick of wood. Grandpa carved him into a puppet so he could walk and talk!"

Pinocchio's fork dropped against the plate, banging so loudly that even Geppetto stopped eating. But Albero was unfazed. "And he burned his own feet off in the fire, and Grandpa had to carve him new ones—and then, when Grandpa was swallowed by the whale, Papa talked his way out of the whale's belly and the fairy made him a real boy!"

"Dad, I really wish you wouldn't tell him these stories," Pinocchio said before turning to his son and explaining, "Albero, those are just fairy tales. Your Grandpa didn't carve me into a puppet—"

"Yes I did," said Geppetto.

"And animals don't talk."

"Yes they do!" said Albero.

Pinocchio threw his hands in the air, and tagged out to Whitney.

"Albero," she explained, "some animals do talk, but only to each other. Do you understand the difference?"

Albero shook his head.

"You see that, Dad?" Pinocchio huffed. "He believes every word!"

"Why shouldn't he? It's the truth."

"You tell him this nonsense and one day he's going to run across a fox, try to talk to it, and the damn thing's going to bite him."

"Oh no, I told him to stay clear of foxes. You can't trust a word they say."

Pinocchio gritted his teeth. "Whitney, will you take Albero into the living room?" She nodded, gathered their plates, and left her husband to straighten the matter. She couldn't help but agree with him—sometimes fairy tales could be quite dangerous if children were to believe them.

Geppetto waited until they were safely out the door before he continued, "I don't see what you're so upset about. You grew up with these stories and you turned out fine."

"Well, as a matter of fact, I did get a promotion today—"

"Promotion," Geppetto huffed. "What's so important about a promotion? I don't even understand what you do at that company."

"I've explained it a hundred times, Dad. We argue for laws to be changed—"

"Argue all day? My goodness, what a job! And now you bring your work home and argue all night, too!"

"I'm not arguing; I'm telling you. He's my son and I don't want you filling his head with this absurdity. Just stop with the fairy tales, will you do that for me, Dad? Please!"

Geppetto nodded. "I promise you, no more fictions." He wandered into the kitchen, shouting back, "So what is it you do with this promotion?"

"Well, tonight I leave for Avalon Island to go meet with some very important—" He froze. *Tonight*. He checked his watch. "Oh, no!" he cried as he leaped up from the table. His flight left in ninety minutes, and he still hadn't told his wife!

* * *

"A promotion?" Whitney asked as she stood outside the hallway closet.

Pinocchio had buried himself headfirst, digging around for a suitcase. He replied, "Junior partner!"

"Just like that? Analyst to executive—"

Pinocchio was too excited to hear the skepticism in her voice. He scooted back out, a dusty garment bag in hand.

"Yes, can you believe it? To think, I was actually worried this would never happen—but Cassandra said—"

"Who's *Cassandra*?"

"My shaving kit!" Pinocchio leaped up the stairs, continuing the conversation through doors and walls. "She's a woman with green eyes—she invited me out to have a drink today but I told her I couldn't because I had to be home for dinner. But now that we're going to Avalon together, I think I might get to have one after all!"

"And what's Avalon?" Whitney asked.

"It's a whole island!"

"Most islands are, Pinny."

"I mean it's a whole island that's a casino! It's in the Caribbean. Mr. Stevens is sending me there to meet with a group of congressmen—*shampoo!*"

Pinocchio tore through the medicine cabinet, tossing bottles and containers across the floor, which Whitney tried her best to pick up. "Pinocchio, don't you think this is all a bit sudden? Yesterday you couldn't even get your supervisor to email you, and today you're going to the Caribbean to lobby?"

"Cassandra said it happens that way sometimes. Doors close fast and you have to be quick if you want to get on the elevator."

Cassandra's no philosopher, she thought. Whitney didn't like this. Even though she had forsaken a corporate career for the nonprofit world, Whitney still had a sense about these things, and she knew full well that a man as seasoned as Stevens didn't just promote unknown associates to full lobbyist unless there was an angle. She also had a good idea what that angle was ...

"What did he say about the article?" she asked.

"Who?"

"Charles Stevens."

"He loved it! He said it opened his eyes to what a value I am to the firm!"

Whitney took his hands into hers, slowing the furious pace of his packing. "Pinny, pay attention to me."

He looked up, his confused face meeting her concerned one.

"Whatever happens down there—" She stopped herself. It was obvious what was happening—Stevens was using Pinocchio's accidental fame to advance some agenda of his. She dreaded to think what it might be, but Pinocchio was excited, ready for an adventure, and dare she say it—*proud. Who was she to take this away from him, to sully this little miracle with her doubts and concerns?* He was on his way to talk face-to-face with powerful men, and any fear he showed would be deadly to his career, and that fear would be because of what she said to him right now. She couldn't warn him—but she did want to remind him in a subtle, even cryptic way, that if he found success, it would only be because he was an honest man.

"Be yourself," she said.

"What do you mean?"

"I mean just that. When you meet with these men tomorrow, say what you mean, and do what you say. That article was written about you because you're honest. So just be honest, and everything will work out OK. Promise me, Pinny."

Pinocchio nodded. She smiled, and handed him the shampoo bottle that had been hiding in plain sight the whole time. "So tell me a little bit more about this *Cassandra*. I've never heard you mention her before ..."

"I don't talk to her very much. Dan Spence says she's a 'maneater.' I didn't know what that was, so I figured it was best to stay away. But she seems nice."

"They always do. Be careful, Pinny." She leaned over and gave his forehead a kiss. He moved to return the favor when the sound of a taxi's horn interrupted.

"That's my ride!"

He shoved bottles and razors into the suitcase as he flew down the stairs. Whitney threw out one last caution before he disappeared through the door: "And don't gamble too much!"

He paused. "What do you mean?"

"You said you're going to a casino."

“They gamble there?” She nodded. “So THAT’S what she meant!”

“Who?”

“Cassandra. She said if I was good, I might get lucky on this trip. Well, goodbye!”

CHAPTER 4

Outside of Washington, Pinocchio Learns the Insider's Game

After changing planes in Miami, it took the little puddle-jumper just twenty-six minutes to reach the airfield of the Caribbean paradise called *Avalon*. As the door opened, a blast of humidity rushed into the cabin, literally taking Pinocchio's breath away. He inched his way to the front of the plane, joining a menagerie of retirees, golf pros, and dentists—each one sporting a new straw fedora that bordered on the obscene.

Navigating down the plane's rickety steps, Pinocchio shielded his eyes from the sun. The weather was a perfect eighty-eight degrees and there wasn't a cloud to be seen. The roar of a twin-engine jetliner drowned out the cheerful instructions of the ground crew who guided the gaggle off the tarmac. Little better than a thatch-roofed waiting room, the terminal served to transfer the passengers to a commuter bus emblazoned with the impressive logotype of the Avalon Resort and Casino.

Pinocchio had never been to the tropics before, and between the noise of the airfield and the crash of the ocean beyond, he felt dizzy. The plush seat on the bus was a welcome relief from the airplane's thin fabric bleachers. Moments later the bus rounded the last turn, and the majesty of the resort itself came into view. Rising some forty stories above the wave-licked sand, Avalon was a vision in fantastic plaster. Four medieval turrets reached upward, dotted with enough windows to render them ineffective for siege defense. Behind every window lay an oversized suite complete with a painted-marble Jacuzzi, microfiber sheets and all the simulated luxuries expected in a simulated vacation.

Behind the castle, the artificial greens of an eighteen-hole golf course covered what should have been sand. To the west lay a series of pools, hot tubs, and the much-advertised dolphin paddock—every manner of distraction meant to keep the kids busy while their parents enjoyed the trappings of the adult amusement park within.

The bus glided to a stop under a glowing archway. A glass wall, which continually opened and closed, blasted the chilling breeze of air-conditioning. With hydraulically actuated teeth, the Avalon seemed to devour entire tour groups in itty-bitty bites.

The scale of the structure impressed Pinocchio, but the casino floor inside astonished him. Rows of game tables stretched so far that they seemed to vanish into infinity. Above the hum of gamblers was the sound of coins crashing into metal plates as a thousand slot machines paid out ever so much less than they took in.

A thin man dressed as a squire ushered the group to the reception desk, where a labyrinth of red velvet ropes shuttled the guests one and two at a time to a smiling, blue blazer-clad hostess, who tip-tapped away at a hidden computer, trading credit cards for key cards. Another smile, and another guest checked in. Pinocchio took his place in line and patiently awaited his smile.

"Astounding," said a man behind him. Pinocchio didn't mean to eavesdrop, but the heavyset gentleman had such a distinctive voice: "Nothing like what we have in Vegas."

"That's just the point, Congressman. Look at the money here. Every penny spent by an American, and not one cent of it taxable."

Congressman? Pinocchio dared a peek. There, not eight inches from him, stood the legendary fifteen-term congressman from Tennessee, Frank Barnes. Pinocchio had met the man only once on that day when their fates literally collided. Now, here he was, in the flesh—and perspiring profusely under a wool suit. *What should he do?* Pinocchio was here to talk to this man, after all. He was so busy trying to decide, he didn't even notice that the congressman was already talking to *him*.

"Son!"

Pinocchio snapped out of it. "Yes sir! Congressman Barnes, do you remember me?" he asked with an outstretched hand "My name is Pinocchio."

Barnes took the hand, but his eyes never met Pinocchio's. He tried to continue, "Yes, son, but—"

"I overheard your discussion just now about tax dollars, and—"

"Well—"

"And, oh, how rude. I'm with the firm of Kronos, I mean the Kronos firm. Place. *Group*. The Kronos Group!"

"I'm sure—"

Pinocchio only then noticed his hand hadn't been shaken. He yanked it away and thrust it into his bag, pulling out an oversized presentation folder. "Our firm has taken a very unique view on the issue of overseas gaming—"

"Look, son—"

"If you would just turn to page three hundred and twenty-six ..."

"SON!"

"Congressman?"

"You're next."

Pinocchio followed the congressman's sharply pointed finger to an open queue, where a blue blazer should have been smiling—but wasn't.

"Oh."

Pinocchio's embarrassment only amplified when the folder slipped from his hand and went crashing to the ground in a spectacular explosion of PowerPoint graphs. Everyone in line behind him groaned. Unsure what else to do, Pinocchio fell to his knees and began scooping up pages. The groans turned to open displays of aggression.

"Come on!"

"Just move!"

"GO!"

That's when the most marvelous thing happened. Frank Barnes, the wise old lawmaker from Tennessee, knelt down and began scooping up paper.

"A little over-eager, aren't you, son?" he asked.

Pinocchio couldn't help but agree. "I just, when I heard your voice—"

"I know, I know. But there's a reception later. I think that would be the time—"

The mob was ready to guillotine them. Barnes had had enough. "What are you, sheep? Just go around us!" he declared.

As the line began to filter around, Barnes chuckled. "So are you new at this, Pinocchio?"

Pinocchio didn't think he could be more surprised than he was a second ago, but Barnes proved him wrong. "My name!"

"Is *Pinocchio*, right?"

"You remembered it—you pronounced it right, too!"

Barnes smiled as he shoved the last of the crumpled presentation into Pinocchio's bag. "*The Last Honest Man in Washington*," he said. "Now there's something to be proud of." Without another word, the congressman made his way to the check-in counter, leaving behind a junior partner with a handful of paper—and a sudden crush.

"How did you manage to do that?" Pinocchio looked up to find Cassandra standing over him. She seemed so very tall from down there. He hastily zipped his bag and stood up just as Stevens and Dominic approached.

"Mr. Stevens, I'm so sorry," he said.

"Hush," Stevens replied, watching as Barnes disappeared around the corner. He smiled. "You're a natural at this, Pinocchio. It only took you thirty seconds to get a congressman on his knees." He offered Pinocchio a warm hand. "That usually takes me weeks!"

* * *

True to Avalon's theme, the wait staff at the reception wore shiny metal armor. They waddled from table to table, clinking and clanking as they filled the glasses of America's most powerful men.

Never in his wildest dreams would Stevens have imagined how well Pinocchio could work a room. He had barely introduced the boy when lawmakers were all over him, chuckling, smiling, toasting—*actually toasting*. For the past forty-five minutes Stevens hadn't said so much as a word. For the past fifteen he hadn't moved so much as a muscle. He stood quietly in the corner and watched as Pinocchio worked political magic.

Pinocchio was anything but smooth, however. He spilled drinks, he stumbled over words, he mispronounced names, but for some reason, the elected officials just seemed to eat him up. Somehow, the juxtaposition of such a modest—dare he think it, *innocent*—man simply dazzled. The members were as entranced as Stevens was. Ordinarily a lobbyist has to chase a senator down, almost shouting his spiel as she makes her way to the golf course, but not Pinocchio. What started as a group of three freshmen congressmen snowballed until the entire room orbited around him. The few who ventured away to enjoy some on-the-house gaming did so not with a polite handshake, but with a warm slap on the back or a pat on the elbow. A few even bothered to stop by Stevens's lonely corner to thank—*thank!*—him for bringing the charming young Italian with him. Stevens didn't want to admit it, but he was entranced too, so much so that he scarcely noticed the shapely young woman slinking up beside him.

"Having a good time, Cassandra?" he asked.

Cassandra nodded. "I've never seen anything like it," she said. "Have you?"

Stevens shook his head, afraid to break his stare. "What do you know about him?" he asked.

"Pinocchio? We've talked a few times. I mean, what you see is what you get." Pinocchio dropped a drink, splashing ice across the room. Within seconds, he and the distinguished gentlemen from New York, Idaho, and Illinois were on their knees gathering it. "He's just that way."

Another roar of laughter erupted from across the room.

• • •

"I used to work in a carnival," Barnes mused. "Did you know that?"

"No, I didn't!" said Pinocchio. A carnival sounded exciting and he was eager to hear the details.

"I was sixteen, and I ran away to join the circus. Of course, the circus knew a lot more about child labor laws than I did back then, so it didn't work out; but there was a carnival in town, and they didn't ask too many questions. The next day I was pulling levers on the *Tunnel of Love.*

"It was a great time—there were pretty girls in every town we went to, and for some reason, the guy pulling the lever seemed really interesting to them. Eventually they put me in the *Fool the Guesser* booth. The guy who ran it was this skinny little guy named Raisin. Can you believe that? A skinny guy named Raisin."

Pinocchio shook his head and let Barnes continue, "Well, Raisin taught me a lot about people. It's not really that hard to guess someone's weight—or their age—but you were still wrong, oh, maybe thirty percent of the time. But the prize was only worth a quarter, so the game always made out."

"But," Pinocchio interrupted, "if the prizes were so cheap, why did people play?"

Barnes laughed.

"The same reason they play any game at the carnival—to beat the game! They didn't care about some sawdust-stuffed animal; they just wanted to see if they were smarter than I was. But your big money came from the tips. When you saw a couple, you *always* played for the lady, and you *always* guessed wrong. Guess her age or her weight low, and she loved you for it. It was flattery, pure and simple. The guys, well, they knew that thanks to you, they were getting a little love that night, so they tipped you really well. See, they were in on it." Stevens sighed. "It was a great game; hell, it was a great job. I do miss those days."

"So why did you leave?" Pinocchio asked.

Barnes flashed the charming smile that helped get him elected for fifteen consecutive terms. "I didn't. What do you think politics is, Pinocchio? If you tell them what they want to hear, they'll love you for it." Barnes swallowed the rest of the drink, and began chewing the ice. Pinocchio took that as his opening.

"Congressman, about the bill—"

"Yes," Barnes interrupted, "we should chat about the bill." He scanned the room, locking eyes with Charles Stevens who watched the exchange intently. "I'll tell you what, Pinocchio, I'm going to go talk to your boss. Why don't you go upstairs and call your wife." He smiled. "You can tell her everything is going great."

Pinocchio smiled back and made a beeline for the elevator. Barnes took a moment to refill his drink. By the time he made his way to the corner where Charles Stevens was standing, his smile was long gone.

"Charming guy," said Barnes. "So tell me, Charles, how long do you intend to hold this kid over me?"

"Not too long," Stevens replied. "Just until we pass House Resolution 1976."

H.R. 1976 was a bill that had been floating around for some years. On the surface it wasn't very important—just a resolution to allow logging rights to an area known as the Oldwood Forest. The only problem was that the Oldwood Forest was the nesting ground of the endangered speckled owl, the very same species Barnes had fought so hard to protect thirty years ago. As the head of the Internal Land Development Committee, Barnes had successfully kept H.R. 1976 from a vote for the last few years, but it wasn't until that moment he realized The Kronos Group was lobbying for it.

"Come on, Charles," Barnes said, "you really expect me to vote for that thing?"

"Not at all," Stevens replied. "I expect you to keep your constituents happy and vote against it. All I want is for you to let it pass committee. Let the members decide."

Barnes smirked. "And I suppose if I do, this whole accident business goes away?"

Stevens nodded.

"Then I'll make you a deal, Charles. Send me an expert witness to give testimony and I'll put it up for a vote."

"We've already got several PhDs lined up—"

Barnes shook his head. "No, I want Pinocchio."

"Pinocchio?" Stevens asked incredulously. "He's no expert; why him?"

"Because I want my members to hear the truth about that bill, and something tells me *the last honest man in Washington* is the one to give it to them. That's the deal, Charles. Send me Pinocchio, I'll open debate on 1976, and you bury the accident story. If it passes or not is up to you. Do we have a deal?"

* * *

Pinocchio could barely contain his excitement as he practically sang into the phone, "Oh, Whitney, you should have seen it! They were hanging on my every word!"

"That's great, Pinny!" said Whitney.

Never much of a drinker, Pinocchio couldn't help but pop a bottle that someone had thoughtfully placed in his room. He threw open the doors to the balcony and let the tropical humidity soak him from head to toe. He went on about the party for five solid minutes, pausing only to sip on the expensive champagne.

Whitney didn't want to admit it, but she was relieved. Secretly, she had wondered if Pinocchio would find his footing in such a crowd—eighteen congressmen and a room full of millionaires—but hearing Pinocchio's excitement, she felt foolish for doubting him. It was the same thing she had seen in him so many years ago on that Northern California campus—everyone wants to love Pinocchio. He was one of those rare men who was completely honest; not brutally so, but gently so. She should have known that these men who were so accustomed to dishonesty would find Pinocchio as refreshing as she did.

Pinocchio was in the middle of a rundown on the aperitifs when he was interrupted by a knock.

"That's Mr. Stevens!" he exclaimed. Though the details had grown tedious, Whitney still wanted to hear more, but she knew Pinocchio was there on business. He blew her a virtual kiss and set the receiver into the cradle as gently as if it were his beloved herself. Pinocchio took a moment to compose himself then threw open the door.

Pinocchio was dumbfounded when he was greeted not by the senior partner of The Kronos Group, but by a most delightful figure whose sheer sarong did more than hint at the bikini underneath.

"Can I come in?" Cassandra asked innocently.

Pinocchio hesitated. Not only was he rendered mute by the sight of his colleague in so little, but he also knew Charles Stevens was on his way. Still, ever the man of manners, Pinocchio welcomed her inside. She spotted the open bottle of champagne and asked for a glass, making herself at home on the balcony. Reluctantly Pinocchio joined her.

"You were just magnificent in there tonight, Pinocchio," she said.

"You really think so?"

She nodded. They sipped champagne and listened as the waves lapped the shore beyond. It was the most romantic setting that could be imagined for a married man and a maneater in a bikini, which Pinocchio was trying his best not to look at. Many strange feelings began to wash over him—he wasn't really doing anything wrong, yet he felt guilty. *What would Whitney say if she could see him now?* Pinocchio didn't even want to think about it. His answers dwindled from single words to nods and shakes. He guzzled his wine in the hopes that the empty glass would signal that it was time to call it a night; instead, Cassandra marked it as the time for a refill. When she returned, she chose a spot so close that she almost stood on top of him. He was praying for something—anything—to break the moment. An earthquake would do, maybe a fire in the hotel, or—*a knock at the door.*

Pinocchio practically flew across the room to answer it. He was beyond relieved to greet the grandfatherly smile of Charles Stevens, who made his way inside and requested a glass of champagne. Pinocchio poured nervously, wondering how long it would take the old man to notice the bikini on his balcony. Much to Pinocchio's horror, he didn't. Stevens sipped the champagne, taking the time to savor the way the effervescence danced across his throat.

"Ah. That's the good stuff, right, my boy?" Stevens asked.

"Yessir," Pinocchio replied.

"Do you like champagne?"

"Yessir."

Stevens laughed. "Pinocchio, you're a partner now; you can call me 'Charles.'"

"Yes, Charles ... sir."

"Well, I had the bottle sent up to celebrate."

"Celebrate what?" Pinocchio asked.

It was then that Stevens noticed Cassandra, who was listening with some interest from the open balcony.

"Oh. I didn't realize you had company," said Stevens. "Hello, Cassandra."

"Charles," she replied, nonchalantly.

Stevens shot a knowing smile Pinocchio's way, which only served to confuse the junior partner. "Cassandra," Stevens continued, "would you mind giving us a few minutes?"

She nodded. The lobbyists watched as she slinked her way across the suite and pulled closed the French doors that, much to Pinocchio's horror, led to his bedroom. Stevens motioned for the balcony, leading Pinocchio out by the arm. He pulled the doors closed behind him and threw a final look toward the bedroom.

"Watch out, Pinocchio, she's got you under her thumb."

"She does?" Pinocchio asked.

Stevens nodded. "And if you play your cards right, you can be under the rest of her, too." Stevens chuckled at his own wit. He lit a cigar and let the nighttime heat envelop him. "Pinocchio, we want you to testify."

Pinocchio nearly dropped his drink. "You want *me* to testify in front of Congress?" he asked. Stevens nodded.

"But, Charles," Pinocchio continued, "I'm no expert! What would I say?"

"We checked your records," Stevens replied. "You have a degree in ecology. That's good enough for the kind of questions they'll be asking." He poured the junior partner the rest of the champagne. "This testimony will make you, Pinocchio. Millions of people will hear what you have to say. All I'm asking is for you to be yourself. If you do, the bill passes, the firm benefits"—seemingly out of thin air Stevens produced a carefully wrapped box and handed it to a speechless Pinocchio—"and you benefit, too."

Pinocchio hesitated before finally taking the box from Stevens's hands. It was heavier than he expected. He was out of breath by the time he had unwrapped it. He instantly recognized the logo on the cover—a crown, embossed on a rich-feeling black leather. He threw a glance Stevens's way before opening it.

There, in dazzling white gold, sat the most beautiful watch Pinocchio had ever seen. It was the exact same model as Stevens's, who took care to turn his wrist ever so gently toward the sparkle-eyed young partner.

"You earned it, lad."

Pinocchio's heart raced as he lifted the timepiece. He tore off his old digital with such haste he nearly snapped its flimsy rubber wristband. As he slipped the Swiss-made beauty into place, his breathing stopped altogether. He marveled at the movement—the second hand swept across a blindingly brilliant face as smoothly as the pour of warmed honey. He dared to brush across the bezel, his finger smudging the high polish of the gold. By the time he turned his gaze back to Stevens, he was blurry with tears.

"You were curious about how the system worked?" asked the senior partner. "Well, now you know. It's called pragmatism. In Washington, pragmatism is power. Pragmatism, and knowing how the system works. You have the power now, and you need the tools to go along with it. That watch is a symbol, the kind of thing that makes you who you are in the eyes of the people that matter."

"Things ...," Pinocchio asked, "things make you who you are?"

"The clothes make the man, Pinocchio. Nobody would listen to you if you were naked."

Pinocchio tried to match Stevens's intoxicating grin with one of his own, but he was in no condition to smile. He turned his attention back to the watch and his long-neglected champagne, which suddenly went down just a little less smoothly. He stood in an uncomfortable silence for what must have been an hour, though Stevens didn't seem uncomfortable at all. The breeze blew through his silver hair, revealing the image of a youthful, if wrinkled, face.

The senior partner relished the sparkle of the wine, the scent of the cigar. Pinocchio began to wonder if it were these simple pleasures that were energizing him, or the place itself. The aroma of the cigar brought back to Pinocchio memories of his own father, who used to enjoy the tingle of a smoldering pipe and the kiss of anisette across his tongue on the rare evenings when the mosquitoes were not unbearable in the Italian summer.

Though in later years Pinocchio had grown to despise the sting of smoke, he could not help but admire the pure masculinity of it all—here was a man, not unlike Geppetto, with dues paid and youth conquered, enjoying the well-earned rewards of life. His drink may have been more expensive, his smoke more aromatic, but still, the memory of the moment was so strong, so familiar—it was as if time had reversed itself and allowed the innocent boy, so admiring of the old man, to come back once more and borrow a moment of real manhood with a man who had been there, who had earned it. Once again, Pinocchio was in awe.

"Your job here is over for now," Stevens announced. "We're going to put you on the road for a few weeks to schmooze some of the committee members, but for tonight, I just want you to enjoy everything my island has to offer."

"Your island?" Pinocchio asked. "You *own* Avalon?"

"Part of it," Stevens replied. "An investment group approached me with the idea ten years ago, so in a way yes, I own it. I own everything on it." Stevens raised his glass and clinked a toast to the utterly speechless junior partner.

"Well, I'm going to call it a night," said Stevens. "Remember, *mi casa es su casa*."

Pinocchio didn't have the faintest idea what that meant. He nodded politely as the old man patted him on the shoulder and showed himself out. Cassandra stepped back onto the balcony and interrupted Pinocchio's fruitless smartphone search for a translation.

"It's Spanish," she said. "It means 'my house is your house.'" She brushed a hand across his cheek. "By the way, that means he owns you, too."

She leaned in and planted a kiss on his forehead, which was the most he would allow her that night. As Cassandra made her way out the door, she set her glass on the table and stole one last look at the confused—and still married—young partner on the balcony. She did feel guilty for eavesdropping on her boss, but she was also incensed that after her years of work, the old man had decided to reward not her, but this fool, whose only real accomplishment before that night had been that he had smashed a station wagon into a congressman. Cassandra didn't want to feel jealous, but then again, she didn't want to end the evening lonely either. It seemed in neither matter did she have a choice that night.

CHAPTER 5

The Many Travels of a Junior Partner

Over the next eight weeks, Pinocchio spent exactly five nights at home. The rest of his days quickly devolved into a haze of hotel beds and dry turkey sandwiches as he became a regular visitor to the nation's many fine airports and train terminals. In two months Pinocchio had gone from being a nobody—a worthless analyst working on worthless reports—to a man of some repute in the decision-making circles of the country.

After Houston he found himself in Detroit, where he convinced two key senators that additional auto safety rules would push manufacturing overseas and kill American jobs. On a hunting trip in Oregon he espoused the virtues of unrestrictive gun laws and posed with a Wisconsin congressman's trophy buck. In South Carolina it was tobacco regulation. In Seattle it was airline regulation. He stopped an army base from closing in Louisiana and he funded a nuclear waste storage facility in Nevada. Pinocchio was fast becoming the man to know in Washington, and he did it all from a suitcase he had hastily packed two months earlier.

As he pushed his way into yet another unlit guest room—he checked the stationery on the desk to learn it was in San Francisco—he collapsed on the bed. In the last few weeks he had met more people and collected more business cards than he could remember. He had seen the country through the portal windows of God knows how many planes. Every airport seemed just a little different, but somehow still the same. Each one took him on a train, or bus, or monorail, shuttling him from one jet to another, from one assignment to the next. The daily calls with the home office seemed to confirm his progress, and Mr. Stevens's tone had grown only more excited in the past few days. But still, Pinocchio couldn't help but admit there was something about it all that he just didn't understand. Even as he was becoming an insider, Pinocchio had never felt more like an outsider in his life.

Of all people on this earth, it is perhaps our friend, Pinocchio, who best understood what it was to be a stranger. Though he would never admit it, or perhaps because he simply didn't remember, ever since he first leaped into consciousness fully aware, Pinocchio had wondered how it was that he fit in. What a shock, my dear friends, to be thrust into a world with the skills of a boy but the understanding of a baby! To be able to speak but not have the experience to know when to hold your tongue. To be able to walk, but lack the falls, scrapes, and cuts that allow us to walk tall. To be able to think, but not to understand; to give love, but not know how to welcome it.

Pinocchio had spent his whole life wondering what it was the rest of the world knew that he didn't. Everyone who laughed at a joke he didn't get, who smiled a knowing smile, who touched each other playfully and tenderly, who seemed to be able to speak without words—what was the secret that the whole world seemed to share?

Pinocchio was fortunate that he was so curious to learn; otherwise, he could possibly have been the loneliest soul on the planet. At times, he wondered if he still might be.

But Pinocchio also knew he was fortunate. He never doubted the love and support of his father, and as he grew older, he began to recognize the scope of the sacrifice poor old Geppetto had made to bring him to this country, to give him the chance at a life beyond the judging eyes of those who had known him at his most awkward. Pinocchio remembered when they first arrived in their new homeland, standing in a line at a New York airport, waiting to meet a federal officer who would stamp their passports and say they could enter this new country—how tightly Geppetto held his hand. He did so as if to reassure him, but strangely, Pinocchio was not afraid—he was excited, anxious. It was only with the hindsight of age that Pinocchio realized Geppetto was holding his hand because it was *he* who was afraid. Pinocchio was an eager boy, but Geppetto had never even traveled but a few miles from the very house he was born in.

Yet he smiled. He looked at Pinocchio and smiled. Pinocchio never forgot what he said that day. "This is the place, boy. We used to come on ships. They put us on an island and gave us a ticket to a bigger island. Now we come on planes, but for the same reasons. People come here for the chance to be someone else. Now, we can too. Who else do you want to be?"

"But I don't want to be anybody else, Dad! I want to be Pinocchio!"

Geppetto laughed. "And now you can be, my boy. Now you can be."

Who *had* he become? Was Geppetto still proud of him? Pinocchio stepped onto the tiny balcony overlooking the bay. Sea air had always agreed with him. He considered for a brief moment moving back to California and resolved to discuss that with Whitney.

His dear Whitney! She was, besides his father, the only person who had ever looked at him as if they had something in common—a normal birth and a normal childhood. She laughed with him, not at him, and he knew the difference. But it was more than that; when she looked at him, she saw not a naive child, but a man. Perhaps this was why she never seemed surprised when he accomplished what he considered to be miracles—landing the job in DC, buying a home, changing a diaper, the newspaper article, the promotion.

She knew, better than he did, just who he was and what he was capable of. It filled her with pride to see him step into the potential she had long before predicted he would. Could Whitney ever truly know what her simple faith had given him? Is it the fate of all wives that they should never know just how much husbands the world over owed their manhood to their strength? What amazing creatures women are, and what would become of men without their silent guidance?

But then there was Albero. Geppetto used to say that fatherhood was the time when one faces *the abyss*—and this is when he becomes a man. On the day when Pinocchio first learned he would be a father, he faced it with the same brave front I suspect all men master at some point in their lives. But secretly, Pinocchio was terrified.

He had once before faced an abyss—a place of infinite sadness where, when confronted with it, one is forced to choose between strength and surrender. What Geppetto never told him was that when his son was born, he would face that test every day. Every day when he awoke, for a moment he was content, happy, and warm in the embrace of his wife. But as soon as the realization hit him, the terror returned. Of course, a small child by itself is no cause for alarm. Other than the occasional tantrum, scribbled-upon wall or accidental fire, children are mostly harmless. It was something else—it was the weight. Pinocchio was afraid of the potential the boy held, and of the possibility that he alone would be the one to ruin it. After all, how could he ever guide his son through a world that he himself did not fully understand?

What was the secret that everyone else seemed to share?

Whitney shared it. She was a natural mother. She took on late nights and early mornings. She faced sleeplessness, sickness, scribbled-upon walls, and the occasional fire as if they were part of the simple course of life—nothing at all unusual. All the while, Pinocchio was dying. Even in the simple act of holding his son in his arms he felt the fragility, the smallness in his body. He felt clumsy, careless. Pinocchio had long since doubted his ability to rock the baby to sleep, let alone master the "papa hug."

The "papa hug" was the kind of hug that only men of advancing age can offer, and only to their sons. It is a full-bodied crush of an embrace that seems to draw on not only the strength presently in their arms, chest and shoulders, but indeed all the strength that they have ever pulled from their arms, chest and shoulders. Such a hug would crush the air out of a man's lungs, and if one of them had only thought to slip a lump of coal into his chest pocket, he would soon have a diamond. No, my dear friends, no force on earth or heaven can quite match the power of the "papa hug."

Pinocchio wouldn't dare even attempt it. He wondered, *How dare he pretend to be a father?*

But still, there was something so pure in his son's eyes; his face was so soft and young. He was so unafraid of the world, so ready to try everything and taste everything, consequences be damned. He was most curious and trusting, and he looked upon his terrified father as a mortal gazes upon a god. Every now and then, sometimes just once a day, Pinocchio simply accepted his son's admiration and felt, in that moment, not like a fraud who was putting up a brave face, but like a man. The fact remained, however, that for the rest of the day, Pinocchio was petrified.

Abyss.

The word brought back a vague memory. It was a feeling of having the breath crushed out of him, of heaviness so great that to even heave his chest would cause his ribs to shatter. It was a putrid acid that soaked through his clothes and burned his skin red. He had not thought of it in many years, but now, he was overcome with the feeling of it. Pinocchio shook it off and wandered into the bedroom to watch some television.

Pinocchio thought to call Whitney, but checking his watch, decided better of it. It was already a quarter past twelve on the West Coast and he didn't want to wake her. He lay back down and watched the end of the local news while flipping through a brochure for that hybrid wagon they had looked at just before he left for Chicago. It had been two months that they had been without a car, and Whitney had tasked him with putting the family back on the road when he returned. Mr. Stevens was promising him a bonus—and two weeks back in Washington, so it was as good a time as ever. He checked the price—it was reasonable given Pinocchio's new salary, but still the idea of spending that much money on a car terrified him. He reached for his phone, dialed Whitney's number, and quickly hung up. He would have to wait to hear her reassuring voice until the next day.

Pinocchio turned the brochure over and re-added the cost of the options they had agreed on. The little wagon was a most unusual-looking car, but it seemed to have everything they wanted, and Whitney let Pinocchio decide on the color. Even a deaf man could have heard the tension in her voice when Pinocchio announced it would be another two weeks before he would be back home. She thought that he had forgotten about the car.

Quite the contrary, it was foremost on his mind. To him, the new car was a way to soothe the frazzled feelings that had resulted from Pinocchio's sudden and excessive absence. He unfolded the glossy brochure and gave the entire idea one last nod. This was going to be a great surprise—a way, in one swift stroke, to restore Whitney's faith in the new job, and in her husband too. He smiled as he imagined the look on her face when he came pulling up in the beautiful new wagon. What a wonderful gift for the family—the start of a new life together, one where money was no longer a worry, no longer even a concern. This was what Pinocchio needed to get her back on his side. There was no way he was going to screw this up.

CHAPTER 6

Pinocchio Runs Afoul of a Terrible Beast

Surrounded by glass, dripping in chrome, the showroom was opulent, glitzy—and utterly terrifying. Pinocchio crept timidly through the door, and like every other buyer brave enough to actually walk in, his eyes were immediately drawn to the mechanical magnificence that rotated lazily in the center of the sales floor.

The salesmen called it "*The Beast.*"

The big German coupe perched arrogantly atop a glass turntable, shimmering like a disco ball under the lights. It was massive; it was intimidating ...

It was utterly hideous.

Like something cats hissed at and villagers chased with pitchforks, the car was tragically exaggerated in every sense. Three rows of headlights angled toward the gaping, shark-mouth grille, which seemed wide enough to inhale stray dogs. The bulges in the fenders were almost obscene. The paint was thicker than a Texas oil slick and was so shiny that one needed a pinhole viewer to glance safely at it. Pinocchio could tell that this was a car he most certainly couldn't afford. It was a pity he was so totally entranced by it.

Summoning all his courage, he crept cautiously up to the big coupe, hypnotized by the sheer size of the thing. Something about it seemed to speak to him, but he was still surprised when it actually did.

"Welcome to success," it said.

Unsure how else to react, Pinocchio backed up and scanned the room. There wasn't a soul in sight. He shrugged, and continued forward—

"Welcome to success."

He locked eyes with the car, which only ignored him, turning its chrome grin away in seeming disgust.

"Are—are you talking to me?" Pinocchio asked.

The car responded, albeit a bit rudely, "Nothing broadcasts your status quite like the beauty, the power, and the soul of a German-engineered sports coupe."

"I'm Pinocchio. What's your name, car?"

"And nothing exemplifies German engineering like the M650."

"Pleased to meet you, Mr. M650. Are you for sale?"

"With the power of two turbochargers and the fine craftsmanship of a custom leather interior, each trip in the M650 is a journey to a dream."

"I said, are you for sale?"

"Available in both coupe and convertible, the M650 ..."

"Hello?"

"A stunning array of colors ..."

"HELLO?"

"Touch screen navigation ..."

"HELLO?"

"Hello, yes!" said the Englishman. Turning, Pinocchio was surprised to find that the most unusual-looking salesman had slinked up beside him. He was well tailored, save for his electric-blue hair, and he wore his biggest Cheshire smile. He extended a hand and said, "Pleased to meet you, Mr. ...?"

"Pinocchio."

"So tell me, what do you do for a living, Mr. Pinocchio?"

"I'm a junior analyst—" He corrected himself. "Partner. I'm a junior partner at The Kronos Group."

"I see. Swiss?"

"No, Italian."

"Not you, the watch. Swiss?"

"Oh yes, my boss gave it to me for—"

"Excellent. A man who can afford that watch deserves a car to show it off in—so let's do some business, shall we? What kind of car are you looking for?"

"My wife says we need something sensible, with room for the family."

"Sensible, room for the family ... Hmm. Well it just so happens that the Germans are the masters of value transportation." The salesman gently led Pinocchio to a sad little corner of the showroom where, crouching in the shadows, sat an oddly proportioned little box of a car. "This is the Two-Class," he said. "It's a crossover sports-utility hybrid. Good on gas, five-star safety rating ..."

And terribly boring. They were both thinking it.

"What about that one?" asked Pinocchio, pointing back toward the coupe. "Is that a sensible family car?"

The salesman grinned. "Absolutely. When I think of family transportation, I think of a twelve-cylinder luxury coupe, and the M650 is the absolute top of the line. When you drive that car, people listen to you."

"They listen to you?" Pinocchio asked.

"They can't help it! That engine is the loudest thing on the road."

Pinocchio had subconsciously wandered back over to the turntable. Like a great spinning planet, the gravity of the car seemed to be pulling him closer. "*Welcome to success.*" It beckoned.

The salesman tapped at a control panel and the turntable froze. Powerful spotlights bathed the car in an otherworldly glow and for the first time, Pinocchio could take in its astonishing size. The back seat, what little there was of it, seemed best reserved for distant relatives you didn't like very much. The driver's seat, on the other hand, was superb. Set a full twelve feet back from the tip of the car, it offered a commanding view. Pinocchio was instantly mesmerized.

"Hop in," the salesman offered. The automatic door opened gracefully, accompanied by the pleasing hiss of hydraulics. Pinocchio held his breath as he slid onto the softest material he had ever felt. Every surface Pinocchio touched was covered with that same leather: The steering wheel, the floor mats, even the cup holders were swathed in the supple tan.

"Hand-rubbed," the salesman continued. "Over twelve hides worth of top-grade, barb-free leather."

"You mean it takes twelve cows to make this car?" Pinocchio asked.

"Don't be silly." The salesman chuckled. "It takes twelve cows to make the *front seat*. Care to fire it up?" he said as he closed the door, locking Pinocchio in the seven-mile-per-gallon rocket ship. He handed over a beautiful titanium key fob, which also happened to be wrapped in leather. "All you need is this, and push the start button."

Pinocchio held his breath as the engine roared to life, rattling the showroom windows loose from their frames.

"GREAT SOUND, ISN'T IT?" the salesman screamed. Terrified, Pinocchio quickly switched the engine off. As he did, the large touch screen in the center of the dash flickered awake, showing the bladed, propeller logo of the carmaker, and its hallowed tagline, "*Welcome to Success*."

Pinocchio was woozy. The salesman had seen that look before. He felt the pen heating up in his breast pocket ...

"So, Mr. Pinocchio," he continued, "let's talk options."

* * *

Whitney heard a rumble. The water in the sink was jumping. The glasses vibrated. The pictures swayed. A Northern California expatriate, she knew the signs of an earthquake. She leaped up from the desk and ran out the nearest door, screaming Albero's name the whole way.

Children have a sense for such things. Though barely audible over the low rumble, Albero could hear his mother's panicked voice.

"Grandpa," he said, "something's wrong."

Geppetto closed his book and jumped to his feet, calling back to his daughter-in-law, "We're outside!"

The rumble intensified, shaking leaves from their very branches. Whitney raced around the corner and found Geppetto and Albero standing under the tree. Neighbors were running out of their homes in the same confused state.

"What is it?" asked Geppetto.

Whitney shouted, "Earthquake! Stay clear of the house!" She scooped Albero up and, taking the old man by the hand, led them to the middle of the cul-de-sac. A dozen neighbors joined them, hoping the rumble would subside.

But it grew louder.

It arched to a high-pitched scream as the ground bounced beneath them. This was no earthquake—something was coming, and it was coming around the corner!

"Mama," Albero cried, "I'm scared."

Indeed, so was she. So was everyone. All eyes focused on the corner, where any moment, the specter of a skyscraper-crushing lizard was sure to emerge.

They braced, they prayed, and they watched as the beast appeared, its roar as deafening as war itself—

* * *

The only thing loud enough to drown out the growl of the motor was the stereo. It was a very expensive option, but like the car itself, one that Pinocchio had convinced himself he deserved. He rounded the corner of the pastoral Virginia suburb and was surprised to find almost the entire neighborhood crowding into the street.

The coupe pulled proudly into the driveway, parked and at last the engine stopped. No one dared to break the stunned silence that fell upon the neighborhood—mostly they were just pleased to have feeling in their ears again. Everyone approached the monster as they would a beached shark—a thing of curiosity, but a thing that might still prove deadly. Whitney was as shocked as anyone to see who emerged from the driver's side door.

"Hi-lo!" said Pinocchio.

"PINOCCHIO," Whitney shouted, "WHAT ON EARTH IS THAT?"

Pinocchio jumped. "Why are you screaming?" he asked.

"AM I? I CAN'T HEAR A THING!"

Whitney took a moment to let the stillness of the suburb creep back into her head. She took a deep breath and chose stern, but careful words. "Pinocchio," she asked, "what is this thing?"

"It's the M650!" he answered.

"It's *what*?"

"It's our new car."

Blood raced through her veins, as near to a state of boil as the human body could manage, and judging by the cautious room afforded her by the neighbors, they could see it too. "I thought we talked about a *family* car," she managed through gritted teeth.

"This is a family car. It has a great big back seat. All you do is slide the front—oh! He showed me how to do it—" Pinocchio fumbled with the key fob, finally selecting a button, which set off the alarm.

Spectators scattered as the shriek blasted the neighborhood, rattling windows and alerting dogs as far away as Baltimore that the M650 had arrived.

* * *

"I can't believe you bought that car!" said Whitney.

"I don't see why you're so upset."

Whitney had vowed she wouldn't start a fight, at least not until after Albero had gone to bed. She served the potatoes with a seething rage, practically throwing a plate at her husband.

"How much?" she demanded.

"How much what?"

"How much did you spend on that, that *thing*?"

"We don't have to talk about this now."

Another plate landed in front of Geppetto, who had already decided this was the worst dinner since the dam burst in '63 ruined what had otherwise promised to be a great meal.

"But my promotion!"

"Getting a promotion doesn't mean we need to spend every penny on opulent purchases! That damn thing has a leather trunk!"

"But it's a successful man's car—and I'm a successful man now!"

Whitney fumed. It was an awkward silence. Geppetto did his best to shrink into his chair and chew as quietly as he could, hoping against hope that nobody would ask his opinion.

"Dad," Pinocchio asked, "what do you think of the car?"

Geppetto was trapped. He could feel every eye in the room watching him. He chose his words carefully. "I agree—"

"Ha!" Pinocchio celebrated prematurely as Geppetto continued, "With Whitney."

"What?"

"My boy, that's a single man's car. You're a family man now, and you need a family car."

"Oh, I can't believe this!" exclaimed Pinocchio.

As he watched the drama play out, Albero couldn't understand why his mother didn't appreciate what was, in his opinion, the most astounding motor vehicle ever manufactured. He could see the hurt in his father's eyes, and decided someone needed to defend him.

"I like the car, Daddy!" he proclaimed.

"Well thank you, Albero," said Pinocchio. He smiled for the briefest of moments before turning back to the confrontation. "*Someone* in this family understands!"

"My boy," said Geppetto, "it's not that we don't understand—"

"I don't," Whitney added.

"But to buy a car like that, it comes across as a little selfish."

Whitney stormed into the kitchen, determined to let her temper cool. Pinocchio crumpled his napkin, turned to Geppetto and asked, "Why did you have to say that?"

"You wanted my opinion!"

"When I said 'opinion,' I meant 'just agree with me!'"

"Well, I'm sorry, Pinocchio, I guess I'm just too old to know everything anymore." Geppetto pushed the plate aside and leaned over the table. "It is a very nice car, Pinocchio, but the measure of a man is not in what he owns."

"It is in this town, Dad."

Whitney returned, threw herself into a chair and sawed at the chicken, shooting an occasional glare Pinocchio's direction.

"Honey," he said, "when you see the way the custom luggage fits in that trunk—"

"Pinocchio, I don't want to hear one more word about that car," Whitney barked. "Not one more word, understand? Let's just enjoy this meal, and later we can talk about how you're going to take it back. OK?"

It wasn't OK, but Pinocchio knew he had pushed it too far. He turned his attention back to the plate in front of him. He gnawed at his green beans, Whitney stabbed at her chicken, Geppetto poked at his potatoes, and for the rest of the meal not a word was spoken.

* * *

As Pinocchio crept into the bedroom, he was alarmed to find Whitney still awake. She sometimes liked to stay up late and read, but tonight Pinocchio had no desire to continue the argument, which would most certainly happen when she saw he had brought the owner's manual to bed with them.

He slipped under the covers, doing his best not to tussle the bed. They ignored each other for ten full minutes before Pinocchio finally said something ...

"You know the key fob is made of titanium—"

Whitney slammed her book on the nightstand. Pinocchio did not take that as a good sign. She flipped off her light and yanked up the covers, presenting him with her back—and a wall of silence. Pinocchio slid under the blankets and dared not even breathe, but he couldn't help himself.

"I just wanted the best for us."

Finally, Whitney rolled over. "What did you say?" she asked.

Pinocchio clarified, "Our last car was so rickety. The salesman told me this was the best car they made, and that means the safest. I just wanted you and Albero to ride in the best."

Whitney sighed. "Oh, Pinocchio, I know you meant well, but I don't need a big fancy car like that. These smooth-talking salesmen, you know ..." She trailed off. *It wasn't his fault; it was her fault.* She knew her husband, and she knew how suggestible he could be. She should have been there with him, and since she wasn't, it seems she'd now be shuttling Albero to kindergarten in a twelve-cylinder German sports car.

"Let's just forget all about it, alright?" She sealed the offer with a kiss on the forehead. "I'm proud of you, Pinny," she said, "but I do wish you hadn't blown up at Geppetto in front of Albero like that."

"But, Whitney," he said, "those stories he tells!"

She pressed her finger to her lips ever so gently. "Shh. I know, I know. And you're right, but, Pinny, that temper of yours! It doesn't come out very often, but when it does—it's going to get you into trouble one day." She gave him another kiss—a little sugar with her medicine. "Your father is getting old, Pinny, and there's no telling how many years he has left. I just don't want you two saying goodbye when you're angry like that. That's all." Another kiss. "OK?"

How could he disagree? The fight was over, and ultimately, she was right. Pleasantly surprised to have peace in the house again, he reached over and turned off the light. As he did, Whitney caught sight of the shiny silver band around his wrist.

"Is that a new watch?" she asked.

"Mr. Stevens gave it to me to celebrate the promotion." Pinocchio beamed. "It's Swiss!"

She nodded, then rolled over, looking forward to a little sleep. But something about the watch bothered her. She always thought of watches as a gift you get at the end of a career, not at the beginning.

CHAPTER 7

Geppetto's Forgetfulness Costs Him Dearly

"That boy!" Geppetto exclaimed.

The only soul within earshot was the shabby old cat curled on the chair. "He asks for my opinion, then gets mad when I offer it!" Geppetto opened a can of his favorite tobacco. He shredded a few flakes and tapped them into his pipe. "Oh, my boy, what has this city done to you, to make you forget who you are?"

The shabby cat didn't know, and frankly, wasn't interested. He simply wandered into the bedroom and did his best to tune out the old man's ranting. Geppetto sighed. He struck a match and drew lightly on the pipe. Ribbons of cherry smoke danced up to the ceiling. He cracked the door and stepped into the crisp Maryland air. Frost had already begun to form on the leaves. Fall was not far off. The threadbare old slippers didn't do much to keep out the chill.

"Men!" he addressed the moon. "They count too much. They know the cost of everything but the value of nothing."

The cold air was heavy on his lungs, and he pulled the door closed behind him. He poured a glass of wine, took a sip. It was warm and bitter, perhaps aged just a few months too long—just like the slippers on his feet, *and just like the old fool wearing them*, he thought, *a once fine thing dated past its usefulness.* He shuffled into his bedroom, one sole hanging lazily from a slipper. The old shabby had taken his place on the bed. Geppetto brushed through his graying hair as he climbed under the sheets. *But he's right. I'm just an old man with his old-world ways.* Perhaps that car wasn't something he was meant to understand—just like the job Pinocchio raved about, and a world where spending time in airports and hotels made a man more important than one who spent time at home.

"I was afraid it would be like this. When he told me he took the job here, but I hoped—" He looked down at the old shabby. "Eh! It doesn't matter what I hoped. It doesn't matter what I think. He is his own man, and he will have to find his own way now, right or wrong." He took another long draw. Smoke filled the room, tickling and teasing the nose on old shabby.

"You must remember, Pinocchio. You must remember who you were ..."

It was late, and Geppetto's eyelids were getting heavy. Old shabby had long since drifted away to slumber.

"I'll pray you do."

He closed his eyes and let darkness drift in. A peaceful rest fell over the old man, and at long last, he relaxed. His face curled into a smile, his shoulders sagged into the pillow, and his fingers let slip the briarwood pipe that he had enjoyed since his youth. It tumbled to the bed, spilling glowing embers across the cotton sheets. The embers settled into every fold and wrinkle, quickly finding new fuel for the insatiable appetite of fire.

It nibbled, it chewed, and then ... it devoured.

* * *

Albero's infancy had been mercifully uneventful, but owing to a year's worth of worry-filled nights, Whitney had become a light sleeper. She was the first to wake to the ringing phone.

"Hello?" She listened carefully, possessed, as every mother is, of the ability to instantly rouse from a deep slumber and focus. The man on the other end of the line was calm—strangely so—as he announced his title and the reason for his call. At once Whitney grabbed Pinocchio and shook him awake.

"What? What is it?" he asked.

She thrust the phone to his ear. "It's the fire department! Your father!"

* * *

Pinocchio could see the emergency lights from a half mile off. The eerie glow beckoned onlookers who seemed to have gathered from all over the neighborhood. The deep rumble of the coupe's engine caught the attention of even the most dedicated fire and emergency workers, who, until that moment, had been busying themselves shifting piles of smoldering wood from one side of the lot to another. Pinocchio yanked the coupe onto the sidewalk and hustled through the curious crowd.

The extent of the devastation caught Pinocchio by surprise. All that was left of Geppetto's once-quaint little two-bedroom was a redbrick fireplace. It stood almost defiantly above what had now become an empty lot, ironically the only piece of the house to survive the fire.

A fire captain waved him over, judging by his pajamas and house shoes that he was a relation, and helpfully pointed him in the direction of an ambulance. Pinocchio hurried over to find his father wrapped in a blanket, sucking fresh oxygen from an angry-looking contraption of rubber hoses and plastic, a singed shabby curled under his arms.

"Dad!" Geppetto raised a singed eyebrow, at first relieved, but also confused when his son, his little boy, came running up. For the first time in his life, Geppetto needed Pinocchio to take charge. He needed his son to slip a reassuring arm around him and make it all better. He needed him to say—

"What the hell did you do?"

They were not the words Geppetto expected. He took a deep breath of fresh oxygen and answered—

"Hurumph. Hurph-hur-hurr!"

"That's not what the fire marshal just told me."

"Whuss urg-urg?"

"Smoking in bed. I warned you, didn't I?"

It sounded suspiciously like a lecture, which was the exact opposite of what Geppetto needed to hear at that moment. He angrily flung the oxygen mask to the ground, and shouted through grinding teeth, "This is not the time, boy."

"You're lucky you weren't killed!"

Geppetto didn't have a good response to that—Pinocchio was right, though a little boorish about it. Whatever pride Geppetto had left crumbled into the smoldering ruins of the little house his son had once bought for him, and all that remained of a life spent building beautiful things along with it. He didn't mean to, but he broke the gaze he and his son had locked into and ever so slightly hung his head.

Pinocchio was caught off guard by the response. Wells of anger suddenly ran dry as he began to realize just how scared his poor father truly was. He felt ashamed of his angry first response. *Why did he do that?* It was not Pinocchio's way to feel anger first, but it was becoming a disturbingly common occurrence. As he looked over his father, the tatters of his bedclothes hanging loosely under the blanket the firemen had thought to provide on the chilly night, he realized just how helpless the old man really was. But as Pinocchio looked back over the ashes, the anger slowly returned. Everything Geppetto had in the world he had just carelessly destroyed.

Carelessness.

It was the one thing Geppetto had always railed against—and an attribute that, unlike anger, unfortunately came easy to Pinocchio. Many times over the years he had faced down Geppetto's angry stare when this careless act or that one had gotten him kicked out of school, or in trouble with bullies, or even the law. Now, standing amid an army of people who had been awoken and inconvenienced because of his own carelessness, Pinocchio felt what could only be described as betrayal.

"Can I take him home?" he asked a paramedic. The paramedic nodded, handed over some forms, which Pinocchio snatched away from Geppetto's outstretched hand. "Just go to the car, Dad."

Geppetto obliged, obediently. Pinocchio took a moment to tersely thank the rescue workers and get some questions about insurance claims answered before marching his way back to the coupe, only to find his father standing helplessly next to it.

"Why didn't you get in?"

"The door was locked."

Indeed it was, but it didn't keep Pinocchio from being upset about it. He mashed the key fob and the door swung open, nearly pushing the old man into the grass. "Just get in."

* * *

If it weren't for the roar of the engine, the ride home could be described as silent. Geppetto sat motionless as Pinocchio pressed the coupe to its limits—his mood swinging wildly between rage and worry as the highway slipped by beneath them.

What was to become of the old man? Was he to come live with the family? Albero would love it, but with Whitney and Pinocchio both working, who would be there to watch him?

"Thank you for coming, son," said Geppetto.

"Dad, please don't talk to me right now."

Geppetto obliged. A million thoughts raced through his head too, but the one he couldn't get over was why his son never asked if he was alright?

CHAPTER 8

The Occasion on Which Pinocchio First Showed Himself to Be an Asshole

It had been a month since the fire, and Pinocchio was fast learning one of the cardinal rules of the father-son relationship: *There is such a thing as too much.*

Ever since Geppetto had moved in, it seemed his need for constant communication had grown only more constant by the day. Every night Pinocchio was subjected to endless variations of stories he had heard as a child, and they were less charming with each retelling. Pinocchio had never been more thankful that the office was keeping him later and later these days. He was almost joyous when he called Whitney and told her not to hold dinner, for he knew that with every meal came an anecdote, and Pinocchio was certain one of them was giving him heartburn.

What puzzled Pinocchio was the fact that he alone harbored this resentment. Pinocchio complained bitterly into the night, holding that last thought as he bit into his pillow—*the old man was driving him crazy*—but somehow, Whitney didn't seem to mind having him.

Albero was even worse. Not only was the child unfazed by the old man's almost heroic repetition, Albero even went so far as to encourage him! T*ell me again about the fox and the cat, Grandpa! So whatever happened to the woodcutter, Grandpa?* With Geppetto home all day, there was nothing Pinocchio could do to spare his own son from the nonsense that had, in Pinocchio's opinion, skewed his mind and made him an outcast in this modern world. From the window he watched as the old man sat under the old oak tree and poisoned the mind of yet another helpless boy. As the days became weeks, Pinocchio's annoyance turned to genuine rage at the thought of it: another generation of naive Pinocchio, doomed to wander lost in the world, all because this doddering old fool couldn't help but fill his mind with nonsense.

He cringed.

Pinocchio checked his watch. It was 7:52 a.m. For once in his life, he was not late. He took one last look out the window ... *If it weren't for that tree*, he thought, *I could almost see the Capitol.*

Pinocchio grabbed his keys and headed out to the big coupe. As he tore down the cul-de-sac he tried to focus on the day ahead. *Thank God*, he thought, *thank God for Charles Stevens*. If he hadn't given Pinocchio this chance, he would still be muddling through as a junior analyst, putt-putting to work in some clunker, his mind awash with silly stories and childish thoughts.

Thank God for Charles Stevens.

* * *

"*And how tall did you say the tree was?*" The voice on the phone was barely audible over the engine's roar.

"Thirty feet, at least," Pinocchio answered. "I want the whole thing gone. How soon can you do it?"

"Cutting down the tree is no problem; we can send someone this afternoon, but the stump, that's another matter—"

The traffic was tightening up. Pinocchio leaned on his horn and scooted into the left lane.

"What about the stump?"

"Well a tree like that has big roots; we'll need at least a day to dig it up. That's going to leave a good-sized hole. Are you going to want us to landscape or—"

The traffic finally stopped altogether. Pinocchio checked his watch, sighed.

"Then just get someone out there to take the thing down. The sooner the better." Pinocchio read the man his address and hung up without so much as a goodbye. He sat up, straining to see the accident that was making his life a living hell. Finally, he reached his breaking point.

To the astonishment of the other drivers, he threw the wheel to the left and mashed the accelerator, rocketing the big German coupe down the breakdown lane. He let a smile slip across his lips, which dropped the moment he saw the flashing lights in his mirror.

"Damn it."

Pinocchio drifted to a stop and did his best to ignore the cheers of the vindicated drivers all around him. He didn't even want to acknowledge the officer tapping at his open window but found few suitable options.

"Yes, sir?" Pinocchio asked, humbly.

"Just what did you think you were doing there?"

"What do you mean?"

"Speeding in a breakdown lane. Do you think the rules don't apply to you?"

"Well, no," Pinocchio stuttered, "but I can explain! You see—"

I didn't want to wait for traffic! No, Pinocchio thought, that's a terrible reason. It would be much more understandable if ...

"It was an emergency!"

"Really?" The officer seemed unimpressed, which only led to a more impassioned defense.

"Oh yes, you see my wife, well, my wife is ... she's in the hospital!"

The officer already had his notepad out. "Is that so?"

"Yes! I was on my way to work, and they called and said if I don't get there soon, she won't make it! You see, I'm the transplant donor, and she only has minutes!"

"That's just awful," the officer said.

"Yes it is! I'm her only chance, and it's a matter of life and death!"

"Well"—the officer continued to write—"that is an emergency. What hospital is she at?"

"Huh?"

"You just said they called."

"I did?"

The officer didn't so much as blink as he asked, "Son, is your wife really at the hospital?"

Pinocchio hung his head.

"But I'm in a hurry!"

"I can see that you are," the officer replied, "so let's make this quick. License and registration, please."

* * *

Pinocchio tapped at the wheel and checked his watch—thirty-eight minutes he had been sitting there. Even as the traffic jam cleared, the taunts from passing traffic had not diminished in the slightest.

Ten minutes later, the platter-hatted officer stepped out of the patrol unit and back to the big coupe. He handed over an obscenely long scroll of paper.

"I'm going to ignore that little fiction you told me earlier, but I am citing you for speeding and for reckless driving. Drive safe now, Mr. Pinocchio." The cop started to leave, but turned back, offering, "Oh, and just some friendly advice—you might want to get that thing on your nose checked out."

"My nose?" Pinocchio asked.

"My sister had one just like it, turned out to be cancer." Pinocchio grabbed at the mirror and looked. Sure enough, there sat the reddest, most monstrous welt that he had ever seen—right at the tip of his nose. At least a quarter-inch long, it stuck out like a beaming lighthouse. It was so big he couldn't believe he hadn't seen it before—

"Just some friendly advice." The officer continued, "Have a nice day."

The valediction was a monstrous lie. How could Pinocchio be expected to have a nice day when he had just won himself two tickets *and* cancer? He stared at the welt, squeezing into the mirror for a closer look as he eased back into traffic ...

That's when he felt the crash.

Pinocchio snapped around, his heart stopping when he saw it; what was left of the patrol car's hood was folded neatly against its windshield, steam billowing from the engine. It seemed Pinocchio had shifted the big coupe into "Reverse" instead of "Drive" and backed directly into the officer, who was still idling behind him. Pinocchio felt the blood drain from his face as he heard the tap at his window that was becoming unfortunately familiar.

"This isn't your day," said the officer. "I'll need you to step out of the car."

* * *

For the next few hours Pinocchio sat at his desk fuming about the trio of tickets he had earned that morning—that, and the welt. He took picture after picture, capturing it from every angle and at every length. He searched the web, looking up all types of cancer before deciding he had the deadliest form and that he would be dead within the week.

A knock at the door broke his trance. "Come in!" he shouted. Nancy DelGreco strolled in, a pile of envelopes in her arm. She froze when she saw it.

"Bee sting?" she asked.

"What?"

"My second-oldest is allergic, too. Cortisone works, or I've got some calamine lotion—"

Pinocchio cupped his hands across his face and mumbled, "What do you need, Nancy?"

"Just dropping your mail. There's a letter in there from the insurance—"

"Leave it!" he snapped before offering a rather insincere, "Thank you."

She shook her head and turned, throwing back an afterthought. "Charles wants to see you when you get a moment."

"Charles?" asked Pinocchio.

She nodded as she pulled the door closed behind her. Pinocchio was aghast. How could he see Stevens like this? A Band-Aid was the most obvious remedy, but that would only raise more questions than it answered. Suddenly brilliance struck—he grabbed the phone and mashed a three-digit extension.

"Cassandra," he asked, "do you have a makeup kit with you? Would you mind bringing it in here? You'll see why. Thank you!"

He hung up and flipped through the ever-growing portfolio of snapshots before resigning himself to a doctor's visit that afternoon. He turned to the pile of mail Nancy had just dropped off, paying particular attention to a thick envelope from the insurance company.

Cassandra breezed in without so much as a knock, stopping dead in her tracks when she caught sight of the monster.

"Allergies?"

"I don't have allergies! I don't know what it is! Did you bring the kit?" Cassandra nodded. "Well," he continued, "I have to meet Charles in a few minutes. Do you think you can cover it up?"

Cassandra slinked over for a closer look. "I can make the color match, but this thing is huge!"

"I know it's huge!" he barked.

Cassandra winced—something that did not go unnoticed by Pinocchio. He took a softer tone, which was the closest he would come to an apology that day. "Just do the best you can."

She took a seat on the edge of the desk as Pinocchio buried himself in the insurance report, muttering and cursing as she worked magic with her base and powder.

"Damn it, Dad," Pinocchio grumbled.

"Stop shaking your head!" Cassandra ordered. "Just tell me what's wrong."

"It's the report on the fire. Look at this nonsense. A hundred and sixty-six clocks, two hundred music boxes, a whole room full of scrap wood ... That place was a tinderbox!"

"That's a lot of clocks," said Cassandra.

"You should've grown up with it—every hour the damn things would click, cluck, whistle. As soon as I got to college, I swore I'd never have a clock in my room again."

"How's it going with him at home?" she asked, seemingly innocently.

"Not good," Pinocchio replied. He pushed himself back, pinching the bridge of his nose. "Oh, Cassandra, what am I going to do with that man? All day he sits around telling Albero those ridiculous stories, which he just repeats over and over. He calls me three, four, five times a day, asking for this or that. He gets up at four in the morning, shuffling around, waking up the whole house. *How am I supposed to get back to sleep for two hours?*"

Cassandra could tell he wasn't really looking for an answer. He clearly needed to vent, and she was happy to offer an understanding ear—and a sympathetic frown—as he prattled on, "I was thinking, you know, once the insurance paid off we could get him back out of there, but now they're saying the house was worth less than we owe on it. I can't afford to re-build it! I'm stuck with him!"

Cassandra took it all in. "How old is your dad?" she asked.

"Eighty."

"Eighty?!"

Pinocchio nodded. "He had me at an old age. Why?"

"It's just, have you ever considered getting a little help with him?"

"Help?" Pinocchio was curious, but skeptical.

"Well," she explained, "what you're describing—I mean forgetfulness, repeating himself, hoarding—he might not be well enough to live on his own anymore. You and your wife both work ... maybe it's time to consider a home."

"What do you mean, like a retirement home?" he asked. She nodded. "Dad doesn't need that! He's not senile!"

"Pinocchio, don't get mad at me," said Cassandra. "I know what I'm talking about. We put my mother in a home after she fell down the second time. It was a hard decision, but it was the best thing for her. Folks get old; their minds give out—it's not your responsibility to care for them."

"But he's my dad!" Pinocchio protested.

"And you're not a nurse," Cassandra answered.

Pinocchio realized she had a very good point. "How's she doing?" he asked.

"Who?"

"Your mom."

"Oh, Mom's dead."

Pinocchio was horrified. "She's *dead*?"

"It wasn't the home that killed her, Pinocchio. She was just old."

A retirement home. Pinocchio hated the thought. He wanted to say something. He wanted to ask about costs, and details, and about how her mother felt about being abandoned by her family, but he couldn't find the right words. Everything sounded too offensive to ask. Frankly, he was offended by the idea of it too. But still, it had so much logic ...

Cassandra could practically see his mind spiraling and finally rescued him. "It's just an idea," she said. "Now let me finish with this nose of yours. It's a pity."

"What's a pity?" he asked.

"It's just such a handsome nose."

"Don't start, Cassandra."

"I'm only kidding," she said. She dabbed on a final touch of rouge and announced, "There. Good as new!"

Pinocchio grabbed his phone and snapped a few shots. It was a stunning transformation—other than being 30 percent larger, the nose looked almost normal.

"Wow! Thanks!" he exclaimed.

"No problem." Cassandra gathered her kit, and asked, "So what does Charles want to see you about?"

"I don't know," answered Pinocchio. "I'm hoping it's a new project."

Two projects in a month, she thought. Cassandra didn't want to be jealous but couldn't help herself. She headed for the door, then paused in just such a way as to make it seem like her next thought was a spontaneous one. "One last thing about your dad. You said he burned down his house because he was smoking in bed?"

"Yeah ..."

"And right now he's at your house."

Pinocchio was dumbstruck. His mind raced with images of Albero and Whitney in their housecoats, sitting on the bumper of an ambulance, their own house in flames ... and suddenly it didn't seem so far-fetched.

"Well," she continued, "good luck with Charles." She was nearly at the door when he shouted,

"Cassandra!"

As she turned back, she was surprised by the look in Pinocchio's eyes—a steely determination, something she was not used to seeing in the shy young man. He asked,

"What was the name of that home you sent your mother to?"

CHAPTER 9

The Village of the Weeping Pines

Pinocchio had hoped to avoid a big scene that evening, so imagine his surprise as he pulled into the quiet Virginia suburb to find his entire family waiting to greet him in the driveway. Geppetto had gotten it into his mind that the reason the men had shown up to cut down the tree was to make way for a guesthouse on the property. He knew his son's penchant for drama, and packing the bag was likely little more than showmanship—the family would go to a nice dinner, and then Pinocchio would give over the news—*Geppetto was going to stay with the family permanently!*

Whitney was under no such illusion. She knew her husband too, and she saw how crazy having his father at the house had made him. Pinocchio had been under so much stress with the new job; she knew getting Geppetto his own place would be the best thing for everyone. But that Pinocchio had apparently found such a place and was going to surprise his family with it was cause for a celebration. As the big coupe pulled into the driveway, Whitney unplugged her ears and raced to greet her husband, who replied with a rather terse, "What are you guys all dressed up for? You're not going."

His cold tone didn't stop Whitney from looping a hug around his neck. "Albero's been talking about 'Grandpa's new house' all day. He wants to come." She finished the hug with a big kiss on the cheek.

"Honey, the old man's been through enough. Don't you think he'd like a little privacy—"

"You're not going to rob Albero of this. He wants to see Grandpa's new house—and so do I." She turned to the boys and commanded, "Let's go!"

Geppetto and Albero clambered into the back seat, each taking a moment to offer the newly appointed senior of the family a thanks and a hug. As the big coupe pulled onto the expressway, Whitney even held his hand. Pinocchio couldn't help but think what a rotten thing it was for her to do.

* * *

For two hours the family drove and drove. In the back of his mind, Pinocchio had hoped Albero would find his way to slumber—a long drive to rock the child to sleep was a trick he and Whitney used to use when Albero was still in diapers—but he was just too excited to sleep tonight.

"Does it have a swimming pool?" Albero asked.

"It does have a pool ...," Pinocchio answered. He didn't have the heart to add that it was filled with Epsom salts.

"I thought you said it was close. We've been driving for hours," said Whitney. She was right. Pinocchio glanced at his watch as it ticked past 7:45. He knew the "Welcome Center" closed at 8 p.m., and he was out of options. He hung a right and the sign for Geppetto's new home filled the windshield—*The Weeping Pines Retirement Center.*

A shocked silence filled the car. Even Pinocchio didn't bother to say anything as he stepped out and began fishing Geppetto's bags from the trunk. A man approached with a wheelchair. Geppetto desperately rolled up the window, only to have Pinocchio yank open the door.

"Come on, Dad."

Geppetto stepped out cautiously. The man slid the wheelchair up behind him, bumping against his knees. Geppetto bit the man's head off. "I don't need that thing!"

"Dad, maybe you'd be more comfortable—"

Whitney intervened. "Sir, he can walk." Stepping out of the car, she leaned close to Pinocchio and angrily whispered, "You're not seriously going to leave him here, are you?"

"I told you I didn't want you to come," he replied. "Let's not make a scene; let's just get him in and we'll talk about it in the car."

Geppetto had already noticed that the concrete pond—which, according to the sign posted beside it, was a "lake"—didn't have a single tree. Half a dozen blank faces stared at him from the cafeteria. An elderly woman with tennis balls on her walker shuffled by. Pinocchio put on his widest politician's grin and took Geppetto's arm. "Wait until you see your room!"

Geppetto was too overwhelmed to do anything but follow as his son and a man pushing an empty wheelchair led him inside. A moment later, an orderly in powder-blue scrubs reappeared and snatched Geppetto's bags from the sidewalk. Whitney could only watch, arms folded. She finally slipped back into the car and balled her fists.

"Mama, is this Grandpa's new home?"

To the innocent queries of children, one can only answer with what they need to hear, which is not always the truth. "For a few days, Albero. Just for a few days." It wasn't necessarily a lie, maybe just wishful thinking on her part. Deep down, Whitney knew that nobody really ever left a retirement home, at least not when they were conscious and she wondered just who could have put this rotten idea into her husband's mind?

* * *

On the drive home neither Whitney nor Pinocchio wanted to talk. Albero, on the other hand, demanded answers.

"When's Grandpa get to come home?" he asked.

"Soon," was Pinocchio's vague reply.

"Tomorrow?"

"Soon, Albero."

"Can we go visit him?"

"We should let him get settled in for a few days, then we can go and visit him."

"When?"

"Soon."

Whitney shot Pinocchio an icy glare. He didn't want to take his eyes off the freeway, but he could feel the ice. Finally, he asked, "What?"

"I can't believe you put him in a place like that."

"Can we talk about this after Albero goes to bed?"

"You know he actually thought you were going to build a guesthouse in the backyard—"

"Are you nuts?" Pinocchio exclaimed.

She continued, "Then why did you cut down the tree?"

"So we could see the city—"

"Did you see the look on his face when that wheelchair—"

"Whitney, that's enough." Pinocchio's tone was forceful. "This is the best thing—"

"For who? For you?"

"For us! What, did you want to wait until he burned our house down, too? Face it, Whitney, the man was losing it—he was a hoarder."

"A hoarder?"

"You didn't see the insurance report! There were so many goddamn cuckoo clocks in that place—"

"Watch your language!"

Both sets of eyes glanced toward the back seat. Albero wore a confused, almost frightened look. No child likes to see his parents fight, and he still hadn't heard a satisfactory answer to his question, "When does Grandpa get to come back home?"

Pinocchio still didn't answer, choosing instead to continue the argument, albeit at a much lower volume. "I'm not going to talk about this anymore. He's my father, and this was my decision."

"And what example are you setting for him"—Whitney nodded toward the back seat—"that when someone starts boring you too much, you ship him away? Is this what we have to look forward to one day?"

"Whitney, he almost killed himself! I'm not going to put this family in any more danger—"

Albero's screaming was the first warning of the danger they were suddenly in. Pinocchio snapped his eyes back to the road as the mass of fur bounced off the hood and tumbled into the air. A chorus of terrified screams filled the car as Pinocchio leaned on the brakes—a delayed reaction that was too late to save the unfortunate deer.

The coupe wobbled and swerved as Pinocchio managed to bring it to a halt. He crept over to the side of the mostly empty highway and jumped out, examining the damage, what little there was of it. The coupe's build quality rivaled a Panzer tank and a few scratches aside, seemed to survive the collision like one. Twenty yards back, the deer was not so lucky. Before anyone could protest, Albero was out of the car and running down the side of the road to see to the fallen creature. Whitney was fast on his tail, calling his name and being ignored. The panic in Whitney's voice was enough to snap Pinocchio out of his insurance-claim haze.

The deer was a sad sight, its legs twisted and broken, and a small puddle of blood forming around its ear. It struggled to breathe, and its eyes darted around, both confused and frightened, not even realizing what had just happened. Albero brushed against its back gently, and was speaking to it in a relaxed, reassuring tone when his parents finally caught up to him.

"Albero, get away from it!"

"He's hurt, Mama!"

Pinocchio didn't hesitate before sweeping Albero up and away from the injured creature, to which Albero protested with a cry: "No, Papa! He's hurt!" Albero struggled and squirmed against his father's tightening grip. "Albero, stay away, it's dangerous!"

The deer heaved—a best effort to get back on its feet before collapsing back to the ground. Startled, Pinocchio and Whitney jumped. "He's asking for help!" Albero declared.

"You see?" said Pinocchio. "This is what Dad's doing!"

The deer heaved again, its breathing growing more labored. Blood began to drip from its nostrils.

"Help him, Papa!" Albero shouted.

"Pinocchio," Whitney added, "call someone!"

"Who? 911? Animal control?"

"I don't know!"

"Well, I don't know either; I've never hit a goddamn deer before!"

"For the last time, watch your language."

Pinocchio sighed. "Its legs are broken. It's not going to make it." Pinocchio handed Albero to Whitney and fished for his phone.

"Who are you calling?" she asked.

"The police. I don't know who else—"

"His family," Albero interrupted.

"What?"

"That's what he told me. He wants to see his brother before he dies."

Pinocchio and Whitney exchanged confused looks. They stepped even farther back as the animal made a vain final attempt to get to its feet. Finally, the heavy breathing faded, its black eye clouded over, and the animal fell perfectly still. The three stood in silence as the phone rang in Pinocchio's ear. Finally, the nonemergency police dispatcher answered. Pinocchio relayed the event, the location, and assured the officer that everyone was all right, a statement that drew a sharp rebuke from Albero. He finally managed to squeeze his way out of his mother's grasp, and crept up to the unfortunate creature. Neither Pinocchio nor Whitney protested as he knelt, brushed the matted fur, and whispered something that neither of his parents could make out. He stood, took Whitney's hand and the three of them silently made their way back to the car. Pinocchio took one last look at the scratches across the top of the hood, and they drove away, the argument, as well as any other conversation, ended for the rest of the night.

* * *

That week, Pinocchio and Whitney spoke less than at any time since before they had met. Pinocchio's workdays were growing longer, and when he wasn't in the office, he was working at Cassandra's apartment. A painful truth had taken hold in his mind—Pinocchio was forgetting how to talk to his wife, yet talking to Cassandra had become disturbingly easy.

Most of the few hours he was at home were spent waxing the scratches out of his beloved coupe. Bedtime was anything but restful as both he and Whitney lay perfectly still and treated the middle of the bed with the reverence of a demilitarized zone. Dinners, what few of them there were, had become a study of tension. By the one-week anniversary of Geppetto's departure, the situation had begun to boil over. By that Thursday night, it exploded.

CLANK! CLANK! CLANK!

Enormous scoops. Then more. Each time, Pinocchio pounded the heavy sterling spoon against his plate until not a fleck of white remained on the silver. With each *CLANK*, he lifted his eyes from his plate and glared at Whitney over the arch of his glasses. Oh how she hated that! It was like being lectured by a stern professor; only this professor hadn't spoken a word, and she had no idea what she had done to deserve such a dressing-down.

His plate overflowing with mashed potatoes, Pinocchio next went to work on the gravy. Normally so careful in the way he served, tonight his gentle pour was something more suited to Jackson Pollock. Gravy spilled off the edge of the plate and dripped in thick gobs onto the linen tablecloth. Still Whitney said nothing.

The next victim was the wine. It wasn't the most expensive wine, just a tall-bottled Chianti from Italy, and Pinocchio poured nearly the entire bottle into his glass.

That was the last straw.

"You're drinking too much," Whitney said.

"If you didn't want me to pour half a bottle, why did you put out these ridiculous glasses? Look at this thing!"

"It's a *burgundy* glass. They're supposed to be tall. But you're only supposed to fill it less than half—"

"Hey! It's my house and if I want to drink a full glass of wine, I will. OK?"

"Papa," Albero asked, "can I have some mashed potatoes?"

"You can have them when I'm done."

At that, he resumed the clanking. Gravy and flecks of potatoes flew everywhere.

"Albero," said Whitney, "why don't you go watch TV? I'll bring you something to eat in a minute."

He didn't have to be asked twice. He leaped up and ran into the living room—as far away as he could from the fight that even he could feel brewing. Pinocchio folded his hands and stared at the disaster of a table.

"If you're not going to talk about this, I will," said Whitney.

"What's the point?" Pinocchio replied. "Nothing changes."

"Well, I won't have these childish outbursts in front of our son. You're acting like an idiot."

"Well that's perfectly motherly of you," was his snarky reply. "You're just a perfect mother, aren't you?"

"Don't take it out on me. I didn't do anything."

"Didn't you? Ever since they made me a partner, it's like everything I say goes in one ear and out the other. It's like you're not even proud of me; it's like you *resent* this little bit of success I'm having."

Whitney didn't mean to laugh, but she couldn't control it. "Resent you?" she snickered. "What are you talking about? I've never been anything but proud of you, but—"

"Yeah, see? But what?"

"Look, I let it drop about your father. Maybe you were right. But these hours you're working. Your son misses you, and"—she paused—"I miss you too."

The sentiment was lost on Pinocchio. "I don't want to have this discussion again," he said.

"We never finished this discussion!"

"It's what they expect. What'd you think, they pay me all this money to kick back and relax?"

"No—"

"There're a hundred guys in this town who would scoop up this job in a second if I gave the partners anything less than—everything!"

She sighed. "So how long is it going to be like this?"

"As long as it takes," he replied. "A few years."

"A few *years*? Pinny, you can't keep this up for years."

"I can keep it up for a hundred if I have to. Partner, Whitney, full partner. That's what they've got picked out for me.

Do you know how much a partner makes? It's everything I ever wanted, to be a real lobbyist!"

"There was a time when all you ever wanted was me, and after that, to be a dad. This job is changing you, Pinny."

"What do you want me to do? Just quit?"

"No, I don't want you to quit. We're with you, Pinocchio, but we need you to be with us, too."

"Well, you're going to just have to get along without me for a while, because I'm not leaving. These guys respect me—"

Whitney had held her tongue long enough. She let into him with the ferocity that only sincerity can bring.

"No, Pinocchio, those guys use you! You don't see it, but ever since that article came out, they've made a sideshow of you and your talents. You're just a puppet to them. Then there's all this time you spend with that woman—"

Pinocchio leaped to his feet, nearly flinging the table over. "You leave her out of this!"

But Whitney held firm. "You owe me an answer, Pinocchio. What's going on?"

"What do you mean?"

"Are you—" She swallowed hard. "*Are you having an affair?*"

Pinocchio didn't get the chance to answer. Roused by the heated conversation spilling into the living room, Albero made his presence known with a simple, "Mama?"

His face wore the same terror that Whitney had seen a week ago as Geppetto was escorted away. Pinocchio didn't want to look at him. More accurately, he couldn't stand to look at him. "Go to your room, Albero," Pinocchio ordered.

"Mama, what's the matter?"

"Albero," Pinocchio repeated, "I told you to go to your room."

"Mama?"

Pinocchio had finally had enough. He whirled around and marched toward the frightened boy, screaming, "Albero, go to your *GODDAMN ROOM!*"

Whitney leaped to her feet and snatched Albero into her arms. The fierceness of her response startled Pinocchio, who quickly replayed the moment in his head, and was instantly sinking beneath a wave of guilt. Whitney had only to turn her head—the look in her eyes was one of pure revulsion. Pinocchio had never seen this look before, and only a glimpse of it was chilling. He knew, at that moment, he had crossed a line.

His instinct was to apologize, to cower, and to hide. But there was another feeling fighting back—a most human emotion, one of pride, one of resistance, one of reciprocity. It was the politician in him, and it was ordering him to *stand his ground.*

He had made a command decision—to retreat was to show a weakness he knew he could never recover from. The two emotions crashed into each other with a fury he had not known since the wreck that had taken Whitney's little station wagon some months earlier. His only recourse was to leave. He grabbed his keys as he pushed through the door, and that was the last Whitney and Albero saw of him that night.

* * *

Cassandra was asleep when a knock at her door startled her into consciousness. Of all the faces she expected to see through that peephole, Pinocchio's rain-soaked visage was at the bottom of the list.

She asked for a moment to get herself together while the junior partner waited patiently at the door. She was terrified he might leave, little knowing that he really had no place else to go. There was no time for makeup, but certainly a moment to switch from her dowdy cotton robe to a silk kimono just short enough to leave something to the imagination—though admittedly not much. She checked her hair and her breath, then threw the mirror a quick smile before peeling the door open, and asking this most married young man what he was doing at her door on a Thursday night.

"Whitney and I had a fight. Can I come in?"

She offered a token resistance, which was the custom, but both of them knew full well that she was going to open the door. She kicked aside the trashy novel she had been enjoying and offered wine. Pinocchio was already a full glass in that evening, but he didn't resist. He took a seat in the middle of the sofa—an unusual move, as he had always insisted they sit at the table to work. Cassandra floated down as close to him as ever she had been, offering a sympathetic ear, as well as a marvelous view of her legs.

Pinocchio let it all flow out, everything from the day he landed in Washington up to the very words of the last argument. Cassandra listened, nodded, and took every opportunity to lend a reassuring pat on the knee. As one glass of wine turned to three, he found himself turned directly toward her, his fingers wrapped around hers and his mind, for once, completely at ease. For the first time in a long time, he began to notice the depth of the green eyes that watched, intently but also gently, as he let the problems of a man pour from his heart. She seemed not only to listen, but also to care. Pinocchio leaned closer and closer, the lightness of a wine-soaked haze allowing a level of intimacy that the clear-minded man never would. He felt so alone, and in this moment, this woman now seemed his only link between sanity and madness. Pinocchio felt himself beginning to let go of the old-world rules that had kept their relationship professional up to this point, and for the first time in his life, he began to wonder what it might be like to misbehave for the very sake of it.

But should he? For Pinocchio, the worst part about acting like a bad man would be that everyone saw him as a good man. How could they have known just how human he had become? It was not that he wanted to sin, but he realized for the first time in his life that he was capable of it—not just capable of the deed, but actually getting away with it. The woman sitting so dangerously close to him was beyond attractive to his eyes—she was alluring.

Cassandra could see the want in his eyes. She had seen it many times before. To her, this was the thing that gave her power. She knew what would come next, and she had no pity for those who would suffer the consequences, for in love, war, and politics, all things were fair. She seized the moment. She leaned over, pushing her body against his. This was Pinocchio's last chance to protest. He didn't.

Their lips pressed. He could feel the warmth of her skin as she offered a kiss as tender as he would ever find. Pinocchio let instinct take over. Images of his wife faded quickly from his periphery as Cassandra loosened her kimono ...

Was there any other way, my friends, for Pinocchio to realize his lifelong dream of becoming a real man, than in the arms of another woman? The entire affair from the very first smile she had shot his way to the one that now moved her lips to his had been a lie, and like all simple-minded men, Pinocchio had allowed himself to believe it. In this way he became a man that night, for as we all know, it is a child's folly to lie to one's self, but a man's folly to actually believe it.

CHAPTER 10

Pinocchio Learns the Consequences of Selfishness

By Tuesday of the next week, Pinocchio had become a genuine recluse at the firm. Alone in his office, he studied the binder all day. It wasn't until late in the evening that he finally pulled his door locked behind him and drove his big coupe into the Washington night. In that time, Pinocchio had not a word to share with Cassandra, never once suggesting they get together to work on the project, or to have dinner, or to spend the night.

What Cassandra couldn't have known, what no one but the parties involved could have known, was that Pinocchio was splitting his research time. Half his day he spent on the bill, but the other half he focused carefully on the handwritten note he had found waiting for him when he finally returned home that fateful evening.

It read:

My Dear Pinny,

I shall never forget the day I met the man I loved.

I was a student at Berkeley. I used to sit on the grass and read—but that afternoon it had rained and the grass was wet, so the only place for me to sit was on a bench, right next to a nerdy, but still handsome young Italian man. I remember he was so shy that he could barely speak. I even thought he might have been an exchange student. He asked me to borrow a pencil, but what he really wanted to ask was my name. We spent the whole afternoon together. He was so curious about me, and so honest about his curiosity—it was very charming. That night, we shared our first kiss, and I knew that that ecology student and I were going to spend the rest of our lives together.

I fell in love with him, though it wasn't always easy—like the time he went to Washington DC for a job interview and ended up buying a house without even asking me.

But his love was as solid as the Redwood Forest, where we spent so many dates. I may have fallen in love with a boy, but I knew I had married a man, and never was that more clear than after Albero was born. My husband was a wonderful father. He loved our son even more than he loved me, and his father, and the earth.

I do not know where this man went, and I miss him terribly.

For a long time I knew something was different, but tonight it became clear to me what that was. You have become selfish. Your job has changed you, has made you do things I never thought possible before this year—and the worst part is, you do it in spite of yourself. The man I know would never have thrown his father out of our home. The man I know would never have left me to spend the night God knows where and with God knows who. But most terribly, the man I know would never have frightened our son the way you did tonight. The man I know would not do this, but you did.

I do not know you anymore, Pinocchio, and I cannot bring our son up with a stranger in the house, and so I have decided to leave.

Perhaps you will find yourself again—and if you do, you may decide to come and find your family again. I hope so, because our family is broken, Pinocchio. Your lies have splintered it into a hundred thousand pieces like that dear old tree in the backyard that you too once loved. I do not know what can heal us now. I do not know if we can ever be healed.

If you ever come back for us, Pinocchio, you must come back as your true self. If you come back to me, you will have to become a real man. I do not know how you will find that, or who will guide you, but you must, Pinocchio; otherwise who knows what will become of you?

—Whitney

Once, when he was little more than a child, Pinocchio killed a bird with a slingshot. He remembered the image of the bird flapping around, unable to heal itself, unable even to understand what had happened. It was not unlike the tired heaving of that poor deer—there was an awful finality to it, a sense that he had done something that could not be undone. As he read the letter over and over, that same feeling crept back into his mind. It was as if he had attempted a jump that in retrospect, he knew he couldn't make, and landed on a broken arm—the energy of the moment long since yielded to the foreboding of a terrible injury. It was the same feeling he had when he returned home from Cassandra's apartment to find his family gone, and only this note left in their place.

Pinocchio had done something terribly wrong, and he didn't know how to even begin to undo it.

Dan Spence came in with another pile of papers. Pinocchio offered the slightest of nods before turning back to the letter and planning his evening—another night on the sofa, with the television as his only distraction, and a takeout dinner his only meal for the day.

He decided to concentrate on the bill. He opened his well-worn copy, flipping almost instinctively to the section he had highlighted earlier. Pinocchio couldn't get a particular phrase out of his mind—"to be released from the requirement of the EIS, given the time-sensitive nature of the project." *To be released from the requirement of the EIS.* There was no other mention of the term in the entire document. He wanted more than anything to ask someone what it meant, but being the "professional witness," it seemed silly that he wouldn't know it. He decided to give the web a try.

According to Google, "EIS" was either a financial consulting firm out of Miami, or an "environmental impact study." Pinocchio had heard the term before, but didn't know much about it. He drilled down further. There were pages on wind farms, mining operations, ocean research—and a number of links to the big local story of the week, the whale that had been trapped in the tuna net. Pinocchio read quickly through them, but there weren't very good pictures of the animal, so he moved on. Whales had always interested him, but he was determined to focus on work right now. Finally, he came across a page that made a little more sense—a summary of a lawsuit filed on behalf of a shale oil driller that was seeking to waive the requirement that an environmental impact study be performed prior to logging in a national forest.

To be released from the requirement of the EIS.

"How about lunch?"

The sound of Cassandra's voice startled him. He hadn't heard the door open, yet there she was, leaning over his desk, looking as fresh as a spring day. Her eyes wandered over to his monitor, which still had a window open on the local news.

"Reading about that whale, hmm?"

Pinocchio quickly locked his computer. "No, just—"

"You can go see it if you want. The fishing boats out there are running tours."

"No, I'm just researching—" He quickly changed the subject. "What do you need, Cassandra?"

She pulled back a bit and dropped the smile. "I was just wondering if you wanted to get lunch."

Pinocchio checked his watch. "No, I really have a lot of work to do." Cassandra nodded, stepped back to the front door and pushed it closed, a simple gesture that sent splinters of fear down Pinocchio's spine.

"Pinocchio, what's going on? You don't talk to me anymore; you're distant, ever since that night—"

Pinocchio had been avoiding this conversation for a week. Now it seemed he was out of excuses. "Whitney left me."

"What?"

"Last week. Took Albero too."

"Pinocchio, I'm sorry—"

He waved her off. He didn't want to, or wasn't ready to confide in her any more than that. She understood and she made her exit. Pinocchio took one last look at the note, then shoved it into a drawer and unlocked his computer. He couldn't take any more emotion at this moment—not sadness, not loss, not even anger. The time had come to bury himself in work, and that's exactly what he intended to do. Still, something Cassandra had just mentioned—*a tour of the whale.* It was lunchtime and he wasn't particularly hungry. Maybe a distraction was just what he needed, and besides, there was something strangely familiar about the sight of this whale ...

CHAPTER 11

Pinocchio Encounters an Old Nemesis

It had been a good week for fisherman Will Sanford. Ever since the whale first appeared, the sleepy little hamlet of Deale, Maryland, had become something of an amusement park. The commotion had scared off a lot of fish, but the endless line of reporters, Greenpeace volunteers and lookie-loos who came asking for tours had more than made up for it. Ordinarily Will's boat wasn't available for hire. Frankly there wasn't much to see off the coast of Deale—and certainly not from the deck of a choppy little launch like the *Cunnyfish*—but this week his rate was fifty dollars a tour.

Will tapped away on his cell phone, barely noticing the funny little man wandering up the grimy dock in a suit and tie. *Just another customer.*

"Looking to see the whale?" Will asked.

"Uh, yes!" Pinocchio replied. "Fifty an hour?"

"Cash only. You got cash?" Will asked. Pinocchio nodded. "Good. How long do you want?"

"Two hours?"

"Two hours? He's right over—" Will caught himself. "I mean, if you think that'll be enough."

Pinocchio thought it over. "Yes, you're right ... make it four."

Will grinned. "Come on aboard." He skipped up to the wheelhouse as the tourist stumbled aboard, trying his best not to slip on the wet deck. Will knew this would be a quick trip. The smell out there was unbearable—it wouldn't be twenty minutes before the tourist had had enough and asked to go back—easy two hundred bucks.

Pinocchio felt the salt breeze sweep across his face as the *Cunnyfish* chugged away at five knots—close to its top speed. As they crept closer to the small flotilla of boats and rafts that had gathered around the whale, Pinocchio noticed the stench. The sea was getting rougher, and the tiny boat bucked and strained. The ocean crested the bow and soaked Pinocchio from cuffs to collar.

"Why are the waves so big?" Pinocchio asked.

"It's the whale," said Will. "He keeps kicking and kicking. You'd think he'd be exhausted, but that guy just don't give up."

Will eased off the throttle and a huge puff of black smoke shot from the engine.

"What's going to happen to him?" Pinocchio asked.

"Not sure. Ordinarily they just cut the net and let them out, but ordinarily they don't fight like this. Whales are smart. They know when people are there to help them. But this monster's good and pissed. Nobody can get near him. He just smashes these little skiffs into nothing. He'll either suffocate or die of starvation."

"He'll die?"

"He can't go on like this. He'll wear himself out. Even if someone does manage to cut him free, it'll be too late. He's a goner. Probably in a day or two. Lucky you caught him now. You from out of town?"

"DC," Pinocchio answered. "How close can you get?"

"Not very. That tail could snap us in two."

The engine settled to a hum as the boat slowed. The waves were getting bigger and bigger.

"Can you see him?" Will asked.

"No ..."

"I've got binoculars up here."

Pinocchio climbed up to the wheelhouse and Will handed him a well-used pair. As he squinted through the cracked lenses, he took the extraordinary sight into view ...

The whale's white spine broke just above the water—and it was easily forty feet long. It sat motionless as a pair of rigid inflatables crept up. Pinocchio could see the tangled net wrapped around him, cluttered with trash and dead tuna. It was a pathetic sight. A bearded man aboard one of the inflatables leaned over and gingerly began to cut through the net. At once, the mighty tail reared up. As it splashed down, the little inflatable nearly flipped, tossing the bearded man into the air. Pinocchio's heart froze. The beard's crewmates hauled him in by the seat of his pants as the second inflatable slinked away.

"Angry beast," said Will.

"OK." Pinocchio sighed. "Take us in."

"All done for the day?"

"No, I mean take us in closer."

"Closer?" Will was aghast. "You saw what that thing does!"

"It'll be OK."

"Look, pal, it ain't my boat—if something happens—"

Pinocchio reached into his pocket and fished out another pair of fifties. Reluctantly, Will pushed on the throttle and the boat surged forward.

The whale was closer now, so close that Pinocchio could clearly make out scars, bruises, and a lump of pink, irritated pustules around his blowhole. His tail drooped lamely. Pinocchio could feel exhaustion in the creature, but as they drew closer, the overwhelming feeling welling up inside him was fear.

Pinocchio focused in just beneath the waterline. As the whale drifted in and out of the water, his eye rose and fell, water pooling and dripping with each heave. Reduced to humility by a malfunction of man, it was as if the ocean were giving the mighty beast the tears he himself could not make. The lenses of the binoculars fogged up. The beast was not alone—

Pinocchio was weeping.

Suddenly the great eye opened and instantly locked on Pinocchio. He froze—it was as if the monster knew he was there before he even saw him. Though scared out of his wits, Pinocchio was excited by the connection that he seemed to have with the creature. This was, of course, not unnoticed by Will, who hastily turned the boat around.

"No!" ordered Pinocchio. "Stay here!"

"He'll capsize us!"

Pinocchio, however, wasn't sure he would. He lowered the binoculars and stared right back into the eye. He could not tell if the stare was a plea for help or a declaration of war. Pinocchio loosened his tie and announced, "I'm going in."

"In where? The ocean?" asked Will.

Pinocchio nodded. "Just wait here for me. I'll be right back."

"You can't go in there! He'll kill you!"

"I just need to get closer."

Will couldn't believe his ears. Suddenly $300 seemed less like a fortune and more like something he'd be putting in a coroner's report. "Look, pal, we never talked about this. If you dive in, I'm turning around and leaving you here."

Pinocchio reached into his wallet and counted. "I'll pay you a thousand dollars—*IF* you're still here when I get back."

"A thousand?" Will thought it over. He imagined his conversation with the coroner again. This crazy guy dives off his boat, against his good warning—it's not his fault if some nutjob ...

"Give me another five hundred now," he ordered.

Pinocchio took the wad of cash and neatly tore all ten bills in half. He handed one half to Will, who stared incredulously at the tattered edges. "You get the rest when we get to shore. Deal?"

How could he refuse?

Pinocchio balled up his socks and took a good look at the water. It had been some time since he'd swum at all, let alone in a rough sea. He leaned over and splashed water across his face. A quick jump later, and he was paddling through the Atlantic Ocean.

Will ran to the edge and watched as the strange man, still wearing a shirt and slacks, bobbed back to the surface and caught his breath. "Why are you doing this?" Will shouted.

"It's hard to explain," came the reply, "but I think I know this whale."

The water was frigid, and Pinocchio could already feel his muscles starting to cramp. Six years he'd been sitting at a desk, and it had done his physical condition no favors. As he pulled closer, Pinocchio could smell the warm decay radiating from the net. The great eye never broke its gaze, and as Pinocchio closed to within a few feet, he could see the pupil dilate.

Pinocchio stopped just a yard away. The stench was overwhelming. He did his best to breathe through his mouth, which only made him breathe harder. Finally he reached out and brushed the smooth, scarred skin of the whale.

"So, boy, you've come back."

The voice was like thunder—a boom that bellowed through the depths and seemed to freeze solid the very sea. Again, it spoke,

"That's right, you know me; I know you—Pinocchio."

Pinocchio gasped upon hearing his name. *"You're the only meal that ever got away."*

The whale was warmer now, almost hot. Pinocchio bobbed back and peered into the unblinking eye. The whale's voice was familiar, something less than a memory—more like a feeling. His words hit like a boxer's blows just above Pinocchio's sternum. He pushed aside the fear, touched the beast again and asked, "Who are you?"

"What a question, boy! You already know the answer—I am terror. I am the wrath of an angry earth and I eat men like you. I have been here since the sunrise of man. I have swallowed the Jonah and all the sailors who have tried to hunt me, and I have turned ships to splinters of wood."

The beast rolled back, laboring for a breath.

"But that was so very long ago, wasn't it? Nobody fears me these days. There is too much information, too many websites, too

many people writing, talking, shouting. You are so convinced of your knowledge of the world, aren't you? You remember nothing about me, just that my kind is dying, that we are gentle, and that we sing lullabies to the sailors who dump their sludge in the ocean and kill my brothers and sisters. But you will remember. I am the reckoning of nature, and you, of all your kind, are right to be afraid of me, Pinocchio."

Pinocchio crept closer and said, "I do not fear a crippled whale caught in a net."

"No, you fear your memory of me. What you fear is the past."

The monster was right. Pinocchio did not know how, but somewhere deep inside his belly, he felt a memory of something terrible—that same feeling of being crushed in the dark. But even as he listened to the monster's words, Pinocchio couldn't help but pity the beast. He looked again into the giant eye, which drifted aimlessly. It was tired, drooping. Pinocchio could only see a hint of the spark that once bejeweled the whale's gaze—now replaced with this dull, gray longing. It was the same look he saw in Geppetto not so many days before, a look of regret. It was that look, more than the rows of sharp teeth, that struck a dagger of fear across Pinocchio's heart.

"Show me your teeth," Pinocchio demanded.

The beast's eye met Pinocchio's, and for an instant, the spark reignited. The whale curled his giant lips into a terrible grin. His teeth were rotten and porous, caked with layers of what Pinocchio could only assume to be dead fish and hardened seaweed. The odor burned his eyes, an acidic haze ...

Acid!

It was the smell that finally brought it all back. Pinocchio knew that odor and he knew these teeth. Could it be? He looked back into the beast's eye—the sparkle had become a gleam—his grin an evil glower. Pinocchio was sure of it now—he and this whale had met once before.

"Yes! Yes, I do remember you! *Oceanus* they called you, isn't that right? What a cruel soul you were! You swallowed my father, and when I came to rescue him, you swallowed me too!"

Oceanus grinned wide. "Ah, not so dull as we look, are we, Pinocchio? That's right, you escaped me once—you were the only ones to ever escape me."

"You were a monster then and you're a monster now. I should let you stay here and die in the sun."

The water settled quickly as the net pulled the tired whale back into the sea.

"Let me die in the sun?" the whale bellowed. "You don't understand, do you, boy? It was because of the fear I brought into your world that you became a man. Had I not swallowed you, you would have ended your days as a lonely soul—lost in a wilderness of guilt. But look how you have grown! Look how you have forgotten! You do not know guilt again, and you do not know love again, and you are lost again, and now we meet again. But this time, boy, I cannot save you, just as these fools cannot save me. Ha! Let me die in the sun, Pinocchio, and be about your business! You have an appointment to be a meal for someone else. A whale bigger and more deadly than Oceanus has come to gobble you up—and no pepper, no smoke, no tricks can take you from him. You are doomed, Pinocchio, doomed as Oceanus is doomed. I have failed. Not for a hundred years have I welcomed sleep, but now, I think it paradise."

The great eye closed as the whale rolled back into the sea. His fins drooped, his back slouched, and he began to sink—a last gasp of air slipping from his lungs.

"No!" cried Pinocchio. He tugged at the net, desperate to rouse the beast from what he knew would be a final slumber. Pinocchio could not understand what he was feeling—the fear was still there, but so was an overwhelming sense of loss. Pinocchio dashed back to the boat, where Will was already revving the engine.

"I need a knife! Quickly!" Pinocchio shouted. Without thinking, Will threw open a footlocker and grabbed a rusty, dull blade.

"What are you going to do?" Will asked as he handed it over. Pinocchio didn't answer—he quickly snatched the blade and raced back to the net, which was sagging lower and lower in the ocean. As Pinocchio hacked and chopped, he cursed the dullness of the old blade. The net was well-made, forcing Pinocchio to saw at each braid before it finally gave way. The whale was already completely submerged, and Pinocchio kicked and strained to keep above water. The weight was immense, but Pinocchio was determined, and it seemed that with his will alone he could lift the beast to safety.

Pinocchio burst back to the surface and gasped. The flotilla had pulled in closer. The bearded man leaned out of his inflatable and offered a much better, much sharper diver's knife. Pinocchio grabbed it and dove back under. The net had sunk almost thirty feet and it seemed to writhe and kick as a hundred tuna struggled to get free. Pinocchio chopped and chopped. His lungs felt heavy. He grabbed at the tiny hole he had managed to open and tore ...

All at once, the net snapped open and floated free. Pinocchio arched his back and burst back to the surface, filling his chest with the kiss of fresh air. Suddenly, the ocean heaved, pulling Pinocchio under as a huge wave surged upward. The wave broke—and the massive grin of whale burst onto the surface. He quickly slipped back under, only to reappear a moment later, launching itself into the air, crashing down onto the flotilla that had tried so hard to free him.

Pinocchio floated helplessly as the monster glided up to him. The tired old whale was gone, and in his place was terror itself.

"You are a fool, boy. You always have been. So shall we finish our business?"

Terrified though he was, Pinocchio closed his eyes and thought his words out carefully—

"You will not swallow me, Oceanus," he said. "You may be a cruel soul, but a soul you are nonetheless. I saved you, and for that, you will not swallow me today."

Oceanus laughed a laugh so heavy it seemed to shake the entire ocean.

"What a man you have become, Pinocchio! You are right. I will not swallow you today, but be warned—you and I have not had our last meal together. When that time comes, you will beg me to show you fear once again, and that, I shall oblige."

The whale turned, and in a flash he was gone. Pinocchio floated back to the surface. As he emerged, the flotilla let out a mighty cheer. Pinocchio gave the lamest of waves before pulling himself back into the old fishing boat. The engine was running, but Will was nowhere in sight. Pinocchio made his way up to the bridge and discovered the skipper curled in the tiniest of tiny balls under the control deck.

Will dared to open his eyes, both relieved and furious to see the strange little man standing over him.

"How—who—*are you CRAZY?*" Will demanded. He stood, dusted himself off and resisted the urge to throw this maniac back into the sea. Instead, he accepted the rest of his payment and pointed the boat back toward the Maryland shore. Even if the whale hadn't gotten free, Will decided in that moment that his days as a tour boat operator were behind him. Not a word was spoken as they chugged their way back to port.

"You are a fool, boy. You always have been."

* * *

Anyone looking for Pinocchio that afternoon had only to follow the seawater trail from his car to Charles Stevens's office.

"Pinocchio, lad, come on in! Ready for the big—" Stevens stopped twelve inches short of a handshake. "My God, what happened to you?"

"I fell into the ocean."

The answer made about as much sense as did any of Pinocchio's answers, so Stevens accepted it. He handed the junior partner a brass-plated Kleenex box and continued, "Well, I'm glad you're OK. Ready for the big day tomorrow?"

"Mostly. I just had a few last questions—"

Stevens took his seat and kicked back. "Shoot."

"In the bill there's a mention of something called an '*EIS*.' Do you know what an *EIS* is?"

Stevens shook his head.

"It's an *environmental impact study*. It's supposed to show what could happen to the environment if a large project like this logging goes forward."

"So?" Stevens asked.

"Well don't you see, Charles? If they waive that, then this company can log whenever and wherever it wants, and there's no way of knowing what damage they could do."

"Pinocchio," Stevens answered, "I'm not so sure that's our concern."

"But we're repping the bill—"

Stevens walked over and slipped an arm around Pinocchio's soggy shoulder. "Understand, lad, we don't write the bills. We're lobbyists, not legislators. Our only job is to represent them, *to advance our client's agenda, to get the bills before the people's advocates.* Now, whether or not the bill is a good idea or a bad one, well, that's for those advocates to decide. They can vote the bill up, or they can vote the bill down, and we have no say over that. All we can do is offer them the choice."

"Charles, I agree, except—"

"Except what?"

"I'm not just lobbying on this one. I'm a witness. I'm a *sworn* witness."

"So?"

"If they ask me, I have to tell the truth."

"And what truth is that?" Stevens asked.

How could Charles not see it? "That we don't know what this logging will do to the environment!"

Stevens let go of Pinocchio's shoulder, shook the salt water off, and poured a drink. "That watch held up nicely," he said.

"What's that, Charles?"

"You said you fell in the ocean. Look at that watch; not a leak, not a scratch. That's a diver's watch. I don't know how many people actually go diving with something as expensive as that, but still—imagine if that thing had filled up with water. How mad would you be?"

"I don't know," said Pinocchio, a little confused. "Pretty mad I suppose."

"I'll bet you would be. I'll bet you'd be so mad that your deluxe diving watch failed the one time you put it in the ocean, that you'd go to the manufacturer and demand your money back. Hell, you might be so mad you'd decide to sue them. You'd take to the Internet, the airwaves, radio, television ... you'd warn every single potential customer not to buy one. Do you see what I'm saying, Pinocchio?"

Pinocchio shook his head.

"Kronos is that watch. We're tasked with an impossible job: to advance a bill like this—bills that don't have an icicle's chance in hell of passing. But we take them on anyway. That's why these clients pay us so much. We're the ones who can stand up to the ocean, stand up to the environmentalists, stand up to the resistance, and get the job done no matter what it takes. Sometimes it means we have to put our own feelings aside and just do what we have to do."

"But ...," Pinocchio said, "it's dishonest."

"Honesty and politics, lad, water and oil. Nobody cares about the truth, Pinocchio; they care about getting the job done." Stevens stood over him, a stern look in his eye. "Are you willing to do what's necessary to get that job done?"

Pinocchio's hesitation was obvious. Stevens sighed. "Haven't we treated you well here, Pinocchio? Didn't we bring you into our family and make you one of our own? Do the right thing tomorrow."

"But, Charles," said Pinocchio, "I'm not sure what the right thing is."

"The right thing, Pinocchio, is to lie."

The word hit Pinocchio like a punch to the face. "Lie?" he clarified. Stevens nodded. "But, Charles, I can't lie!"

"Think of it like you're telling them what they want to hear. You're married, right?" Pinocchio nodded. "What do you tell your wife when she asks you if she looks fat?"

"I tell her she doesn't."

"And is that the *honest* truth?"

"Of course it is!" said Pinocchio. "She goes to the gym twice a day!"

"OK," said Stevens, "what about your little boy? What do you tell him when he asks about Santa Claus?"

"He's never asked about Santa Claus."

Stevens slumped his shoulders. "Pinocchio, haven't you ever just told a little white lie?"

Pinocchio thought about it. "The other day I told a police officer that I was speeding because I had to get to the hospital."

Stevens grinned. "Perfect!" he continued. "And what happened?"

"I crashed into his car and got three tickets."

Stevens threw his hands up. "Pinocchio, nobody expects a politician to tell the truth. No matter what they say, people automatically believe the opposite. So if you go out there and tell the truth, nobody will believe you. If you want to be believed, you have to say the *opposite* of the truth. That way you're not making a liar out of yourself. Ask yourself, what's more important—telling the truth, or being honest?"

"So what you're saying," Pinocchio pondered, "is that to be honest, I have to lie."

Stevens nodded.

Pinocchio didn't say another word, but that's not to say he didn't have questions. *Lie in order to tell the truth*—something just didn't seem right about it. He left a trail of salt water from Stevens's office to his own where he pulled the door closed and spent the remainder of the day buried in his books. There was still so much about Washington that he just didn't understand.

* * *

It was nearly midnight when a knock startled Pinocchio awake. The door creaked open, and Nancy DelGreco stepped inside.

"Mr. Pinocchio?" she asked.

Pinocchio bolted to his feet. "I must have dozed off. Sorry. What are you doing here so late, Nancy?"

"Mr. Stevens asked me to book him a last-minute trip. Don't you have a hearing tomorrow morning? You should be at home, resting."

"I just wanted to study up," he answered. "I'll be leaving in a few minutes."

"Well, since you're here—" Nancy stepped inside and placed a delicately wrapped package on his desk. "This is for you."

"What is it?" Pinocchio asked.

"A gift—in celebration of your big promotion."

Pinocchio excitedly tore into the paper and was shocked when he saw what was inside: a little brass plaque that read:

Oh Lord, thy sea is so great and my boat is so small.

It was the one from Nancy's desk. He was at a loss for words—even at a loss for thanks. "I figured you could use it," she said. "Seeing as how you're the one swimming with sharks now."

Pinocchio smiled, a gesture that had become far too unfamiliar these days. "Thank you, Nancy." He set the plaque on the desk and admired it for a moment, before asking, "Nancy, are you honest?"

It was a puzzling question. Before she could answer, Nancy noticed a wine bottle standing next to the plaque—it was full, but it was open—and she knew Pinocchio was not a drinker.

"What's bothering you, son?" she asked.

Son. Geppetto had always called him *my boy*. For reasons he couldn't explain, he suddenly felt tears filling his eyes and a quiver in his lips. Nancy had the overwhelming urge to comfort the man—to hug him and remind him that everything was going to be OK. Office gossip was rampant at Kronos, and she had heard about Pinocchio's troubles at home. She decided to remain professional for the moment, and just listen.

"I'm scared, Nancy."

At that, her professionalism melted. She covered the distance between them in two steps and hugged the man as he had not been hugged in years. It was a force as powerful as a "papa hug," but tender, caressing. Pinocchio bawled like a child awoken from a nightmare, but the hug had the desired effect—for the briefest of moments, everything seemed like it was going to be OK.

"Tell me what you're scared of," she said.

"Mr. Stevens says I have to lie tomorrow. I have to lie to Congress."

"Well, you wouldn't be the first."

"But it'll be the first for *me*. I've never told anyone this, but I've *never* lied. Never. Not as long as I can remember. Now I'm scared that if I tell the truth, Charles will fire me."

Nancy didn't hesitate. "Yes, he will." She broke the embrace, cupped his ears and drew his eyes to hers. "You asked, Pinocchio, so I will tell you that, yes, I think I am an honest woman. I am an honest person who works for a dishonest person—just like you. Because of that, after thirty some-odd years I am still just a secretary. My life isn't a glamorous one, but I had a husband who loved me, and he gave me five children and eleven grandchildren. Mr. Stevens, on the other hand, is on his fourth marriage. Is the difference that I'm honest? I don't know, but I do know that you're right to be scared. I can't tell you what to do tomorrow, Pinocchio, other than to listen to your conscience."

"My conscience?" he asked.

"It's the one thing that will never guide you wrong." She gave him a reassuring kiss on the forehead, headed for the door, continuing, "Your heart, on the other hand, can. Good-night, Mr. Pinocchio."

She stood to leave, pausing when Pinocchio said, "I didn't know your husband died. I'm sorry."

"Oh, don't be sorry, Pinocchio; he died before you were even born!"

"You never remarried?" he asked.

"Now why would I want to do that? When you really fall in love, it's forever."

Nancy pulled the door closed behind her. Pinocchio stood in silence, debating whether or not to pour himself a glass of that wine. He tossed it into the trash can on his way out the door.

CHAPTER 12

Pinocchio the Politician

It has been my observation, dear friends, that the important events in our lives fall into two categories. The first is the events that we wake up expecting. They are planned weeks, months, even years in advance. We greet those mornings with double-checked alarm clocks and slip into carefully laid-out clothes. We eat a light breakfast, our nerves being too active for us to actually enjoy anything, and we go to our first day of a job. We go to get married. We go to a baptism, or a graduation, or a birthday party, or a retirement party. The event has become all that we are, so much so that we cannot remember our lives before the event—and we cannot imagine our lives without it.

The other is the unexpected kind. We wake to an angry alarm clock and haphazardly toss on whatever we pull from the closet. We hurry through a stale bagel as we rush out the door, imagining the day will end exactly as the one before, and the one before that ... and then it happens.

We hear the crunch of metal as a truck runs a light. A letter arrives from the IRS. Our boss calmly asks us to come to their office. The phone rings at three in the morning. There is surprise. There is dread.

They are two very different experiences, the planned and the unplanned, and every now and then, they intersect. Sometimes, the big event *is* the surprise.

That day was a big one for Pinocchio, for it promised an event he had planned for weeks, anticipated for months, and dreamed of for years. That day, Pinocchio—once a penniless immigrant from Italy—was going to testify in front of Congress.

That day, Pinocchio was finally going to *be* somebody.

The big coupe started easily. Pinocchio took one last look at his perfectly combed hair before he eased out of the driveway. It was 8 a.m., and he wasn't scheduled to speak until eleven. Pinocchio was taking no chances with traffic that day.

Forty-five minutes later, Pinocchio pulled into the Union Station parking garage, three blocks north of the Capitol Building. He had been there many times before, but today felt different. In just over two hours, the chairman of the committee would announce his name, the large oak doors to the chamber would open, and in would walk—him! What a triumph it would be—the pinnacle of his career—and at such a young age! Pinocchio was on top of the world, and he felt lower than the dust, for he knew the moment of his greatest triumph was tempered by an even greater failure. After all, what good is such a moment without someone you love to share it with?

Pinocchio was finally willing to admit that he was lonely without his family—and that was the only honest thing he would say all day.

* * *

Dominic watched the committee meeting from the comfort of Stevens's office. "You sure your golden child is ready for this?" he asked.

"You worry too much, Dominic," Stevens replied. It sounded like a confident answer, but Stevens was pacing. He continued, "That kid has Barnes wrapped around his little finger. This will go quick."

A knock, and Nancy entered with a tray of drinks. Charles Stevens finally took a seat. He didn't tell Dominic about his conversation with Pinocchio the day before, and as he thought about it, he knew he hadn't reason to relax just yet.

* * *

At the Weeping Pines Retirement Center, Geppetto sat polishing his glasses while a heavyset orderly adjusted the television set.

"What channel is it on?" the orderly asked.

"I don't know," Geppetto replied. "They just said it's the government channel." He slipped his glasses back on and shoved his rocker square in the middle of the screen, eliciting angry howls from the rest of the audience.

"Oh hush!" he shouted. "My son's going to be on the TV."

The channels climbed higher and higher. Talk shows ... reality shows ... fashion shows ... but no government shows.

Geppetto checked the clock on the wall—a useless gesture, seeing as how it hadn't ticked in months.

* * *

Whitney hadn't planned on watching Pinocchio's testimony, but when her mother asked if Albero was going to watch his papa on television the next day, the matter was settled. All morning he had been going on and on about *Papa's TV show*.

Mother loaded coffee cups and cereal bowls into the dishwasher while Albero, like so many generations before him, sat cross-legged on the floor of the living room, eyes glued to the tube. "You know, Whitney," she said, "when men have important things in their lives, they tend to go a little crazy. I'm sure once this hearing is out of the way ..."

"It's complicated, Mom," said Whitney.

"I didn't assume it was simple. A week you've been here and you still don't want to talk about it—do you?" she prodded.

"Not really, well—" She paused. "I don't know."

Mother poured her another cup of coffee. "Pinocchio is a very complex man," she said, taking her daughter's hand. "Do you want to tell me what happened?"

Whitney took a deep breath. "I don't know anymore. That thing with his father, that thing with this woman, and"—she nodded at the screen in the living room—"that testimony." Whitney thought about it for a moment. How could she say that she didn't love him? Of course she did, but she didn't have enough love in her heart for both of them. Must she set herself on fire just to keep him warm?

"I never thought I could say this about Pinocchio, but he's become hollow."

* * *

"Max, you're not watching the committee?"

Jessica Gund was a freelance photographer who had been kicking around the *Washington Star* offices for the past month. She was an attractive lady who for some unexplainable reason had shown an interest in the middle-aged, twice-divorced Max Wiggs. Max, however, hadn't taken the hint. He didn't even glance up from his computer as he asked, "What committee?"

"Frank Barnes," she replied. "It's coming on C-SPAN in like five minutes. George Washington is testifying."

"He passed away a few years ago," Max quipped, "or so I heard."

Jessica rolled her eyes. "Not *the* George Washington, genius. *Your* George Washington. The cherry tree? Mr. 'I cannot tell a lie'?"

That got Max's attention.

"Pinocchio?" he asked. Jessica nodded. "What is Pinocchio doing at a committee hearing?"

"He's some sort of expert witness," she replied.

"It's on in the break room?"

Again she nodded. Max leaped up, knocking over a two-day-old cup of coffee. It did not smell wonderful.

* * *

Logically, Pinocchio should have been confident. After all, he knew exactly how this was going to turn out. The committee, Stevens had assured him, was a formality.

So why was he a nervous wreck?

An image flashed into his mind—Geppetto's old house in Italy—that heavy wooden door that creaked and caught on the uneven wood floor. He really had to shove that door to get it open, and even then, he usually had a bruise before an opening he could squeeze through.

Pinocchio was crying. Tears blurred his eyes, but he could still make out Geppetto racing toward him, his apron covered in sawdust, his glasses dangling from his neck.

Trouble, a bad day. Teacher had taken the boy to task over a homework assignment. A bad grade. Worse still, the boys all teased and taunted him. He had fought back, and one of them had tripped him during the scuffle and he had hit his head falling backward. It hurt, but having the boys see him cry hurt more.

Geppetto listened, checked his head, and then straightened him up. He looked at the boy sternly.

"Now, now! Stop crying!" said Geppetto. "The world is not at its end!"

"Dad, I don't want to go back," Pinocchio wailed. "The teacher hates me, the boys hate me, and I'm no good at anything!"

"You're right."

Instantly, Pinocchio stopped crying. He looked at his stern-faced father as if he had just spoken some foreign tongue.

"Wha-what do you mean?"

"You're no good at anything! You say it with such conviction, it must be true! I believe you. But worse still, you believe you."

"Why are you saying this, Dad?"

"It's one thing to lie to yourself, Pinocchio, but quite another to believe it. If you say you can't do something, you're right. But if you say, 'I can do something,' you're still right. Don't you see, boy?"

"But the teacher—"

"Posh, posh! The *teacher said! Teacher said! So unfair!* This is life, Pinocchio. There are rainstorms on the trail; everyone must face them. Some people have umbrellas, and some people don't. Only in heaven is the field even."

Pinocchio wiped his eyes. He had all but forgotten about the bump on his head. Geppetto had his full attention as he took a knee and spoke so tenderly, "You are a special boy, Pinocchio, more special than you can ever know, but that doesn't mean you have charm or magic. You have a gift, but you still must prove yourself worthy of it, even against the bumps, the rainstorms, the laughing boys and the silly teachers. Earn it, boy, and your gift will never let you down."

Returning to the moment, Pinocchio could hear the muffled proceedings behind the doors. Whatever testimony was being spoken was so very important to whoever was speaking, but to Pinocchio, it was noise. He wondered, *Will I just be noise as well?*

He fidgeted on the hard wooden bench, the last survivor of the Eisenhower administration. He checked his speech for the third time that hour—the pages were all still in order, so he went back to his fidgeting. A bead of sweat curled up in his palm. As he wiped it, he caught a glimpse of the watch on his wrist. No matter how many times he looked at it, it still fascinated him. *Thirty minutes, tops,* he told himself, then it would all be over. *I can handle thirty minutes.*

The heavy doors creaked open and an acne-scarred page mispronounced his name. Pinocchio stood, took a deep breath, and followed the uniformed boy into the chamber. He remembered Geppetto's words: *The field was only even in heaven.* It was all just another uneven field, and Stevens was just another angry teacher. The congressmen? Just more teasing boys. Whatever happened in the next thirty minutes, he swore, he would never come home crying to his father. Now was the time for him to be a man.

* * *

Pinocchio had never been to a congressional committee chamber before, and he was surprised by how small it was. The four rows of church-like pews and the two-row gallery above were practically empty, save for a troop of Boy Scouts seated in the front row. The committee members ignored him as he took his place—all except Barnes, who gave him a friendly nod. As Pinocchio sat down, the chair squeaked loudly against the wooden floor. He looked up to find a stenographer lording over him.

"Stand up," the stenographer ordered.

"I'm sorry, I didn't realize it would be so loud—"

"No, you need to swear in before you testify. Can you stand up please, sir?"

Pinocchio was embarrassed, but relieved. He stood, his hands bolted to his side like a toy soldier, and he waited for what seemed like a lifetime. Finally, Barnes swung his gavel and the murmuring of the congressmen fell silent.

"The committee will come to order," Barnes thundered. "The Committee of Interior Land Development was formed for the purpose of investigating matters of importance related to the preservation and disposition of the natural resources of the United States of America ..."

Though Barnes had read the invocation a hundred times, Pinocchio was riveted. He continued, "The committee calls Mr. Pinocchio from The Kronos Group."

The moment was here! It was a B-rated committee at best, but for the first time in a very long time, Pinocchio began to feel genuinely excited.

That's when he noticed the Bible.

It was old, almost an antique. Pinocchio could see how heavy it was by the way the stenographer held it. His pulse raced as he began to imagine what they expected him to do with it.

The stenographer looked at him with a pitiless expression and demanded, "Place your left hand on the Bible and raise your right hand." Pinocchio did as he was told. A cancerous lump formed in his throat as the stenographer read the oath, "Do you, Pinocchio, swear that the testimony you are about to give will be the truth, the whole truth and nothing but the truth, under penalty of perjury?"

Pinocchio nodded. Every eye in the room seemed to drill into him as the stenographer announced, "You have to say '*I do.*'"

The lump had metastasized. It had already spread to his chest as Pinocchio muttered, "I do." Barnes shook his head and scribbled a note. *What was he scribbling? Did he know? Did everyone know? Maybe it wasn't too late to change his mind. Maybe if he just turned and walked out—*

"You can take your seat," Barnes ordered. *Well that ended that plan.* He glanced again at his watch. *Thirty minutes*, he told himself, and he also noticed once again what a beautiful watch it was.

* * *

For the first part of the testimony everything went flawlessly. Pinocchio's prepared remarks had chewed up almost half his scheduled slot, and to his delight two congressmen had nodded off. The questions he was being pitched were softballs. *Does his firm stand behind this bill?* Well of course it did! *Does he believe that the proposed logging would lead to an increase in commerce?* Yes, it was the very purpose of the bill. If things kept going like this, there was a very real chance that Pinocchio would actually survive this.

Barnes had been strangely silent. He had spent the entire time scribbling, looking up every now and then to offer an agreeable nod. Nobody on the committee seemed especially convinced by Pinocchio's testimony, but then again, nobody seemed especially argumentative either.

Pinocchio could already see the handshakes and cigars waiting for him back at the office—that is until the heavyset man from Nevada spoke up. "Mr. Pinocchio," he began, ominously, "though I'm sure your firm has only the country's best interests at heart, there is one thing that troubles me."

It was the word "troubles" that troubled Pinocchio. He dropped his smile and assumed his most authoritative posture. "And what is that, sir?" he asked.

"I suppose the most obvious question is—why there?"

But the question didn't seem at all obvious to Pinocchio. "Why, *there*, sir?" he clarified.

"Yes, young man," Nevada replied. "Considering all the lumber reserves in this country, some of which are just begging for a job-creating project like this one, why does your client feel the need to log in the middle of the Oldwood Forest?"

It was a dirty trick of a question, and Pinocchio didn't much care for the title of "young man." He sat as tall as he could, and belted out the kind of political answer that would make Charles proud. "Mr. Congressman, we feel that the proposed project will bring benefit to the surrounding community in the form of jobs, increased tax revenue—"

"Yes, yes," Nevada cut him off, "we heard all that. But nothing in these materials represents what I'd consider to be compelling evidence that cutting down trees in the Oldwood would benefit anybody other than the loggers, so I'll repeat my question: *Why there*?"

"In my honest opinion—"

"Your honest opinion?" Nevada asked. "Have we heard anything otherwise today?" The committee began to chuckle as Pinocchio realized the mistake he had just made. Nevada continued, "Well, in your *honest* opinion, do you feel this logging project will bring any harm to that environment?"

"Harm to the environment?" Pinocchio asked.

"Yes, Mr. Pinocchio, harm to the environment."

The chuckling had given way to open laughter. *What a rotten question!* Pinocchio thought as he checked his watch—four minutes to go. He raced through his mind, shuffled his papers—*there had to be an answer!*

"Well?" Nevada demanded.

Nothing. Pinocchio had nothing. He ran back to Charles's training—*always deflect a question with a question.*

"Can you define *harm*, Congressman?"

Nevada replied with a blank stare, so Pinocchio tried again.

"Then can you define *environment*?"

"Just say *yes* or *no*," Nevada demanded. He was clearly through fencing with the lobbyist.

Back at The Kronos Group, Charles Stevens was at the edge of his seat and Dominic squeezed his glass so tight it nearly shattered as he whispered, "He's losing it."

In Bethesda, Whitney reached over and took Mother's hands in hers, pleading openly, "Come on, Pinny, do the right thing."

But Pinocchio was out of options. He felt the lump in his throat punch through his windpipe as he muttered,

"No."

Nevada grimaced. "So if we pass this bill as written," he clarified, "it's your position that this limited logging project will not lead to any significant deforestation of our national forests."

"That's correct," said Pinocchio.

"Chemical contamination?"

"None."

"Threats to endangered species?"

"Endangered species, sir?"

"Yes," the congressman continued, "the Oldwood Forest happens to be the nesting area of the endangered speckled owl—"

"Speckled owl?" Barnes asked, his interest suddenly piqued. Pinocchio searched his memory banks—he had heard of the speckled owl before. *Where had he heard of it?* Of course! H.R. 30110! Frank Barnes's first bill saved the speckled owl—no wonder he was suddenly so interested. But if what Nevada was saying was true, this bill would doom the raptors. There would be no way Barnes would ever let that happen, would he?

Pinocchio wondered if that was why Charles sent him here to testify. Pinocchio was possibly the one man Barnes would ever believe if he told him the speckled owl would be safe. But there was no way to know that, was there? The only way to know for sure what the impact would be was to perform an environmental impact study, which would be standard in the case of any proposed logging on government lands ...

Pinocchio flashed back to the last conversation he had with Charles Stevens, how quickly he brushed off Pinocchio's concerns about the EIS. Pinocchio knew that this bill, as written, would exclude the company from having to perform an environmental impact study ...

It was suddenly all so clear—the only reason their client would want to do that would be if they knew for a fact that their logging would cause harm.

This bill had nothing to do with logging—it was designed to reverse Frank Barnes's signature accomplishment. If Pinocchio allowed it to pass, he would sentence the speckled owl to death. But why him? Why of all the people Charles could have sent in to testify, did he choose a junior analyst with questionable-at-best expert qualifications?

The longing look in Frank Barnes's eyes gave him the answer, and his heart sank as he remembered—the crash. Charles took interest in Pinocchio only after the crash—and one detail of the encounter seemed of keen interest to the managing partner ...

Frank Barnes was in the car with a woman who wasn't his wife.

Charles hadn't sent Pinocchio to this committee because he was an expert in ecology; he sent him as a reminder. Charles had dirt on Barnes, the kind of dirt that ended careers, and he would use it if Barnes dared to block this bill—the one bill that could allow a timber company to log in the cherished, untapped lands that Barnes himself had saved so many years ago. Pinocchio wasn't there to testify; he was there to intimidate. Whitney was right—he was nothing more than a puppet!

As the implications of what was happening raced through his mind, another thought emerged—Pinocchio still had a choice. Charles had told him that the bill had already been decided, that his testimony was a mere formality; yet why was he so concerned that Pinocchio might actually tell the truth? It wasn't for Barnes's sake; it was for the sake of the other committee members—like this man from Nevada. Barnes's hands were tied. He *couldn't* stop the bill, but the members of the committee could easily vote it down. If Pinocchio spoke up now—if he told the truth—they would do just that. It wasn't how he wanted it, or how he ever could have imagined it, but Pinocchio had finally gotten his wish—in that moment, he was an important man, and the fate of an entire species rested on his next few words.

The Swiss watch rested heavy on his wrist. He thought of all the things he would give up if he told the truth. He thought of the coupe, of Cassandra, of his big corner office and of the cameras pointed his way—all of it gone in a flash. He had already given up so much to get here—his family, his integrity. He would lose everything to save a few owls.

A few miserable owls.

Only in heaven is the field even, he thought. It may be white, but the Capitol is far from heaven. Pinocchio looked the congressman from Nevada square in the eye and answered,

"No, sir. This project will not put the speckled owls in any danger." It was an outright lie. He even embellished it. "The technology being proposed here is specifically designed not to harm the environment—and native species especially. This committee can rest assured that our client has considered every possible side effect from this logging project, and has determined that it will not impact the area's ecosystem in any way, shape, or form. This project, members of the committee, is one hundred percent safe."

As he finished, Pinocchio felt a sudden weight pulling his face down. At first he thought it was shame, but as he tried looking back up at the committee members, he was surprised to find that he literally couldn't—something was physically pulling him down. He strained every muscle in his neck to lift his head, and when he finally succeeded he was met with gasps.

Pinocchio felt cross-eyed. He strained to draw focus, and was horrified to see that the welt seemed to have grown by a full two inches! He touched it—it was harder than ever—not at all like a pimple or welt. It weighed a ton. As he rubbed it, it seemed to grow longer still. He could hear murmurs from the audience behind him, but the committee members had all been shocked into silence. Finally, the gentleman from Nebraska asked in a most concerned tone, "Mr. Pinocchio, are you alright?"

Pinocchio didn't answer; in fact he couldn't answer because he honestly didn't know! The welt grew longer still, drawing his face down until it hit the table with a decidedly hollow tap. Pinocchio knocked at it, swearing with all that he was worth that he was tapping at a piece of wood.

"Somebody get a medic in here!" Barnes shouted. Pinocchio leaped to his feet which, to his astonishment, didn't seem to work anymore. He collapsed back into the chair, his elbows hitting the table with a metallic "CLANK!"

"What's happening to him?" someone cried.

"My God, help him!" shouted another. As the cameras flashed, Pinocchio grew keenly aware of the zoom of the C-SPAN camera, moving closer and closer to his face.

"Ex-excuse me, please," Pinocchio muttered as he again tried to stand. His feet seemed to be bolted to the floor. All of his joints had frozen. He could barely move his mouth. His eyes were locked on the monstrosity growing from the tip of his nose. He swatted at it and tried his best to cover it with his numbing hands when all of a sudden—a branch appeared at the end of it ... then a leaf ... then a nest ... and finally, in the nest, two birds' eggs, one of which promptly hatched a flittering robin that flew across the room and smashed into a closed window. As the helpless little chick fluttered and stumbled across the floor, a voice from the Boy Scout troop broke the terrified silence.

"IT'S WOOD! HE'S MADE OF WOOD!"

Shocked gasps turned to howls as the room erupted in laughter. Humiliated and scared, Pinocchio drew every ounce of focus to his incapacitated legs and lumbered out of the chamber. He burst into a crowded hallway, drawing the same shocked gasps from everyone he passed as he stumbled his way into the nearest men's room.

He crawled up to a mirror, nearly fainting when he saw the face that looked back at him. Pinocchio's skin had hardened and turned to a smooth, sanded surface. His mouth was hinged at his jaw. His eyes were painted a bright white, and what was left of his nose was a twenty-four-inch wooden branch, complete with bark and leaves.

"My God," he cried, "what is happening to me?"

The door burst open and two Capitol police officers ordered him to freeze—only to do the same when they saw him.

Unsure what else to do, they drew their weapons. Terrified, Pinocchio leaped across the bathroom, aiming for a small open window just above the stall. The officers were too stunned to do anything but watch as the wooden man clambered out of the open window and vanished from view.

Pinocchio landed nose-first in a patch of neatly trimmed grass. As he lifted himself up, the branch nose caught in the soft dirt and snapped in two, leaving him just a two-inch splinter at the end of his face. By the time he had come to his feet, the cameras had found him and chased him all the way down Delaware Avenue until he was finally able to reach the Union Station parking garage, which was mercifully under lit. The big coupe was easy to find, sticking a full three feet out of the parking spot. Pinocchio jumped in, floored it, and through some miracle, was able to guide the speeding behemoth out of the garage, and into the relative safety of the dense DC traffic.

"It's wood! He's made of wood!"

CHAPTER 13

Pinocchio the Puppet

Every employee of The Kronos Group was glued to their monitors as a video clip of the hearing played on an endless loop. But inside Charles Stevens's office, a hurricane was raging.

"Where is he?" hollered Stevens.

"We just sent someone to his house; it's empty," replied Dominic. "What the hell happened to him, Charles?"

"You think I know?" Stevens barked.

Nancy stepped in and pulled the door closed behind her. Charles Stevens glared at his longtime secretary and demanded,

"Well?"

"Well what?" she asked.

"I've seen you two talking. Who's he working for?"

"How can you ask me that?" she snapped. "I've talked to that boy maybe twice for two minutes."

"Has he called?"

"No, but everyone else has. Every cable network, and most of the newspapers, the loggers, and a dozen environmental groups I've never even heard of"—she slipped on her glasses and reviewed her handwritten notes—"and Frank Barnes called."

"His office called?" Stevens clarified.

"No, he called personally. Twice."

Charles Stevens ripped off his glasses as he sank into his leather throne. "If we lose this vote, we lose this bill," said Dominic. "You know what's at stake."

"I know, Dominic," Stevens replied. He pinched the bridge of his nose. "This is a nightmare."

"Well, we have to do something," Dominic insisted.

Charles Stevens let it all sink in—then, as if waking from a stupor, he grabbed the nearest piece of stationery and started scribbling.

"Let's release a statement," he said, shoving the paper into Dominic's hands. "Nancy, call Barnes's office, get me a meeting with him—today. Sound calm when you do it."

Dominic read the note. He looked Stevens square in the eye, and asked, "Are you serious?"

"I'm serious as a heart attack, Dominic. Release that statement—and find that damn kid! Scour the earth if you have to!"

* * *

The big German coupe handled very well at high speeds, even as its driver was barely able to steer. Pinocchio's pulse quickened, itself frightening as the sound coming from his chest was not the usual *thump! thump!* Pinocchio was used to, but the distinctive tick of an old wind-up clock—any moment Pinocchio expected to hear alarm bells.

Pinocchio tightened his grip, the creaking of his fingers terrifying him even more. He shifted, only to have his heavy wooden clog slip off the clutch—the grinding of the precisely machined gears was somehow worse to him than the noise his knees made as they knocked against each other, *Clock! Clack! Clock! Clack!*

This isn't real, Pinocchio told himself, *you're in a dream. Just wake up. WAKE UP!* But how does one wake themselves up? *A pinch! Yes! That's it!* He pinched and pinched, but what was once soft flesh on his forearm was now solid maple—and it simply refused to fold. He closed his eyes and squeezed. As he did, the wood creaked and groaned. He opened his eyes—he was still awake, and flying down the freeway at over a hundred miles an hour.

"What is happening? *What is happening?*" he screamed. The phone buzzed angrily—it was Nancy. Pinocchio knew he was in a lot of trouble; suddenly even his most treasured job seemed insignificant. Pinocchio mashed the end-call button. His heart ticked faster and faster—*Tick-Tack! Tick-Tack!*

Was he dying? Was he cursed? The only thing he could be sure of was that this was not a dream. It had to be a disease, or a virus or a—*YES! A virus!* It had to be a virus—and who could cure a virus?

Pinocchio yanked the wheel hard to the right, pushing the big coupe across three lanes. He didn't even bother with the red light at the foot of the off-ramp. There was a hospital just a few miles away, and by every definition he knew, this was an emergency.

* * *

Pinocchio fidgeted on the edge of the examination table. He gnawed on a fingernail, which promptly splintered and cut his lip.

"Ow."

He paced, sat, paced again. He tried to ignore the whimpers emanating from the next room. A cheap painting of a Parisian café hung crookedly off the opposite wall. As Pinocchio reached over to straighten it, it collapsed to the ground in a magnificent shower of glass.

"Mr. ... *Pinocchio*?" Doctor Carnegie asked as he swept open the curtain. Pinocchio made a lame attempt to conceal the shattered painting as he answered, "Yes, that's me!"

Judging by his silver-streaked hair and the relaxed manner with which he reviewed the chart, Pinocchio was certain that this was someone who could help. Carnegie slid off a pair of glasses, only then noticing the ruins of Paris on the floor.

"I'll—I'll pay for that," said Pinocchio.

"No need," Carnegie replied. "Looking at that ugly thing was probably making people more sick. So, Mr. Pinocchio, what seems to be the problem?"

"Doc," Pinocchio pleaded, "I'm in bad shape."

"Well, let's just see ..." Carnegie grinned and motioned back to the table. Pinocchio took a seat and did his best to breathe normally as Carnegie held his wrist and counted his pulse. The only problem was ... *there was no pulse.*

He thumbed around for a moment, finally reaching for the other wrist. Still nothing. "That's odd," Carnegie mumbled.

"What's odd?"

"Nothing." Carnegie brushed it off. "Can you unbutton your shirt?"

He slapped a stethoscope onto Pinocchio's chest, and was surprised when it landed with a loud *TAP!* His ears were greeted by a strong beat, a perfect *tick-tack* every second, on the second.

"Pulse, sixty. Well, your heart's fine."

"It is?" Pinocchio began to relax a bit.

"Skin's a little clammy, though. Running any fevers?"

"I don't think so ..."

Carnegie slid a thermometer under Pinocchio's tongue and counted to thirty. "It's twenty-two point one degrees ...," he announced, baffled. "What the hell?"

"What?" demanded Pinocchio.

Carnegie tapped the thermometer several times before tossing it away and unwrapping another. Thirty seconds later, it showed Pinocchio's temperature was a balmy—*22.1 degrees.*

The patient's forehead was cool to the touch. Carnegie's eyes drifted to the thermostat on the wall, which plainly showed the room temperature—*22.1 degrees Celsius.*

Carnegie stepped back and re-reviewed the chart, asking, "Mr. Pinocchio, what did you say the problem was?"

"I don't know!"

Carnegie slipped a penlight from his pocket and checked Pinocchio's eyes, one by one. The pupils didn't dilate; in fact, they barely moved at all. If he didn't know any better, he would swear they were painted on. He moved to the patient's lips—

"Open your mouth, and say ah!"

But Pinocchio's mouth was dry as a bone.

"We should ..." Carnegie rubbed his chin. "Let's take some blood." He unwrapped a needle, and tied off a tourniquet. Tapping at the inside of Pinocchio's elbow returned another knock, but no vein. He tapped and tapped, muttering to himself the whole time. Finally, he gave up and plunged the needle into the thickest part. It stuck—and wouldn't come free. He gave the needle a strong tug and promptly snapped it in half. Staring at the jagged sliver of metal, he turned the arm over, only then discovering that his elbow joint was little more than a sanded wooden dowel.

"Well, uh, well ... it seems you have some ... hardening of the skin. Your circulation is not good at all, and your body temperature is nonexistent. See, according to this, you really shouldn't be alive ..."

"I'm dead?" screamed Pinocchio.

"Well no, no! Your heartbeat is as regular as a clock."

"Actually, Doctor"—Pinocchio unbuttoned the rest of the shirt, revealing a brass latch on the left side of his torso. Carnegie's eyes bulged as he unlocked it, filling the room with the sound of clicks, ticks, and tocks—"something is wrong with that too."

Carnegie tossed the stethoscope and stumbled backward, collapsing next to the Parisian café.

"Doctor?" Pinocchio asked as he tapped Carnegie's shoulder. There was no response. The whimpering from the next stall was growing louder—and so was the ticking from Pinocchio's chest. Unsure what else to do, he latched up the cabinet, grabbed his shirt and ran.

* * *

Doctor Carnegie had scarcely lost consciousness when the nurses had him up on the examination table—his heart not quite as *ticky-tocky* as the puppet's. As they tended to their colleague, nobody seemed to notice that their wooden patient was making a daring getaway.

The hall echoed with the *clickity-clack* of clogs as Pinocchio burst from the front door and ran past a line of parked ambulances. He made his way to the nearest grouping of trees beyond the parking lot, his hand-stitched Italian suit flapping like a velvet cape. It finally caught on a branch and tore wide open.

Pinocchio's initial confusion had given way to out-and-out panic. He had already ruled out a dream—that needle surely would have woken him. Whatever was happening was worse than an illness. It felt like something else, something sinister.

It felt like a curse.

We must pity Pinocchio, dear friends, for the helplessness that was filling his heart was becoming all too familiar. The moment he had begun to understand his place in the world, he was suddenly thrust into chaos. Who could explain to him why his heart now ticked when he *knew* it was supposed to beat? No doctor could cure him any more than they could cure the bark on a tree. He cursed, and he cried, and he took out his frustrations on the nearest spruce.

Pinocchio's little clock/heart ticked faster and faster until, overwound and overworked, it threw a gear and stopped altogether. Pinocchio collapsed onto the nearest log. He wiped the sweat from his brow—and his arm stuck to it. He took a whiff as he yanked it away—

"You've got to be kidding me," he said.

Sap. He was sweating sap.

He caught his breath, only to realize he wasn't actually breathing. He couldn't breathe. *He didn't have lungs.*

Silence followed—the kind of silence that the imagination fills with dark possibilities, and Pinocchio had always been blessed with a vivid imagination. He tapped at his chest, then pulled open the little door and looked inside.

"Oh, great!"

A mess of loose gears fell through his hand and scattered across the ground. Pinocchio got down on his hands and knees and scooped up as many as he could find. He thought to put the little clock back together, only to realize he knew nothing at all about clocks. He gathered the pile into his pocket, and cradled his head in his hands. Whatever was happening to him was not only illogical; it was fantastical. Somehow, he was still alive, even though what was left of his heart was now a pile of springs and bolts. He needed answers, and there was one man who might know them ...

"Dad," he said, "Dad would know what's happening."

Pinocchio grabbed his phone, sweeping his wooden finger across the screen. It didn't move. He swept again. Again.

Many years ago, somewhere deep in the laboratories of Silicon Valley, the idea of a touch screen cellular phone was born. All it took was a little warmth—the kind of warmth the human body gives off naturally. Without it, the device would remain safely locked in one's pocket, free from accidental dials and texts. But Pinocchio's fingers were as cold as the chilly forest air around him—not one drop of warm blood flowed through his body. He swiped, and tapped, and pounded, but the screen simply would not answer.

He set the phone down and stared blankly at a tall spruce. The spruce sat across from him, its branches heavy with amber leaves, quiet and unmoving—*and staring back at him.*

Pinocchio wiped the sap from his eyes. It was unmistakable. The scars in its bark formed the slightest semblance of a face, and it looked right at him. For reasons he couldn't fully explain, Pinocchio had the thought to speak to it.

"Hello," he said.

"What the hell?" the tree shouted. It looked left, then right, then back at the strange little man who seemed, somehow, to speak his language.

Pinocchio looked back at the tall tree, which leaned in closer, almost as if it were examining him. Again, Pinocchio spoke, "Hello, tree."

"AAAAAAAAARGH!" the tree screamed. Terrified, it leaped back, brushing its crinkly branches against a much shorter little spruce standing beside it.

"Watch where you're going!" ordered the stumpy tree.

"This *thing* just talked to me!" said the tall one.

The pair stared at Pinocchio for what seemed like an eternity. Pinocchio just stared back, unsure what else to do.

"You've got to be kidding me," the stumpy tree said. "You brought me all the way over here for this?"

"I'm not joking," the tall tree replied. "He just talked."

"You're an idiot," said the stump. He turned back to the forest, ignoring the pleas of his taller companion.

"I swear," the tall tree protested, "he was just talking! Little man—say something again!"

"Something again!" came Pinocchio's reply.

The stump looked at Pinocchio, then turned to the tall tree and screamed. They threw their branches around each other and shivered, never taking their gaze off the terrifying little man.

"You see?" asked the tall tree.

"What the hell is it?" wondered the stump.

"I think it's a doll," was the tall tree's reply.

"I'm not a doll!" Pinocchio protested.

The tall tree gathered his courage and asked, "Do you—do you have a name?"

"I'm Pinocchio!"

"Hear that?" said the tall tree. "It says its name is *Pinochle.*"

"No, Pinocchio! I'm a human being!"

The stumpy one tiptoed ever so close to the little human being.

"Don't touch it!" the tall tree warned.

"I'm not stupid," stumpy responded. "I just want to see if it is human."

"Humans can't speak tree," said the tall one.

"Children can," said stumpy, "but this doesn't look like a child to me."

"I'm not a child," said Pinocchio. "I'm a lobbyist."

"A what?" stumpy asked.

"It's like a lawyer," replied Pinocchio.

"Well whatever it is, it's not human. Look ..." Stumpy leaned in close and tapped against Pinocchio's hollow head, exclaiming, "He's made of wood!"

The trees traded curious glances. "Are you from the forest?" the tall one asked.

"No, I'm from Italy," Pinocchio replied.

"Maybe it's an old statue—," said the tall tree.

"Or a robot that can talk," stumpy added.

"No!" Pinocchio protested. "I'm a human being! My name is Pinocchio and I live in Virginia!"

"Human, eh?" added a new voice. Pinocchio turned to find a most ragged little fox slinking up behind him. His gray eyes were more wolf than fox, and his fur was matted and stiff. He walked with a limp, and he smiled out of only one side of his mouth—the other side being occupied with a stick of straw, which he chewed on continuously.

"Humans, yes, what a vicious sort, always cutting things, shooting things"—the fox shot a glance at the trees—"and chopping things. I don't know if you are human, little man, but if I were, I wouldn't admit it."

Stumpy agreed. He turned to the tall tree and asked, "Didn't humans chop down your cousin last month?"

The tall tree nodded. "He was one hundred and two years old."

"Well," the fox continued as he circled the group, "that's a shame. Now what would humans want with such old wood anyway? Probably makes damn good carvin'."

"Yeah." The tall tree nodded, as he began to creep a little closer to the puppet. "I wonder what they would make out of a tree like that?"

"A chair, maybe?" said stumpy.

"Or a barstool for their fancy new restaurant, perhaps?" the tall tree threw in.

"Or maybe," the fox continued, "maybe they want to make a little ... talking ... puppet."

Pinocchio's eyes followed the surly fox as he slinked around behind him. As he turned, he saw that the entire forest, not just trees, but dozens of birds, raccoons, and deer had gathered around him. Each of them seemed to agree.

Something sniffed at his knees. Pinocchio snapped around to find the fox just inches from his face.

"Hmm. Good joints ... but not strong enough to stand on their own. That's it, isn't it? You're a little marionette whose strings have been snipped!"

"Or he ran away!" shouted a squirrel.

"Or maybe he killed his owner and cut his own strings," a fern added.

"Well one thing's for certain," the fox continued. "We can't have any renegade puppets running around here, looking for other trees to cut down."

Pinocchio was flabbergasted. "I wouldn't do that!" he screamed.

"There's only one way to be sure," the fox declared. "Get him!"

At that, the trees snatched Pinocchio's arms and legs, tearing and tugging him in every direction. Pinocchio howled.

"Get some rope!" the fox ordered. A trio of raccoons complied, tossing the twine they had lifted from a camper's supply. The shrubs, their tiny branches well-made for the task, tightened the knots around his ankles and wrists. When the commotion settled, the two trees held the ends of the strings, dangling the struggling Pinocchio like the marionette he once was.

"Stop it!" Pinocchio shouted. "Let me go!"

"He wants to run away!" taunted the fox. "You heard him, trees! Make him run!"

As the trees tugged at the strings, Pinocchio's feet danced up and down, running in place like a jogger stuck in the mud. The forest erupted in laughter as the fox sat on the ground, clapping.

"Dance! Dance!" he cried out.

Pinocchio jumped higher with each yank. The forest clapped and cheered as the fox chanted, "Come and see! Come and see! The little man who once was a tree!"

"Let me go!" Pinocchio's pleas fell on deaf ears. A flight of robins arranged a crown of twigs on his head. For five whole minutes the trees danced him around when the theater was interrupted by a booming voice.

"ENOUGH!"

The creatures turned their gaze upward, where two grand owls were perched on a maple. "Put him down at once," the owls ordered.

"What business is it of yours, rat-hunters?" shouted the fox.

"You fools!" barked the owls. "Don't you recognize your own kind when you see him?"

The trees were taken aback. "What do you mean?" stumpy asked.

"Look at him," the owls replied. "What do you see but wood—carved and shaped by man, but wood nonetheless." The pair spread their wings and soared through the air, landing on either side of the helpless puppet. Pinocchio marveled at how graceful and magnificent the owls were in flight, yet how they hobbled awkwardly along the ground, their grand wings folded into perfect little humps on either side of their bullet bodies.

The owls each pressed an ear to Pinocchio's chest.

Tick-Tack ... Tick-Tack ...

They nodded at each other, then pecked their strong beaks at the latch, opening the cabinet for all to see. The entire forest came in for a closer look.

"Does this look like the workings of a human to you?" asked the owls.

The fox, however, was unconvinced. "That's a human trick!" he cried. "Don't let these old coots fool you; this thing is as human as can be."

The twins leaped into the air and circled the gathering before swooping down and snatching up the snarly old fox.

"Put me down, you old coots!" the fox cried. He snapped and bit, but the owls had him in a terribly strong grip. They split up, one carrying the fox into the darkening sky, the other landing back at Pinocchio's feet. He stood majestically in front of the forest and spoke.

"What have we become, dear friends, if we cannot know our own kind when they come before us deformed and broken? Is it any wonder that man creeps further and further into our world, knocking our trunks, burning our leaves, and tearing our roots? I am ashamed of you, friends, ashamed that you would treat this poor creature so!"

"But what is he?" trumpeted an elk.

"Let us learn," came the reply. The owl turned, and with four quick snaps, cut Pinocchio free of the ropes. The owl extended a wing, which though suspicious, Pinocchio accepted. "What is your name, puppet?" the owl asked. Pinocchio hesitated. "It's alright, friend. These creatures fear me because they know I never stop watching them—all day and all night I sit and I watch, and I know all their secrets. I know where they hide, I know when they sleep, and I even know which creeks they like to drink from. They know that owls are not to be made an enemy of, so I assure you that no harm will come while I stand for you. Tell me, puppet, what are you called?"

"I'm Pinocchio," came the muffled reply.

"I see," continued the owl, "and tell me, Pinocchio, how did you come to be?"

"I don't know," Pinocchio answered. "I don't know how any of this is happening! I'm just a lobbyist."

"What's a *lobbyist*?" asked a shrew.

"It's like a lawyer," answered stumpy.

"But a puppet cannot be a lawyer, Pinocchio," the owl continued. "How did you come to be alive? Do you not remember?"

Pinocchio shook his head. The owl stepped back and gave the wooden man a good once-over. "You don't fit into this world"—he regarded the expensive suit and polished shoes —"but then again, you don't fit into the human world either. So where do you fit in, Pinocchio?"

Before he could answer, Pinocchio was interrupted by a gravel-voiced moss pile. "There's magic at work here, owl," the moss pile said. "This is the fairies' doing!"

The rest of the forest nodded in agreement.

"If that's true," replied the owl, "then the fairies can help him."

"Fairies?" asked Pinocchio.

"Yes," said the owl, "but for many years they have been absent from these forests. If you are here due to a fairy's spell, then only she can help you. You must find that fairy."

"But how—where—a fairy?" Pinocchio stuttered. "I don't even know what a fairy looks like! How am I supposed to find one?"

The owl leaned in, and whispered, "You need only follow the truest part of yourself, Pinocchio—that is your imagination. Now come, let me show you the way out of the forest."

The owl lifted into the air and pointed west. The trees, bushes, and creatures stepped back, clearing a path for the wobbly puppet. With the owl's assurances still fresh in his mind, Pinocchio followed his lead.

As he made his way through the forest, Pinocchio began to notice things he had never imagined: A mother squirrel scolded her children for playing in the road; two spiders haggled over the price of a tree branch; a sparrow, upset over a lost promotion, cried to his wife. Pinocchio had always assumed that life in the forest was random, wild. Never before had he seen how much the creatures of the woods lived a life seemingly every bit as sophisticated as man's.

"Fear not, Pinocchio," said the owl, "the fairies will help you to be a man again, and when they do, you may finish your work on the hill."

"I thought you didn't know who I was?" Pinocchio asked.

"Of course I know. We owls never forget our friends. Aldous Kronos was our friend, and we know that you now stand for his name."

"How did you know that?" Pinocchio asked. The owl landed on a branch just above him, and spread his wings. That's when Pinocchio noticed the most unusual speckled pattern on the owl's chest. "You're—you're a speckled owl!" Pinocchio exclaimed.

The owl nodded. "Most of the forest is so very unconcerned with the politics of man, but we owls learned long ago that the business of man can sometimes become the business of owls. Time is short for you, Pinocchio, and if that bill passes, it is short for us too. You must find the fairies, and then you must go back and stop that bill. It is more dangerous than you could know."

Though he still didn't fully believe everything that was happening, Pinocchio was beginning to take a few things on faith. "Where will I find a fairy?" he asked.

"Fairies are notorious drinkers," said the owl, "so I would try a pub." It was not the answer Pinocchio was expecting, but he rolled with it.

"Any particular pub?" Pinocchio asked.

"McFadden's on 24th and Pennsylvania is your best bet," answered the owl. "If you hurry, you can probably catch happy hour."

"I'll head that way," said Pinocchio. He quickened his step and marched toward the clearing.

"Do hurry!" the owl called out after him. "They get so very irritable when they're drunk!"

"Come and see, come and see,
the little man who once was a tree!"

CHAPTER 14

The Circumstances Under Which Max Wiggs Found His Purpose

Woodward and Bernstein—that's who Max Wiggs wanted to be.

Ever since he was a kid, Max was interested in newspapers. The press room—as he imagined it—was a menagerie of chain-smoking, world-battered reporters chasing the beat. Telephones buzzed off the hook and the clatter of typewriters drowned out all but the angriest of senior editors as he called the evening deadline—and he, Max Wiggs, was the chain-smokingest, most world-battered of them all. Night and day he would hound congressional aides for leaks. A scoop here, a quote there—before long, he would break the story that would make his career. Then, a book deal, an Oval Office exclusive, a write-up in *Esquire*, maybe even a photo by Leibovitz.

Woodward and Bernstein ... not exactly.

The fact is, the typewriter was a relic ten years before he ever set foot on a story floor. There were telephones, but they didn't ring—they beeped and they buzzed—and even that was muted by the carpeted walls. And Max was no journalist; he was a freelance gossip columnist who wasn't exactly burning up the pages these days. His last four articles had been rejected—one more and he'd lose his desk.

But everything was about to change for Max Wiggs. That morning, the moment came that every Washington correspondent dreams of—the big call into the senior editor's office—it didn't come from a middle-aged man with rolled sleeves and a cigar hanging from his teeth, but rather it took the form of a quiet, almost peaceful, *ding!* on Max's computer that announced a new email had been received.

To: mwiggs@Washstar.com
From: palderman@Washstar.com
CC:
BCC:
Subject: Come into my office when you get a moment ...
This message has no content.

Max sighed. *Romance is dead*, he thought.

A video of Pinocchio's surreal transformation had already gone viral, and now everyone was coming to Max. It was a sensation. Everyone was talking about it. *Who was he? Where did he come from? Was it a hoax? A stunt?* Max's little article seemed to give Pinocchio a kind of legitimacy. Everyone wanted to know how they had met, and if Max knew what the puppet really was.

Max grabbed a notepad and knocked at editor Phil Alderman's door. "You wanted to see me, Phil?" he said.

Phil was typing, and barely glanced up as he came in. "Easter Island," said Phil. "Ever been there?"

Confused, Max replied, "Uh, no. You?"

Phil shook his head. "Easter Island, my friend. The greatest man-made ecological disaster to ever hit the planet—until Chernobyl, Fukushima ... Anyway, you see this statue here?" he pointed to his screen. Max nodded. "Easter Island was once covered with trees, hundreds of thousands of tall, tropical trees. But the government of the island decided that in order to please the gods, they had to make these statues. To get them into place, they cut down trees so they could roll the damn things all over the island. In less than twenty years they had cut down every single tree. Every one. No more fruit, no more birds. All that was left were hundreds and hundreds of these statues. Fascinating, hmm?" Phil leaned back in his chair. "Your article went viral."

Max nodded. "That's good news, sir."

"Good?" Phil exclaimed. "It's phenomenal! Every paper, blogger, and network is tearing apart Fairfax trying to find this 'wood-man,' and you're the only guy in the Beltway who seems to know anything about him. We need to find this 'Mr. Pinocchio,' and find out what his deal is. You, my friend, may just have an exclusive on your hands. What do you say?"

"Phil," Max replied, "I'll take the compliment, but I don't know how to find him. Wish I did."

"I'll give you a promotion to staff writer with a one-year contract. Salary, benefits after thirty ..."

"Sir, I appreciate that, but I'm serious—I don't know where he is."

"You've got to find him, Max. I'm sending you out on a genuine assignment."

Max paused. "You mean, like real investigative sort of stuff?"

"We have a fine history of journalism at this paper, Max. The *Star* has brought down big companies, whole industries, even senators and presidents. This is one of the few places you can work where you get to go home and say, 'The country is better because of what I did today.' The world is full of ugliness, Max, and it's our job to expose it. Whatever this guy is, he can't stay hidden. He needs to be exposed for the country's sake—hell, for his own sake."

"What do you mean by that?" Max asked. Phil slid his keyboard aside and leaned close. "You know who he worked for, right?"

"The Kronos Group—lobbyists."

"Right. And do you know what he was lobbying? On the surface it was logging rights for some national forest. What that bill really does is wipe out the EPA."

Max was stunned. "How?" he asked.

"Ordinarily a logging company like this would need to have an impact study done before they got to break ground. But buried deep under a bunch of procedure, this bill eliminates that requirement. That sets a precedent. Think about it—why push a bill for what should have been a rights contract with some minor government agency? It's the language in that paragraph. *In cases of construction projects where an EIS is considered to be onerous, the proposing party can waive their own requirement and bring in a private firm to conduct the study.* No time requirements, no scope, and best of all, no EPA oversight. It'll be Easter Island all over North America. This bill opens the door for a lot of amazingly bad things, and your boy is caught in the middle of it."

Max took it all in. "Well, if that's true, why would Frank Barnes even let it get out of committee? Everyone knows what a green-lover that guy is."

"That"—Phil smiled—"is the story. This puppet friend of yours is just a sideshow. Who knows what he is? Personally, I think it's a publicity stunt. But find out why friend-to-the-earth Frank Barnes is about to wipe out nearly fifty years of environmental protections, and you've got a scoop."

Max nodded. "Where do I start?"

"Start at his house."

Max grabbed his pad—he hadn't taken a single note, but somehow, he remembered every word of the conversation. Just as he reached the door, Phil called him back. "Time is ticking, you know."

"Why do you say that?" Max wondered.

"Because Charles Stevens is going to be looking for him too. If they get to him before you do, you'll never find out what he has on Barnes."

Max pulled the door closed behind him. He raced back to his cube, snatched a laptop and hustled down the hall. Max Wiggs, staff writer for the *Washington Star*, hurried out the door. He was hot on the trail of a scoop, and ready to take on some big game in the process. It seems romance in journalism might not be so dead after all.

CHAPTER 15

Pinocchio Finds the Blue-Haired Fairy

A puppet walks into a bar ...

It was an old joke that stunk as bad as the cigarette smoke hitting Pinocchio's nose as he pushed his way into the pub. It had in fact been some fifteen years since Pinocchio had set foot in a place like this, and even though it had been nearly that long since the District of Columbia banned indoor smoking, time had done little to diminish the aroma.

The crowd was lively for a Tuesday afternoon, with both ties and tongues loose as baby bureaucrats and junior staffers tussled for the attention of the lone bartender. The light, what little of it there was, was a dim neon, covering the heads in the crowd with an ethereal glow. Pinocchio hated bars—nothing but bad memories of even worse decisions—and he was debating the wisdom of his even entering when someone shouted, "Shut the damn door!" Suddenly committed, Pinocchio made his way to the bar, nestled in between two gossiping interns and did his best not to be noticed.

He wasn't successful.

Every person who walked past him paused ever so slightly. *A puppet walks into a bar* ... Pinocchio thought. He didn't see the humor in it.

"What do you want?" the bartender asked.

Pinocchio gulped as he answered meekly, "A fairy."

"What's in a *fairy*?" the bartender asked, barely hiding his annoyance.

"Oh, you mean to drink?" Pinocchio replied. He ordered the first beer he saw on tap, some local swill he had never heard of before. As the bartender set—tossed, really—a mug in front of him, Pinocchio continued, "Maybe you can help me out." He unfolded a five-dollar bill and set it on the bar. "I'm looking for a fairy."

The bartender pushed the fiver away, his annoyance turning to anger. "Nobody talks that way anymore, pal."

The bartender's bark was loud enough to catch the attention of the gossiping interns. "What did you say you were looking for?" they asked. "The Fairy? Is that a bar?"

"Shh!" Pinocchio pleaded. "It's not a bar. It's a—" *How could he put this?* "It's a mythical creature. Tall, blue, has great big wings." As he described it, Pinocchio held his hands above his head, as if the measurement would be the thing that jogged their memories.

The interns seemed genuinely concerned with his plight—a side effect, Pinocchio deduced, of the amount of alcohol in their systems. Questions led to questions, which only grew louder, eventually drawing a crowd. Before long the entire bar was abuzz with rumors about a fairy that had been sighted here or there—someone even insisted he saw one crossing the Arlington Memorial Bridge that very morning.

Pinocchio gulped down the last of his beer and reached for his wallet. His chubby fingers fumbled as he tried to pull a credit card. Pinocchio was so engrossed in the transaction that he didn't even notice the slender little Englishman sliding up beside him.

"That was kind of you to offer me a drink," said the Englishman.

"I didn't offer you a drink," said Pinocchio.

"Yes, I noticed that," the Englishman replied. "You've been slim with your offers lately, but don't worry, darling, I won't take it personally." He turned to the bartender and mouthed, *Make mine a double.*

The bartender was as amused as Pinocchio, which is to say, not at all. "I told you before," said the bartender, "if you want to open a tab, you need a credit card."

"That's alright," the Englishman replied, "my wooden friend here is buying."

"Shh!" Pinocchio commanded.

The Englishman leaned in close and asked, "What did you say?"

"I'm trying to keep a low profile," Pinocchio whispered.

The Englishman patted him on the shoulder, nodded, then climbed onto his barstool and shouted, "Did you say you wanted to buy drinks *FOR EVERYONE?*"

"Shut up!" Pinocchio barked, yanking the man back to his seat. Pinocchio produced a credit card and tossed it at the bartender. "Here, get him his drink!"

The Englishman smiled before turning to the bartender and repeating, "Make mine a double."

The bartender poured a thirty-two-year-old Scotch that seemed to call to him. The Englishman lifted the glass and savored the aroma. As he knocked it back he was teleported to heaven itself. He rapped the empty glass on the bar, growing impatient as the bartender leisurely poured another.

"You're welcome," Pinocchio muttered, doing his best to end the encounter. The Englishman, however, would have none of it. "What's your name, friend?" he asked.

Pinocchio didn't even raise his eyes. "Look, I'm just meeting someone here, OK? I really don't want to talk."

"Well, let me help you!" the Englishman insisted as he slid his stool closer. "Anyone who buys me a whiskey that expensive is a good friend, and I don't let my friends down."

"I'm not really looking for a new friend," Pinocchio replied.

"Quite right, quite right," said the Englishman. "But what about an old friend?"

"What on earth are you talking about?" Pinocchio asked.

The Englishman shook his head. "You're starting to hurt my feelings here, Woody. Look at me." Pinocchio had been doing his best to *avoid* looking at the man, but he chanced a peek, at least as good a peek as the neon glow would allow. "Don't I look the least bit familiar?"

The Englishman hadn't shaven in weeks, and his clothes were sufficiently disheveled as to make a hobo look sharp. But still, something about him did seem familiar. Maybe it was that bright blue hair, or the sound of his accent. As Pinocchio studied him, he locked eyes with the man—those intense, half-crazed eyes of his—and it registered. "Yes, I do remember you," said Pinocchio. "You're the car salesman."

"*Sales consultant*," the man corrected. "Hey, how'd it work out, anyway? Did your wife like it?"

"She left me, actually."

"Because of the car?" the Englishman clucked. "I told you to go with the red."

Pinocchio rolled his eyes. "Look, I have to go."

The Englishman's firm grip sat him right back down.

"Where are you gonna go?" he asked. "I don't think home's a good idea, seeing as how half of Washington is looking for you right now." The salesman waved to the bartender. "One more round," he whispered. "Besides, you don't really have a home to go back to anyway, do you, Sticks?"

Pinocchio started to answer, but the arrival of more drinks interrupted him. The Englishman swallowed most of one in a single gulp and continued, "I suppose you could talk to your father, but that means you'd have to go to that little penitentiary you dumped him in, and that's not a very pleasant choice either, is it?

"You could call that green-eyed bird you've been plugging, but, well, she works for the company, doesn't she? She's just as likely to rat you out as take you in." The bartender poured the salesman a double, which went down as fast as a single. "Yes, you're really quite alone now, aren't you, Pinocchio?"

Pinocchio was beyond speechless. He watched in amazement as the Englishman finished a third pour, then a fourth. Suddenly he turned his gaze to Pinocchio's perplexed eyes and declared, "You know you're beautiful."

"Excuse me?" Pinocchio asked.

The Englishman merely raised his voice, repeating to the long-legged woman passing by, "*I said you're beautiful!*"

She hurried by with nary a shrug.

"She'll be back," the Englishman declared. "Or maybe not." He turned back to Pinocchio and observed, "You're stunned. Out of words, don't know what to say, utterly stupefied." He shoved a glass into the puppet's hands, continuing, "Drink up, mate; it brings clarity."

Pinocchio focused as hard as he could on the fragile tumbler. He managed to get most of the whiskey into his mouth before the glass shattered between his wooden fingers. The taste was as foul as anything he could remember. He shook and coughed while the Englishman broke into an obnoxious chortle. He smacked Pinocchio across the back, as if that would somehow make him cough less.

"So," the Englishman continued, "you're wondering, how could this simple sales professional—handsome though he may be—know all these little private facts about you?" He leaned in close—close enough for the odor of a half-dozen whiskeys on his breath to send Pinocchio back into a coughing fit. "A little bird told me," the Englishman whispered. "Well, two little birds, actually. And come to think of it, they aren't so little."

That caught Pinocchio's attention. "You mean owls?" he asked. The Englishman nodded.

"That's right, Sticks. I'm the fairy."

* * *

Dominic burst into Stevens's office and shouted, "We found him!"

"Where?" Stevens asked as he leaped to his feet.

"He just used his credit card at some place called McFadden's."

Stevens looked to Cassandra. "Do you know it?" She shook her head. "Well it's not that far," Stevens continued. "Get Coachman and his boys over there right away."

The very mention of that name sent a shiver down Cassandra's spine. Leonard Coachman was an imposing man, over six feet tall, with a sidewall haircut that he had worn since his days as a marine. Officially Coachman was Charles Stevens's security guard, but everyone in the firm knew what he actually did—at least they knew to be afraid of him.

As he gathered up papers, Stevens could feel Cassandra's stare. "Don't look at me that way," he said. "The bank sent us the alert—it was his company credit card." Cassandra nodded, even though she knew the firm didn't issue company credit cards. Stranger than that, she knew Pinocchio didn't drink.

* * *

"I just don't understand!" said Pinocchio. The pair had since moved to a booth in the far corner of the bar—just below the speaker. Pinocchio appreciated the darkness but didn't appreciate having to shout. "The fairy was a lady—a beautiful blue lady!"

The fairy sighed. "What kind of foolishness is that? Don't you think the sight of a floating blue ghost might frighten a child? Who does that? Sends a terrifying apparition to an infant's bedroom? I have blue *hair*." The fairy grabbed a lock of his hair and dangled it over Pinocchio's nose. Pinocchio shoved it away. "Azure hair, actually," the fairy continued. "Everyone gets that wrong."

"Dad said the fairy was dainty, graceful, well-mannered—"

The fairy interrupted with a loud belch.

"We English ARE mannered," the fairy said. "You can tell by the accent." He took another gulp. "Like it or not, darling, I'm your man."

Pinocchio buried his face in his hands as a waitress appeared. The fairy ordered another round, then inquired as to her name and what time she got off work. The waitress only shook her head.

"She'll come around," the fairy mused. "Yes, couldn't believe it myself when you wandered into the dealership. I thought for sure you'd remember me. Who can forget a face like this?" He grinned, searching for some hint of a smile on Pinocchio's face. Not finding one, he continued, "I have to say though, that was one beautiful car. How do you like it?"

"Wings!" Pinocchio exclaimed.

"Come again?"

"The fairy had wings. Show me your wings and I'll believe you."

The waitress interrupted, setting two drinks in front of the fairy and one in front of the puppet. "So is it midnight then?" the fairy asked, getting a sigh as his only response. The fairy's eyes followed her as she stomped away.

"Hard to get," he mused.

"You didn't answer me," said Pinocchio.

"Did you ask a question?"

"Show me your wings," Pinocchio demanded.

"Wings?" The fairy slammed down his drink. "Wings? You want to see my wings?" He reached into his back pocket and fished out a crumpled, half-torn sheet of pink paper. He flung it on the table, and declared, "I don't have wings, but I did get the boot. Twice. They fired me because of you!"

"You got fired from the dealership?" Pinocchio asked.

The fairy nodded. "Wasn't aggressive enough, they said. What a country. I sell you a top-of-the-line sports car with every option, and somehow I wasn't aggressive enough. Do you know their reason? Because I tried to talk you out of it. Serves me right for having a conscience. They even kept my commission! Bloody thieves. That's the second job you cost me."

"What was the first?"

"Take a guess," the fairy replied.

Pinocchio, unfortunately, was not very good at guessing.

"I'm not a fairy anymore," said the Englishman. "They took my wings."

"OK," said Pinocchio, "I don't believe a word of this, but I'll humor you; how did they take away your wings?"

"With a hacksaw. Bloody mess it is ... with magic, you moron! Fairy magic! They wave their wands and *poof!* No more wings. No more fairy. Even immigration has the decency to give you a ticket home. No, sir, just 'poof,' and no wings, and there I was. No job, nothing. A total nobody in a strange country—all because of you."

"Me?" Pinocchio was flabbergasted. "How am I responsible?"

The fairy couldn't help but laugh. "You're joking, right?" he asked.

Pinocchio shook his head. "Alright then," said Pinocchio, "if you did have wings once, tell me what it's like to fly."

"I don't remember," the fairy replied. "What's it like to crash?"

"What do you mean by that?" Pinocchio asked, defensively.

The fairy stared right through the little puppet. "I dreamed my whole life about having a family. A wife, kids, a nice home. Warm. Clean sheets. A porch. Trees in the backyard, leaves to rake. These are the simple things that you people take for granted because they come so easy to you. They never came easy to me, Pinocchio." He downed the rest of his drink before going on, "You ask what it's like to fly, I tell you, imagine the most beautiful thing you've ever seen—a mountain, an ocean, the first time your wife smiled at you ... that. That's what it's like to fly. Now look at me." Pinocchio did just that. The fairy continued, "I'm a has-been. All I can see is what was once beautiful, and nobody cares about that now, do they? Do you think I like this life? Barflies and beer taps? I was envious of you, Sticks. I wanted a *family*. I would have given anything to have what you had, and watching you throw it all away ..." He began to weep. "I may be just a washed-up celestial body, but I'm still only human."

It was a remarkably tender moment between the puppet and the fairy. As he watched the suddenly vulnerable Englishman wipe tear after tear from his eyes, Pinocchio couldn't help but embrace the man. The guilt was overwhelming. All Pinocchio could think to do was offer an apology, no matter how empty it seemed. "I'm ... I'm sorry," he said.

Pinocchio felt at any moment he might begin to cry as well. But before he could, the fairy laughed.

It started with just a giggle—so slight that Pinocchio at first took it for a sob. But as the fairy tried in vain to conceal the smile creeping across his face, he burst into a raucous cackle. "You really bought it, didn't you?" he howled. "Could you see *me* with children?"

Pinocchio rolled his eyes. The fairy got into a few more chuckles before taking a more serious tone. "You should be sorry, though," he said, "so apology accepted."

Pinocchio reached for his whiskey only to see it snatched away by the fairy. "So what now?" Pinocchio asked.

"Well that depends on you, Sticks," the fairy replied.

"Will you stop calling me *Sticks*?"

"No," the fairy replied as he finished the drink and tossed the glass on the table. "So what's it to be, then?" He continued, "Do you want to be a man again? Are you ready to prove you're worthy of that?"

"How?" Pinocchio asked.

"You always wanted to be a politician," the fairy replied. "Well now's your chance. You're gonna have to campaign—only this isn't like any election you've ever seen. You've been kicked out of office—expelled from Congress on an ethics charge, and now you're asking for a second chance. To get it, you'll need to go to the ends of the earth and beyond. The drawback I'm seeing is that you don't really believe any of this yet, do you?"

"No," Pinocchio replied, "I don't."

"And see, that's the problem. The place you need to go can only be reached on a journey of faith. You're going to have to believe the unbelievable." The fairy leaned back and scratched his chin for a moment. "You need advisors."

"Who?" Pinocchio sighed. "You?"

"I'm a good strategist, but what you need is a body-man, someone who can whip you into shape and make you ready to answer the tough questions, because if we're going where I think we're going, and seeing who I think we're seeing, believe me, Woody, the tough questions are coming. We need to find your conscience."

"The cricket?" Pinocchio asked, drawing a grin from the Englishman. "So you do remember," he said.

"No," Pinocchio replied, "he's from my father's stories. Apparently there's a talking cricket that's supposed to teach me right from wrong, or something."

"So you don't believe in him," pondered the fairy, "but you want to go find him anyway?"

Pinocchio nodded.

"Well, let's get out of here, then," the fairy ordered. "We've a long way to go if we're gonna find the cricket you don't believe exists, and you've a long way to go if you're gonna prove your great worth. In fact, you can start right now."

"How do you propose I do that?" Pinocchio asked.

"Well, you have a credit card, right?" Pinocchio nodded. "Then you can pay this bar tab."

Pinocchio sighed as he tossed the card on the table. "You see, darling?" the fairy mused. "Everything has its purpose."

CHAPTER 16

Pinocchio and the Blue-Haired Fairy Set Out in Search of the Talking Cricket

The big coupe hurtled down the freeway with the fairy at the wheel. It would take the average driver just over an hour to clear the capital traffic. The fairy did it in seven terrifying minutes.

"Seriously," screamed Pinocchio, his hands glued to the dashboard, "where are we going?"

"I haven't the faintest idea," answered the fairy.

"You said we were going to find a cricket!"

"No, we're not going to find a *cricket*, Sticks."

"Stop calling me Sticks!" Pinocchio demanded.

"Then you stop calling me fairy!"

"What should I call you then?"

"You can call me George. It's my name after all."

"George, the fairy?"

"*Pinocchio, the lobbyist*? What was going through your head when you picked that job?"

"I don't want to talk about it," answered Pinocchio.

"When I'm driving, we talk about what I want to talk about."

"Then let's just not talk at all!"

"Fine. We'll just listen to the radio." George found a classic rock station and began to hum along.

"Did I ever tell you I can't sing?" he asked. "It's true. I'm wretched. But there are four hundred and eighty-six songs in the Rolling Stones catalog, and I'll bet I know the lyrics to every single one of them—" He screeched out what might have been the chorus to "Shine a Light" before continuing, "Your call."

Pinocchio switched the radio back off. "I wanted to make a difference, OK?"

"By lobbying?"

Pinocchio hadn't thought about this for a long time. "After I graduated, Kronos was the only job offer I got. I had a family to support. Whitney wanted to be close to her mother in Bethesda, and I knew about Kronos and the owl bill—I just thought I could do some good."

George nodded ever so slightly, then turned the radio back on. "What?" Pinocchio asked. "That answer not good enough?"

"It's an answer," said George, "I'll give you that."

"Oh the hell with you!" Pinocchio huffed. "I don't even know why I'm talking to you. I don't even know why I picked you up! That's the last time I listen to a goddamn owl!" Pinocchio crossed his arms and turned away, glaring out of the window.

"Sticks, Sticks," George said as he cracked open a bottle of bourbon, "you've got to learn to relax." He took a sip and handed it to Pinocchio. "Stress is a killer."

Pinocchio snatched the bottle away, tossing it in the back seat. "What are you, nuts? Drinking and driving?"

"See what I mean? Your blood pressure must be through the roof."

"Just pull the hell over!"

"You got it."

George yanked on the wheel, aiming for an exit. The tires protested, but the fairy just managed to bring the big coupe to a stop at the foot of the ramp. The hazard lights flashed, the Stones blared, and the passengers sat silently, George staring at Pinocchio, and Pinocchio pondering the miracle of survival. After five long minutes, George reached back and grabbed his bottle. He took a gulp and said, "I thought you'd be an artist."

"What?" Pinocchio asked.

"You always loved colorful things. Art was your favorite subject, your father was a carpenter, and so it just seemed natural."

Pinocchio was stunned. "How did you know art was my favorite subject?"

George looked to the heavens and asked, "Does he just not hear me?" He turned back to Pinocchio. "You honestly don't remember, do you?"

Pinocchio shook his head. George continued, "Well, you can't fake your way through this one, Pinocchio. If you ever want to feel your own skin again, you're going to have to remember. You're going to have to believe, and above all"—he took another sip—"you're gonna have to atone."

He offered another drink, which Pinocchio declined. "Thank you, by the way," said Pinocchio.

"For what?"

"For calling me *Pinocchio*."

The fairy chuckled. "No problem. And thank you for telling me where to stop. Look"—he nodded toward a rusty, dusty shack just beyond the road—"we're here."

"Where?" asked Pinocchio.

"You wanted to find a talking cricket, right?"

"He lives in there?"

"Well, sort of."

They stepped out of the coupe and up to the abandoned shack. "I should tell you," George continued, "a lot has changed for him, so if you want him to come with us, he may take a little convincing. That, and ..."

"And what?"

"Well, he's not actually a cricket."

Pinocchio pushed aside a withered foreclosure notice and knocked.

"It's abandoned," said George. "Why are you knocking?"

"I don't want to be rude."

"Rude?" George burst out laughing. He leaned into the door, which collapsed into a cloud of splinters. Pinocchio was trepidatious, but a natural curiosity overtook him. He stepped inside and called out, "Cricket?" Silence answered him. He continued, "Cricket? Cricket?"

His shouts were interrupted by a faint rustling inside the walls. Pinocchio couldn't quite place the sound—leaves brushing against the house, maybe? He traded glances with George and they took another nervous step in.

"Cricket, are you here?"

The voice that answered was hollow, echoed—like a thousand whispers talking as one. It said, "*There is no cricket here ...*"

"Who said that?" Pinocchio asked.

"*Crickets are not welcome here. We don't care for crickets here ...*"

Pinocchio looked up toward the ceiling and called, "I—I am looking for an acquaintance of mine—a talking cricket. I think he used to live here. Can you help me find him?"

The voice answered from above and below, from the left and the right ... "*There are no crickets here. We don't welcome crickets here ...*" The rustle in the walls grew louder, faster. The voice seemed to be all around them.

"*We don't care for crickets here ...*"

"Who are you?" Pinocchio demanded.

"*In fact, we EAT crickets here!*"

George grabbed Pinocchio and pointed at the floor as a thousand black specks materialized from every corner, crack, and crease in the floor. Up above, a thousand more rained in from the ceilings, the walls ... The entire room shrank inward as blackness crept in all around them.

"We EAT crickets here," the voice continued. "And we eat wood, too!"

They were cockroaches—hundreds of them! They poured into the room like water on the deck of a sinking ship. George and Pinocchio grabbed on to each other and raced toward the door. It was too late. The sea of black slammed the rotted door closed and covered the walls.

"We eat wood here!" it continued.

"George!" cried Pinocchio. "Let's get the hell out of here!"

"*George!*" cried the voice. "*George?*"

At once, the roaches halted. They stood in place and gazed curiously at the duo. The duo, on the other hand, was frozen with terror.

"*George?*" the voice continued. "*We didn't know it was you. Poppa! Poppa!*" the voice cried into the darkness, and a single voice answered—a tiny voice, but a slow, deep, gentle voice.

"Yes?" it said.

"Poppa! It's George! George is here!"

"George?" the single voice asked, and at that, the black sea cleared the floor. From down the hall appeared a shadow—the shadow of a single, solitary little bug—not much bigger than the thousands of roaches covering the walls, floors, and ceilings, but one who moved with certain, if aged, authority.

"George," it said, "is that you? My goodness, it's been decades ..."

The single roach crept into the light, crawling closer and closer—finally standing toe to toe with the two of them.

"It is you, it is! And is that ... Yes! My God! It's *Pinocchio*!"

The little bug scurried up Pinocchio's leg and looked into his eyes. Like all roaches, he was a perfectly disgusting little creature, at once both dry and slimy, harmless yet terrifying. As he leaned closer, Pinocchio could swear he saw a smile creep across the creature's face. "It is you, Pinocchio! I can't believe it!"

"You ... *know me*?" Pinocchio asked.

"Well, of course I know you, Pinocchio," said the roach, "but I can tell you don't know me, so perhaps I should once again make my acquaintance. I am your old friend, your mentor, and your voice of reason. I am the talking roach."

* * *

So precise were the roaches' movements, Pinocchio could have mistaken them for a military drill team. He watched in amazement as they filed neatly into the living room and sat in a perfect circle around their Poppa.

The Poppa relaxed in an old bottle cap he had fashioned into a rocker. He packed his pipe with the tiniest shred of tobacco and asked, "Do you mind if I smoke?" Pinocchio shook his head. The roach struck a match at least an inch longer than himself and lit the pipe. "My boy!" he said, "I didn't dare hope you'd come to see me, but I'm very glad you did."

"Who is this, Poppa?" asked a roach.

"Come over and see for yourself," Poppa said as he patted at his knee. Pinocchio watched as the tiniest of the tiny roaches stood up from the circle and scurried over, taking a seat on his Poppa's lap. He continued, "Do you remember the stories I used to tell about my friend, the puppet?" The tiny roach nodded. "Well, this is he. This is Pinocchio."

"*Puppet! Puppet!*" chanted the swarm of roaches.

The tiny one smiled. Instinctively, Pinocchio smiled back. He then turned back to Poppa and asked, "Are these your children?"

Poppa nodded. "They're my life. One thousand and fourteen wonderful blessings."

"Where is their mother?" Pinocchio asked. But before Poppa could answer, something tapped at his cheek. He turned to find the tiny roach standing on his shoulder, scratching curiously at his wooden skin. "You really are made of wood!" he exclaimed, before turning back to his Poppa and saying, "But you said he was a *real boy* now!"

"Squeak!" Poppa shouted. "Come down from there and leave the man alone."

The tiny roach did as he was told. "You'll have to forgive young Squeak," Poppa continued. "He's a bit on the curious side."

"He's smaller than the others," Pinocchio observed.

Poppa nodded. "Of course! Squeak is my youngest—he was born almost seven minutes late." Squeak climbed back into his Poppa's lap. "But don't let his size fool you, Pinocchio. He may be tiny, but he's big in spirit, isn't that right, my boy?"

Squeak giggled, then hopped away.

"But I'm afraid he's right," Poppa continued, "you were a real man once, weren't you? My boy, what happened?"

"I don't know," Pinocchio replied. "I honestly don't remember you, or George, or ... anything!"

"But then why did you come here?"

Pinocchio sighed. "George brought me. He said I had to find my—" Pinocchio scratched his chin. "I can't believe I'm asking this. Are you my conscience?"

Poppa laughed. "Of course not!" he replied. "Your conscience is something inside of you! There was a time, yes, when I helped you find its voice, but those days are past. It seems you've taken your own counsel these days." He turned to the roaches sitting on the floor and asked, "That's not working out for him, is it, children?"

"Conscience! Conscience!" replied the swarm.

Poppa continued, "Whatever you have done, Pinocchio, has broken the spell that made you human. Now it is up to the fairies to decide if you can be made whole again. But to find them, you'll have to go on a long and dangerous journey to a land that can only be reached in your imagination—*The Great Beyond.*"

"I don't understand," said Pinocchio. "George is a fairy, so why didn't he just take me there?"

"You should ask him," Poppa replied. "Where is he, anyway?" Pinocchio turned to find the fairy snoozing away on the floor, a bottle clutched to his chest. Squeak had found him, too.

"George!" called the tiny roach. "Wake up, George!" He kicked at the Englishman's cheek, snapping him back to consciousness. When the fairy saw the little roach, he shrieked as he swatted at it.

"Get away, you bloody ... *rodent*!"

"Stop!" Poppa commanded as he rose from his chair. He snapped his fingers, ordering Squeak back to his side. "George, so help me, if you ever swing at one of my children again—"

"Well, tell him not to kick me!" the fairy replied.

Poppa folded his arms. "I see you're still hitting the bottle," he said.

"And I see you're still hiding in the dark," George retorted. "So are you gonna help this twig, or what?"

"He hasn't asked for my help," said Poppa.

George shot Pinocchio an incredulous glare and demanded, "Well? Ask him!"

Pinocchio shrugged his shoulders and wondered, "What? Ask him what?"

"He doesn't get it." George sighed, explaining, "You can only get to The Great Beyond in your dreams, mate, and you need a clear conscience to have good dreams."

"If you go in a nightmare," Poppa added, "you will not like the place you end up."

"That's why you need *this* little thing," George continued. "You need to dream well to guide us there."

"Little thing?" asked Squeak. "What little thing?"

"Your pappy," George replied, pointing at the swarm, "he needs a grody little roach!"

George's sarcasm didn't sit well with his hosts.

"What's wrong with roaches?" demanded one of the youngsters.

"We're survivors!" declared another.

"We're strong!" added a third.

"And loyal!" said yet a fourth.

"Whatever," said George. He turned back to Pinocchio. "So ask him. He's your only ticket, Sticks, so you'd better hope he says yes." But before Pinocchio could say anything, Poppa announced, "I can't come with you."

"What?" demanded George. "We came all the way—"

"I have to think about the children," Poppa replied. "It's too dangerous for them."

The children, however, didn't agree.

"We can make it!" insisted one.

"We won't be a burden!" added another.

"We want to go!" said a third.

"He needs our help!" said the fourth.

Poppa sighed. "Children, go and play in the other room," he said.

George waited until the last of them had cleared the door to begin his assault.

"You bloody coward."

"You can call me all the names you want—," said Poppa.

"And I will!" barked George.

"Stop it, you two!" Pinocchio ordered. He knelt down and got as close to the roach as he could. "Poppa roach, I wouldn't ask if it weren't important, but I must be a man again. Will you help me?"

Poppa's shoulders sagged. "You asked about the children's mother—" He took a deep breath. "It is very tricky for roaches to find a home. If the humans don't see you, they don't know you're there. That's why we stay hidden."

He sat back in his bottle cap and continued, "When my wife and I decided to have children, we moved into a nice house. A young family lived there, and they kept it very clean. We knew as long as we stayed in the walls, the children would be safe there. But when little Squeak was born, he was very sick. For days we kept watch over him, hoping that he would get better on his own. By the third day, we were desperate. My wife said only a certain root would heal him. I promised to go gather it as soon as the sun set. But then Squeak took a turn for the worse. As he coughed and coughed, I held him in my arms and prayed that he would make it until nightfall. But what I didn't know was that my wife had already made up her mind not to wait. Before I could stop her, she slipped through a crack in the wall. I could see that the lights in the room were on, and it took the humans only a second to spot her. She tried to make a break for it, but they were fast with their spray can ... I watched as they gassed my wife to death."

The roach began to weep. Pinocchio could not help but join him. "Oh, Poppa," he said, "I'm so sorry."

Poppa did his best to compose himself before he continued, "There was no time to mourn. My children were in danger, so I gathered them and we left that very night. We spent weeks on the road, no shelter from the rain. Finally we found this abandoned shack. It may not look like much, but it's free of humans, and it's ours."

"But for how long?" George asked. "They'll find this place. They always do. Some house-flipper will scoop it up and the first thing he'll do is call an exterminator."

"Maybe," Poppa conceded. "But for now, it's home." He turned back to Pinocchio. "I miss her terribly. I look at Squeak, and all I see is her smile. The children are all I have left. Please, Pinocchio, please don't ask me to put them into danger. I would do anything for you—except that."

Pinocchio reached out and brushed the roach gently across his antennae. "I won't ask," he said. And with that, he stood and headed for the door. George was flabbergasted. "What?" he asked. "So we're just leaving?"

"I can't ask him to go," said Pinocchio. As he turned back to offer his goodbyes, Pinocchio saw the beaten, defeated look on the roach's face. Without another word, he left, George following closely behind.

"Only looking out for his *own* kind," George mumbled. "Rather selfish, isn't it?" Pinocchio didn't answer. By the time they reached the car, George could see that Pinocchio was deep in thought.

"I'll dream a good dream," Pinocchio offered. "We'll make it, just you and I."

"I thought you didn't believe in all this," said George.

"After what I just saw in there," Pinocchio replied, "I'm starting to."

* * *

From the window, Poppa watched as his visitors made their way back to their car. It was then that he noticed little Squeak standing beside him.

"Aren't we going with them?" he asked.

"We cannot, son," Poppa replied. "It's a very long, very dangerous journey."

"But he needs our help," said Squeak.

"I know he does, son."

Squeak looked back to where his brothers and sisters had gathered. They nodded to their chosen representative, who pressed the point. "Poppa," said Squeak, "we *want* to help."

"Children, we have a home here—"

"But that man needs us!" Squeak interjected. "You always taught us that helping each other is our first, best job."

"That's true," said Poppa, "but he's not one of us—he's not family."

"If he's not family, then why did you call him 'my boy'?"

Poppa didn't have a good answer to that one. He turned back to the window and watched as George angrily pointed Pinocchio out of the driver's seat. Poppa looked back at the swarm, which waited breathlessly for his answer ...

* * *

"For the love of God," cried George, "we'll be here all day! Just move over and let me drive."

"Absolutely not!" said Pinocchio. "You've been drinking, and I'm scared enough when you drive sober."

As they tussled for control of the driver's seat, another voice interrupted them.

"Gentlemen," he said, "if we're expecting to get anywhere, we're going to have to learn to work as a team." They turned to find Poppa—and 1,014 of his children—standing proud and tall on the back seat. Poppa continued, "All of us."

"So you changed your mind?" asked George.

Poppa nodded. "I'd do anything for my boys." He turned to Pinocchio. "Even the big, clumsy wooden ones."

"Hear that?" said George. "Even he says you're clumsy. Now scoot over and let me drive!"

Pinocchio finally relented, and the coupe roared away with the fairy behind the wheel.

"So where, exactly, are we going?" Pinocchio asked.

"You can't run a campaign without finance," said George. "We're going to see your donors. We're going to meet the Fairy Queen."

"And how do we get there?" Pinocchio asked.

"We'll need a boat," George replied, "and it would be preferable if the captain didn't ask too many questions."

A grin crept across Pinocchio's lips. "I think I know just the boat ..."

* * *

It had been a bad month for Will Sanford.

The damage from his little whale charter venture had cost him almost a month's salary. Worse still, ever since he was freed from the net, the whale had been trawling the coast, eating everything in sight. Will hadn't caught a thing for weeks.

Will blamed it all on that pipsqueak from Washington. If ever there were a man he hoped not to see again, it was him. Will did his best to block every thought of the man, from his stupid grin to that annoying, high-pitched voice.

Unfortunately, he didn't succeed.

"Ahoy there!" Pinocchio called as he and George wandered toward the SS *Cunnyfish*, a backpack in hand.

"You!" screamed Will. He suppressed the urge to run over and punch the man in the face. "What do you want?"

"I want to charter your boat," Pinocchio replied. Will would have laughed if he didn't so badly want to cry. "You've got to be kidding me, right?"

"No," said Pinocchio, "I'm serious."

"Stop right there!" Will demanded. Pinocchio didn't comply. He and George marched right on board and proceeded to make themselves at home.

"No, no, no!" Will demanded. "I don't want your business—do you have any idea how much you cost? Hey!" he snapped at George as he fingered a bottle of Scotch. "Put that down!" George grudgingly obliged. Will continued, "You know that little shenanigans you pulled cost me thousands of dollars!"

"Shenanigans?" George puzzled. "Who uses that word anymore?"

"Alright," said Will, "that's it! Both of you, off my boat right now!"

"You don't understand, Mr. Sanford," said Pinocchio, "I need your boat. I'll pay very well!"

"Not for ten thousand dollars!" Will declared.

"Twenty?" asked Pinocchio.

"No way!"

"Mr. Sanford, be reasonable."

"Reasonable?" Will's voice kicked up three octaves. "This from a man who dove into the ocean to swim with whales?" A crash in the cabin caught his attention. His eyes whipped around to find that George was surfing through his footlocker. "Hey!"

"George, get out of there," Pinocchio ordered. He turned back to Will and asked, "So what do you want?"

"I want you off my boat, and I want to never, ever see you again."

"He might want a car," George suggested. He held up a dog-eared brochure for a big German coupe. "I found this in your locker."

"That's mine!" Will barked. He snatched the booklet from his hands.

"It's a proper beast," said George. "I used to sell them, and I happen to know one you can pick up for next to nothing."

"What are you talking about?" asked Will.

"Yes," Pinocchio added, "what *are* you talking about?"

"I'm talking about a trade."

"For what?" Will asked. George pointed across the harbor to a parking spot where sat the beast itself—*Pinocchio's* beast. "What do you say, mate? One car, one charter."

"No way!" shouted Pinocchio. George grabbed his arm, twisted. "You really want to keep that thing?" he whispered.

"Yes!" Pinocchio replied.

"Pinocchio," said Poppa as he climbed out of the backpack. "That car has brought you nothing but trouble. Think about it."

Pinocchio didn't argue. He gritted his teeth as he slipped the key fob out of his pocket. Will's eyes bulged.

"Are—are you serious?" Pinocchio nodded. "Wait," Will continued, "before I agree, tell me where you want me to take you?"

"An island," said George.

"Is it far?"

"No," said George. "Just one good sleep."

"So, a night?" Will asked. Pinocchio nodded. "And you have the title?" Pinocchio nodded again. "OK, deal—on one condition: no funny business, no swimming with sharks, nothing."

"No swimming. No funny business," Pinocchio replied.

"Promise?"

Pinocchio checked his nose. *Not a fraction of an inch.* "You have my word of honor."

CHAPTER 17

A Congressman and a Lobbyist Pull at Pinocchio's Strings

Frank Barnes loved to play ping-pong with the media. They served a low, bouncing ball of a question, he answered with a low, bouncing ball of a position. Barnes's sound bites were witty, wily, and endlessly quotable, which made him a favorite among the 8 p.m. talking heads. He had become an institution—so much so that on the second-floor balcony of the Capitol rotunda was an area unofficially known as "Barnes's Corner." Like deer to bait boxes, every night the networks came to "Barnes's Corner" knowing that by 8:10, they would have at least one good clip. Serve, return ... *Ping-pong.*

But tonight was different. All anybody wanted to know about was the man in the committee. Barnes didn't have answers; in fact, he was just as curious as the reporters. By 8:15, he had had enough. He stormed out of "Barnes's Corner" as a barrage of flashbulbs followed him. By the time he arrived at the congressional subway station, Barnes had over one hundred text messages waiting in his inbox, including several from his office. It seems two men were waiting for him there: One was a reporter from the *Star*, the other was the senior managing partner of The Kronos Group.

Barnes arrived at the Rayburn Building and found Josh, his office assistant, on duty at the reception desk.

"Where are they?" Barnes asked.

"I showed the lobbyist into your office a few minutes ago," Josh replied. "The reporter wandered away. I didn't recognize him. I think he said his name was *Wings*."

"Wiggs, actually," Max corrected. Barnes turned to find the *Star* reporter, crooked tie and all, sprinting down the hall.

"How are you, Congressman? Max Wiggs, Washington Star." Barnes sneered. Max continued, "Now before you throw me out, I'll tell you that I am absolutely not here to talk about the wooden man."

"Good," said Barnes. "That just bought you two minutes. Now what *are* you here to talk about?"

"The EPA."

* * *

It had been a while since Charles Stevens had waited in a congressman's office. In fact, it had been a while since he had actually lobbied. Watching the coverage of Barnes's ping-pong, he saw the discomfort with which the congressman had handled the questions. Reading body language was a skill Stevens had learned as a teenager selling newspaper subscriptions. Barnes shifted his weight, checked his watch—*he actually checked his watch on television!* Barnes was out of his comfort zone; it was as plain as the liver spots on his cheeks. Stevens checked his own watch. He had the distinct feeling that Barnes was stalling for time, and now he was growing impatient.

But there was something else moving in him at that moment, as foreign an experience as being made to wait for a lawmaker—*apprehension.*

The effort behind this bill was simple; it had to pass Barnes's committee. Stevens knew that environmentalist Barnes would block it unless, politically, he couldn't. So all Stevens had to do was find the right leverage, which came the day Pinocchio told him about the car accident. Stevens couldn't believe his good fortune, and the newspaper article was the icing on the cake. Thrust into the spotlight, overnight Pinocchio had gone from being a nobody to being an important man. Stevens knew he would do anything to hang on to that. Pinocchio was putty in the old man's hands, and Barnes's hand was forced. The path seemed clear: Pinocchio would testify, Barnes would be silent, and the bill would pass with nary an eyebrow raised.

But now everything was falling apart. Stevens had leveraged too much to make this bill happen. It was not like him to be so chancy and now it was *he* who was out of his element. For a man who liked to control every outcome, know every angle, this was uncharted territory for Charles Stevens. Now he would have to resort to some good old-fashioned lobbying if this bill was to have any chance at all.

On the plus side, this was a game he knew how to play well. Lobbying, after all, was really rather straightforward; first, you had to show genuine curiosity in the lawmakers' causes—they all had one—then, once you'd earned their trust, you simply lined their pockets. Congressmen like Barnes, had to fight every two years just to keep their jobs. As a result, they were always hungry for campaign funding. It was never too early to begin thinking ahead to the next cycle. Politicians, even well-loved ones like Barnes, lived and died by their campaign accounts.

But what happens when finance isn't enough? There were still those occasions when some stubborn lawmaker simply refused to vote Stevens's way. It didn't matter how much money he invested, no matter how right his arguments, no matter what research he had, or what polls he could produce. It was rare, but it still happened. In those instances Stevens played what he called "the invisible game."

The invisible game was all about leverage. The rules were simple: *We have something on you. Vote our way or we release it to the media and your career is finished.* But it was a dangerous game to play, even for a master like Stevens. Usually a career-ending photograph or compromising series of texts was enough to turn the heart of even the most radical of activists. But the invisible game had risks. If forced to use the leverage, it wouldn't take much for the victim to reveal the motive behind whoever released it. When cornered, after all, birds and squirrels tend to use their beaks and claws. The invisible game had sent more men to jail than Stevens even cared to count.

The invisible game Stevens played with Barnes and Pinocchio had blown up in his face, and now the only option left was to pass the bill. If it failed, there would be inquiries. There would be publicity. There would be lawsuits. There would be a scandal. If the truth about Stevens's leverage ever saw the light of press, Barnes would be finished, and Charles Stevens had no doubt he would take him down with him.

The bill must pass. No matter the cost, the bill must pass.

Stevens checked his watch again. 8:32. *What the hell was keeping him?*

* * *

"So if what you're telling me is true, Mr. Wiggs, you're taking on a much bigger adversary than just The Kronos Group," said Barnes.

"That's exactly my point," Wiggs continued. "We don't really know who is behind this, but it's not a logging company, I guarantee it. I don't believe a lobbyist as smart as Charles Stevens would back a bill that had these kinds of ramifications unless he knew every single angle. I think we need to know who his clients are."

"Good luck," said Barnes. "Kronos will never disclose that, and I can't make them, so what do you suggest I do?"

Wiggs thought about it. "Charles Stevens is waiting in your office. Why don't you talk to him *off the record*."

"And then give you the gist of it? Come on, Wiggs, you know better than that."

"No, sir, I mean for your own education. If you suggest removing the impact study waiver from the bill, you'll at least know where he stands. If he agrees, then I'm wrong. But if he objects—"

"Mr. Wiggs, I thank you for your opinion, but I am going to make up my own mind—and you may *not* quote me. Come back the day after tomorrow and maybe then I'll have a bite for you."

Barnes didn't offer so much as a handshake as he turned and pushed into his office. Max slumped into a chair. He had a million things to do at that moment, but he couldn't resist hanging around to see exactly how long the two men were going to talk.

* * *

Stevens was out of his chair, hand outstretched before the door was even closed. "Frank!" he called. "Good to see you!"

"I've been expecting you, Charles." Barnes accepted his hand and offered a limp shake.

"Frank, with everything that's been going on, I thought it might be a good idea if you and I—"

Barnes cut him off. "If we what, Charles? If we talked? Have you seen what they're saying on social media?"

"We'll get Pinocchio back," said Stevens. "I'm sure there's a perfectly reasonable explanation, but right now, I think we need to talk about what it's going to take to salvage this. Kronos still needs that bill passed, and we're willing to do whatever we need to do to make that happen."

"Oh, I don't believe this," said Barnes. "Your plan falls apart on live TV, and now you come into my office and try to bribe me? You must be crazy. No goddamn newspaper article is going to save you this time."

Stevens stepped back. "Are you threatening me, Frank? Because if you are, you must be one hell of a tactician, and honestly, I don't think you're a tactician."

"Well, you don't want to know what I think you are," retorted Barnes. "You got us into this mess, so you get us out. That, or I will bury that bill of yours right in the trash."

That *was* a threat. Barnes was the committee chair, which meant that if he so decided, all he had to do to shelve the bill was wave his gavel.

"Damn it, Barnes, we made a deal!"

"No, you made an offer. I don't recall ever accepting it. Truth be told, Charles, I despise what you do, and the way you do it. I don't like the fact that just being *Charles Stevens* means you'll automatically be shown into my office whenever you please. I also don't like the way you strong-armed me into this, or the way you manipulated that boy. Aldous would have never done that."

Barnes could tell the name struck a nerve in Stevens. He continued, "Isn't it sad, Charles, that after all you've done, all the bills you've passed, and all the money you've made, that you still can't get out from under his shadow? Aldous has been dead thirty years, and yet somehow he still has more pull in this town than you do. All you've got left are threats, and they don't scare me much anymore. Go ahead. Release the photos. I think at this point I'd rather end my career as an idealistic womanizer than a lobbyist's puppet."

Stevens was speechless, motionless. For a moment, he even forgot to breathe. Barnes continued, "What, no argument? Very smart. See? You *do* know something about Washington after all. Bring Pinocchio back to the committee by Friday, and I'll allow a vote on the bill. Otherwise, I'll shelve it and let the media ask all the questions they want."

"But, Congressman, I don't—"

"Know where he is or what happened to him? I know that. And that's exactly why I want to hear from him—and him alone."

Barnes took Stevens by the arm, motioned him gently out of the office, and pulled the door closed, leaving a stunned Stevens to stare in disbelief. He turned to the assistant and said, "I think I left my briefcase in there."

On cue, Barnes reached out, handed him a brown leather case, and closed the door shut again. Wiggs was as stunned as the lobbyist as he watched the entire scene unfold. Stevens stormed down the hall, Wiggs in hot pursuit. He stepped into the elevator and leaned on the "door close" button, but Wiggs was too fast for him. He forced the door open and slipped inside.

"So what's the next move on this bill, Mr. Stevens?"

"No comment," was Stevens's cold reply. Wiggs didn't let up. "So was it just money?" he asked.

That one got a reaction. "What did you say?" Stevens asked.

"I'm just trying to figure out what possessed you to take this bill on. From what I can tell it's nothing but dirty, stinking, bird-killing deforestation, which is kind of strange fare for a firm that built its reputation on *saving* owls."

Stevens's only response was a glare. "Nothing?" Wiggs asked. "Well, what about Pinocchio?"

"What about him, Mr. Wiggs?"

"Will he come back and finish his testimony?"

"No comment."

"Do you have any idea where he is?"

It took every ounce of self-restraint to keep Stevens's fist from landing on Wiggs's nose. Instead, he bit his lip and repeated, "No comment."

CHAPTER 18

The Puppet, the Fairy, and the Roaches Journey to The Great Beyond

Out in the open sea, the *Cunnyfish* proved to be just as slow as she looked. Will kept one eye on the wheel and the other on the owner's manual to his new car, which Pinocchio had grudgingly handed over—he had never seen an owner's manual wrapped in leather before.

On the foredeck, George and Pinocchio watched as the waves pushed by. "So how does this work, exactly?" Pinocchio wondered.

"It's simple," said George. "The Great Beyond is a place between worlds. To get there, you just need to dream about it. Everyone you want to take has to dream, too." He looked up at the wheelhouse. "Even him."

"So you're saying that to find this island, everyone on this boat has to be asleep?" George nodded and took another swig of the Scotch.

"Then who's gonna steer the boat?" Pinocchio asked.

"Pinocchio," said Poppa, "you're never going to get there until you welcome a little faith into your heart. You have to trust us."

Pinocchio swallowed the lump in his throat. "OK, Poppa, I trust you."

"Good," said Poppa. "George, would you please go relieve our captain?"

"With pleasure," George replied as he swallowed the last few drops of Scotch. Pinocchio watched as he snuck up to the wheelhouse, slid behind the distracted captain, and broke the bottle over his head.

"Hey!" shouted Pinocchio.

Will slumped forward and collapsed on the deck. As George dragged the snoozing captain down below deck, Pinocchio raced to intercept him.

"What are you doing?" he demanded. Poppa was already by his side.

"Everyone on the boat has to dream good dreams," Poppa said. "The last thing Mr. Sanford was thinking about was his beautiful new car. He'll dream quite well."

As George dragged the hapless fisherman below, Pinocchio took a long look at him, suddenly aware of the chaos he had brought into the man's life.

"I'm sorry, Will," he whispered.

George emerged from the cabin brushing his hands across his pants. "He sleeps in there? God it stinks."

"It's a fishing boat," said Pinocchio.

"Enough to make me a vegetarian."

"That's enough," said Poppa. "Let's get going."

The three of them lay down on the deck, doing their best to form pillows out of coats and ropes. Pinocchio was exhausted, but between his nerves and the uncomfortable deck, he doubted he'd be able to sleep.

"Now close your eyes," George whispered. "Allow yourself to drift away ..." Pinocchio was surprised at the gentle tone of his voice. All day he had heard the coarse grumblings of a chain-smoker, but as his volume softened, somehow so too did his melody. George continued, "Find that place where dreams and touch are one ... feel the lightness of your body, and the heaviness of your soul."

With every word Pinocchio found himself drifting into unconsciousness. His eyes *were* heavy. The rocking of the boat fell into a relaxing rhythm and the clouds above parted. A star appeared, followed by a dozen more.

"Feel your heart beating, and let the sound of it fill your mind. Look beyond the sea, beyond the stars, and see the mountain in the mist."

Pinocchio *could* see something. Just above the fog there appeared a mountain crest, tipped with the white of snow. His body felt warm, much warmer than it had been on the beaches of Avalon. The boat was perfectly still now, gliding across a glass-smooth ocean. If Pinocchio hadn't known any better, he would have sworn they were flying.

Pinocchio drifted into a great nothingness. Space didn't matter. Weight didn't matter. He opened his eyes and found that blackness was all around the boat. He stood, walked to the edge of the deck, and peered over. His reflection stared back at him, but he barely recognized it. His skin was soft and unwrinkled. He wore not a suit, but a child's clothes. His hair was sloppy and uneven, and his smile was broad and innocent. His reflection was not of a puppet, or a man, but a boy.

Another boy walked up behind him and joined his reflection in the water. His shape was familiar, as was the sound of his voice.

"Papa?"

It was Albero! Pinocchio turned to greet him only to find an empty ship. He turned back to the sea to find the reflection of youth was gone. In its place was a creaky, ugly old wooden man. His face sank. Tears clouded his vision. Then he saw the shape of another man standing over him. As he wiped the tear, the glowering face of Charles Stevens came into focus.

Pinocchio stared at his boss. As Stevens smiled that grandfatherly smile of his, his eye twinkled. Pinocchio looked back at his own reflection; the cracks in his arms, the flaking of the paint. Another tear welled up and dropped into the water, rippling it. As the water settled, Pinocchio could see that the twinkling eye of Charles Stevens had grown darker, larger. His smile grew unnaturally wide, revealing, tooth by tooth, a ten-foot grimace.

A voice filled his head, a voice so very familiar, and so very dreaded. It said, "*Welcome to MY world, little man.*"

* * *

The violence of the collision jolted him awake. Pinocchio leaped to his feet, stumbling over the fairy. "Get up, George!" he shouted. George mumbled and grumbled, swatting the puppet away.

Another collision rocked the boat, scattering screaming roaches across the deck. Another crash. The sky was clear; the waves seemed calm. It didn't feel like a storm—it felt as if something was ramming the boat.

"George!" Pinocchio hollered. Finally, George leaped to his feet just in time to be knocked back down by another crash.

"What the bloody hell?" he said.

"Something's wrong!" Pinocchio shouted. As Poppa gathered the roaches back into the safety of the backpack, he ordered, "Go wake Sanford!"

George raced below deck and shook the slumbering captain. Will only smiled and rolled over, content to sleep off the concussion.

"Damn it," George grumbled. He reared back and slapped him across the face. Finally, the hapless Will Sanford blinked himself awake. "What's going on?" he asked.

"Wake up, wanker! Your boat is out of control!"

Will leaned forward, surprised to find himself covered in Scotch. Another crash sent the two of them to their knees. With a restored sense of urgency Will shook off the headache and raced upstairs. He grabbed the wheel and pulled starboard. George lent a hand, and it took their combined strength to even get the wheel pointed straight.

"What happened?" asked Will.

"Don't ask me!" George shot back. "You're the bloody skipper!"

Another, more violent collision threw them to the deck. The wheel slipped away and resumed spinning. Will grabbed it, snapping off a handle.

"Something's ramming us!" he cried. George gripped the wall of the boathouse, crawling to his feet just in time to see a huge gray mass slip beneath the waves.

"What the hell was that?" he cried.

Another crash. Another. Fear had completely overwhelmed Will as he struggled to stay on his feet. He started crying. George saw the panic in his eyes and realized he had seen the same thing. "Oh no," he whispered as Will let the wheel slip. The boat lurched to the left. Another crash. Will leaped from the bridge and raced across the deck, knocking Pinocchio over as he passed. He tore at an orange cube stored just under the deck box and screamed, "He'll kill us all!"

"What are you talking about?" shouted Pinocchio as he grabbed at the hysterical skipper, only to be knocked away. Another crash. Will was in full panic as he ripped the raft from its storage case and tore open the inflate valve. The raft unfolded quickly, nearly pushing Pinocchio over the side. Will flung it into the ocean, then made a beeline for the edge of the deck. Pinocchio seized him and held on with all his strength.

"What? What is it?" he demanded.

Will's eyes wore absolute terror. "It's you!" he shouted. "It's you he's after!"

"Who?" asked Pinocchio.

Will finally broke free and launched himself over the side. Pinocchio watched helplessly as the captain pulled himself into the only life raft on the little fishing trawler.

"Damn it!" George shouted.

Another impact.

The edges of the deck snapped free from the keel.

Another.

The flimsy metal of the wheelhouse buckled.

Another.

Pinocchio grabbed the backpack and raced to the bow, just in time to meet George. "What is this?" George demanded. Pinocchio didn't have time to answer. One final crash and the boat exploded in two, flinging its passengers into the air. Pinocchio did his best to hang on to the backpack as a thousand tiny screams pleaded for help. As the surface of the ocean raced up toward him, time seemed to stand still. Then ...

Crash!

The pounding of a concussion began to overtake him. He looked up to see George drifting limply in the sea some twenty feet away. He still had the backpack in his hand. He gasped for air, but the sensation of water filling his throat was the last thing he remembered before the darkness was absolute.

* * *

The world was spinning like a falling kite when Pinocchio finally woke. Against his better judgment, he lifted himself to his feet and assessed the situation; George was sprawled across a stone wall, a bottle clutched firmly in his hands. His snores were loud enough to mute the waves that were hitting the shore below, blasting the fairy with a fine mist. Most of the roaches were huddled in a pile next to their backpack, while Squeak was curled under Poppa's arms like a dozing puppy.

Pinocchio looked over the wall that surrounded the landing. The rocky shore was some fifty feet below. He had no idea how they had gotten this high. In fact, he had no idea how they had managed to land the boat ...

The boat!

Pinocchio searched frantically, but it was nowhere in sight. He raced from one end of the wall to the other, tripping over George and knocking his bottle to the ground.

"What are you doing, Sticks?" George demanded.

"The boat!" Pinocchio shouted. "Where's the boat?"

Roused by the commotion, Poppa woke. "What's going on?" he asked as he gently nudged the children from their slumber. George, on the other hand, was in no mood for panic. He rolled back over to find some more sleep, instead finding that the other side of the wall was a cliff. "Whoa," he said as he caught himself. "How did we get up here?" But before Pinocchio could answer, Squeak announced, "I found the boat!"

"Where?" asked Pinocchio.

"Down there," the tiny roach replied as he peered over the far edge. George, Pinocchio, and Poppa raced over. All that was left of the SS *Cunnyfish* was a flotsam of broken wood and debris. The four let out a collective sigh.

"Now what?" demanded George.

Pinocchio replied, "I guess we find another boat and keep going."

"Another boat yes," added Poppa, "but we don't need to go any further." He turned and pointed to the island behind them. "Gentlemen, welcome to The Great Beyond."

When Pinocchio saw it, he was awestruck. Unlike the gaudy Avalon, there was a purity about this place. Trees bloomed in the deepest reds, oranges, and yellows. Beyond the clearing mist lay a small mountain range. At the base sat a grand white structure whose domed roof seemed to glow as if burning.

George had been here a hundred times before, but each time the majesty of it humbled him. Suddenly aware of his sloppy appearance, he declared, "I can't go to the queen like this!"

"We'll clean you up," Poppa said, "but right now we should worry about how we're going to get home."

"Home?" wondered Pinocchio. "I thought we wanted to get here!"

"You do not understand, Pinocchio. This is an island of dreams. It has no port, no beach, and there is no safe place to dock. We may meet the queen, she may even grant your wish, but you will grow old and die here unless we find a boat that can make it past the dangerous shoals and get us back off this island."

"First, I want to know what hit us last night," said George.

"That was Oceanus," said Pinocchio. "It's me he was after."

"Is he a whale?" asked Squeak.

Pinocchio nodded, asking, "Did you get a good look at him?"

"Not last night," said Squeak, pointing, "but I was wondering if it was that whale right over there."

Pinocchio ran back to the wall. There, in the ocean fifty feet below, lay Oceanus. He smiled and let loose a mighty snort from his blowhole. Pinocchio could do little but watch. In his mind he heard that mocking laugh as the beast sank back beneath the waves, and the ocean calmed once again.

"That son of a bitch!" said George. "He sank our boat!"

"Well, we know he's there," said Poppa, "but he can't get us on land. We will have to contend with him soon enough."

"Do we have anything to eat?" asked Pinocchio.

"Quite right," Poppa replied. "We should gather some supplies and find a way off this plateau. We need to make our way to the Great Hall."

"How long do you think it'll take?" Pinocchio wondered.

"Ten or twelve hours," said George. "And who knows what's waiting in that jungle for us."

CHAPTER 19

Pinocchio Is Hunted

"Geppetto, where is your son?" Charles Stevens asked.

The old man didn't respond. He continued to gaze at the flickering television as if his unexpected visitors weren't even there. Stevens persisted, enlisting a warm, kindly tone. "We have to find him, Geppetto."

Still no answer. A well-built man reached over and switched off the television. It was quiet at the Weeping Pines Retirement Center, quiet enough that all three men could hear the crackle of tobacco in Geppetto's pipe as he took another draw.

"Geppetto," Stevens continued, "we want to help him, but we can only do that if we know where he is."

Geppetto finally lifted his eyes and acknowledged his visitor. "You cannot help him, Mr. Stevens," he said before tapping down his tobacco and returning to his absent gaze. The well-built man sighed, noting, "Finally, he says something."

Stevens shook his head. "Do you know where Pinocchio is?"

"Yes," Geppetto replied, "but you will not find him."

"Why not?" Stevens asked.

"Because you don't know how to get there."

"Geppetto, he's in trouble—"

Geppetto grinned as he cut him off. "That is true, Mr. Stevens, but I think you're here not because Pinocchio is in trouble, but because you are, too."

Dropping the grandfather act, Stevens's brow furrowed and his voice sharpened as he demanded, "Where is he?"

"You don't listen," Geppetto replied, coolly. "You cannot follow where he went. He is safe among friends. That is all that's important." Geppetto emptied the ash from his pipe and refilled it. He struck a match and let the sizzle of tobacco do the talking for him.

Stevens had had enough. He snapped to his feet, hollering into the old man's ear, "Stop talking in riddles, Geppetto! WHERE IS HE?"

Geppetto didn't wince. He took a calm drag on his pipe and offered the most honest and the most cryptic answer he could.

"He is beyond our world, and beyond your reach. He is in the land of dreaming—a place where no man can go—certainly not I, and certainly not you. He was sent there to plead with the fairies that they might release the spell and make him a human once again." Geppetto puffed out a perfect string of smoke circles before continuing, "My son will return when he is ready. When he does, he will return a man, and nothing you or any of your people do will bring him back before that."

Shaking his head, Stevens made for the door. Dominic followed. "Well I can see why Pinocchio threw him in here," Stevens exclaimed. "The guy's off his rocker."

"I'm not so sure," said Dominic. "My father was a pipe smoker. Did you see the way he packed that tobacco? That takes skill, concentration."

Stevens rolled his eyes. "What are you, Sherlock Holmes?"

"I'm just saying, I don't think he's senile at all; in fact, I think he's telling the truth."

His loafers squealing against the linoleum, Stevens stopped, turned, and looked his partner square in the eye. "So you think that Pinocchio is—at this very moment—in a land of fairies? I just want to be clear; that's what you think?"

"I didn't say it was true," Dominic replied, "but *he* thinks it's true. Besides, you saw what happened at the testimony. Is anything Geppetto said really that far-fetched?"

Before Stevens could respond, something bumped into him. He looked down to find that an elderly woman (in an even more elderly wheelchair) was blocking his path. Like most of the center's residents, the woman looked lost, confused. But as Stevens moved to step around her, she suddenly reached up and seized him by the wrists. Stevens was stunned by her quickness, and even more stunned by the sound of her sandpaper voice.

"Do you hunger?" she asked.

Stevens broke free and hurried away. Dominic, however, was immobilized by the very sight of her and refused to budge. By the time Stevens reached the end of the hall, Dominic was all alone some thirty feet behind him. As Stevens reached for the door, again he felt a viselike claw lock on to his wrist. Somehow, the old woman had kept up with him. Stevens yanked at his arm, but could not manage to break the grasp.

"Let go of me!" Stevens demanded.

But the old woman held firm, declaring, "You eat, and yet you hunger!"

The grip tightened. Fear, a sensation wholly unknown to a master of the universe like Stevens, now flowed through his body like water through a pipe. He called for a nurse. The old woman continued, asking, "Why are you hungry, *Charles Stevens*?"

Already panicked, upon hearing his name, Stevens was gripped with terror. His voice cracked as he screamed—

"NURSE!"

A linebacker-like orderly raced around the corner. With a gentle touch, he released the petrified lobbyist from the woman's grip and took her wheelchair by the handles.

"She has dementia," the orderly explained. "I'm sorry if she startled you."

As he wheeled the old woman away, he passed two other residents in their own rickety wheelchairs, their backs twisted like driftwood, their moans echoing through the hall as they clawed at the railing.

"It's a goddamned madhouse," Stevens muttered, as he bolted for the front door.

* * *

As Charles Stevens's limousine rolled out of the parking lot, Cassandra could sense that her boss needed some good news.

"Well, I found the wife," she said. "She's staying with her mother in Bethesda."

Stevens wasn't impressed. "Do you really think we'll have better luck with her? She doesn't have any more idea where he is than we do." He pinched the bridge of his nose. "What on God's green earth is Pinocchio up to?"

"It's possible he's just scared," Dominic replied. "He doesn't know what happened to him either. For all he knows he's sick, maybe even dying—"

"And finishing the testimony is probably the last thing on his mind," Cassandra added.

Stevens watched the traffic drift by—a thousand grinning faces in a thousand mid-grade cars. How happy they seem, he thought, how content, how blissfully unaware that the man in the limo next to them, a man of some considerable wealth and influence, was on the verge of losing his mind.

"The fact is he could be anywhere," Stevens continued. "Forty years I've worked in this city, and I've never seen the like. An expert witness falls victim to a voodoo curse smack in the middle of testimony, then just up and disappears. I've got four days until the biggest vote of my career, and what am I doing? Chasing old men and ex-wives! This is madness!"

THUMP! Stevens's fist bounced off the leather seat.

THUMP! THUMP! THUMP!

"I take it the kid is with her?" Dominic asked, trying to stay focused.

"What kid?" demanded Stevens.

"Pinocchio's," Dominic replied. "Didn't you know he had a son?"

Stevens shook his head. As the limo eased onto the Beltway, everything faded into a high-speed haze as desperation washed over the senior partner. Stevens knew that there was one option still on the table. In forty years he had resorted to it only once, and it had nearly turned disastrous—the kind of disaster that ends with shortened careers and lengthy sentences. He had resisted even exploring it up until now, but even as he announced, "We're out of options," he was still desperately searching for one that had eluded him. He grabbed Cassandra's pad and began scribbling. "Driver? 18th and K," he ordered.

He tore off the sheet, thrusting it into Dominic's hands. "I'm dropping you at the office. Have Nancy pull these files and then take the next commercial flight to Avalon."

"Me? Where are you going?" Dominic asked.

"Bethesda."

Stevens tapped a contact up on his phone and without so much as a greeting, began issuing orders to the muffled voice on the other line.

Suddenly the limo lurched to the right, knocking Cassandra into the senior partners.

"Take it easy, driver!" Stevens shouted.

"Sorry, sir, he cut me off!"

Stevens turned his attention back to the phone. Dominic offered Cassandra a reassuring pat on the shoulder.

"Why are we going to Avalon?" she asked.

"If I had to guess," he said, "it's because we can't be arrested there."

* * *

"Watch out!" cried Jessica.

Max leaned into the brake pedal and braced his passenger. The wallowing sedan juddered to a halt, missing the big limo by mere inches. Max's heart pounded.

"Are you OK?" he asked. As he turned, he was mortified to find his arm was resting across her chest. He yanked it away and blurted, "Sorry!" They looked back toward the car that had nearly wiped them out—a large black limousine that seemed somewhat out of place at the Weeping Pines Retirement Center. As it zoomed past, Jessica locked eyes with the young woman in the back seat. "I know her," she said.

"You do?"

"I don't know her name, but she's one of the analysts at Kronos."

"Damn," said Max, "they beat us here."

Jessica nodded—she didn't believe the old man would tell them anything. But then again, Charles Stevens could be convincing when he needed to be. "Let's hurry."

CHAPTER 20

Pinocchio Discovers That Anything Is Possible in the Land of Dreams

There was not but what could not be in The Great Beyond. Water flowed up the raging falls and crashed into the cliff above. A herd of trees raced by. The streams boiled. A winged salamander circled the sky, searching the island for a mate.

Under the mistaken impression that he knew where he was going, Pinocchio and the roaches followed George up a trail. As the sun crept behind the mountains, they found a clearing and made camp. George gathered mud-soaked logs, which made for the best burning in The Great Beyond, and the roaches gathered poisonous berries, which were perfectly edible.

As the fire burned a hot blue, Pinocchio reveled in the warmth. He was surprised at how cold the tropics could get.

Poppa loaded his pipe and kept a watchful eye as the children played in the forest.

"Shouldn't be too much longer," George announced. "Half a day, maybe more. We'll get going first thing in the morning." He uncorked a bottle of some brown liquor and offered Pinocchio a swig.

"No thanks," said Pinocchio.

"Come on, it'll keep you warm."

Pinocchio shook his head and concentrated on the fire. His suit was a tattered shell of its former self, his sharp, doweled joints having long since worn through the thin fabric. All eyes turned to the sound of laughter in the forest. The roaches were having the time of their lives.

"They need a home," Poppa mused. He wasn't so much starting a conversation as thinking aloud. Regardless, Pinocchio replied,

"What about the shack?"

"Abandoned foreclosure," Poppa replied. "George is right. It's a matter of time before the bank unloads it, then in come the workers, the contractors, and the exterminators. No, it's temporary, to be sure."

Pinocchio sat up, brushing aside another offer of whiskey. "So what kind of home do you want?"

Poppa took a deep draw on his pipe. "Not a house, not somebody else's old home. I don't know, Pinocchio. Someplace warm with plenty to eat, places for them to run, play—someplace we can be safe." Pinocchio noticed Squeak had joined the conversation, listening with wide-eyed wonder at every word his father said. "I didn't want them to have to live on the run. When I was a boy, I used to dream that I could be more than this, more than a scavenger. But that's the thing about maturity. As we get older, we learn to give up, to surrender to our limitations. This is one of the reasons I love children. They remind me of who I once wanted to be."

"But you should never learn to give up!" said Pinocchio. "If that's a lesson you've learned, you have to *unlearn* it!" He turned to Squeak and asked, "What do you want to be when you grow up?"

"I don't know," said Squeak.

"Sure you do. If you could be anything—anything in the world?"

Squeak thought it over. "I—I want to be a *flyer*."

"A *flyer*?" Pinocchio asked.

"Other bugs get to fly, like bees, and butterflies. Roaches only get to crawl on the ground. I want to fly."

"Well," said Pinocchio, "I think you can."

"Barmy," said George. "You're filling the kid's head with nonsense."

"Oh hush, George!" Poppa shot back. "I forget, why did you lose your wings again?"

"Because of Pinocchio," answered George, drawing a disbelieving stare. "Well, that, and because I was sleeping with the boss's daughter."

"Uh-huh," Poppa replied.

George sat up. "OK," he said. "I admit it. I got distracted, but you should have seen this girl. Just, body like ... anyway, I lost track of Pinocchio when we went to Hollywood."

"Hollywood?" asked Poppa. "What on earth were you doing in Hollywood?"

"I wanted—" He paused. "Never mind."

"No," insisted Pinocchio, "tell us."

George sighed. "I always had this thing. I wanted to be an actor."

Poppa snickered. "See?" said George. "See? That's why I don't tell anybody about it. People used to tell me I had a handsome face. Fairies spend half our time giving speeches anyway, so I just thought it was inevitable. Anyway, the relationship wasn't working out, so I headed back to Virginia. By the time I found you again, it was too late. So they sacked me."

"Do they hire a lot of actors with six-foot wings?" Poppa asked.

"Well, what about you?" George demanded. "You're supposed to be the voice of reason. Where were you when all this was happening?"

"I was raising my family!" protested Poppa. "It's not easy for a single parent—"

George cut him off. "So what you're saying is that it's alright for you to be distracted but not me? Now isn't that just like a roach—"

"That's enough!" cried Pinocchio. "This constant bickering, back and forth. You sound like a pair of old ladies." He sighed. "I mean, the truth is, it wasn't your responsibility, Poppa, or yours either, George. I'm a grown man, and I made my own decisions."

"Decisions that had a lot of consequences," Poppa added.

"I know that," Pinocchio replied. "And now you're all here because of it." He took a deep breath, continued, "I haven't said it yet, but I am grateful to you. All of you. You believed in me once. Hell, you believed in me when I didn't even believe you existed. I owe you better than that."

He turned to Poppa. "I believe you'll find a wonderful home with everything you and the kids need."

He turned to George. "And you should go back to Hollywood. Honestly, I think you'll be a great actor."

Finally, he turned to Squeak. "And you go find your wings, Squeak. There is no impossible in this world. Believe me. If you want to fly, you will."

"And what about you, Pinocchio?" asked Poppa. "What do you want to be?"

Pinocchio sighed. "I just want to be *somebody*."

Poppa grinned. "Then somebody you will be, my boy." *It wasn't the right answer, at least not all of it.* "Now let's all get some rest. Tomorrow will be a big day."

Everyone seemed to agree. George even went so far as to cork his bottle rather than finish it.

When Poppa finally rolled off to sleep, George whistled at Squeak and pointed. "You, little roach, come here."

As Squeak tiptoed over, George crouched as low as he could, whispering to the tiny bug, "Do you really want to fly?" Squeak nodded. "Then I'll take you. If I get these wings back, we'll go as fast and as high as you want."

"I don't think Poppa would like that," said Squeak.

"I'll bet he won't." George grinned as he rolled back over. "We'll go anyway."

* * *

The front tires squealed as the sedan roared out of the parking lot. Jessica was nervous. "I've never flown in a helicopter," she said.

"Well, I've never seen the paper hire one before, so I say eat it up."

Max leaned on the horn. The sedan jumped two lanes of traffic and caught the on-ramp. "Read me those directions the old man gave you," he said, "word for word."

Jessica thumbed through her notes. "Close your eyes, my child, and imagine—"

"My child?" asked Max.

"You said word for word."

"I guess. *Move it!*" Another honk and the sedan was barreling down the 50 West Highway.

Jessica continued, "Imagine the energy of all things as you sleep the deepest sleep—"

"Sleep? You want the pilot to sleep?"

"I think we're supposed to sleep."

"OK ..."

"Until you walk in the place where dreams and touch are one. Breathe freely, and let the wind carry you across the seas of time—"

Max groaned. "Tell me again why you don't think the old man is senile?"

"Max, he smoked that tobacco to perfect ash—"

"Oh, this is nuts, Jessica! We're supposed to get on that chopper, go to sleep, and let *dreams* guide us to the land of the fairies? Are you listening to yourself? My God, listen to me! Here I was thinking I'd be a real reporter one day ..."

Traffic slowed. The sedan didn't. Max hit the gas and careened down the breakdown lane, drawing honks and unpleasant gestures.

"Yeah, yeah, I know," he muttered. Jessica stared at him. "What?" he asked.

"Nothing. Just seems you're in an awful hurry to get to somewhere you don't think really exists."

"When you get to be my age, Jess, you're prepared to make a few leaps of faith. You, on the other hand, are a trusting soul, aren't you?"

"Why, because I let you drive?"

"No, for asking to get on this story. I started out with a great little insider piece; double-dealing and payoffs. Now I'm mixed up with fairies and magic spells. This is starting to feel like the story that finally put the paper out of its misery."

"Well, it'll be an adventure anyway."

She was right. Max smiled as he nearly clipped a hatchback merging back into the fast lane. "I hope we find him before Stevens does."

CHAPTER 21

Pinocchio Meets the Fairy Queen

It was almost dusk when the expedition finally reached the edge of the jungle. Pinocchio was the first to step into the clearing. He froze when he saw it. There, at the base of the mountain, stood the most marvelous structure he had ever seen. Built of white marble that shimmered in the evening sun, the hall had an almost Roman quality about it. A long staircase led up to a row of columns that lined the entrance. At the center sat a majestic white dome a hundred feet tall. On any other island, the structure would seem out of place, but nothing was out of place on The Great Beyond.

"That's it," George announced, "the Great Hall." It had been many years since he had been here, and he never dreamed he would be back. George stepped into the lead, taking the marble steps two at a time as he led the expedition inside.

The interior was even more immense. Rows of long wooden tables stretched from one corner to the other, enough room to seat thousands. Pinocchio's footsteps echoed in the seemingly abandoned hall, the only activity being the crackle of a large firepit.

Suddenly the hall was bathed in the bluest of light. The walls glowed. The tables shimmered. It was a light so powerful, Pinocchio could almost hear its hum. Then, without form or direction, came a voice that seemed to speak from every corner of the space. It thundered with authority, yet it spoke in a sweet, almost soothing tone.

"You are the first, Pinocchio ..."

Pinocchio cowered upon hearing his name. The roaches burrowed themselves inside their bag, which George used to shield his eyes.

The voice continued, "No human has ever entered the realm of the fairies, but then again, you are no longer human, are you?"

Squinting, Pinocchio looked up and beheld the most beautiful angelic shape drifting toward him on translucent wings.

"Yet The Great Beyond is a place so very familiar to you, is it not?" she said. "This is the home of your dreams, those you long to remember, and those you tried to forget."

Her feet brushed the ground and she stepped toward the trembling entourage. Pinocchio felt his pulse quicken, ticking like a stopwatch as she approached. Awestruck, George fell to his knees, as did Poppa. Pinocchio, however, was both too terrified and too fascinated by the beautiful creature to do anything but look.

"I am the Fairy Queen, and I welcome you to my realm. Come, my child, let us honor the dangerous journey you took to come see me. Sit, eat. We will hear your questions soon enough, and perhaps we can find that thing that you seek today."

As the glow dimmed, Pinocchio was shocked to find that a great feast had appeared on the table before him. The queen took her seat in an ornate wooden throne at the end of the hall, and though she was so very far away, her voice was as clear as a whisper in their ears.

"Please, my children, eat."

As George reached for the wine, Pinocchio and Poppa shot him a disapproving look.

"Don't look at me like that," said George. "She offered."

George had a point, and they hadn't eaten much for the last two days. As George set the backpack on a chair, the roaches streamed out. They looked to Poppa, who nodded, then proceeded to devour a platter of breads and cheeses. For half an hour not a word was said as the entourage gorged. After a while, Pinocchio noticed the queen had not eaten a thing. He kicked George gently under the table.

"What?" barked George. Pinocchio dropped his voice to a whisper. "How do you address her?"

"Who?" George asked, loudly.

"The queen."

"What do you think you call a queen? Call her *Your Highness*."

Pinocchio took a sip of wine, cleared his throat, and asked. "Your Highness, are you not hungry?"

"How would one know when one is hungry, Pinocchio?"

It was a strange question that Pinocchio did not know how to answer. She continued, "Some eat when there is food at hand, whether they are hungry or not. Would you agree?"

Pinocchio nodded.

"Then the answer to your question is not whether I am hungry; it is whether you are."

"I don't understand," he said.

The queen rose, crossed the table and stood over him. "Are *you* hungry, Pinocchio?"

"Yes," he answered.

"But a puppet does not need to eat."

Pinocchio hadn't thought about this. In fact, he hadn't actually eaten in days. "I suppose you're right," he said.

"Yet you ate anyway," she continued. "Now look what you have done!"

As if on cue, Pinocchio felt a rumbling in his stomach. He unlatched the cabinet door, and a puddle of chewed-up meat, gravy, and wine hit the ground with a most unpleasant splash. What was left of the mess clung to the fragile gears of his heart, clogging the movement. Pinocchio reached in and hastily wiped at it, but as he did, he felt a spring come free.

"Oh no," he said.

Once again he watched helplessly as his fragile heart exploded in a cloud of flying gears. As Pinocchio collapsed to the ground, George and Poppa leaped to their feet, lifting the motionless puppet to a chair.

"Children! Hurry!" Poppa cried. The roaches sprang into action, gathering fragments of Pinocchio's heart and laying them on the table; a gear here, a spring there.

The queen sank to her knees, picked up a gear, and held it up to Pinocchio. As he stared at it, he noticed something different about the stamping on that piece. It was a logo, one that he had seen countless times before: a five-tiered crown with a brand name under it. He saw that logo every time he had looked at the expensive Swiss watch that Charles Stevens had given him some months before.

"A man is his purpose," said the queen, "and you have made your purpose *things*, so a thing you have become."

He looked at the gear again. The queen held it still closer, close enough for Pinocchio to make out the stamping under the crown logo. George read it aloud. "Swiss Made." He shrugged. "At least it's quality. Imagine if your boss gave you a quartz."

A raised eyebrow from the queen silenced him. She set the gear on the table, which was quickly snapped up by the roaches who were busy at work in the cabinet. The last piece in place, they gave the crown a hearty wind, and the clock began to *tick ... tick ... tick*.

Pinocchio came to his feet, as did the queen. She reached out and brushed the painted hair that covered his ears. He could not feel the warmth of her touch, only imagine it.

"What has become of you, Pinocchio?" she said. "And what has become of the ones you love?"

* * *

Whitney knew they were in trouble. She also knew that, for the moment anyway, it was best to play along. Children could read anxiety in their parents' faces like words in a book. If she showed the slightest hint of fear, it would spread like wildfire. She had to play along—not for her sake, but for young Albero's.

Well, mostly it was for Albero's.

As the executive jet dropped below the clouds, Albero spotted the island. "Is that where we're going, Mama?"

"It is, son," Whitney replied. "That's our island."

"Is Daddy going to be there?"

In her heart of hearts she knew he would. Whether it would be his choice or the choice of the same sharply dressed men who had forced her onto this plane, it didn't matter. Somehow, she knew he would come.

The pilot announced, "Folks, we are just a few minutes out. If you haven't already, please take your seats and put your seat belts on tight. We have arranged a car to pick you up when we land. In twenty minutes you'll be enjoying our resort. Thank you and I hope you had a smooth and peaceful flight."

Smooth? Yes. Peaceful? Not quite. Whitney tightened Albero's strap, pulling the curious boy away from the window. She chewed her fingernails. She was positively ecstatic at the thought of no longer being in the air. She glanced back at the ogre in the seat behind her. He hadn't moved but an inch or two since the plane had taken off.

"You heard him," she said. "You better put your seat belt on."

Reluctantly, he agreed. She held her son's hand and braced herself for whatever would meet her when she landed.

* * *

While George and the roach dined away, the queen led Pinocchio on a walk through the forest.

They strolled the length of a gentle creek, which at points, turned angry and fell into rapids, only to settle down again just a few yards beyond. The sun hung low in the west. The air was cool and heavy.

"You have come a long way to see me," said the queen. "Tell me, my child, what it is you wish of me."

Pinocchio took a deep breath. "Your Highness," he said, "I want to be a real man again."

The queen smiled. "To be a *real* man, Pinocchio, is no simple affair. Yes, we can use our magic to make you a human again, but does this make you a man?" She sat by the creek side and traced her fingers across the water. "Do you know why it is that you became a puppet again?"

Pinocchio shrugged his shoulders. "Because I told a lie?"

The queen shook her head. "One lie, Pinocchio? You think that is all it would take to break a fairy's magic?"

Pinocchio looked away. A thousand possible reasons had come and gone from his mind since that day, but none of them made much sense. He listened to the stream and how the *tick-tick-tick* of his heart seemed to drown it out. He placed a hand over his chest and felt the mechanical thump pushing against it as it grew louder and louder. "I don't know," he said, "but I've lost everything."

"Listen to yourself, Pinocchio. Every*thing*. It is not *things* you should cherish, but life! Life begets life, Pinocchio, and it fills you with purpose. If you welcome others into your life you allow yourself to be welcomed as well. Find this and you will find the place you are supposed to be. It is not a new place; it is a return to a place you once knew, but that you forgot when you fell in love with *things*, just as you forgot how you came to be.

"A man is his purpose, Pinocchio. If you would be a man again, you must remember yours."

Pinocchio sat on the ground and pulled his knees up to his chest. He had never told anyone what he was about to say. "All I ever wanted was to fit in. I wanted to know why everyone else seemed to understand each other so well while I didn't understand them at all. I thought if I belonged to *something*, if I were *somebody*, it would all make sense."

"Then you have chased a false purpose, and in the process you have made yourself a puppet. Think, Pinocchio, on who now pulls your strings. It was not fairy magic that made you what you are any more than it was your loved ones who abandoned you."

Pinocchio thought on this. She was right. Geppetto's stories turned out to be true after all, so why did he think him senile? And Whitney ... she didn't leave him; he ... he *left her!* It was not his body, or even his humanity that was broken; it was his family! All his life Pinocchio had carried an aching fear that he would be alone, and now, thanks to Charles Stevens, he actually made it happen.

"May I ask a question, Your Highness?" Pinocchio asked.

"Of course."

"Do I have a mother?"

The queen smiled. "Of course you do, Pinocchio, and as your father often told you, you have known her all along. All of nature is your mother—from the trees in the forest, to the fish in the streams—even the angry whale that has so often haunted your dreams. Each is a part of who you are, and more to your worries, *why* you are. You are a child of nature, Pinocchio. You have a beautiful mother, and a brave father, but you have abandoned them; thus you have made yourself an orphan. These things were ordered not by nature. Think now on who has done this to you."

My God, Pinocchio thought, I've done it to myself!

Pinocchio took the queen by the hand. "Will you help me, Your Highness?"

The queen smiled again. "You do not need my help to find what you seek, just as you did not need a map to find this island."

"But I can't do it alone."

"You are so very far from alone, Pinocchio. Though they are far away, you still have a family. On this very island you still have friends—"

"One thousand and sixteen, to be exact," George declared. Pinocchio looked back to find the Englishman, backpack in one hand, a glass of wine in the other, walking toward the creek.

The queen nodded. "These friends have risked much for you, my child. How can you say that you are alone when so many souls have pledged to your happiness?"

Pinocchio felt ashamed. He had not thought of things in this way. He looked at George, bleary-eyed as he sipped on his wine, Poppa riding on his shoulder, and 1,014 little children peeking out from the backpack. He thought about Max Wiggs—the article he had praised as a blessing, then condemned as a curse—why did Max choose him of all the people in the city to write about?

He thought about Cassandra—she never really meant to hurt him, had she? If only she could understand the depth of the love Pinocchio and Whitney had shared! Who was he to condemn her? If he had lived the life she had, he might be no better—and no worse than she.

Pinocchio began to shiver. The queen took him by the hand and led him back into the hall where the fires continued to roar. After a few minutes, Pinocchio felt very warm again. For the first time in weeks, he did not feel alone at all.

"I have been a fool, Your Highness."

"Do not despair, Pinocchio. Today you have taken the first step in that you recognize your faults. Now, to the best of your abilities you must undo the hurt you have caused, and there may come a point when you will be forced to choose another's happiness over your own. If you choose well, you will find your purpose again, and your humanity will follow. Seven days you had to find yourself again. Here, in The Great Beyond, the magic is very strong. Stay with us, my child, and together, we will help you find your path again."

"And my friends?" Pinocchio asked. "Can they stay also?"

Poppa and George exchanged curious glances. They hadn't expected this. Neither had the queen. She turned to George and said, "You too have amends to make, but you have proven yourself worthy by guiding your friend through great danger. If you wish it, we will welcome you back to our realm."

George was overwhelmed. Tears poured down his unshaven cheek as he asked, "I can be a fairy again?"

The queen bowed her head. Poppa patted him on the shoulder and said, "Congratulations, George!"

George stood, drink still in his hand, and twirled around. "Are they there?" he asked. "Can you see them?" George stumbled around the hall like a dog chasing his own tail, trying desperately to catch a glimpse of the most brilliant pair of wings that ever an Englishman had worn.

"They're—they're beautiful!" said Pinocchio.

Overcome with joy, George leaped up and soared across the hall. Despite being out of practice, George was a graceful pilot, and he came to land so gently that it seemed to Pinocchio that he had been flying for decades. He glowed with an energy Pinocchio had not seen in him before, but suddenly was so familiar.

"Yes!" Pinocchio exclaimed as he leaped from his seat. "Yes! I do recognize you now! You were there! You *were* the blue-haired fairy!"

"Azure, mate," George corrected, and as he winked, Pinocchio could swear he heard a bell tinkle.

George bounded into the air, barnstorming through the hall. The roaches clapped as he buzzed the room, unable to contain the joy that rushed through him like warm blood. He was alive again.

The queen turned to Poppa and asked, "And you, father roach?"

Poppa turned his attention from the aerial acrobatics and asked, "Your Highness?"

"Your heart has never been in question for me. You accepted the duty nature had chosen for you, to guide her son through times of trial and doubt, and you have earned your reward."

Poppa blushed as best as an insect could. "Oh, Your Highness, I do not need any reward. Just to see Pinocchio safe, and to have my boys and girls with me, I have everything I need right here."

"Except a home," she said. Poppa's pipe drooped ever so slightly. She continued, "Yes, father roach, long have you wandered since your wife, beautiful creature, was taken from you. Now I ask you to stay with us, here on the island of The Great Beyond. The forest here is lush, and your family will find all you need. For generations can you flourish, no longer threatened by ignorant man. If you wish it, this shall be your home."

Poppa had always prided himself on his quiet dignity, but as he listened to the queen's words, he could not help but be touched. Now it was George who offered a gentle pat on the shoulder. Poppa looked down at the roaches gathered about his feet and asked, "Children, what do you think?"

Always obedient, the roaches deferred. But Poppa knew he could count on at least one of his children to speak up.

"Squeak?" he asked. "What do you want to do?"

Squeak looked to his brothers and sisters, whose nods were growing more pronounced. "Poppa," he said, "we want to live here!"

Poppa turned back to the queen and said, "Your Highness, we would be honored to stay with you."

She smiled. "Then welcome home, my friend."

The roaches let out a cheer such as had not been heard in the hall in many years. Poppa jumped up onto Pinocchio's shirt and as best as he could threw his arms around his neck.

"Thank you, Pinocchio!" he cried.

Suddenly the celebration was interrupted by the unmistakable sound of a cellular phone.

"What on earth?" Pinocchio asked. He fished through his pockets and was shocked to find his smartphone had come back to life.

"No way!" exclaimed George. "You get service here?"

"You'd better answer that," Poppa warned.

"I can't," said Pinocchio. "My fingers—they can't swipe the screen."

"Mine can," said George as he snatched the phone away. He swiped and handed the plastic brick back to Pinocchio who answered, "Hello?"

"Pinocchio!" said Charles Stevens. "Where have you been?"

Pinocchio surveyed the hall, and replied, "It's kind of hard to explain—"

Stevens cut him off. "Who got to you?" he asked.

"I—I don't understand, Charles."

"That little magic show you put on for the committee. Who put you up to it?"

"Charles, no one! I mean, it's hard to explain. I promise, as soon as I'm back—"

"Back?" asked Stevens.

"I can't leave here, not for a few days."

"We need you back before Thursday. Barnes said if you finish your testimony, he'll put the bill up to a vote; otherwise, he'll bury it. You don't understand how important this is. This bill *must* pass. Tell me where you are and I'll send a plane."

"Charles, I can't come back before Thursday!"

A long pause followed. Finally, Stevens sighed, and continued, "I was good to you, wasn't I, Pinocchio? Didn't I make you feel like you belonged with us? Didn't we make you part of our family?"

"No," said Pinocchio, a second wind of courage filling his sails. "You used me, Charles. You *cost* me my family."

"So you refuse to come back, is that what you're telling me?"

"Yes," Pinocchio replied.

"I can't believe you're making me do this, Pinocchio, but I have no choice."

On the other end of the line Pinocchio heard what sounded like tussling as Stevens's voice was replaced with another.

"Pinny?" Whitney asked.

"Whitney?"

Everyone in the hall froze when Pinocchio said her name.

"Pinny, where are you?" she asked.

"Whitney? What's happening? Where's Albero?"

Before she could answer, the line was filled with clicks and more tussling. Finally, Charles Stevens replied, "He's here too, Pinocchio."

"Charles," said Pinocchio, "what have you done?"

"This is how the game works, Pinocchio. You promised me you'd pass that bill, and you must. I don't care where you are, what you think you're doing, or who talked you into what, but that bill must pass. If that happens, everyone will be OK. Now listen, we're on Avalon Island, and there's a charter plane waiting for you here. Do not do anything stupid like call the police or that reporter friend of yours. Just come here—I don't care how you do it—and finish what you started."

The line clicked dead, possibly the most agonizing sound Pinocchio had ever heard. He stared at the phone for a moment, hardly believing what had just happened. Finally, he announced, "Stevens has Whitney and Albero."

"What does he want?" asked Poppa.

"He wants the bill passed," Pinocchio replied. "I have to go."

"But you can't leave," said George.

"I don't have a choice, George. He's got my family!"

The queen agreed. "Your family is in danger, Pinocchio, and you must go to them."

"But the spell!" George protested.

"It cannot be undone, George. You know this."

Without any hesitation, Pinocchio stood and marched toward the doors.

"Pinocchio, stop!" the queen commanded. He did, reluctantly. She stood by his side and took his hand. "Listen to me, my child, for what I say may save your life. You face now a wicked enemy, but remember that you have allies. Remember who you are, Pinocchio, but"—she pulled him closer—"our magic cannot help you anymore. If you do leave this island, forever wood will you remain."

Pinocchio bowed his head. "I have made my choice, Your Highness."

The queen laid a gentle kiss on his forehead. Pinocchio let her hand slip from his and continued out of the hall. George and Poppa watched in disbelief, shaken only by a command from the queen,

"Well? Go after him!"

CHAPTER 22

Pinocchio Confronts His Fear of the Sea

With Poppa riding on his shoulder, George raced after Pinocchio, shouting, "Wait! Where are we going?"

"*We* aren't going anywhere," Pinocchio replied. "*I'm* going to Avalon, and I'm going to put a stop to all this."

"Well you'll need us!"

"No!" said Pinocchio. "I have to do this on my own."

"You're just going to jump into the sea?" asked George. "It's a two-hundred-foot drop!"

"You think I don't know that?"

Pinocchio peered over the cliff's edge. The sea below broke violently. It had been a long time since he had made such a jump, and even then it was terrifying. Even assuming he missed the rocks that lined the shore, from this height the surface of the water would be like concrete. There was a strong chance Pinocchio would shatter his fragile wooden body as it hit the ocean. But what was the alternative? Pinocchio could not wait for help—no one even knew where he was, let alone that his family was in danger.

"Sticks," said George, "let's think this through."

"I don't have time to argue," Pinocchio replied. George could see from the look in his eyes that Pinocchio was serious. Still, George knew that with backup Pinocchio at least stood a chance. Alone, he didn't. Whether he liked it or not, Pinocchio needed help. "We have to come with you," he insisted.

"You'll never survive the drop," reasoned Pinocchio, "and I can't carry you all the way."

"I can fly—"

"It's hundreds of miles, George. You'll never make it."

"Maybe the roaches can form a raft or—"

"George, listen to me—" Pinocchio reached out and took his arm. His grip had a tenderness George had not expected from the wooden, hinged hand. Had he not known better, he would have sworn he could feel a pulse in his fingertips. "You were right," Pinocchio continued. "I owe you a lot, more than I can ever repay, but this is my fight, not yours. Make things right in your own life, and I promise I'll make things right in mine."

George thought to offer resistance, but he knew it would be fruitless. As he stepped back, he took the puppet's hand and shook it as a friend would do.

Pinocchio turned to Poppa, who rode proudly on George's shoulder, and the bag where his children poked out and watched the entire exchange with two thousand compound, teary eyes.

"Poppa," he said, "I have only ever called one man *Poppa*, and I owe it to him not to risk your, or your children's lives anymore. You have given me my conscience back. Now, you can stop wandering. Accept the queen's offer and make this your home. I owe you my life a hundred times, but this time, I must go alone. Just know that if I make it, it's because of you."

Pinocchio extended his tiniest digit. With a hearty grasp (and a heavy heart), Poppa embraced the wooden pinky and shook. He had nothing more to say, and neither did the puppet. So much danger loomed, but in fear lies a calm, that intuition that tells us everything will find its way to right in the end. It always does.

George offered one more suggestion. "At least let us try to put a raft together, or find something that floats—"

"I'm a wooden puppet, George," said Pinocchio. "Wood floats."

With that, Pinocchio thrust himself off the cliff and hurtled toward the rocky coast below. George and Poppa held their breath, squinted through the mist, and hoped beyond hope to see a splash.

"He'll make it, won't he, Poppa?" asked young Squeak.

But Poppa didn't answer. He never liked to tell his children lies, and he was afraid of the truth himself.

* * *

"Hello? HELLO?" Whitney shouted.

There was no answer. She knew someone was there—she had heard voices just a few moments ago. She banged on the door and jiggled the handle—locked. It was useless. Whitney turned around and slumped against the door. Roused by the commotion, Albero came running into the sitting room. "Mama?" he asked. She assured him everything was all right.

Whitney surveyed the suite: three bedrooms, two baths, a full kitchen, and a sunken sitting room. The wet bar in the corner was stocked with expensive bottles. The furniture was modern and well-made. "Give your father credit," she mused. "At least his enemies have good taste."

"Mama, where are—"

"Shh!" Whitney silenced him. The voices in the hall were back. Whitney pressed her ear against the door. She could make out three voices this time, all male, and all very serious. Footsteps ... Another voice, a female this time ...

Whack!

The heavy door smacked Whitney in the forehead. She stumbled back, landing on a sofa. "Mama!" Albero shouted. "Are you OK?"

"Get over here, Albero," she ordered. She squinted at the men entering the suite. She stood, holding Albero close as she faced her abductors: three men—all wearing wool suits—and one woman in a green sarong. They stood in silence for what seemed like an eternity. Finally, Whitney spoke.

"Are you going to tell me who you are, or do I start guessing?"

The tallest man answered, "Honestly, Mrs. Pinocchio, I'd like to hear your guess."

"Three suits and a bikini ...," Whitney deliberated. She pointed at each of them and proclaimed, "The drummer, the bass player, the harmonica"—she turned to the bikini—"and the bimbo who can't play an instrument. So what do you guys call yourselves?"

The big man was not impressed. "I call myself Charles Stevens."

"Pinocchio's boss?" Whitney asked. Stevens nodded. She turned to the woman in the bikini and demanded, "Then who are you?"

"My name is Cassandra. I'm a friend of your husband."

Whitney couldn't believe it. The very woman she had grown to hate so much was now standing in front of her. She turned back to Stevens. "Why did you bring us here?"

Stevens ignored the question. Instead, he strolled over to the bar and offered, "Would you like something to drink, Mrs. Pinocchio?"

"No!" she barked.

"How about your boy?"

"He's five years old. So, also no."

Cassandra chuckled. The sound of a glass slamming down on the bar silenced her. "I meant milk or cola." Stevens continued, "Obviously, I don't offer liquor to children."

"Of course not," Whitney replied. "You have morals."

Stevens smirked. "Well, you must be hungry. I'll have some food sent up." Again, Whitney declined. Stevens took a seat opposite the sofa. His tone was gentler now—he was the grandfather again.

"Mrs. Pinocchio," he said, "we may be together for some time, and I'm sorry about that. As you can see, we have gone to great lengths to make you comfortable while you are here. Anything you want, anything that can make your stay more pleasant, we are happy to provide. There are clothes in the closets and toys in the bedroom."

"Mr. Stevens—"

Stevens paused her with a raised hand. "You can call me Charles," he said.

"Mr. *Stevens*," she continued, "why did you bring us here?"

Stevens glanced at Cassandra. *Was he looking for her to answer*, Whitney wondered, or for her permission to answer? Finally, Stevens replied, "Mrs. Pinocchio, we need to find your husband—"

"I don't know where he is," Whitney said bluntly. "Nobody does."

"I believe you," Stevens continued. "We think he's hiding. Why? We don't know, but we need him. It's very important that he goes back to Washington and finishes his testimony. So we figured that by bringing you here, it might entice him to do just that."

"And where's *here*?" she asked.

"You're in a private suite at a casino resort. That's all you need to know right now. But I assure you that you're perfectly safe."

"We can't leave?" she asked.

Stevens shook his head. "We'd prefer not, no."

"So we're hostages, then."

"That's not a word I would have chosen," Stevens said, "but yes."

"Mr. Stevens." She sighed. "My husband and I separated two weeks ago. I'm not even sure if he *wants* to come."

"Yes, I heard," said Stevens, "but speaking bluntly, Mrs. Pinocchio, we were out of options."

"And how long do you intend to keep us here?"

Stevens stood and buttoned his jacket. "We will not keep you here forever, Mrs. Pinocchio," he said as he headed for the door. "On that you have my word."

But Whitney persisted. "And what happens if Pinocchio doesn't come?"

Stevens didn't answer. He didn't need to. He simply shot her an icy glance before storming out of the room, goons in tow. Cassandra lingered for a moment before Stevens barked at her to follow. "*I'm sorry*," she whispered as she turned and left. The door closed and Whitney could hear the latching of deadbolts. The tears she was holding back during the stand-off came free now as she collapsed into a pile on the floor.

"Mama, are you scared?" Albero asked. But she didn't want to answer. She gripped her son even tighter, brushing his soft brown hair.

"Oh, Pinny," she cried, "where are you?"

CHAPTER 23

Pinocchio Makes the Acquaintance of an Erudite Tuna

The current was exceptionally strong. Though he had been a skilled swimmer in his youth, Pinocchio's new wooden body lacked the strength to pull him but a few yards every minute. Worse still, his wood had started to become saturated. It weighed him down and made the effort of swimming that much tougher. Add to that the exhaustion of a man who hadn't slept in days, and it was starting to become obvious to Pinocchio that he might not make it to Avalon. The boy who had worn a hopeful smile his entire life suddenly found himself face-to-face with something he had once considered an impossibility ... hopelessness.

The very word brought tears to his painted eyes. He was alone in an endless ocean, exhausted and sinking. His family was in danger—a danger he had put them in, and now he was helpless to save them. He needed a miracle, and like men do at those times, Pinocchio began to pray.

"This is all my doing," he whispered. "I have been so selfish, I know, but please, let me save my family! I will fix everything I screwed up, and I will make the world right again, I promise. Then, you can do with me as you wish; feed me to Oceanus, let me rot alone in a forest, but please, God, help me save those I have hurt."

Pinocchio listened for an answer, a sign, anything to prove that someone was listening. He wept as he murmured, "*Oh Lord, thy sea is so great, and my boat is*—"

"Not at all!" a voice interrupted.

"Who's there?" shouted Pinocchio.

The stranger answered, "I am there, although from my perspective it would be more appropriate to say that I am *here*. *You* are there."

Pinocchio turned around and found himself face-to-face with a very large, very blue, very curious tuna. The tuna continued, "But then if I asked you, I suppose you would answer the same way ..."

The tuna circled the confused puppet, rubbing his chin and musing, "One cannot be both *here* and *there*, but one cannot be neither here *nor* there." He stopped and smiled. "So the question is quite paradoxical."

"What, what *are* you?" Pinocchio asked.

"Why I am a fish!" the tuna replied. "I am a Thunnus thynnus, though a more vulgar common description is that I am a tuna. I welcome you to my water—quite a place to call home, wouldn't you say?"

"Uh, it's very nice," Pinocchio replied, "but right now it's kind of the last place I want to be."

"So I heard," said the tuna. "I did not mean to interrupt. It is quite rude to eavesdrop on private conversations, and what more private conversation can one have but with himself? But I was genuinely concerned that a man who was praying out loud while swimming in the ocean might be in need of some assistance. You prayed about a boat, and like I was saying, your boat is not at all, as you have no boat. But then again, as a wooden man, perhaps you consider yourself the boat, in which case your boat is poorly designed. In either case, I think you are right to pray, Pinocchio."

"You know my name?" Pinocchio asked. "You seem to know quite a bit—"

"Of course we know quite a bit!" the tuna interrupted. "We tuna swim in schools, so we tend to be well-educated. We focus our time on matters of the mind, pondering solutions to incalculable problems, the kind that it seems you have. But cheer up, my sad little friend, for being a thinker, I think it is all possible that I can help you. After all, I do believe you once helped me ..."

"I ... helped you?" Pinocchio asked. Pinocchio took a closer look at the smiling fish. He did not look familiar.

"Why, it is true!" said the tuna. "They said you had forgotten much—a form of amnesia that I would assume to be a side effect of your rather sudden transformation, but I had no idea it had gotten this bad, for we met mere months ago. But then again, it was such a different part of the world; perhaps in these surroundings I appear different. The light often does that, you see; it is the refraction of the water. But regardless, Pinocchio, it is true that we have met. You see, it was a day not unlike this one, except for the fact that it was much earlier in the afternoon, and I was swimming in the Atlantic

Ocean, which is as I'm sure you know, so much farther from where we are now.

"So there I was, swimming in a strange ocean, quite unaware of the danger about, when I saw a huge creature bearing down on me. If I had not known any better, I would have guessed it was a whale, but of course that was a ridiculous thought, as I knew that whales did not frequent the trade tides. So imagine my surprise when I was suddenly accosted by one, and what a chase he gave! Without boasting I can say that I am quite the swimmer, but so too was this dreadful whale, and closer and closer to the shore we pushed. That was when, much to my delight, I found myself entangled in a net. I was certain that I was saved, for whales are known to avoid fishing nets. But this dreadful whale was clearly not much of a thinker, for so diligently was he following me that before I knew it, he was caught in the net as well! Can you imagine such a thing?"

The tuna's story suddenly seemed interesting. "You—you were in the net?" asked Pinocchio.

"Indeed I was, as were several other tuna, one unsightly and rather ill-tempered whale, and much to my chagrin, a half-dozen simple-minded dolphins."

"Oceanus!" said Pinocchio. "His name is Oceanus!"

The tuna was taken aback. "Ah, so your memory is not so bad! Yes, Oceanus, what a beast. For days he thrashed, kicked, and bit at the net, but to no avail. As the rest of us discussed plans to work together to free ourselves, Oceanus merely sulked, refusing to cooperate. Every time one of us swam over to try and talk some sense into him, he swallowed them, rather rudely, I might add. Eventually we decided that he wasn't even worth talking to and did our best to ignore him.

"So after a week of planning, we still had not settled on a concrete strategy for working ourselves free of the net, a failure I might add I lay squarely on the desk of the dolphins. Entirely overrated as thinkers, they are. Why were they in the net to begin with? Tuna nets are made for tuna, not for dolphins. You never hear of a tuna being caught in a dolphin net now, do you? Of course not! Indeed, I halfway hoped that the whale would snatch me into his mouth and end the pain of having to listen to the pathetic wallowing of those dolphins, 'Oh, what of my children!' It's enough to make you sick. In either case, a strange thing happened just then. I watched with some curiosity as a man in a rather expensive suit swam up to the net, exchanged words with the whale, swam back to his boat, retrieved a knife, and cut the entire gaggle free. Spared, I fled the scene and headed straight back to these glorious blue waters, eager to forget the entire affair. So imagine my shock when, upon my arrival, I learned that the entire ocean was abuzz about the plight of the young wooden man who had freed the whale. There were stories that this same whale had once before swallowed that man, and as I heard your prayer earlier, I realized that it was you."

The tuna smiled. "That's right, my friend. I know who you are. Though I'm sure it was an unintended consequence, you saved me from a terrible death at the teeth of that monster, but what is most remarkable is that you did so in the act of saving the monster himself. I must ask, why?"

Pinocchio thought about it for a moment. "He was a terrible creature, but I could not let him die when I had the power to save him."

It was then that Pinocchio realized—he and the tuna were not alone. Dozens—no, hundreds—of fins, beaks, scales and gills listened with rapt attention. The tuna turned to the crowd and declared, "You see? This is what I mean." He turned back to Pinocchio. "Such a person you are, Pinocchio, and such a species is man! At once capable of such kindness, but you are also quick to pollute the waters and fish until there are no fish left to eat. What a difficult case you are, my friend. What are we to do with you?"

"I do not know."

"Well, we have already decided. You see, all that the ocean destroys, the ocean can mend. Long have we known that the secret to life is in the cycle. But until you came along, we had considered that man was the exception to this rule. But we know now that is not the case. All that man can destroy, man can mend as well. It is the way of things, the way of nature, and you, my friend, though you have so often railed against it, are part of nature."

A porpoise spoke up. "We are under a great threat now," he said.

"The whale comes for us," said a dolphin.

"But he is not of the ocean," added a salmon.

"And," said the tuna, "we believe you can stop him."

Pinocchio knew who they meant. "Charles Stevens." The school nodded in agreement. "His bill will kill so many of us," said the tuna, "but you can help us, Pinocchio."

"I cannot," said Pinocchio. "I want to stop him, I want to save my wife and my son, but I do not believe I can. My friends, I have failed."

The tuna swam up and lifted the soggy puppet out of the water.

"You are heavy, my friend, but not from the water. No, no, it is the weight of guilt that pulls you down. Your heart is swamped with it. It is right to be, for from the stories I have heard, so much hurt have you brought. But remember what we tell you here: Whatever the sea can destroy, the sea can mend. So too for man, and so too for you, Pinocchio. You are not defeated. You just need a little help. Allow me to help you by saying—I believe in you."

Back in the Great Hall, George set down a martini and whispered, "I believe in you, mate."

Hearing this, Poppa chimed in, "I believe in you too, my boy."

At the Weeping Pines Retirement Center, an old woodworker slipped off his glasses and sighed. "I believe in you, son."

In a noisy helicopter circling the Caribbean Sea, a disheveled reporter added, "So do I."

A thousand young roaches, the employees of a Washington lobby firm, neighbors and friends, and a million tuna, dolphins and salmon, all agreed. They whispered to themselves a simple prayer of their own—four little words that at once had more power than all the words of anger and cynicism that have ever been spoken in every language for all time: "I believe in you."

But the most powerful prayer came from a luxury suite, behind a locked and guarded door on a little tropical island. They were spoken by an estranged wife and her dear son, who had nothing to back their words but a shattered faith in a man they once thought they knew. At this moment, it was as if he were standing in the room, with his trademark smile and kind, but determined eyes, and all the hurt that had separated him from his family had melted away like ice in the desert. When they spoke, they did so with absolute conviction.

"I believe in you, Daddy," said the boy.

The wife voiced a slight variation. "I love you, Pinocchio."

At once, Pinocchio seemed to lift free of the ocean, and his body, now dry and light, found a renewed strength. He armed himself with a smile as he realized his heart was strong, light, and ticking as surely as a Swiss-made watch.

The learned tuna grinned such as a tuna had not grinned before. "You see, my friend? Science is not always the answer."

"Oh, thank you, tuna! Thank you, friends! You were right. Now I am ready to take that monster on, and rest assured, the bill will end or I will. But—"

"Yes?" asked the tuna.

"I still am far from the island, and time is very short."

"My dear wooden friend, such little faith you have in the planning abilities of tuna. We have already considered this, and we realize that for all our cognitive abilities, all our reason and rationale, there is one thing we have that can best help you. You see, every campaign needs volunteers—a ground game, if you will, and we tuna just happen to be very good at organizing." Suddenly, a dozen tuna gathered about Pinocchio's feet and lifted him out of the water as the learned tuna continued, "We are also accomplished swimmers."

And with that, the school fired through the water like a fleet of blue torpedoes, their wooden passenger holding on for dear life.

* * *

With every wave they crested, a blast of salty mist smacked Pinocchio across the face. His heart was pounding like a timpani.

"Not far now, my ligneous friend!" announced the tuna. "Another day, maybe less."

"Fool!" a dolphin bellowed. "You've not accounted for wind resistance. That puppet is like a sail!"

"To jinx with your wind resistance!" the tuna replied. "I'm counting the shoals. It will be precisely thirty-one and a half hours."

"Unless we hit a storm," the dolphin countered.

Frustrated, the tuna shouted, "It's early spring! Storms don't hit these waters until midsummer." He turned to his passenger and declared, "We shall see no storm."

In the distance, a bank of menacing clouds hovered on the horizon ...

* * *

It was as bad a storm as any of the fish could remember. The waves were growing higher, and Pinocchio was finding it harder to hold on.

"I can't explain this!" cried the tuna. "These chaotic weather patterns may have knocked the trades off-cycle."

"Nonsense, this is cyclical!" shouted the dolphin. "It's a result of last season's relatively warm spring. The melt cooled the temperatures—we see it every seven years."

"There's no record of a warmer spring," the tuna argued.

"*Relatively* warmer!" was the dolphin's reply.

"Enough!" cried a salmon. "I've been listening to you two for a hundred miles! Whatever brought this storm, we're in it now, so let's just focus on how to get out of it!"

The tuna shook his head. "Do you see what I mean about salmon?" he asked.

The dolphin agreed, "Very planar thinking."

"Still," the tuna continued, "simple problems sometimes require simple solutions. If we can't swim through the storm, we simply swim under it." He turned to his passenger and asked, "How long can you hold your breath?"

Water crashed across Pinocchio's face. "I don't—I don't know!" he replied.

"We must try," the tuna continued. "It won't take but a few minutes. Can you hold on that long?" Pinocchio nodded. "Then brace yourself!"

Pinocchio gulped, ballooning his cheeks as the tuna dove headfirst into a crashing wave ...

All of a sudden the fury was gone. Though under the surface the ocean was calm and steady, Pinocchio felt the crush of the water all around him. He tightened his grip as he felt the air in his lungs growing stale.

"Pinocchio!" the tuna cried. "You're choking me!"

But Pinocchio could not let go. The rushing water seemed to tug at every fiber of his clothes, every splinter in his body. He wanted to scream for help, but dared not open his mouth. He gripped with all his might, but his strength was fading. Desperate, he dug his fingernails into the tuna's slippery scales. He could feel himself beginning to slip ... and away he fell.

The tuna shot away like a missile in the water. "Wait!" Pinocchio screamed, but the school was going too fast to hear him. He hung there, helplessly watching the fleet disappear into oblivion. Bubbles of air floated past as the heavy seawater rushed into his throat. He thrashed about, desperately trying to reach the surface, but only managing to sink deeper.

Then all of a sudden, he felt nothing at all.

A kind of peace came over him, and he began to wonder if he had drowned. He tapped his fingers—he could still feel them—so he was certainly still alive. But he was puzzled by the fact that he was not breathing.

"You don't need air, boy," a bellowing voice declared. "Little wooden men don't breathe."

Pinocchio knew that voice—a deep, angry, old roar booming all around him. He turned, and found himself inches away from the angry scowl of Oceanus.

* * *

"I can't agree with you," said the dolphin. "When I look at Camus's language, I don't get the sense that he's paying homage to the classics at all. I think the myth is a device."

"Is this that postmodernist nonsense again?" the tuna demanded. "That was a wasted movement."

"Postmodernism was an era, not a movement," the dolphin replied. "To call it a movement indicates it had a beginning and an end."

The tuna felt his blood boiling. "We'll finish this up above," he said.

"Fine with me," the dolphin replied.

The tuna turned upward and blasted to the surface, the entire school in tow. The sun shone warmly, leaving no trace of the storm. "How'd you do back there?" the tuna asked. Nobody answered. The tuna turned his head and found that his wooden passenger was gone. "Pinocchio?"

"What's the matter?" the dolphin asked.

"It's Pinocchio," said the tuna. "I think he fell off."

"My God," whispered the dolphin, "he must have drowned."

"He drowned?" asked the tuna, a salty tear clouding his eye. "Oh the poor boy! He's a goner for sure."

"Stop it, you two," the salmon interrupted. "He's a puppet."

"Then the salt water must have been too much for his metal joints!" the tuna concluded. "They rusted away and he couldn't hang on!"

"And he's too buoyant!" the dolphin added. "He floated to the surface and was dashed by the waves!"

"I should have known that he lacked the strength to withstand that kind of pressure," the tuna continued. "Curse my speed and agility! Curse it!"

The salmon rolled his eyes. "No, you idiots, I mean he can't have drowned—he's made of wood, and he can't have rusted because *he's made of wood*! If you two had been less focused on your stupid argument we wouldn't be in this mess, now would we? So put a cork in it, and let's go find him!"

"Something already did," a swordfish announced, staring off into the distance. They turned just as the geyser spouted. There was no mistaking the stench from this particular whale's blowhole.

"Tuna," said the dolphin, "I hope you're as fast as you say you are."

"So do I," the tuna agreed, as he raced off toward the fountain.

* * *

Pinocchio hung motionless in the air for a moment, bracing himself for the fall ...

Crash!

He plummeted back into the water and was once again eye to eye with the beast. Oceanus's laugh heaved the very ocean as he taunted, "*Man, proud man, dressed in a little brief authority—now turned back to wood!*"

The whale slid his head underneath the helpless puppet, and with a snap of his neck tossed Pinocchio back into the air ...

Crash!

As Pinocchio landed on his shoulder, he felt his wooden joints straining under the force.

"*Oh what puppets may do, what they do, what they daily do, not knowing what they do!*"

Another toss, another crash.

"*Many years, little man, many years have I waited for this moment ...*"

"Oceanus!" Pinocchio begged. "Listen to me!"

"Your pride falls, boy. He that is proud eats himself up. He that is humble ..." Oceanus moved in closer and whispered, "I shall oblige. Look at you, little man—arrogance undone what miracles did. Only man, only the foolishness of man can unravel the dream of nature. You think you have met your reckoning? Not yet, little man, you have not yet begun to know what pain is."

"I beg you—"

"*As I begged you to cut me from that net? That is what you think.*"

"My family—"

"Is in grave danger. Yes, I know. And now you ally yourself with the fish, and the crabs, and the dolphins to save them. Little lobbyist, little beggar, how it must tear you apart to know that those who can save them you condemned to death." Oceanus smiled. "Do you realize you are nothing?"

Before Pinocchio could answer, a chorus of voices shouted, "OCEANUS!"

The whale turned to find that an army a thousand strong had encircled him. Its ranks were filled with all manner of creature, and leading the charge were the dolphin and the tuna.

"Ah!" Oceanus roared. "What a gift you bring me, Pinocchio, the other lost meals! Dolphin, tuna, you wait your turn."

"Oceanus, you must not harm this man!" screamed the tuna. "He is the only one who can stop the danger."

"The danger?" Oceanus demanded. "And you think he shall? Fools, all of you!"

"He will!" declared the dolphin. "I heard his prayer."

Oceanus fell back and looked Pinocchio over. "Proud man prays on his knees?" the whale asked. "What humility the infinite brings. Beg and pray, little man, run to the danger, run away." He turned back to the school. "I am nature's greatest wrath! I heed not your warnings, and I answer not your demands. The danger you speak of I alone shall negate."

The whale knew he was outnumbered. He looked back at Pinocchio and declared, "*This boy is nothing, and I have no appetite for nothing today.*" And with that, Oceanus disappeared into the darkness of the ocean.

Pinocchio bobbed in the water, confused, but relieved. The tuna extended a fin. "Grab on, my friend. That whale will not menace you again."

The dolphin swam alongside, a newfound sense of cooperation in his offer. "Take mine, too. Together we will get you to your family."

Pinocchio did as he was instructed, taking the tuna's fin in one hand and the dolphin's in the other. He held tight, the great school in tow, as they raced toward the little island on the horizon.

CHAPTER 24

The Political Mortality of Dominic Bayard

Dominic had never liked flying, and the storm he had just navigated didn't help matters. By the time he stepped down to the tarmac, Dominic Bayard was quite possibly the most irritable man on Avalon Island. He didn't want to smile at the purser, he didn't want to make small talk with the driver, and he certainly didn't want to tip the valet. All Dominic Bayard wanted was a straight answer from his senior partner, Charles C. Stevens.

In their suite, Stevens and Cassandra were glued to the television when the knock came.

"Charles," Dominic demanded, "what in the name of—"

Stevens rose to greet him. "Good flight, Dominic?"

Dominic answered by throwing his briefcase to the floor.

"What am I doing here, Charles? What are *you* doing here? Do you have any idea what's going on back in Washington? Our phone has been ringing for two days, and the media built a tent city on our doorstep! Nobody can go to lunch without—"

"Did they follow you?" Stevens asked, calmly.

"How?" Dominic shot back. "In a jet fighter? No, they didn't follow me!"

"You sure?" Stevens asked. Dominic thundered across the room and ripped the television from the wall, not even blinking when it exploded in a shower of sparks.

"The world is falling apart, and you two are down here in the sun and fun! Do you know what the rumor is, Charles? They think you've fled. They think you've gone to Belize. Every client we have—a client list I've been building for thirty years—is scared, and when clients get scared, they walk. Thirty years! Now explain to me this instant what you're doing, and why you brought me down here!"

"Did that make you feel better?" asked Stevens.

Dominic shook his head. "The Italian," Stevens continued, "he's on his way here."

"You found him?" Dominic asked.

"No, but I'm sure he's coming."

"How can you be sure of anything right now?"

Stevens rose and headed for the door. "Well?" he said. "Don't just stand there; come and see."

"See what?" Dominic asked.

"Our insurance policy."

Startled by the sound of the lock, Whitney stood and pulled Albero close to her. In walked Charles Stevens, Cassandra, and some other man she hadn't seen before.

"How are you today, Mrs. Pinocchio?" Stevens asked. The other man seemed surprised by her name. "Is there anything you need?" She shook her head. "Very well," Stevens continued. "Ring if you do." He pulled the door closed behind him.

Out in the hall, Dominic had nothing but questions.

"Who is that, Charles?"

"Pinocchio's wife and son," Stevens answered.

"And how did she get here?"

"Coachman brought her in a chartered plane."

"That's not what I meant."

Stevens turned, and stared down his partner. "You know what's riding on this, Dominic. We need Pinocchio. This was my only option."

"My God," gasped Dominic, "are you saying you *kidnapped* them?"

"Calm down," Stevens commanded as he ushered him back into his suite.

"How can you tell me to calm down?!" screamed Dominic. "You'll finish us all! That's a federal offense!"

"This is part of the game."

"That's a five-year-old boy in there! I never learned that part of the game! My God, we're lawyers, Charles; we're not mercenaries."

Stevens sat down, sipping casually at his drink as he explained, "I want the firm, Dominic. I want Aldous's shares. I don't care about the other clients; this bill is everything."

Dominic collapsed on the sofa. "Those are *my* clients—"

"Barnes flat-out told me that if Pinocchio doesn't finish his testimony, he'll bury it. No Pinocchio, no bill. *Three hundred million dollars*. I had no choice."

Dominic looked to Cassandra. The terror in her eyes said it all. He turned back to Stevens and asked, "What if he doesn't play ball, Charles? What if he goes back to Washington and rats us out?"

"He won't," Stevens insisted.

"And if he does?"

Stevens lit a cigarette. "Coachman's taking the two of them out on the yacht tomorrow. If Pinocchio does what he's supposed to do, when they make port in Miami, they go home. If he doesn't, they simply won't make port."

Cassandra came to her feet. "You'd hurt them?" she demanded.

"Be quiet, Cassandra!" Stevens ordered. "This doesn't concern you."

But Dominic came to her defense. "It concerns all of us, all three! We've skirted the rules before, but this? I've got a family, a career—lobbying is my life."

"It's over unless that bill passes. Go tell that to your family."

Dominic snatched the cigarette and smashed it out. "I won't be a part of this."

"If that's how you feel." He lit another cigarette. "Did you bring the files, by the way?"

"What?" Dominic asked.

"I asked you to bring some case files. Did you?"

Dominic picked up his briefcase, slipped out two folders, and threw them at Stevens. "Here."

Stevens thumbed the edges like a bound stack of dollar bills. "Like it or not, Dominic, you *are* part of this." Stevens held up the files—a type-printed label announced Coachman—Accounts Payable. "You're an accessory."

As Dominic began to realize the implications of what he had done, his anger boiled. Politics is an ugly business, built on changing loyalties, so it was not beyond the realm of possibility that his trusted partner would someday turn on him. But never in his wildest imagination could he believe Stevens was capable of something like this.

Cassandra's mind was not far behind Dominic's. For four years she had watched Stevens with the envious eyes of an outsider, always wondering how he was able to pull off what seemed impossible. Was this it? She had seen blackmail, betrayal, even bribery before, but never kidnapping. Every shred of respect she had ever felt for the man suddenly evaporated, and what took its place was pure revulsion.

Cassandra had spent her entire career hiding her tears. She had always viewed crying as a sign of weakness that the old men she worked for would never understand. It took all her will to hold them back now, which did not go unnoticed by Dominic. If he could have, he would have run across the room, embraced her, and told her it was all going to be OK. But he couldn't do that. The only thing he could do was smile—and nod. She understood what he was saying without his even needing to say it. The consequences of what Stevens had done were too terrible to behold, so she nodded back. With that, Dominic and Cassandra had formed a pact and bound themselves to a dangerous action—one that might save their skin, but one that would definitely save their souls.

Dominic took the first step. "I resign," he announced.

Stevens was expecting his partner to say almost anything except that. "What?" he asked. "You resign from what?"

"Kronos," Dominic replied. "Effective immediately. I'm taking the next plane off this island, Charles, and I fully intend to take Pinocchio's family with me."

"That won't happen, Dominic."

"How are you going to stop me? Are you going to throw me on that yacht, too?"

Stevens didn't answer. Dominic took one last look at his old partner, and saw only a criminal. He turned for the door. "Are you certain you want to resign?" Stevens asked. "Because if you do, you understand you've lost all partner privileges."

Dominic laughed, not even turning as he opened the door. "Like what, Charles?"

"Like early checkout."

"What on earth are you talking about?"

At that, two oversized guards snatched him up. Dominic reached for his cellular phone, which was quickly removed from his hands.

"Are you kidding me, Charles?" he asked.

"No," Stevens replied. "I am not. This is my island, and everything on it belongs to me."

The men dragged him toward the elevator as the door to Stevens's suite crept closed behind them. "And you, Cassandra?" Stevens asked. "What's your answer?"

Only she didn't.

"Cassandra?" Stevens scanned the room. Cassandra was nowhere to be found, and neither was her purse, her cell phone, or the files that Dominic had brought.

CHAPTER 25

Cassandra Is Redeemed

Oversized guards were everywhere on the island—two more were watching the entrance to Whitney's room when Cassandra raced up, shouting, "He's gone crazy! He's tearing the room apart!"

"Who?" one of the guards demanded.

"Bayard! He's got Mr. Stevens! You need to get up there right now!"

The suits raced down the hall and into the elevator. As the doors closed she estimated that she had about four minutes; the hotel had sixty floors, and she had pushed the button for each and every one of them.

Whitney jumped as the doors flew open. Cassandra raced in, a look of panic on her face. "Cassandra?" Whitney asked, "What are you doing here?"

“Get your things,” Cassandra demanded. She flew across the room, slamming closed windows and blinds. She tossed a purse at Whitney and barked, “Now, Mrs. Pinocchio! We only have a few minutes.”

“Until what?” Whitney demanded. She was not prepared to take much on faith at that moment.

“Until the guards come back. We have to get out of here.”

“I’m not going anywhere until I know what you’re talking about.”

Cassandra marched up to Whitney, who instinctively stepped back.

“Don’t you understand? If Pinocchio doesn’t show up, they’re going to hurt you!” Cassandra took a deep breath, placed a hand on Whitney’s shoulder, and continued, “Mrs. Pinocchio, I know you have no reason to believe me, but I had no idea what Stevens was planning. I will ask for your forgiveness later, but right now, you have to trust me. *Please,* if he finds out that I’m here ...”

All Whitney had for this woman was hate, but sometimes in moments like these, one’s true nature finds a way through such fog. Cassandra had done so much to hurt her family, but in that instant, what she saw in those green eyes was not deceit, but fear. Whitney chose to listen to her instincts. She nodded, lifted Albero, and took Cassandra’s hand as she led them into the hall.

“The express elevator leads to the kitchen,” Cassandra whispered. She peeked through the door. Certain the coast was clear, they quickly made their way down the long, endless hall, finally locating an elevator marked Service Only. Their footsteps echoed off the metal walls as they crept in, not breathing a single breath until the doors closed behind them. They stood in tense silence as the floors ticked by—59 ... 58 ... 57 ...

"I think you should know," Cassandra said, "that nothing ever happened."

"What do you mean?" Whitney asked.

"Between me and your husband. We kissed, that's all."

"I'm not sure what to say to that."

"Mrs. Pinocchio, this might not be the time, but I might not get another chance to tell you all this. I was jealous. I was jealous of him, and I was jealous of you for having him. But I want you to know that I never intended to hurt you, or Pinocchio." She took a deep, unsteady breath, and admitted, "I love him."

Whitney winced at the word, but she understood exactly what Cassandra was saying. Cassandra continued, "There's a commercial flight leaving in an hour. I'll make sure you're on board. When you get to Miami, go straight to the police and tell them what happened. They'll keep you safe."

"What about Pinocchio?" Whitney asked. "What happens to him?"

"Charles doesn't want to hurt him," Cassandra replied, "he just wants his bill passed. He'll bring him to Washington. But if you get to the police first, they'll take care of everything once they're back on US soil."

"What about you?"

"Don't worry about me, just worry about getting home."

The elevator stopped. As the doors opened, the noise of an industrial kitchen filled the metal box. As Whitney started out, Cassandra touched her on the arm and said, "For whatever it's worth, I am sorry." But Whitney didn't want to forgive her. Cassandra had just done a magnificent thing in helping them escape, but it was not enough to earn Whitney's absolution, at least not yet.

Whitney stepped into the kitchen only to be greeted by a familiar face—and two unfamiliar ones. Charles Stevens and his guards were waiting.

"Charles!" Cassandra exclaimed. Stevens shook his head. "I'm disappointed in you, Cassandra."

The guards yanked her out of the elevator while Stevens offered a gentler hand to Whitney. "Mrs. Pinocchio, I'm sorry for this."

Something about Stevens's manner convinced her that she had no choice but to take his hand. She held her breath as Stevens leaned in close to Albero. His brow softened, and he smiled. The grandfather had returned. "Albero," he said, "that's your name, right?" Albero nodded. "I'm your daddy's boss. My name is Charles—"

"Leave him alone!" Whitney barked. It was a mama-voice bark. Instinctively, Stevens backed off for a moment, but it was just enough time for Whitney to set her son down. She put herself between them.

"You're a good mother," Stevens noted. "Is Pinocchio a good father?"

Whitney didn't want to answer—but she also didn't want her silence to answer for her. "Of course," she said.

"I'll bet he is," Stevens reached out his hand. Albero looked up as his mother nodded, nervously. Holding one hand in hers and one hand in the old man's, Albero followed as they led him out of the kitchen.

"Where are we going?" the boy asked.

"To a boat," Stevens answered coolly. "Do you like boats?"

CHAPTER 26

The Roach and the Fairy Form an Unlikely Alliance

"This is no good," Poppa grumbled. He emptied his pipe and paced.

"What are you on about now?" asked George. "You've been doing nothing but whining since he left." George poured himself a glass of wine. It had been two days since they had returned to find the Fairy Queen gone and the hall empty. Rain knocked at the doors, but the fire kept everyone warm and dry. The roaches were asleep—all except for Squeak, who watched with some curiosity as George thumbed through a wallet. "Where did you get that?" he asked.

"It's Sticks's."

"Pinocchio's?" Poppa clarified. George nodded as he examined a platinum card. "Well, leave it be!"

"Why?" asked George. "He ain't coming back for it."

"That's not the point!" Only then did Poppa notice Squeak was hanging on his every word. "And—and you know darn good and well he *is* coming back for it!"

"Back?" George asked, incredulously.

Poppa cleared his throat and nodded at Squeak. "Oh"—George corrected himself—"I mean, well, he wouldn't mind if I take a peek. I'll keep it safe for him."

Poppa marched over and snatched the card from George's fingers. He slipped it back in the wallet and dragged it away.

"I thought you roaches could lift a thousand times your own weight," said George.

"That's *ants* you're thinking of, and it's a myth. They can barely lift ten times," Poppa replied. As he set the wallet aside, a photograph caught his eye. He slid it out and examined it—a family portrait: Pinocchio, Whitney and an infant Albero.

"Oh, so you get to play with the wallet but not me?" asked George.

Poppa ignored him, observing, "It's kind of old-fashioned, isn't it?"

"What is?" George asked.

"A picture in the wallet. Most people just keep their photos in their phones." As he held the portrait, he gently traced the edges of Pinocchio's face. "This must have been right after Albero was born."

George grabbed the photo and gave it a good look. He had never met Whitney; in fact this was the first time he had ever seen what she looked like. "Not bad," he said. "For Pinocchio, that is."

"He's not gonna make it, is he, Poppa?" asked Squeak.

"He might," Poppa said as he patted his lap. Squeak hopped up. "Don't lose hope. He's an awfully good swimmer—a champion in college. Isn't that right, George?"

"Uh, yeah!" George agreed. "Best there is!"

"But, Poppa," Squeak continued, "it's been two days already. The queen said he had to be back here in three or he'd be a puppet forever!"

Poppa didn't know what to say. Fortunately George did. "Your father's right, Squeak, don't lose hope."

"But the queen—"

"No matter what the queen said, there's always a chance when you wish hard enough. That's why they call it a *miracle*."

Poppa nodded in agreement. "Now go lie down with your brothers and sisters." Poppa watched with pride as his youngest son scurried off. He turned to George and said, "Thank you for that."

"Eh, don't mention it."

And as Poppa returned to his pacing, the most unusual thing happened ... a phone rang. Squeak leaped to his feet and rushed around, shouting, "Where is it?"

"It's here!" George declared, hoisting the smartphone into the air. "That's Pinocchio's phone!" Squeak exclaimed.

"Well answer it!" commanded Poppa. George complied.

"Hello?" he asked. Silence. "Hello? Who's there?"

"*Is this ... Pinocchio?*" asked the voice on the other end.

"That depends," George replied. "Who's this?"

* * *

Max and Jessica traded glances. Even through the roar of the helicopter the voice on the other end of the line didn't sound much like Pinocchio—in fact, he sounded British. Max continued,

"I'm a friend of Pinocchio's and I need to find him."

"Friend, eh?" asked the Brit. "I'll have you know that the last 'friend' who called this number kidnapped Pinocchio's family—"

Back in the hall, Poppa snatched the phone away. "Are you crazy?" he asked.

"Oh, so you *can* lift a thousand times your own weight!"

Poppa shook his head. "You don't know who this is!" he exclaimed. "Why are you telling him about Whitney and Albero?" Poppa had a good point.

George brought the phone back to his ear and continued, "Uh, what I meant to say was that Pinocchio doesn't have any friends."

"Well, who are you?" Max wondered.

"I'm Pinocchio's friend. I meant he doesn't have any friends—except me."

Max heard what sounded like a struggle for the phone before a much calmer, much more fatherly voice took over. "Whom am I speaking with?" Poppa asked. "What is your name and relation to Pinocchio?"

"My name is Max Wiggs. I'm a reporter. Pinocchio is a friend of mine, and I want to help him. Is that true about his family?"

"I don't mean to be rude, Mr. Wiggs, but Pinocchio's friends have not proven to be so friendly lately," Poppa replied.

"The article!" Max shouted. "The 'Last Honest Man in Washington,' I'm the one who wrote that!"

Poppa chuckled. "Mr. Wiggs, do you have any idea how much trouble that article caused?"

"I understand, but if you read the article, you know it wasn't my intention to hurt anyone. I wanted to help. Is that true what that other guy just said about Pinocchio's family?"

A pause. "You work for the *Washington Star*?"

"Yes!" Max exclaimed.

"So you know who Charles Stevens is?"

"Of course."

"Then you know it's true."

Max muted the phone and looked at Jessica. "My God."

"What do we do?" she asked.

"Well whoever these guys are, they obviously know where the family is. That's where Pinocchio's going."

Jessica agreed. Max unmuted the phone and continued, "Sir, I think I can help Pinocchio's family."

"How?" Poppa wondered.

"We have a helicopter. If you tell us where they are, we can try to rescue them."

Poppa thought it over. "One condition, Mr. Wiggs."

"Anything!" Max promised.

"You must take us with you."

* * *

"Poppa, that's crazy!" George shouted.

"Just hear me out, George. They have a helicopter. If we beat Pinocchio to Avalon, we can at least make sure his family is safe."

"And how do you expect a helicopter to get here?"

"The same way we got here."

George sighed as he picked up the receiver. "OK, listen close. Close your eyes. Find the place where dreams and touch—"

"Damn it, we already tried that!" Max barked. "Just use the map!"

"We don't have a map," George replied.

"Not a paper map, the one in the phone. It's a smartphone, right?"

"Yes ..."

"Well, it has a map function, like a GPS. Just tell me the coordinates so my pilot can find it."

Poppa and George looked at each other, dumbfounded. "OK, just give me a moment." George relayed the coordinates as Max scribbled furiously. "Let me check with my pilot and make sure we have enough fuel ... how many passengers?"

George counted on his fingers and replied, "One thousand and sixteen."

"We can't carry that!"

"Oh, you mean human passengers! One passenger, and one piece of luggage."

"What do you mean?"

"We'll explain on the flight. I just hope you have an open mind, Mr. Wiggs ..."

* * *

Albero tight beside her, Whitney lay on a hard-cushioned bunk while Cassandra paced the cabin. The sound of the engine was the only indication she had that the yacht was still moving. The cabin was remarkably cold given the tropical weather. Cassandra took a blanket and handed it to Whitney, who snatched it out of her hand, barking, "Why do you keep trying to help us?!"

"I don't know," Cassandra replied.

Albero was still asleep. Whitney tucked the blanket around him, turned back to Cassandra, and said, "Nothing you do or say can erase what you've done, Cassandra. I don't owe you forgiveness, and I won't be your friend. Right now, however, it seems I'm stuck with you, so I will make you a deal: Stay away from my son, and we won't have any problems. Do anything else, and I promise you, you won't wake up tomorrow. Do we understand each other?"

Cassandra nodded.

"Good."

Whitney shivered. She brushed Albero's hair as she whispered, "Please hurry, Pinocchio."

* * *

With new passengers safely aboard, the chopper sprinted toward Avalon. Max's phone was glued to his ear, while Jessica's eyes were glued to the fairy's wings. Finally she asked if she could touch them. George, of course, obliged.

As she leaned across the seat, she accidentally gave the fairy a most intriguing view. The wings were light, lighter than she had imagined, and she wondered how something so fragile could keep a man aloft. She slipped the membrane between her fingers. Almost sandpaper-like, the texture surprised her.

"They're nice, eh?" George said. "When this is all over, we can go for a ride. What's your name, anyway?"

Before she could answer, Max interrupted. "That was an employee at the casino. Sounds like Whitney and the boy tried to make a run for it. He says Stevens has them stashed on a yacht a few miles offshore."

"That makes things difficult, doesn't it?" Poppa asked. Max turned to the pilot. "If we can get the registry number of that boat, do you think you can find it?"

"No telling," the pilot replied. "There could be a lot of boats out there."

"Do your best," said Max. He turned back to his passengers and continued, "Even if we do find it, it's sure to be guarded. How do you plan to get aboard?"

George fluttered his wings. "You leave that one to me." He winked at Jessica and repeated, "They're nice, eh?"

CHAPTER 27

A Daring Rescue

A jiggling lock roused Dominic back to consciousness. Suddenly the door flew inward, and a familiar shape stepped through the threshold. "Pinocchio!" Dominic exclaimed.

"Mr. Bayard?" Pinocchio was as shocked as the man he discovered. Though still groggy, he grabbed Pinocchio by the arm, and slipped into the hall.

"Mr. Bayard, where—"

Dominic hushed him. Somewhere nearby a guard's boots clomped across the carpet. The steps grew fainter, and finally disappeared. Dominic looked the junior partner over. He wanted to cheer but dared only whisper, "Pinocchio! It is you, thank God."

"My family, Mr. Bayard, where are they?"

"In a boat, somewhere off the coast. Cassandra is out there too—" He paused as another pair of boots marched by. "She tried to help your family escape. She's a prisoner, too, Pinocchio. We all are."

"Why is Stevens doing this?"

"Because of that bill. Stevens *has* to have it passed. If he does, he'll own the company!"

"I don't understand," Pinocchio said. "Who owns it now?"

"The third partner—Aldous Kronos's widow. Kronos left the ownership in a trust. His will says that if Stevens can make The Kronos Group the largest firm in Washington by the thirtieth anniversary of his death, then the shares go to him. Otherwise, they revert to the widow. The revenue from this bill pushes him over the top, and the anniversary is next month. If that bill fails, he loses everything."

"Does Barnes know?"

"I don't think so, but it doesn't matter. Barnes agreed that if you—and only you—return and finish your testimony, he'll put the bill up for vote."

"And what if I don't go back?"

"He'll bury it. But that's not really a choice for him." Dominic shoved Pinocchio into a stairway and pulled the door closed behind them. "You don't know this, Pinocchio, but Stevens has Frank Barnes over a barrel. When you two got into that accident, who was he with?"

"His mistress," Pinocchio replied.

"That's right, and if that had come out, it would have ruined his career. Stevens kept that secret in his back pocket, dangling it over Frank's head like some godforsaken sword of Damocles."

"That's how you forced the bill into committee," said Pinocchio.

Dominic nodded, continued, "Why else would a man who made his career saving owls consider a bill that would kill thousands of them? And that's not all. This bill was supposed to be passed under the radar. But your testimony made that impossible. You're a sensation! Everyone is looking for you, and Frank especially. If he can't explain who and what you are, he's finished."

Pinocchio let it all sink in. Frank Barnes was the last great environmentalist on the hill. With him gone, there would be nothing to stop industry from marching all over the planet—wiping out species and laying the forests to waste.

All Pinocchio had ever wanted was to matter, but in that moment, he had never wanted it less. Until thirty seconds ago, saving his family had been his only concern, and if he could do so without testifying, he intended to. But now it seemed Barnes's career was on the fulcrum as well. "What do I do?" Pinocchio asked.

"You go back and testify," Dominic answered. "It's the only way to save your family."

For the briefest of moments, Pinocchio considered what would happen if he did just that. The bill would pass, the EIS would be rendered obsolete, and millions of animals would die, starting with the owls. But on the other hand, Whitney and Albero would be safe, and a good congressman would stay in office. Politics, it seemed, made strange bedfellows—but very ugly children. Pinocchio was convinced there was another way, but to find it, he had to know who were his enemies, and who were his allies. To find out, he started with the obvious question, "Whose side are you on, Mr. Bayard?"

"All I care about is getting Whitney and Albero out of danger."

"So you'll help me?" Pinocchio asked. Dominic nodded. "Then I will go back and testify," he continued. "But the way I want to, and not until I make sure my family is safe. Where's Charles?"

"He's waiting for you, here, on the island."

"Then we need to get to that boat."

"I should warn you, Pinocchio, your family is being guarded by a very dangerous man. His name is Coachman, and he runs a private security company. More like mercenaries, actually."

"So you're saying we need an army?" Pinocchio asked. Dominic nodded, continued, "And that's assuming we can even find the boat. It could be hundreds of miles away by now."

"Then we need sonar, too." A smile crept across Pinocchio's face. "Come along, Mr. Bayard, I know just the guys to call."

* * *

As they jogged up the water's edge, Dominic was alarmed to find the shore empty. "Pinocchio," he asked, "where's your boat?"

"I didn't say I had a boat," Pinocchio replied, "but I do have sonar."

Pinocchio slipped two fingers into his mouth. As he whistled, a pair of eyes poked up through the waves. Two eyes became four, four became eight, and soon over a hundred fish stood ready as Pinocchio led the stunned lobbyist into the surf.

"Pick one and climb on!" Pinocchio ordered. Dominic grabbed a hold of what he guessed was a porpoise, wrapping his arms gingerly around the creature's fin. Someone—or something—greeted him.

"Good day, sir!" the porpoise said.

"He's talking!" Dominic cried. "The fish is talking to me!"

"Mammal, actually," the porpoise corrected.

"He won't hurt you," Pinocchio assured him. "Just hold tight." Dominic nodded, and squeezed as hard as he dared as the armada launched into the bay.

Dominic had to admit, riding the big mammal was a most exhilarating feeling. Waves crashed against his face, the mist both stinging and refreshing him at the same time. His heart raced when he realized the shore was easily a half mile behind them. At any moment the big creature could have dumped him off, or worse, dove under, leaving him stranded in the middle of the ocean, but for some reason that possibility seemed remote. Somehow, Dominic knew he could trust the creature. He pushed his sagging jowls into a smile—in fact, it was all he could do to keep from laughing.

A yacht loomed on the horizon, its floodlights muddled in the surf. As Pinocchio turned back toward Dominic, the *wop-wop* of a helicopter drowned his voice. The chopper roared by, hovered over the boat and switched on a spotlight. Dominic seemed as confused as Pinocchio, who shouted, "Who is *that*?"

* * *

"The registry matches," announced the pilot. "That's the boat alright, but there's no helipad." Poppa leaned over George's shoulder and asked, "You sure you can get us down there?"

George replied, "I can take you and the kids."

"No way!" cried Jessica. "This is our story!"

Just then, a spotlight flooded the cabin with white. The passengers shielded their eyes. "They're armed," said the pilot. "I can see at least two rifles."

"They will shoot," warned Poppa. But Jessica was unfazed. "Max, we have to go with them."

"Please trust us," Poppa implored. "Let us help them."

"We're on fumes, Max!" the pilot added.

Max turned to Jessica. "Do what the roach says."

Jessica sat aside as Max slid open the door, blasting the cabin with the stench of jet fumes.

"Good luck, George!" Max shouted. The roaches' bag firmly in hand, George winked, and leaped free of the helicopter.

* * *

"What do you mean, 'a helicopter'?" Stevens demanded.

"*Exactly what I said, sir!*" The guard on the other end of the phone hinted at panic. "*It's overhead right now.*"

Stevens rushed to the balcony. Storm clouds had darkened the sky, but listening close, he could make out the *chop-chop* of helicopter blades in the distance. "Who is it?" he asked. "Feds?"

"*We can't tell,*" the guard replied.

"Then shoot it!"

"I'm not going to shoot down a helicopter, sir!"

Stevens fumed. He was not used to his orders being ignored, and it was becoming a more frequent occurrence. "I'm coming out there," he said, "and if that chopper isn't gone by the time I arrive, you will be."

Stevens mashed the screen, cracking it. He flung off a silk robe and rustled through a closet. "Coachman!" he hollered. "We're going to the boat!"

* * *

The guards watched as the helicopter disappeared into the darkness.

"Who was it?" asked one.

"Who knows? Important thing is they're gone."

As his companion went below, the guard resumed his pacing, stopping every few minutes to check that the doors were still locked. Another sound caught his attention—the rustling of fabric in the breeze, followed by the *thump* of something landing on the deck. He switched on his flashlight, wheeled around, and met the fist of a blue-haired Englishman. He tumbled to the deck, out cold.

"Good shot, George!" said Poppa.

George winked at the little roach on his shoulder. "Used to box in my younger days," he said as he cradled his hand, "but I forgot about the after bite."

Poppa peered into the backpack and asked, "You kids alright?" The roaches cheered with excitement.

"Let's go again!" Squeak declared. "Again!"

Poppa pulled the drawstring closed, turned back to the fairy, and decreed, "Let's go find her."

* * *

"How far?" hollered Pinocchio.

"We'll be there in five minutes," replied the tuna. The rain was pouring in sheets, and Pinocchio could barely make out the yacht's silhouette on the horizon. He had no idea who was in the helicopter, but his instinct told him that time was growing short. Just then he heard the howl of a speedboat behind them. Dominic recognized the boat instantly. "It's Stevens!" he cried.

"Dominic, take a deep breath!" Pinocchio shouted, before ordering the school to submerge. Dominic flung his arms around the porpoise and, with the precision of a drill team, the fleet dove, burying themselves under twenty feet of sea. Pinocchio watched as the cigarette-shaped vessel zipped overhead then waved the school back to the surface. Pinocchio watched as the speedboat pulled alongside the yacht and tied on.

"Something's wrong," he whispered.

* * *

Whitney could hear the men on the deck above quickening their pace. Whoever had just arrived, she guessed it wasn't a welcome visit. "Cops?" she wondered aloud.

Cassandra shook her head. "No, something else."

They could hear the guard pacing in the hall. Suddenly, there was a commotion, shouting, and the sound of a man collapsing to the ground. Whitney grabbed Albero and held him close. Cassandra pressed her ear against the door—someone was whispering. She could barely make it out. Something sounding like candy sprinkled across the floor. Cassandra held her breath and listened.

"Hi!"

Cassandra snapped around to find the most hideous little roach standing nearly nose to nose with her. Instinctively, she recoiled, but with every inch she scooted back, the roach drew an inch closer. "Get away!" she bellowed.

"Don't be afraid," the roach said. "We're here to help."

Cassandra froze. "You can talk?" she asked.

Squeak nodded. "Are you Whitney?" Cassandra shook her head and pointed to the other side of the room where Whitney was staring at her quite blankly.

"What's the matter?" Whitney asked.

"This bug," said Cassandra, "is here to see you."

Cassandra's eyes led Whitney's to the floor, but there was nothing there. "Whitney," she said, "I swear, he could talk."

* * *

All eyes locked on Squeak as he emerged from under the door. Excited, and out of breath, he cried, "I found them!"

"Whitney and Albero?" Poppa asked. Squeak nodded. "Is anyone else in there?"

"Yes," Squeak replied, "some other woman."

"What does she look like?" George asked.

"Pretty, with green eyes."

George turned to Poppa. "That's Pinocchio's mistress."

"What's she doing here?" Poppa wondered.

"I don't know," said George, "but it sounds like she's in trouble."

"Or keeping an eye on her," Poppa added. He turned back to Squeak and asked, "Did you get a look at the lock?"

Again, a nod. "There's no lock inside, just a keyhole."

Poppa rubbed his chin and commanded, "Kids, into the lock, all of you! Lift the tumblers and let us know when to push."

The roaches scurried up the doorjamb, slipping one by one into the keyhole.

* * *

Cassandra's ear was pinned to the door, ready to jump if another thump hit. "What's happening?" Whitney demanded. Cassandra shushed her. "It sounds like someone's fiddling around with the lock."

* * *

As the roaches heaved, the heavy metal teeth slipped free. "Now!" they shouted. George leaned back and kicked!

* * *

As the door caved inward, Cassandra dove just in time. She darted back and wrapped her arms around Whitney as a tall man with bright blue hair stepped inside. "Who are you?!" Whitney demanded.

"Whitney?" the man asked. She nodded. "We're friends of Pinocchio, and we've come to get you out."

No one dared move, especially Whitney, who stood defiant. "Who's we?" she asked. George simply smiled and looked down. Unbeknownst to the prisoners, the roaches had filed into the room and covered the floor. Poppa, ever the gentleman, bowed his head.

"Mrs. Pinocchio," he said, "my name is Poppa, and this oversized fellow here is George."

"What are you?" Whitney asked.

"I'm a *Periplaneta americana*, but you probably know me as a *cockroach*. I've been a friend of your husband's since he was very young. And these," he said, gesturing to the swarm, "are my children."

The roaches waved. Albero waved back. Whitney grabbed his arm and held it down. "Where's Pinocchio?" she asked.

"He left us two days ago to come here," George replied. "We haven't seen him since. We flew here on the reporter's whirlybird."

"On what?"

"A helicopter," Poppa corrected. "Now please, I know this is all so much to take in, but time is very short. Let us get you to safety."

Albero slipped out of Whitney's grip and knelt down, looking Poppa over curiously. He reached out with his little finger and brushed his antennae. "Are you from the world of growing?" he asked.

"Why yes," Poppa replied. "You must be Albero."

"Pops, we've got to go!" cried George. But Poppa knew the ladies were not ready to trust them yet. He stayed intent on the young boy who, it seemed, knew quite well that roaches could talk. "What do you know of the world of growing, Albero?" Poppa asked.

"Grandpa talks about it."

"And the world of dreaming? Does he talk about that too?" Albero nodded. "Because that is where George is from. Show him, George."

The fairy slipped off his coat and let his wings rise to the ceiling. Cassandra fainted, hitting the deck with a thud. Whitney tried to speak, but words just wouldn't come. Albero, on the other hand, smiled. He grabbed his mother's hand, shouting, "It's true, Mama! They're real! They're really real!"

Whitney gasped for air. "Are you—are you—"

"A fairy," George said flatly.

"I don't believe it," she said.

"Mrs. Pinocchio," Poppa continued, "some things are true whether or not we choose to believe them. Trust your son, and trust us. We are here to help."

Whitney looked down at Albero, then turned back to the roach. He had such a gentle smile—somehow, she knew he was right. She agreed. "Then let's go," Poppa declared. "Quickly, now. George"—he pointed to Cassandra—"pick her up."

George swept the unconscious lobbyist over his shoulder and peeked around the corner. Albero took his mother by the hand, saying, "Don't be afraid, Mama."

* * *

The storm was picking up. The yacht groaned as each successively larger wave crashed into its hull. A guard leaned into the bulkhead, steadying himself. He glanced down the hall, then back to the storm clouds, which had swept the moon from the sky. Another groan, louder this time. He turned just in time to catch a glimpse of a woman—and a little boy—hurrying away.

"Hey!" he shouted, and the pair took off as fast as a little boy could run. The guard bolted after them, only to run into a solid mass of fist. George laid him out with a single blow.

Cassandra was starting to come around. She cradled her forehead, only then noticing her feet were off the ground. She leaped from the Englishman's arms, bumping into Whitney.

"It's alright," Whitney assured her, "they're here to help." Whitney grabbed her hand and pulled her to the other end of the hall. Poppa scanned the deck. The storm was really kicking, and the guards' attention was on the swells cresting the bow. "Now's our chance ..."

The group raced across the rain-soaked deck toward the speedboat tied below. "Perfect!" Poppa shouted. "Everyone in!"

They climbed down the rickety boarding ladder and quickly took their seats. George grabbed the controls, mashed the throttle, but to his horror, the boat didn't move. "There's no key!" he cried.

"Can you hotwire it?" Poppa asked.

"What am I, a hoodlum? No, I can't hotwire it! What if we just cast off—"

Poppa shook his head. "They'll scoop us up the second they find we're missing." He searched the boat frantically, fixing his eyes on a small, neatly packed life raft. That's when it hit him. "We disable the yacht."

"What?" asked George.

"We make it so they can't follow us. I'll get the kids working on this boat, but I need you to sneak back in there and cut the fuel."

"Just don't take off without me!" George grumbled as he climbed back into the yacht.

Poppa threw open the backpack. "Kids," he said, "we need this engine running." As the roaches poured into the control panel, Poppa turned to the ladies and did his best to reassure them. "This won't be but a moment. Are you OK?"

They nodded.

He turned back to the control panel and watched as 1,013 roaches went to work. "Wait a minute," he whispered. "Where's Squeak?"

* * *

"Lift this, break that. Bloody rodent," George muttered. "Can't lift a thousand times his own weight? Damned excuses if you ask me." He kept his voice down, but he still attracted a little attention.

"It's because he trusts you," said Squeak.

George turned to find that the littlest of the little bugs had hitched a ride on his shoulder. "What're you doing?" George demanded. "Your pappy would be furious if he knew you were here."

"I came to help!" said Squeak.

"Well, just be quiet while I find the engine room." The duo tiptoed past a guarded hall and made their way down a narrow flight of stairs. "What were you saying about trust?" George asked.

"I said Poppa sent you because he trusts you."

"Right," George grumbled. "I'll be sent to lighten the load—probably had the key the whole time. Actually, I'm glad you're here. He won't take off without you."

"He wouldn't leave you!" insisted Squeak.

"Don't bet on it, mate," he said as he examined a locked door. "Every creature takes care of their own kind. Believe me, I've seen it plenty—"

Suddenly George went silent. Squeak could feel him tense up as he backed into a corner. A guard was coming down the staircase. George set the roach gently on the floor, pressed his finger to his lips and flapped his wings, disappearing into the darkness above. Squeak was terrified. He backed up against the wall and blended into the shadows.

The guard never saw the blow coming. He collapsed to the ground as George floated back down, cradling his knuckles.

"WOW!" Squeak shouted, barely able to contain his excitement.

George pushed the watertight door open, shoving the unconscious guard inside. "Nobody gets the drop on an Englishman, mate. We're seafarers. Boats are our natural environment and we—"

This time it was George who didn't see it coming. A heavy wrench landed on his skull and sent him straight to the ground. Squeak froze. He shut his eyes and did his best to turn invisible. When he finally opened them, everyone was gone.

CHAPTER 28

The Fairy Is Taken Hostage

By the time he woke, George's head felt the size of a well-grown watermelon. Someone was splashing water on his face, which dripped across his eyelashes, blurring everything. His feet and wrists were bound to a chair. He could feel the yacht rocking back and forth, which wasn't doing wonders for his head.

"He's coming about," said a voice. George squinted. He could just barely make out three figures standing over him. An older man in a suit seemed to be giving the orders.

"Ask him his name," Stevens commanded.

"You heard him," one of the others barked. "What's your name?"

"George," he replied.

"George what?"

"Just George. And you are?"

The man smacked him across the face. "Ow!" George shouted. "What was that for?"

"What are you doing on my ship?" Stevens asked.

"Fishing. The pier was full." Another smack. "Stop that!" George demanded.

"Who owns the helicopter?"

"I don't know," George replied, "I just asked for a ride."

"Uh-huh, and what are these?" Stevens thumbed at his soggy wings. "Going to a costume party?"

George sighed. "I can't explain in a way you'd understand."

Another smack. Stevens continued, "You're not helping yourself, George. You're trespassing on a ship. They call that piracy. You know where Pinocchio is, don't you?"

George tugged at his ropes. "Some hell of a sailor tied these!"

"George?" Stevens continued.

"Yeah," George answered, "I know where he is."

"Tell me."

"OK, but you're just going to keep hitting me." George slumped into the chair. "He's *beyond.*"

"Beyond what?" Stevens asked.

"Beyond the earthly bounds. He's in a place where no ship has ever sailed, and men know only in dreams—"

Stevens threw his hands into the air. "Not this crap again."

"I knew you wouldn't understand."

Another strike, harder this time. Stevens leaned in close, eye to eye with the fairy. "Do you know who I am, George?"

"Let me think," said George. "An *asshole*?"

The man chuckled. "I like Englishmen, always that pub-fight spirit. My name is Charles Stevens, and this is my yacht.

Everything on it belongs to me. When I decide that something is useless, we dump it over the side."

"Your name is Stevens?" he nodded. "I was right."

"About what?" Stevens wondered.

"You *are* an asshole." He turned to the guards, as if to gain their agreement. "Big one."

Stevens stood up and rubbed his chin. "Take the wings off," he ordered.

"What?" asked one of the guards.

"The costume. Take it off."

George shook his head furiously as two of the guards tugged at the appendages. George could feel the edges tearing. "Stop!" he cried. "It's not a costume!"

The men let go. "Sir, he's right; I think they're real."

"Real?" Stevens asked. The men nodded. Stevens turned back to the fairy. "What are you? Tell me!"

George sighed. *This wasn't going to go over well.* "In the time before time, when the earth was one with man—"

"I don't believe this."

"There came unto the land a great light—"

"Speak English!"

"And the spirits were born. With every new life—"

"Enough!" Stevens let fly with a heavy fist, landing it square on George's jaw. "GODDAMN IT!" George shouted.

"Finally!" Stevens said. "A word I can understand. No more of this nonsense. No more magic powder and sparkles. Tell me right now—*where is Pinocchio?*"

"He's on his way here!" George replied.

"How?"

"He's swimming."

Stevens shook his head. "Cut them off."

A guard produced a bright blade, eight inches long, and moved toward the helpless fairy. George howled as he sawed into the thin membrane. "Stop! Please!"

"Oh, so now you speak English?" Stevens waved the knife away. "Where is Pinocchio?"

"He's swimming in the ocean. It's the truth! It's God's truth, I swear it! He got your call, and we didn't have a boat, and he couldn't wait, so he dove into the ocean and began swimming!"

"That's ridiculous!" Stevens exclaimed. "The closest island is seventy miles away!"

"I know," added George, "but he's a good swimmer."

Stevens nodded at the knife man, who began another cut.

"Ow! Please, please! I know it sounds ridiculous, but Pinocchio can swim it, I swear!"

The cutting stopped. Stevens leaned in close, and demanded to know, "Why? Why can he swim it?"

"Because he's made of wood!"

Stevens stepped back. "What do you mean?" he asked.

"You really are daft, aren't you? He's a puppet, a goddamn child's toy! He became a real man, but he broke the spell and turned back into a puppet. That's what you all saw! That's also how I know he can swim it, because he doesn't need to breathe, and he floats!"

"I don't—" Stevens turned to the knife man. "Do YOU believe this?"

The knife man picked up the broken tip of the wing. "Sir, there's nothing I'm *not* believing at this moment."

* * *

From under the table, Squeak couldn't see much, but what he did see petrified him.

George's feet were tied to a chair. Three men surrounded him—and he was screaming. It was at least ten feet to the door, which, to a roach, may as well have been one hundred miles.

George screamed again—higher this time. Something fell to the floor. It was a piece of his wing! It was cut and broken, and it hit with a splatter of blood. Squeak couldn't take it anymore. He had to know what was happening. He crept to the edge of his makeshift shelter and peered up ...

They were hurting him! The men were hurting George!

Squeak couldn't stand to watch. He had to get help. He summoned every ounce of courage that any roach had ever known, and dashed for the door.

As he emerged from the shadows, the starkness of the light hit him. Bright light is not a roach's natural environment, and Squeak had never felt so vulnerable as he raced across the metal floor. The stamping of his feet seemed to echo through the room—certain to draw the men's attention. The gap under the door was just a crack, and he was almost there ...

He made it! Once safely under the door, he looked over his shoulder and was relieved to find that he hadn't been seen. He took two deep breaths and raced into the hall, not even bothering to check if the coast was clear. The yacht was watertight—not so much as a crack in the floor—so if he were spotted, there would be no place to hide. His only chance—and George's—was to make it to the speedboat and get help.

A pair of boots appeared at the end of the hall and headed straight toward him. Squeak scurried to the corner and did his best to disappear into the shadow. He dared not even breathe as the man clomped by, shaking the very floor. The end of the hall was in sight, so he made a break for it.

As he climbed onto the deck, he saw just how violent the storm had become. Six-foot swells crashed over the bow, raining roach-drowning water across the deck. He was near the front of the yacht, and Poppa and Whitney were at the other end. Another wave thundered down, dragging the helpless insect across the teak decking. Gasping for air, he grabbed for a mooring rope. As the water washed off, he climbed to the top of the coil and took a better look. He could just make out the front of the speedboat bobbing up and down in the waves. He brushed himself off and jumped; he landed just inches from another boot. Squeak looked up and locked eyes with what must have been the meanest, angriest human on the entire planet. The man glared at him, a look of revulsion on his face. Squeak had seen that look before. The boot lifted into the air, and came crashing down on the little bug. Squeak screamed!

Just then another wave knocked the ship sideways, spilling seawater some six inches high across the deck. The man grabbed a wall for balance, nearly tumbling over as the wave swept Squeak to safety. His relief was short-lived, however, as the edge of the yacht rushed toward him. His last hope was to grab for the shiny metal pole that ran the length of the deck. It was wide—too wide for his little claws to grab—but he had to try.

Squeak clamped down, clinging with a strength he had never before known as the water rushed over the edge. He lifted himself to his feet and scurried up the pole. He peered over the edge and was overjoyed to find a speedboat staring back at him.

"Poppa!" he screamed.

Poppa's ears, like all fathers, were tuned to the sound of their children's voices. He snapped around and nearly collapsed when he saw his youngest standing perilously high on the ship above.

"Squeak!" Poppa shouted. "What are you doing up there?"

"George is in trouble!" cried Squeak, his voice drowned out by the sound of another crashing wave. It was a long climb down to the boat, and he knew he had already wasted too much time. "Hold on, Poppa!" he shouted. He took another deep breath and launched himself into the sky, tumbling through the heavy sea mist. He aimed for the deck, but as he fell, he suddenly realized he had misjudged it.

"SQUEAK!" Poppa's heart stopped as he watched the little bug fall, heading straight for the angry ocean. Poppa leaped across the boat, reaching out desperately, though he didn't have a chance of catching the boy.

Just then another wave pushed the little bug into the boat. Poppa raced over to him. He squeezed the boy with every ounce of strength he had left, crying over and over, "My God, thank you! Thank you!"

But Squeak knew there was no time for sentiment. "Poppa," he exclaimed, "it's George! He's in trouble!"

"What do you mean?" Poppa asked.

"Those men have him tied up—they're hurting him!"

As Squeak described what he had just seen, Poppa looked to his passengers. The storm was becoming more and more unpredictable. He looked Squeak over. The boy didn't have a scratch or a bruise, and Poppa was beyond relieved. George clearly needed help, but the waves were getting higher, and it was a matter of time before the guards spotted them in the little speedboat. If he risked going back aboard the yacht, that would mean putting Whitney and Albero back in danger, but if he cast off, there was no telling what would happen to the fairy. Worse still, Poppa knew that whatever did happen to him would be his fault—he was the one who sent him back aboard. It was one of those moments in life that he had tried so hard to avoid—a moment when there is no good decision. Poppa swallowed hard and made the best one he could.

"We can't help him, son," he announced.

"What?" Squeak couldn't believe his ears.

"We came here to save Pinocchio's family," Poppa answered. "We swore to it—so we can't leave them. I'm sorry."

"But, Poppa," Squeak cried, "he's in trouble!"

"I know he is," Poppa said as he began to untie the mooring lines.

"You're gonna abandon him?"

"It's hard to explain, son, but sometimes you have to take care of your own."

Squeak stared at his father in disbelief. Though soaked from antennae to toe, Poppa could still see streaks of tears racing down Squeak's face. *George was right*, he thought. He wanted to scream. He wanted to cry. He had never known frustration like this. Drowning in hate, he felt his fists balling up. He looked to the yacht, calculating if he could survive a leap for it. But just as he had decided to try, a hoarse, frightened, yet very gentle voice interrupted him.

"Go get him, roach," said Whitney.

Poppa turned to her, hardly believing what he had just heard. "What did you say?"

"He risked his life for us. If you can help him, we owe him the same."

Poppa was stunned. His eyes met hers; she was afraid, but also resolute. Poppa watched the way she held her son so close; it was the same way he held his. Poppa had spent his whole life afraid of people, with their deadly chemicals and their stamping feet, but now this person was selflessly offering her own safety for a being she had met just minutes before. He grabbed his son by the arm and raced over to her.

"We'll go," he said, "but I must have your word—if there's any trouble, you will untie this boat and make your way to shore. Do not wait for us. Swear to it."

Whitney nodded. And with a whistle from Poppa's mouth, 1,014 roaches formed up on the deck.

"Let's go get him, kids!"

Like a wave cresting upstream, the roaches poured up the ladder and seconds later, were gone from Whitney's sight. It had been years since she had seen selflessness, but today she had seen it plenty. First the fairy had gone aboard to give them a chance, then that infant roach had risked his life to save the fairy. Now the entire family was about the same business. Whitney could not ignore the fact that all of this had come about because she and her son were in danger. All of these good beings—friends of her husband—had come to help. So had Cassandra. Never before that moment had she realized how little of the world she actually understood.

She looked at Cassandra, who was clearly still woozy. "Can you drive this thing?" she asked. Cassandra tried to stand, only to tumble back to the deck. Whitney helped her to her seat and placed her arms around Albero.

"Then you two hold on tight," Whitney ordered. "I'll get us home." She studied the controls—the engine was humming lightly, but she could feel the roar wanting to come out.

She intended to keep her promise to the little roach. If trouble came over that edge before he did, she would set a new speed record in this thing.

CHAPTER 29

Squeak's Revenge

Though slight, George was solidly built and it took the guards some effort to move him. Coachman was waiting on the lower deck and pushed open a door built more for a bank safe than a yacht.

"In there," he commanded.

Through bruised eyes, George surveyed the room; lit with only a single bulb, it seemed to be packed with plumbing and electrical boxes. The drone of the engines was deafening. Coachman unfolded a chair and the guards shoved George onto it, binding his hands to a pipe on the wall. He clenched his teeth and glared as the big man gave orders.

"What's your name, bloke?" George asked. Thinking him unconscious, Coachman was surprised to hear the fairy talk.

"Coachman," he replied, coldly.

"*Coachman*? What kind of a name is that?" George asked. Coachman ignored the bait, though George persisted, "Well, *Coachman*, I have to tell you, you're a right *tosser*."

That got his attention. "What did you just call me?" Coachman asked.

"*Tosser*," George replied. "Haven't you ever heard that term?" Coachman shook his head. "I don't know the American word—something more than a 'son of a bitch,' but less than a complete 'asshole'—the kind of fool who takes orders from an 'asshole.' So less than an asshole, I suppose. Yes, I think that's it! Coachman, you're lower than an 'asshole." George glared at him, grinning a Cheshire grin. "You're a *tosser*."

Stunned, the guards turned to Coachman, who was remarkably cool. He even smiled back. "You're working your mouth pretty hard, considering how untenable your position—"

"Untenable?" interrupted George. "That's a big word for a *tosser*."

Coachman smiled, snapped his fingers. "Go ahead and untie him," he ordered. "Pick him back up." He leaned close to the fairy, and asked, "You just love taking beatings, don't you?"

George didn't flinch. "Maybe I do, but that doesn't make you any less of a *tosser*."

"*Tosser ... Tosser ...*," someone called.

All eyes turned up to the ceiling. They had all heard it, a ghostly, disembodied voice that clearly hadn't come from any of them.

"Who said that?" Coachman demanded.

The voice continued, "We don't care for tossers here."

"What the hell is going on?" Coachman asked. He turned to George, who seemed just as curious as his captors.

"We don't like tossers here."

That's when George recognized the voice. Suddenly his curious look settled back into a smug grin.

"In fact, we EAT tossers here!"

"Look!" one of the guards shouted. They snapped around to find that the walls were flowing. The noise of the engine drowned out all but a ghostly patter as six thousand feet scampered across the metal floor and roof. The light went out, the door snapped shut, and suddenly George's captors were engulfed in bugs—hundreds of them!

The men flailed about in the dark, smashing into pipes and generators, cutting and bruising and stubbing their feet, but still not ridding themselves of the itching, creeping feeling.

That's when the roaches began to bite.

Just a nibble at first—a pinch between the toes, a tug at the nape of the neck—then all of a sudden the insects tore into the helpless, blinded men. Their panic turned to genuine terror as they raced through the room, smashing into each other, as a thousand tiny mandibles tore into their flesh.

Poppa watched with morbid pride as his children tormented and tortured the men. Humans are scared of the dark, but to a roach, it's home. It's a terrible feeling to be so overwhelmed, and it was a feeling a roach caught alone in the light knew all too well. Now, the tables were turned, and nobody fought harder than little Squeak, who bit and chewed and clawed with the ferocity of all his brothers and sisters combined. He had a welling rage in him after what he had just seen the men do, and though a gentle soul, he was at that moment the roach least likely to offer any quarter to the cruel, ugly men. It was reciprocity—payback for the lives of a trillion roaches that had been smashed, crushed, gassed, and drowned by generations of men like these. It was revenge for a motherless childhood, and for a father who lived in fear. Now it was the littlest of God's creatures that had the power, and it was man's turn to be afraid.

Coachman yanked at the door handle and the porthole flew open. The guards tore into the hall and screamed topside, brushing and flinging roaches as they ran.

The sound of their panicked feet grabbed Stevens's attention. He turned just in time to see a guard throw himself overboard. Stevens hurried to the stairway and ran, full speed, into Coachman.

"What the hell is wrong with you?" Stevens grabbed him by the shoulders and shook. For an instant, they locked eyes. Stevens saw the look of terror on his face, and his skin was covered with cuts. "Answer me!" Stevens demanded.

Squeak recognized the voice. He looked up from under Coachman's collar and into the face of Charles Stevens. He felt his anger boil over. He leaped through the air, landing square on the lobbyist's right eye, and with all his strength, he bit. The sensation was not unlike having a sewing needle thrust into his eye, and Stevens screamed and slapped at his face, tossing the little bug to the deck. Coachman broke free and dashed toward the edge. Stevens's eye had already begun to swell, and he watched helplessly as Coachman, his hired muscle, launched himself into the sea. Stevens turned back to the gangway and was run over by the other guard, who made a similarly inglorious exit.

Squeak hid behind a brass railing and watched as Stevens rubbed at his eye, examining with some worry the blood he was wiping away. Squeak allowed himself a smile before he hurried back down the stairs to rejoin his brothers and sisters.

* * *

Whitney already had the line untied when she saw the second guard leap off the deck. She leaned on the throttle and the speedboat rocketed away.

She hadn't ever piloted a boat before, but there didn't seem to be much to it. She guessed that the little speedster could outrun the big yacht, but despite what she promised the roach, she couldn't quite bring herself to abandon her rescuers just yet. She made the decision to circle the yacht for a few moments, though she kept one hand on the throttle, just in case.

She didn't even see it coming.

Another body came flying over the deck and hit the corner of her boat with all two hundred pounds of his weight. Albero screamed as the force of the impact knocked him to the floor. Whitney stumbled, leaning into the steering wheel and guiding the speedster straight into the hull of the cruiser. The fiberglass construction of the speedboat was no match for the $30 million yacht, and what was left of the little speedster quickly began to sink.

Her eyes locked on the strange-looking orange cube that had drawn the roach's attention earlier. She quickly located a yellow tab and pulled with all of her might. The raft unfolded quickly, inflating in an intricate ballet. She wasted no time in pushing Cassandra and Albero aboard.

The speedboat listed, finally slipping beneath the waves much faster than Whitney had guessed it would. Whitney grabbed an almost comically small paddle and began rowing, trying to get as much distance between her and the yacht as she could.

Her eyes focused on something bobbing in the water. She leaned over the edge and found one of the guards—the same one who had hit the speedboat—unconscious and floating helplessly in the ocean. With the storm gaining strength, she knew he likely wouldn't make it. Whitney knew she couldn't risk taking him aboard, but neither could she leave him to drown. She reached into the water and pulled the heavy man up, nearly swamping the raft as she did.

"What are you doing?" Cassandra demanded. Whitney didn't answer. Judging by the warmth in his skin, she knew he was alive, but he wasn't coming to any time soon. She grabbed a life vest and fastened it around his chest. She tightened the straps, gave a good tug, and pushed him back into the water.

"Why did you do that?" Cassandra asked.

"I couldn't let him die there," Whitney replied.

"He wouldn't have done the same for you."

"Well, we're better than them," she said, looking at Albero, "and don't you forget that."

* * *

Poppa watched as the kids chewed through the last of the ropes. George lifted his head, surprised to see the swarm standing over him. "You came back," he gasped, "you came back for me?"

"Of course!" Poppa replied, nodding to Squeak. "You can thank him."

And with the most gentle of smiles, George did just that. He reached behind and brushed the tattered edges of his wings. "Damn," he muttered. "Fifteen years I've been trying to get these back and look: two days. Two bloody days." He turned to Poppa and wondered, "Couldn't you have come just a few minutes earlier?"

As the ropes around his feet finally broke away, he tumbled to the ground. Squeak ran to his side and strained, single-handedly trying to lift the heavy Englishman to his feet. "Come on, George! Get up!" he shouted.

"I'm trying, kid," George replied. He pushed and pushed, only to collapse back to the metal floor.

"Can't you stand?" Poppa asked. George shook his head. Suddenly, and quite to Poppa's surprise, the fairy lifted into the air.

Squeak was the first to see him, and with a mix of astonishment and relief, cried out, "Pinocchio!"

All eyes turned upward. There stood the puppet himself—soaked, ragged, but strong as an ox as he hoisted the fairy over his shoulder. "I don't believe it," said Poppa. "You made it."

Pinocchio nodded. "Where're Whitney and Albero?" he asked.

"They're safe for the moment," Poppa replied. "They're in a speedboat off the starboard."

"You shouldn't have come," said Pinocchio. "You put yourselves in danger."

"Do you hear that, roach?" George demanded. "At least I know how to say thank you!"

Pinocchio glanced at the fairy dangling limply over his shoulders, and smiled. "Thank you," he said. "Thank you all. Now let's get out of here."

* * *

CHAPTER 1

Considering the ferocity of the storm, the upper deck was eerily quiet. Huddled behind a bulkhead, Dominic waited anxiously for the junior partner's return. A lightning bolt cracked the sky. Dominic's eyes turned upward as a thunderclap shook the yacht, masking his attacker's approach. He turned back to the deck just as a heavy pipe crashed down on his forehead. He was out before he hit the floor, and Pinocchio's escape route was suddenly unguarded.

CHAPTER 30

Pinocchio Stands Against the Monster, Charles Stevens

The roaches followed as Pinocchio crept up the last few stairs. He hadn't seen a guard yet, but he knew they couldn't be far. Something moved, casting a creeping shadow behind him. He turned ...

Nothing. Just another ghost in his imagination. Pinocchio was almost to the edge. He decided to chance it.

Suddenly Pinocchio felt George go limp. As he turned to see what had happened, he was met with a fast-swinging pipe—

"Pinocchio!" Squeak screamed. Poppa grabbed him and covered his mouth. It was too late; the big man had already spotted the line of roaches and let fly with the heavy pipe. The kids scattered, dodging the swing. Pinocchio, however, was not so agile. A second blow struck him across the temple, knocking him backward. He lost his grip on the fairy, who landed with a *thud.* His vision blurred; Pinocchio wasn't able to make out his assailant. But as he stepped in for a closer look, Charles Stevens's voice gave him away.

"So the Englishman was telling the truth," he said. "You really are made of wood. I don't believe it."

Pinocchio pushed himself against a bulkhead, pleading, "Charles, listen to me—"

"What are you?" Stevens demanded. "*What are you?*" Stevens stood over Pinocchio as he struggled to his feet. He could see that the roaches had found shelter behind the unconscious fairy. He nodded at them. Poppa, understanding the message, rallied the swarm around George's body. With all their strength, they lifted the heavy Englishman and began to drag him to safety. Out of the corner of his eye, Pinocchio watched his friends slip away, always careful to keep between them and the enraged Stevens. This was Pinocchio's fight, not theirs, and it was a long time coming. Despite the swelling in his head, Pinocchio stood up. Stevens had never noticed just how tall the junior partner was, and for a moment, he was almost intimidated. Pipe in hand, he advanced, but Pinocchio was determined to stand his ground.

* * *

With one last heave, the roaches succeeded in pushing the heavy Englishman over the side. George hit the ocean with a splash and slipped quickly beneath the waves. Poppa dove after him, launching himself into the rough sea. Poppa had never been in water before, and he was surprised to find that he couldn't sink. He struggled and kicked, but his tiny body and the density of the seawater made the act of pushing himself under impossible. He watched helplessly as the Englishman sank deeper and deeper below the surface.

But just when all seemed lost, something grabbed hold and pulled him to the surface. Astonished, Poppa looked up to find one of the guards—bruised, bleeding, and covered with welts—was lifting the fairy. He tossed the fairy into an inflatable raft, then backed away, cautiously keeping an eye on the occupants. It was the same man Whitney had saved earlier, and though he didn't say a word, he seemed most interested in repaying his debt.

Poppa paddled up to the raft and was delighted to find Whitney, Albero, Cassandra—and now an unconscious George—safe and sound. Whitney scooped him out of the water, and gave a hearty "thumbs-up!" Poppa whistled, and one by one, the roaches leaped off the yacht above and into the surprisingly sturdy little raft. Poppa kept count, ensuring each and every roach made it safe and sound. He turned back to Whitney, yelling, "Pinocchio's aboard the yacht!"

"What?" she shouted.

"He bought us time. He's all alone with Stevens!"

All eyes locked on the yacht above as two shadowy forms stood toe to toe on the forward deck.

* * *

"We don't have to do this, Pinocchio," Stevens said. "You're here now, so let's just go back and finish what we started."

"You kidnapped my family!" Pinocchio cried. "What makes you think I would ever help you?"

"I didn't want to, Pinocchio, but you don't know what's at stake here."

"Yes I do," declared Pinocchio. "Aldous's shares. I know all about it."

Stevens took a deep breath and let the negotiator in him come out. "You're right, Pinocchio. Your testimony makes me a very rich man, but I intend to share it. There are only two partners left in this firm: me ... and you. Finish the testimony, and you'll end this day very wealthy."

"Wealthy?"

"That's right, Pinocchio. You can accuse me of a lot of things, but never selfishness." Stevens sensed that he might have hit upon something. He lowered the pipe and slinked closer. "I never had children. I don't have anyone to leave it to, and I always thought of you as a son."

Upon hearing the word, Pinocchio felt a rage ignite within him. "I already have a father."

Stevens ground his teeth. He gripped the pipe so hard his fingers tingled. He reared back and swung!

CRACK!

Pinocchio covered his head as he fell to the ground. The second swing missed, but the third landed square on his back, knocking his chest door open. Stevens lost his grip on the heavy pipe, which rolled across the deck. He glimpsed a thick wooden oar lashed to the side of a lifeboat, grabbed it with both hands, and bore down on the wounded puppet.

Pinocchio was a pathetic sight. He lay there, pleading with his eyes and cradling his "heart." Stevens pushed aside any sense of pity, kindness, or empathy one naturally feels for a fellow man and searched for a reason to strike again.

The reasons came fast, and he swung away.

CRACK! CRACK! CRACK!

The oar shattered, leaving a blunt club in his hands. Pinocchio leaped to his feet and raced across the deck. Stevens followed, but his age-worn reflexes got the better of him, and he went down like an elephant, skinning his knees on the rain-slicked teak. Pinocchio seized the moment, dashing for the other side of the yacht. Stevens grabbed at his ankle, knocking him out of stride. Pinocchio's wooden clogs found no traction in the rain, and he stumbled. The old man jumped to his feet and swung a ferocious kick into his stomach.

"You cost me everything!" he shouted.

Another kick.

"Who were you to think?"

Another.

Pinocchio doubled over, straining for the edge—if he could just reach the sea ...

In the raft below, Whitney could see he was in trouble. Her heart sank at the sight of the battered puppet as he struggled to pull himself up, only to be yanked back out of view. "Pinny!" she screamed.

Poppa had never felt so helpless. He leaped onto George's unconscious body with all his weight. "George, get up! Get up!" There was no response. The blue-haired fairy was out of this fight.

Stevens stood over Pinocchio, the shattered oar growing heavy in his hand. Again they locked eyes. Pinocchio thought once more to reason, but there can be no reasoning with monsters. Stevens lifted the oar high above his head, and with every ounce of fury he had felt throughout his entire life, he swung.

The blow shattered Pinocchio's chest, which vomited watch parts all over the deck.

"Oh no ...," Pinocchio wheezed.

Everyone in the raft saw the blow. Albero didn't need to know the particulars of his father's biology to know that something terrible had just happened. Whitney grabbed him and covered his eyes.

Poppa knew they were too far away for the roaches to help. There was no other choice—one little bug or not, he had to get to that yacht. He looked at Whitney, and with a more fearful tone than ever he had used before or since, pleaded, "Please, take care of my boys."

Whitney pulled the backpack tight to her chest, cradling the children with all of a mother's strength. The ocean bucked. Lightning cracked the sky. Poppa knew he wouldn't make the jump, but he had no choice—

Suddenly, something lifted the little raft up into the air. Albero screamed as they smashed down into the sea. Poppa landed halfway under George. He pulled himself free, and climbed back toward the edge of the raft, only to have Whitney grab him. Poppa knew it was too big to be a wave. Again the raft heaved, knocking the bag out of Whitney's hands. The roaches screamed as the bag tumbled across the floor. Squeak scurried out and raced toward Poppa, who grabbed him tight.

"Poppa!" he cried. "What was that?"

Poppa's answer came as a geyser of steam shot out of the sea, accompanied by a rancid stench.

"My God!" cried Poppa. "It's him!"

Back on the yacht, Pinocchio used what was left of his strength to sit himself up against the bulkhead. Stevens curiously examined a watch gear, then tossed it aside as he stood over the crippled marionette.

"What *are* you?" he demanded.

The gears in Pinocchio's chest ground angrily against each other. Pinocchio was finished. He swallowed the lump of springs gurgling up his throat and coughed out what were sure to be his last words.

"I am my mother's son ..."

Stevens craned to hear. The boat shuddered, nearly knocking him off his feet. A blast of sea spray splashed across his face as Pinocchio continued, "And you know my mother."

"Do I, now?" Stevens replied.

A groan lumbered through the decks below. The boat pitched violently from side to side, the keel straining under the pressure. Another blast of spray. A voice—faint, but unmistakably familiar—filled Pinocchio's consciousness. As the stench from the geyser wafted across the deck, a smile grew on the puppet's face.

"That's right, Charles. You know my mother, and you have made her very, very ... *angry*."

The yacht lurched to the side, throwing Stevens off his feet. Pinocchio's shattered body slid across the deck, crashing into the bow. Stevens pulled himself to the edge and leaned over to see what had just hit them ...

The whale exploded through the surface of the water, his hungry mouth agape. Pinocchio watched in amazement as the monster soared through the air, arcing right toward Charles Stevens ...

Stevens's scream was curdling—and short-lived.

Oceanus snapped his jaws shut and swallowed the lobbyist in one gulp, and at once, the whale was gone.

The wind was instantly calmer, and the boats slowed to a gentle rock. Pinocchio pulled himself to the edge, searching the horizon, desperate to learn the fate of the little raft.

He spotted it, right side up and bobbing wistfully some three hundred feet from the yacht. But just as he did, the voice returned, and once again it had his undivided attention.

"Little man ..."

Pinocchio looked down to find the great eye of Oceanus staring into him.

"Do you know fear, little man?"

"No," Pinocchio declared. "And I never will again."

"Then our business ... is concluded."

Oceanus smiled, slipped beneath the waves, and as suddenly as he had appeared, vanished forever.

The last spring in the puppet's chest snapped free, and he collapsed in a puddle of rainwater. Darkness overwhelmed him. Not even the shouts from the raft, whose occupants were desperately paddling back to the crippled yacht could rouse him.

Such visions filled his mind. At once, he was flying through the air, the infinite greenness of The Great Beyond below him. An instant later, he was over the Capitol dome, nearly brushing the tip of the Statue of Freedom. Now he was in a rocking chair, his aging father by his side, and a pipe in his mouth. Now he was under the great oak in his own backyard, Whitney by his side and Albero playing on the porch. The roaches crawled up the bark of the tree ...

Then, everything faded and he was blinded by the starkness of a white light ... and the sound of a ticking watch.

Tick-tack. Tick-tack.

Pinocchio opened his eyes. Dominic Bayard was kneeling beside him, a shoddily applied bandage across his head, and a tiny screwdriver in his hand. Pinocchio's chest door was open, and the little watch was ticking.

"How?" he asked.

Dominic smiled.

"Bayard. That's my father's name. He's Swiss." He wrapped a bandage around the cracked cabinet, continuing, "You could say watchmaking runs in our blood."

He gave the clock one more wind and Pinocchio felt the energy of a lifetime surge through his little body. At once he was back on his feet, watching as the raft neared. He tossed a rope. The roaches caught and quickly fastened it. Pinocchio and Dominic tugged with all their strength until the raft was bobbing alongside. Whitney lifted Albero as Pinocchio leaped across the deck to grab him.

"Papa!" he cried.

Pinocchio held him tight, squeezing him with every ounce of strength he ever had, or ever would. His ribs nearly cracked, but Albero and Albero alone could take the force of the squeeze, for only a son could survive a papa hug.

Shocked by his father's appearance, Albero could not squeeze back, but this was not to say he resisted the papa hug. Albero simply melted into his father's moment, thus allowing himself to feel safe while for what seemed like hours, Pinocchio promised, in words and thoughts, never to let go again.

And on both boats, there were tears.

Pinocchio finally reached an arm out and lifted Whitney in one heave, snagging her into the embrace.

"I love you so much ...," he whispered. "I'm so sorry."

Much like her son, Whitney was not ready to forgive Pinocchio at that moment. She didn't want to hear him, talk to him, or think about anything other than the fact that they were all alive, and for at least a moment, together.

What a thing, my friends, such a moment can be.

"You know my mother, and you have made her very angry!"

CHAPTER 31

At Last, Pinocchio Finds His Purpose

What was left of the crew was most anxious to see their passengers safely put to shore—and also to make it known what unwilling participants they were in the kidnapping.

The yacht slowed to a crawl as it neared the harbor. Albero was asleep in Pinocchio's arms. Though for most of Albero's life Pinocchio had been afraid to even touch him, now he refused to let him go. Whitney nursed a still-groggy George. She hadn't said much during the trip back.

Pinocchio finally set Albero in a deck chair and pulled a blanket over him. Dominic watched with some relief as the little boy slept soundly, out of danger. Poppa stood on Pinocchio's shoulder and for a moment, the three watched as Avalon welcomed its guests with absolute stillness.

"What will you do with the firm?" Dominic wondered.

"What do you mean?" Pinocchio asked. "You're the senior partner—"

Dominic cut him off. "It's not my firm, Pinocchio. Voluntarily or not, I committed kidnapping and fraud. I'm done for."

Pinocchio tried his best to find the bright side, wondering, "Maybe you could take a leave of absence, or—," but again, Dominic stopped him.

"There're no second acts in politics anymore, Pinocchio. The Internet made damn sure of that. Forty years I've been in this business. This is all I've ever known, and now it's over."

Poppa spoke up. "One thing I never understood about you humans is why you identify yourselves by your jobs."

"Come again?" Dominic asked.

"Why are you *what you do* instead of *who you are*? You call yourself a lobbyist, but Pinocchio tells me you have grandchildren. What do they call you? Surely not lobbyist."

Dominic chuckled. "Of course not. They call me Grandpa."

"I see." Poppa rubbed his chin, continued, "Then maybe it's time to get back to who you are, and in that, find what you are. There is a 'second act,' Mr. Bayard, and it is right in front of you—you're a *grandpa*."

Dominic was floored. He turned to Pinocchio and declared, "Smart bug."

"You're telling me," Pinocchio replied.

Dominic continued, "So you never answered me about the firm."

"I think I'm retired," Pinocchio replied.

"Good idea," Poppa added. Pinocchio froze, staring at the little bug for what seemed like an eternity. Finally, Poppa asked, "What?"

"Nothing," Pinocchio replied. "It's just that whenever anyone agrees with me, I second-guess myself."

"Well," Dominic continued, "I'm not sure retirement is a choice. The committee is scheduled to vote on that bill today. You know what it will do if it passes. You have a chance to stop it."

Pinocchio laughed. "You want me to go back and testify? Like this? Nobody will believe a word I say!"

"You're the only one they'll believe," said Dominic. "The eyes of the world are on that committee."

"Then everyone knows what's in the bill," said Pinocchio. "It can't pass."

"Not this time," Dominic replied, "but what about next time? It won't be Kronos, but some firm will get it through—that is unless you go back there and bury it right now. Like it or not, Pinocchio, this is still up to you."

Dominic was more right than he could have known. Pinocchio was bound to a promise he made to legions of crabs, dolphins, tuna, trees, fairies, and roaches, and so long as the bill was alive, his promise remained unkempt. Pinocchio had no other choice but to go back to Washington and finish his testimony. To get there in time, however, meant Pinocchio would need a favor from a reporter ...

* * *

A phone call was all it took for Max to arrange the charter. By the time the group arrived at the helipad, the blades on the big chopper were already turning. George carried the roaches' bag on one arm and offered the other to Cassandra, whose conservative skirt suit seemed uncomfortably out of place in the tropical heat. Pinocchio held tightly to Albero with one hand, Whitney with the other, and Poppa riding on his shoulder.

"You're all set," Max shouted over the whine of the turbine. "Someone from the charter company will meet you in Miami and take you straight to the plane. You should be back in DC by three o'clock—plenty of time to make it to the committee session."

Pinocchio turned to Whitney. "George will fly back with you tomorrow morning. I trust him with my life."

Whitney smiled warmly at George and agreed. "I do too." Pinocchio squeezed Whitney's hand tight. "I have to do this, Whitney. The helicopter can only hold—"

"Don't worry, we'll be fine," she said. Whitney swallowed hard, fighting back the words she wanted to really say. Instead she asked, "Are the roaches going with you?"

"Poppa is," Pinocchio replied. "The kids will stay with George. And"—he took her hand again—"Cassandra needs to go with me, too."

"I understand," Whitney replied, coolly.

Pinocchio leaned in close, trying to have as intimate a moment as the engine noise would allow. "Whitney, when this is all over, there are a few things I want to tell you—"

He stopped as she dropped her eyes.

"Pinocchio," she said, "I don't know why what happened, happened, but"—she reached over and took Albero's other hand—"but now you need to go do the right thing."

More than anything in the world, Pinocchio wanted to kiss her in that moment—to kiss her goodbye, and to kiss her hello, and to kiss her in such a way as to ask for forgiveness, but now was not the time for kissing. The helicopter was howling, the crowd was getting anxious, and Pinocchio knew—a husband's sense, maybe—that it was not the time to ask for forgiveness. He did smile, which she returned with a forced grin. Though she did feel safe, there was no clarity for Whitney now.

Pinocchio knelt down and squeezed Albero's shoulders. "You and Mama are going to take a plane tomorrow. I'll see you soon, but right now I have to go do important business."

Albero nodded. Though every adult on the helipad was filled with questions, somehow it all made sense to him. He reached out and brushed the smooth, shiny grain on his father's face, the only part of Pinocchio's body not cracked and splintered.

"Are you always going to be like this, Dad?" he asked.

Pinocchio nodded, and said, "But I will also always be your dad. Now I need you to take good care of your mama, and do as Uncle George says. I will see you tomorrow, OK?" Albero nodded. "Now give your dad a hug."

Albero crept tentatively into Pinocchio's arms. Pinocchio squeezed and squeezed, lifting the boy off the ground and pulling his cheek next to his. But Albero was not quite ready to hug back, yet. He hung there, his clothes snagging on the rough surface of his father's arms, stiff and unresponsive. Whitney stood by, cold, emotionless to all who observed her, but inside, she was dying.

Finally, he set the boy down. Albero backed into his mother's arms, his eyes never breaking from the strange wooden creature that once was his father.

Poppa tapped Pinocchio on the shoulder. "Time to go," he announced. Pinocchio, Cassandra, and Poppa made their way through the fragile door of the chopper.

"I owe you big, Max!" Pinocchio shouted.

"Why is that?" asked Max. "You're paying for this!"

"I'll find a way."

"Just bill it to the firm!" Max suggested.

"Kronos? I don't think they would—"

Max cut him off. "They'll do whatever their CEO tells them."

"Dominic?" Pinocchio asked.

Max shook his head. "Dominic Bayard resigned yesterday. And with Stevens gone, the leadership of the firm falls to the next senior partner, which in this case, just happens to be a puppet."

"There's another puppet at the firm?" Pinocchio asked.

Max sighed. "No, Pinocchio, *you're* the puppet. You're the senior partner at the firm now."

Pinocchio glanced at Poppa, who appeared as surprised as he was. "Guess feeding your boss to a whale has some benefits," Poppa said.

"Your father was right about you, Pinocchio," Max continued, "you *are* here for a reason. Now fly safe!"

Pinocchio pulled the door closed behind him and strapped in. He slipped on a headset, and handed another to Poppa, who climbed into the earpiece.

"How much does the senior partner of a lobby firm like Kronos make?" Poppa wondered.

"I'm not taking the job," Pinocchio replied.

"Well, maybe you should, just for a couple of days."

"Poppa, haven't you learned anything?"

"Think about it, Pinocchio, you've still got to defeat that bill, right?"

"Yeah ..."

"And what about the rest of the people who work there? If that firm falls apart, they'll be out of a job. You have to take care of them too."

Poppa had a good point. "What do you think, Cassandra?" Pinocchio asked.

But Cassandra didn't answer. For her, everything had changed in the last seven days—everything she knew about the world and everything she thought she knew about it. She just watched, quietly, as the helicopter lifted into the air and an ocean passed beneath them. Cassandra didn't have an answer, or a thought, or an opinion. She was literally just a passenger now, and for a woman who had played the angles her entire life, it was a wholly unpleasant experience.

* * *

Nancy was right on time. She had received her new boss's phone call not forty-five minutes earlier and pulled up at precisely 3 p.m. The ragged-looking creature who emerged from the executive jet was a sight to behold. But ragged or not, this puppet just happened to now be the most influential man in Washington. Pinocchio and Cassandra hustled down the stairs and jumped into the SUV. Nancy floored it.

"Thanks for coming," Pinocchio said. "Did you get everything I asked?"

Nancy nodded. Thanks to the Herculean efforts of the entire Kronos staff, the trunk of the big SUV was stuffed with boxes of freshly printed reports. "I also brought you a fresh suit," she said.

"You're a lifesaver. Think we'll get there on time?"

"I promise we will." Nancy was a great driver and kept both eyes on the road. Once they entered the expressway, however, she managed to snag a look at the wooden man through the rearview mirror. "So," she said, "what exactly happened to you?"

"It was a long swim," was his reply.

Nancy turned her attention back to the freeway until she heard an unfamiliar voice suggest, "You had better change, Pinocchio; time is short."

"Who said that?" she asked.

"Oh, I'm sorry," Pinocchio replied. "Nancy DelGreco, meet Poppa."

"The pleasure is mine!" the voice said.

Nancy glanced around the car, finally settling her eyes on the passenger seat. There, on the edge of the cushion, sat the most perfectly disgusting little roach she had ever seen ... and it was smiling at her.

Both Nancy and the tires screamed as the SUV veered across the Beltway. "A roach!" she shrieked. "A *talking roach*!"

Pinocchio reached over and grabbed the wheel, managing to get the big truck back under control. "Are you OK?" he asked. Nancy took a deep breath and nodded. "Then take the wheel. I'm sorry, I should have warned you."

"What is that thing?" Nancy demanded.

"His name is Poppa," was Pinocchio's reply, "and he's an old friend."

The little insect hopped up on the dashboard and bowed politely.

"I'm sorry," said Nancy, "I—I—that was rude."

"No offense taken," said Poppa. "It's more common than you'd imagine."

"Are you sure you're OK?" Pinocchio asked. Nancy nodded again. "Then I'll crawl into the back and get changed."

Cassandra emptied the garment bag and handed Pinocchio a pressed shirt and tie. Nancy, meanwhile, shared her attention with both the road and the roach on her dashboard.

"By the way," said Poppa, "Pinocchio has told me so much about you."

"Oh?" Nancy replied. She didn't know what else to say to a roach.

"We don't have time now," he continued, "but when we get a moment, I'd love to hear your thoughts on lobbying firms."

"Lobbying firms?" she asked.

"Yes," he replied, "I understand you've been in the industry for some years."

"Over thirty. But I'm just a secretary."

Poppa turned to her and smiled. "Do you think that's what your husband wanted?"

"What do you know about my husband?" Nancy asked, quizzically.

Poppa continued. "I know that he was an idealist, just like you are, Ms. DelGreco. But one thing I could never figure out is why you didn't take his name."

Nancy was stunned. "He asked me not to," she said. "I loved his name—it was a proud name. Aldous just didn't want me to have the burden."

"Aldous ... Kronos," said Poppa. Cassandra nearly fell out of her seat. "You?" Cassandra asked. "You're the silent partner?" Nancy nodded. Cassandra continued, "And all this time you've worked as your employee's secretary?"

"Aldous asked me to," she replied. "He was a strange man. But I respected his wishes."

"I'm sure he had his reasons," Poppa mused. "Maybe it's because he wanted you close to his protégé, Charles Stevens, to watch, to learn. Maybe also because thirty years ago, not many women ran powerful firms."

"Not many," Pinocchio chimed in.

Poppa continued, "Your husband needed someone who could forge the connections that would make The Kronos Group a powerful voice—powerful enough to make a difference. He needed someone like Charles Stevens. So to entice him, he concocted this scheme with the shares, and because of that, Stevens spent the last thirty years bringing in clients and making political contacts. That whole time, every appointment, every call, and every email came through his secretary—you. In effect, Stevens created the firm your husband always imagined."

"And now that he's gone," Pinocchio added, "The Kronos Group needs new leadership—someone who knows everyone in Washington."

"And more importantly," Poppa continued, "someone as idealistic as Aldous was. Your husband was not a strange man, Nancy; he was a genius. He wanted to build a firm that would be a force for good, and I think he wanted *you* to run it."

Fighting back tears, Nancy shook her head. "No, not me," she said. "I'm just a secretary. I can't run a whole company. Besides, after all this, I'm not sure if there's much of a company left to run. Our reputation is in tatters."

Poppa turned to Pinocchio and declared, "Then our first order of business is to restore it, and that's just what we intend to do. How long until we get to the Capitol?"

CHAPTER 32

Pinocchio Returns to Congress

One skill that separated the rookies from the political pros was feigning interest in committee testimony. Frank Barnes's technique was a simple one—he doodled. Airplanes ... cars ... today it was alien invaders. Though the saucers had barely landed when the first witness took the stand that morning, by the fifth hour the interstellar legions had captured DC and were advancing, unchallenged, up the East Coast.

All of this testimony was a big waste of time as far as the bill was concerned. Thanks to what many assumed to be the greatest publicity stunt in history, what should have been a minor resolution passed by a minor committee had suddenly become the story of the decade. Now all of Washington was tuned in, and everything—Frank's career included—hung in the balance. Nothing these so-called "experts" had to say mattered. The only voice anyone wanted to hear was Pinocchio's.

At 3:08 p.m. an aide handed Frank a note; Pinocchio had resurfaced and was on his way to testify later that day. It was the most exciting—and most worrisome—news Frank had heard all day.

* * *

As the SUV screamed down Pennsylvania Avenue, Pinocchio tumbled around the back seat, fighting his way into a pair of trousers.

"Do you want help?" Cassandra asked. She could see that the zipper was proving a challenge for his wooden fingers.

"No, no!" Pinocchio replied. "I just need some pliers—or a hook! Does anybody have a hook?"

"For God's sake!" Nancy exploded. "Will you just let Cassandra do it?" The truck hung a hard right, the tires screeching in protest. The Capitol dome loomed on the horizon. Knowing they were out of time, Pinocchio reluctantly waved Cassandra into the back seat. He stared straight ahead as she grabbed the zipper and tugged.

"The buttons too?" she asked. Pinocchio nodded. "Funny, isn't it?" she continued. "I used to think of getting you *undressed*." As she straightened his tie, the most unexpected thing happened—Pinocchio reached up and took her hands in his. As he studied her with curious, tender eyes, Cassandra became quite still, not sure how else to react.

Pinocchio had never known anyone quite like Cassandra. She was so desperate to do the right thing and yet so willing to do the wrong thing—aching to be trusted, but lying with every breath. Now here she was, doing everything in her power to atone. He squeezed her fingers gently. Slender and soft, they could not have been more different from his. Her eyes, on the other hand, wore a guilt that looked very familiar.

"I know what you did on the island," he told her. "You risked your life for my family."

"Who—who told you—"

"Shhh ..." Pinocchio placed a finger on her lips. "I just want you to know—I think you're a good person."

Her eyes fell to the floor. "No, Pinocchio," she replied, "I'm not a good person at all."

"But you have to be!" he said as he tapped his nose. "See? Not an inch!"

She forced a smile, which quickly faded. "I tried to fix something that I screwed up, but it doesn't make me any less guilty." Still afraid to look him in the eye, she slipped her hands out of his and with shaking fingers fastened the last two buttons on his shirt. She began to sob. "Oh, Pinocchio, I'm rotten. You know it, your wife knows it, and now all of Washington will know it."

"No!" cried Pinocchio. "Don't you see, Cassandra? Nothing is forever. I'm living proof of that—" Pinocchio again took her hand, holding it to his chest. She felt the *tick-tick-tick!* as he helped her open the latch. Upon seeing what was inside, she gasped.

"Is that your heart?" she asked.

"Yes," he replied. "I still have one." He closed the door and pulled his shirt closed. "And so do you. You're not rotten, Cassandra, you're just lost. You need someone to show you the way, like someone"—he winked at Poppa—"showed me. You might be surprised who that person turns out to be."

Cassandra wiped her eyes, turning her carefully painted mascara into a shadowy mess. "Oh, Pinocchio," she cried, "you're one in a million." She threw herself into his arms and gave the little puppet one hell of a hug. When she finally released him, they sat back and watched the buildings race by. It took Pinocchio almost a minute to notice that she was still holding his hand. She didn't want to let it go, partially because she still needed his reassurance, but also because she knew she would never have this chance again. She held tight until Nancy announced,

"We're here!"

As the SUV lurched to a stop, the delegation leaped out, gathering boxes and briefcases before marching up the magnificent grand staircase of the United States Capitol Building.

"Do you know what you're doing?" Cassandra asked.

"Of course I do," Pinocchio replied. "I'm making it up as I go!"

* * *

Pinocchio had once thought of congressional testimony as a romantic dream. A man strode through a pair of oak doors—opened simultaneously by two crisply dressed guards—and marched through the crowd, which was awestruck, of course, by the identity of the surprise witness. Gavels were swung and heroic words spoken—words that riveted the nation and maybe, just maybe, changed a little history: a little Perry Mason, a little Mr. Smith.

But that was a dream long since faded. Witnesses entered through a side door. The guard (there was usually only one) seemed old enough to remember the day the redcoats torched the place. When the committee members even bothered to show up, they spent the majority of their time chatting with aides. The gallery was empty save for a few sleepy law students or a tour group that had stopped by the Capitol to see their government in action before heading to the National Archives to see it framed. If anyone was paying attention, it was thanks to the unmanned C-SPAN camera that perched lifelessly in the upper deck—a red light being the only indication that anyone cared, and that itself was no guarantee.

But this day was different. Max Wiggs had gotten the word out about Pinocchio's return, and it seemed half of Washington had shown up to see it for themselves. As the door opened, the anxious chatter muted as the crowd beheld a most incredible sight—a living marionette clacking his way into the chamber.

Pinocchio had arrived.

Nancy and Cassandra entered behind him and began handing out slickly bound reports to the committee members. Pinocchio took a seat and tapped at the bouquet of microphones before him, shooting an echoed *THUMP! THUMP!* throughout the gallery.

The specter of the wooden man shocked not only everyone in the chamber, but also the millions who tuned in hoping to witness a moment just like this. As the scope of this thing he had created became clear, Pinocchio wiped a bead of sap from his brow. Pinocchio wasn't caught up in a scandal—he *was* the scandal.

How could he ever have imagined the sensation his testimony had become? Millions had watched his transformation in endless loops on endless video streams. There were discussions in every office and at every dinner table in America.

Everyone, it seemed, was most interested in how he—a man whose only real achievement prior to that had been a throwaway article in a throwaway newspaper—had come to dominate the national conversation. Pinocchio had become a celebrity.

Barnes swung his gavel, opening the hearing. "The committee will come to order," he proclaimed. "We hope today to continue discussion of item H.R. 1976, a resolution to permit limited logging in certain public lands. We have before us an expert witness from The Kronos Group who, I imagine, will fill us all in on what transpired at the previous meeting." Cameras flashed and a murmur filled the chamber before a knock from Barnes's gavel could silence it.

He continued, "Can you state your name, employer, and position for the record?"

Pinocchio glanced at Poppa, who sat quietly in his breast pocket. At last, the voice that had been Pinocchio's conscience ever since he was a boy was content to be silent. All Poppa offered was a nod, which was all Pinocchio needed to hear—or see.

He began, "My name is Pinocchio, and I am the senior managing partner of The Kronos Group, LLC."

"*Senior* managing partner?" asked Barnes.

"That is correct, Mr. Chairman. Dominic Bayard has resigned and Charles Stevens is no longer with us."

"Excuse me, young man," a congressman from Texas asked, "are you saying Charles Stevens is dead?"

"No!" Pinocchio clarified. "But he is really, really incapacitated."

"How is that?" Barnes asked.

"He was swallowed by a whale last night." The chamber buzzed as he continued, "But he might be OK! I just happen to know that it's entirely possible to survive in a whale's belly—for weeks even!"

The statement drew gasps from the audience, which led to another rebuke from Barnes's gavel. Pinocchio continued, "So, according to the partnership agreement, the firm's leadership falls to the next most senior partner—which is me!"

"So," the Congresswoman from Idaho asked, "what are you?"

"I'm a lobbyist!" Pinocchio answered.

"Yes, I know that, but *what* are you?" Idaho persisted.

"Oh!" Pinocchio said. "Why, I'm a puppet, of course, which is really one and the same if you think about it."

"Excuse me?" Idaho demanded.

"I don't mean to be ornery, Mrs. Congresswoman, but you asked two questions with three words—my goodness, they need you on the budget committee!"

The audience laughed.

Pinocchio continued, "Frankly, ma'am, even I don't understand it all, which I guess makes me a poor expert, except I'm actually living it, which I guess makes me the perfect witness. As far as being an *expert witness*, gee, now that I think about it—it kind of makes my head hurt."

Another laugh. Cassandra leaned into Nancy's ear and whispered, "*He's himself again. He'll charm the pants off them!*"

"Mr. Pinocchio"—it was Frank Barnes this time—"I'm not sure this is the time for humor." Pinocchio agreed. He could tell by the congressman's tone that the chairman was offering him a chance. Barnes continued, "The whole country—the whole world, even—has been swept up in this thing. I think

I speak for everyone when I say that you owe us an explanation about last week."

"I do, Mr. Chairman."

Pinocchio set down his papers, and for the briefest of moments, forgot about the cameras, the audience, even the rest of the committee. Instead, he spoke directly to his old friend. "I meant what I said a moment ago. I am a lobbyist, and I am also a puppet, and they are indeed the same thing. What happened last week, well, there is no simple way to put this, so I'll just put it simply ... it happened because I lied to you."

Barnes clarified, "Are you saying that you lied *under oath*?" Pinocchio nodded. "What you're telling me, son, is a very serious crime. Before you go any further, maybe you want to talk to a lawyer, or—"

But as delicately as he could, Pinocchio cut him off. "No, sir. I know what I did was a horrible thing, and I am ready to face it."

Murmurs, shouts, and insults filled the gallery. Even ten strikes from Barnes's gavel couldn't silence them this time.

"Let him finish!" shouted someone in the crowd. Others agreed.

Finally, the commotion died down and Barnes continued, "Mr. Pinocchio, this bill was advanced by your firm. You personally testified for it. From what you're telling me now, you don't seem to want to see it passed anymore. Is that what I'm hearing?"

"Yes," Pinocchio answered.

"But what about your clients?" asked Barnes.

"Mr. Chairman," Pinocchio replied, "over these past eight days I have come to see that there is a consequence beyond me, beyond my clients, my firm, even beyond all of mankind for the decisions that we make. It seems like a lesson I've had to learn before, but this time I think it will take root." Barnes smiled at the pun. "The only good grace left to me," Pinocchio continued, "is this chance to come back here and set it right."

Barnes glanced around the committee—no one seemed to object. Barnes had anticipated anything but this, and it was a very difficult situation. On the one hand, this was clearly a crazy man sitting in front of him. If he opened up the microphone, there would be nothing stopping him from revealing the details of how they first met, and how he too found himself under the thumb of Charles Stevens. But on the other hand, what he had said earlier was true. If he denied this, this *thing* being the chance to explain himself, it would be Barnes suddenly under the spotlight. The feeding frenzy had barely just begun when the puppet showed back up. It wouldn't be much longer before some blogger, some wag, some investigative reporter got to the truth. Perhaps this was a chance for Barnes to set everything right as well. If this puppet could give the public what it wanted, the story would die right here. Once more Barnes was playing "Fool-the-Guesser," only this time the world was his pigeon, and his legacy the prize.

He pulled the microphone closer and announced, "Very well, Mr. Pinocchio. We're all ears. What would you like to tell us?"

Pinocchio wasn't sure how it happened—he wasn't even sure that it could—but as the cameras rolled and the world watched, a smile crept across his chiseled wooden cheeks, and he declared, "The truth."

* * *

With Poppa riding proudly on his shoulder, and Cassandra and Nancy by his side, Pinocchio marched out of Capitol and into the afternoon haze. The glare from the news cameras made it seem as if two suns were shining that day, and the reporters' questions came so quickly Pinocchio could barely sort them out.

"Mr. Pinocchio, how do you feel about the committee voting down the bill?" asked one.

"Elated," he answered.

"You lobbied so hard for that bill—what made you change your mind?" asked another.

"I didn't change my mind," Pinocchio replied. "Only my purpose."

"Sir," asked a third, "some people are calling you the next power broker in Washington—any thoughts?"

"All I did was speak my heart in there."

"Mr. Pinocchio, can you explain your condition?"

"I've never felt better."

"But you are made of wood?"

"Of course I am!"

That opened the floodgates. One after another they peppered him with question upon question. "*Is it a disease or bacteria?*" "*Can it be cured?*" "*Is it hereditary?*" "*Will you ever change back?*"

Pinocchio had always wondered why it was that when confronted with microphones, so many people felt the sudden need to clear their throats. He did exactly that before he spoke.

"My friends," he said, "I will answer every question you have about my body in due time, but I first want to make a couple of announcements. To begin with, I know there has been a lot of speculation about the future of The Kronos Group now that Charles Stevens is gone. I am here to say that the firm will go on, albeit with a different mission. From now on, Kronos will do what lobbying firms were first born to do—the people's work. Never again will we The Kronos Group put profit ahead of principle."

The light bulbs flashed. He continued, "And in order to make this new strategy work, we will need a new leader—someone with experience, expertise, someone who is strong, but morally so—in short, we need someone with wisdom, and I happen to know someone who fits those requirements ..."

A buzz, a flurry, an excitement filled the crowd. Flashes of light, shouted questions, but nowhere was there more confusion than between Nancy and Cassandra as Pinocchio looked their way, continuing, "That is why I am announcing that I will be stepping down as senior managing partner—and Nancy DelGreco will replace me."

Nancy froze when she heard her name. "Nancy?" Pinocchio asked, his voice echoing off the Capitol walls. He turned, and extended a hand. "Would you like to come say a few words?"

It took Nancy's feet a moment to move. That instant was all Cassandra needed to whisper, "I believe in you, Nancy."

Nancy smiled, feeling a rush of pride—the kind of pride that overwhelms a sense of reality and snuffs out any lingering flames of self-doubt. She marched up to the microphones, standing side by side with the wooden man who, a moment earlier, had been her boss.

"Thank you, Pinocchio." She smiled for the cameras as naturally as any politician would, continuing, "Your tenure at the firm was brief, but I think it's an understatement to say, influential." She scanned the crowd. "I recognize some familiar faces out there, but for those of you who don't know me, I am Nancy DelGreco. I'll be happy to take a few questions. Yes, CNN?"

Pinocchio let her take the stage. It was then that he noticed a most interesting thing—from behind, all Pinocchio could see was Nancy's silhouette as the cameras' lights beamed all around her a fluorescent halo. She stood tall. She spoke slowly—and a little deeper, too. As Pinocchio listened to her field question after question, it had never been more obvious—she was made for this job.

"Two birds, eh, son?" Poppa offered.

"That was a great call, Poppa," Pinocchio replied.

"So where are we off to now? Time to begin another adventure?"

"No," Pinocchio answered. "Time to end one."

Nancy paused the impromptu press conference when she caught sight of the two of them leaving. Reporters shouted after her, but she was intent on seeing Pinocchio off to that next important appointment—her last official act as secretary to the senior managing partner of the firm.

"Shall we get you into a cab?" she asked.

Pinocchio nodded and, Nancy leading the way, started down the grand marble staircase. But when Cassandra didn't follow, Pinocchio stopped, turned around and took in the sight of what may have been the saddest woman ever he had seen.

"Aren't you coming?" he asked.

Cassandra shook her head.

"I understand," Pinocchio continued. "Well, don't be late to work tomorrow."

"What do you mean?" she asked.

"You have to set an example. We can't have the associates thinking senior partners just come tripping in whenever." He turned to Nancy. "Seven o'clock, right?"

Nancy nodded, and Pinocchio continued down the steps—at least until someone yanked him almost off his feet. As he regained his balance, he turned to find Cassandra, her hand on his shoulder and shock on her face.

"Senior partner?" Cassandra asked.

Pinocchio nodded. "I think you'll do fine."

She still didn't believe it. "This was your idea?"

Pinocchio shook his head. "Poppa's."

"Then I owe one to him too," she proclaimed, almost in tears. "But I just can't help myself!" And with that, she grabbed Pinocchio by his cheeks and pulled him into the most passionate, the most fiery, and the most innocent kiss ever given to a puppet on the steps of Congress. When they finally broke apart, she caught her breath, turned to the blushing little roach on his shoulder and planted one on him next.

Speechless, Pinocchio wiped at his face, smearing red lipstick across the back of his hand. He turned and found Poppa doing the same thing. A wolf whistle caught his attention. Nancy was at the driveway, holding a cab door open. Pinocchio leaped down the last few stairs.

"Do you know where you're going?" Nancy asked.

"Yes," Pinocchio answered as he closed the door behind him. Nancy watched him slip a wad of cash to the driver, then he rolled down the window and asked his successor, "You'll be alright?"

She grinned.

"I'll be alright. I'll miss you, Pinocchio. But I want to tell you something—" She pondered for a moment, then leaned into the cab, brushed him across the forehead, and smiled sweetly—something Pinocchio did not know the hard-edged secretary could do—before she continued,

"You've been brave today, Pinocchio. You have a good heart and you must forgive yourself your past misdeeds. Men who love their families, and help them when they are sick or in trouble, are worthy of praise and love, even if they sometimes stray, even if they sometimes forget how. You are a good man, Pinocchio. Be good, and you'll remember happiness."

Before he could reply, Nancy banged on the roof of the cab, and the driver floored it. Pinocchio and George tumbled over each other to see Nancy—and the Capitol—disappear into nothingness behind the late-afternoon smog of the city.

They rode in silence for a moment as the weight of what Nancy said sank in. Her words were wise, and like all true wisdom, seemed almost familiar, as if he had heard that sentiment before. Pinocchio was still deep in thought when the cabbie finally asked where they were going. Choked with emotion, Pinocchio politely asked to be driven to the Weeping Pines Retirement Center.

CHAPTER 33

Pinocchio Rights a Great Wrong

Geppetto never used to sleep late, but something about the Weeping Pines Retirement Center just made him tired all the time. It might have been the heat. Old people, he observed, were always either too hot or too cold—the nurses erred on the frigid side and kept the place roasting, even in summer. There was also nothing to do here. He could only watch so much television, and none of the twelve-year-old magazines they had interested him. Depressed and bored, he often thought of his beloved tools. He would give anything to have them again. At least then he could carve something.

But that was not to be. The doctors were dead set against giving sharp objects to the "elderly and infirm" as they called him, so Geppetto had little else to do but smoke his pipe, stare out of the window, and sleep. It had been two months since the fire, and Geppetto was beginning to wonder if his son was right—perhaps he had outlived his useful days. Perhaps this home was the best thing for him, and he just needed to accept it.

Feeling another nap coming on, Geppetto set his pipe carefully in the ashtray before closing his eyes. He wasn't going to make that mistake again; God knows where he would end up this time!

While Geppetto's life had become dull and meaningless, at least in his dreams he could remember a time when it was not so. He could visit that place where all things are still possible, where past and present are one. There, he was young again, with an energetic, curious—and sometimes troublesome—little boy. They were back in Italy, back in the shop, before America, before Washington, before money and cars and watches, and before Pinocchio had forgotten that he loved his father. Every day and every night, Geppetto would go to the land of dreaming, and meet his son in that Great Beyond ...

* * *

"Look at him, Poppa," Pinocchio whispered. "He sleeps too much."

"Well I don't blame him," the roach replied. "It's a thousand degrees in here!"

Though hushed, the voices were rousing. Geppetto recognized them both—one from so many days ago, and one from so many years ago—so long ago that he was sure he was still dreaming. So certain was he, in fact, that he dared not open his eyes, lest the wonderful fantasy be taken from him. Instead, he lay perfectly still in his old rocker and asked through his bleary haze, "Is that Pinocchio?"

"Yes, Dad, it's me," Pinocchio answered. "I've come to take you home."

"And who is with you, son?"

"An old friend," was Poppa's reply.

Upon hearing his voice, Geppetto chanced to open his eyes, and they were met with the most handsome pair of smiling faces he had ever seen.

"Pinocchio! And yes, it is you, my old friend, the cricket!"

"He's a roach, Dad," Pinocchio corrected.

"He is?" Geppetto asked.

Pinocchio and Poppa nodded.

"Well, it is a pleasure to see you again in any case. What a wonderful dream this is!"

Pinocchio smiled. "You're not dreaming, Dad. We're really here. We've come to take you home."

The dreariness of sleep had given way to the blur of tears by the time Geppetto could bring himself to speak again. "Do you mean so, my boy?"

"Yes," Pinocchio answered. "I can't apologize enough for putting you in here. I want you to come back home with me."

Pinocchio reached out to help the old man from his rocking chair, but as Geppetto touched his arm, he recoiled. Not warm, pink flesh, but the hardness of sanded wood greeted him. He fumbled with his glasses and flipped on a lamp. The light shimmered off Pinocchio's painted eyes.

"Oh, my boy! But what day is it?" Geppetto asked.

"It's too late, Dad," was Pinocchio's reply.

"You mean the spell ...," Geppetto continued, to which Pinocchio only nodded. "Albero? Whitney?"

"They're safe," Pinocchio answered. "They're on their way to her mother's house."

"And that awful bill?"

"Pinocchio killed it," Poppa chimed in.

"But that old boss of yours!" Geppetto exclaimed.

Pinocchio reassured him, "He won't bother us anymore, Dad."

Geppetto looked his son over, then glanced quickly at the fine polish of his pipe, marveling at how well-made both were. He returned his gaze to Pinocchio, nodded, then took his hand. "You've done all you can, my boy. Well done. Well done. Now let's go home."

And with that, Geppetto bounded from his rocker and sprinted down the hall—past the moaning wheelchairs—with Pinocchio and Poppa racing to catch up. As he burst through the front door, a cool breeze smacked his face, bringing the pink back to his cheek and the smile back to his lips.

Pinocchio and Poppa were a moment behind him, out of breath. Geppetto turned to them and asked, "What's wrong, boy, forget how to walk?"

"Dad! I—I didn't know you had that much energy!"

"The time for rest is over!" Geppetto declared. "Come along. We've got to get you home. You've a big day tomorrow."

Confused, Pinocchio for a brief moment considered returning the old man to his room, but he knew Poppa would never stand for it. Besides, it seemed Geppetto had a few tricks up his sleeve today. They stepped into the waiting cab, which had helpfully kept the meter running.

Geppetto, still in his housecoat and slippers, patted the vinyl seat, turned to Pinocchio, and asked curiously, "What happened to your coupe?"

* * *

We are tired; we sleep. We are exhausted; we sleep. The difference, dear friends, is how we wake. To awaken after an exhausting adventure is to see the world anew, to be grateful to be alive, to at once want to leap up and gather fallen leaves, but at the same time to crave the softness of the sheets, the heaviness of the blankets, and the warmth of our bed. It had been days since Pinocchio had known sleep, and in that time he had swum an ocean, battled a whale, testified before Congress, and reorganized a company. Pinocchio had earned his rest, and he had welcomed it not minutes after he returned home that night, flipped on a few lights, and collapsed on his sofa. It had been many years since old Geppetto had carried the boy upstairs to bed, but with his son's wooden body as light as an empty seashell, that evening he did just that.

Geppetto also slept, but not until he had a few hours to share a delicious pipe with his roach friend, to hear stories about his son's great adventure, and to trade anecdotes about parenthood—a sacred rite shared by family patriarchs for many generations. All night the old fathers laughed and sipped brandy, while upstairs Pinocchio slept the sleep of a righteous man.

It was almost noon the next day when the sun finally pushed through the curtains and tickled Pinocchio to consciousness. Pinocchio curled under the blanket and breathed deep, heavy breaths. He could hear the faint sounds of the neighborhood beyond the window—lawn mowers, cars drifting lazily by, a sprinkler tapping against the corner of a driveway—but for this moment, all he wanted to do was lie down. It was finally nature's call that urged him out of bed, and bleary-eyed, he shuffled his way to the bathroom at the end of the hall. He kicked something heavy lying on the floor, vowing to pick it up when he returned. His knees didn't hurt as much this morning, and he was exceptionally hungry—which only made sense. He hadn't eaten in days.

He passed the guest room, stopping to peer in upon his father, still dressed in his housecoat and slippers, dozing quietly, a pipe lying carelessly on his chest, spilling black ash everywhere.

"Oh, Dad—," he muttered, only then noticing Poppa sleeping in a matchbox beside him, his own pipe lying on the floor where it had fallen.

As Pinocchio passed Albero's room, he paused for another moment. He pushed the door open, daring to imagine he would find his boy sound asleep in his bed—but the room was quite empty. A window had been left open, and leaves had blown in and curled themselves into a pile of Albero's clothes. Never more did Pinocchio feel the boy's absence. He crossed the room and pulled the window shut, pausing to observe the tree stump in the yard. But something was different about that stump this morning—it was dotted with color. Pinocchio squinted, rubbing the salty tears from his eyes as he focused. Indeed, two tiny saplings—little better than twigs—had sprouted up beside the old stump, each bearing a hint of green leaves.

"I'll be damned," he said to himself. He pulled the window closed, locked it, and promised to water the little plants later that day.

By the time he had reached the bathroom, the urge was overwhelming, and Pinocchio allowed himself the pleasure of a well-saved pee. When he was done, he washed in the sink, splashing water across his face, and wincing at the cool blast. His mouth tasted like an old ashtray. He poured himself a decent swallow of blue mouthwash and swirled it around, accidentally dripping a few drops from his cheek. He checked his reflection—he looked terrible. Stubble had given him a dark, scruffy look and his hair was a disturbed bird's nest. He shook his head, vowed a shower, and splashed more water on.

That's when he realized—puppets don't have hair.

He looked back at the reflection—stubble, hair. He stuck his tongue out—it was moist and soft. He felt his skin—clammy and pink, he watched how it pinched and bunched as he rubbed his fingers across it. He patted down the rest of his body, still afraid to believe it—muscle, bone, nail—it was all there!

He held his breath—he could breathe! But there was one last thing to check. His shirt was wrinkled and matted—apparently he had fallen asleep still dressed. He opened it, button by button, and dared not look as he slipped it open ... dark hair, soft flesh, a growing belly ... but no latch. He pressed his palm to his breast and was ecstatic to feel the *thump-thump* of a healthy, beating heart. He started breathing again, but only barely. He listened closely—*thump-thump!*

"DAD!" he cried.

Geppetto tumbled out of bed, spilling ashes to the ground as he raced down the hall.

"Dad!" Pinocchio repeated. "Get in here!"

Geppetto yanked open the door and beheld a breathtaking sight.

Pinocchio, disheveled and out of breath, stood naked in the bathroom, the water running behind him.

"Dad! Look at me!"

Geppetto could not help but comply. It took him a moment to bring to words what they were both seeing. Finally, he cried, "My boy, you're a real man again!"

He grabbed his son by the shoulders and pressed him into what may have been the most powerful "papa hug" a man has ever known. They laughed, and cried, and laughed some more. Finally, through streams of tears Pinocchio was able to ask,

"But how?"

"*You* did it, son!" Geppetto replied. "A righteous deed has been returned on you."

Geppetto took his son by the hand and stood, side by side with him, staring into the crisp, clean reflection in the mirror.

"Dad, I don't understand. The Fairy Queen said ..."

Geppetto laughed. "But it was not for the queen, was it? It was for you." Pinocchio turned from the mirror and looked at the smiling face of the proudest papa in the Western Hemisphere. "You earned it through your sacrifice, your honesty, and how you protected your family. This is what a man does, and it has brought you manhood again. Don't you see, my boy? What a lie can break, the truth can heal. Now look at you, you are healed!"

"Oh my God!" Poppa shouted. They turned to find him standing at the door.

"Isn't it amazing, Poppa?" Pinocchio asked.

"You're naked," Poppa replied.

"What's that?" Pinocchio asked.

"You're naked," Poppa repeated.

And indeed he was. Pinocchio grabbed a towel, wrapped it around himself and lifted the little bug into the air, dancing and spinning with all the joy he had ever known. Geppetto clapped along.

"I'm starving!" Pinocchio exclaimed. "And this time I'm really hungry!"

"Then I should make us breakfast!" Geppetto replied. "Go get dressed, boy, and let's eat!"

Pinocchio hurried back into his room, anxious to try on real clothes again. As he burst through the door, he froze. On the floor, right where he had kicked it, was the Swiss watch. Gold and glistening, ticking and tocking, it sat there, perfectly still. Pinocchio looked at it curiously, then with shame, then with anger. Placing it on the nightstand, he reached for the heaviest thing he could find, which happened to be an Italian loafer, reared back, and let fly!

The watch smashed into a million pieces. Stubbornly, and earning the reputation for quality that Charles Stevens had paid so dearly for, it continued to count for a few more seconds, until a second volley silenced its mocking tick forever.

Pinocchio placed the shoe gently on the ground, opened the nightstand drawer and removed the box the Swiss watch had come in. Inside sat a rather simple, rather garish old Japanese digital that still ticked away, though without the grace or precision of its former contemporary. It was the watch Whitney had given him so many years ago, and to Pinocchio's eyes, it was the (second) most beautiful sight he had seen that morning. He slipped it on, and began to get dressed. The sound of a voice stopped him. It was a sweet voice, a familiar voice, a *lady's* voice.

"You look wonderful," she said.

With everything Pinocchio had been through that morning, he refused to believe his own ears, and as he turned, he refused to believe his own eyes ...

Looking lovelier than Pinocchio could possibly have imagined or remembered, there, in the doorway stood Whitney. They endured a tense moment known only to lovers who have fought and met again, too afraid to touch each other, but too terrified not to. Finally, Pinocchio broke the distance and took her up into a passionate embrace. Any resistance she had thought to offer on the flight home melted away as his arms wrapped around her waist and his lips met her cheek. The anger, the fear, and the resentment that had washed the love from her heart over the last two months lay shattered on the floor along with the remains of the old Swiss timepiece. In that moment, more so than any she had shared with the man she married, Pinocchio was her world. It went without saying that she was his, so of course Pinocchio decided to shout it.

Finally, after what seemed like minutes, she broke away, ran her fingers across his face, and grabbed his chin firmly in her hands.

"You hurt me, Pinny."

He tried to apologize, but a stern look told him it was the time to listen, not to speak. She continued, "I wondered, for a while, if I could ever find my way back to loving you. Cassandra told me everything that happened."

Again, words came to him, only to be silenced by a finger pressed to his lips. "But so did Poppa, and George, and your father." Finally, a smile crested her lips. "And I saw the testimony. You made me proud, Pinocchio. You made Albero proud. You showed me the way back. I love you, Pinocchio."

Finally, she released him and braced for the words to come—Pinocchio had a knack for saying too much at the wrong moment—but it seemed that a lot of old habits died that morning, for all he had to say, all he could say, all he wanted to say was, "I love you too."

And as he pulled her in for yet another embrace, his eyes beheld what was by far the *most* beautiful thing he saw on that morning of beautiful sights, or any morning before or after—for in the hallway, watching with some confusion the events of that strange day, was young Albero.

Pinocchio released Whitney, and kneeled, beckoning his son to come closer. For a moment he hesitated, but when he saw the sparkle in his father's smile, and the tear in his eye, any question he had was swept away and he ran into his father's arms with all the speed of a sprinter. Pinocchio lifted him up, readying himself for the greatest, strongest papa hug he had ever given. But Pinocchio was in for a surprise that morning, for with a strength no child had ever before known, it was Albero who did the squeezing today. He squeezed his father's neck such that had Pinocchio not been a strong man, accustomed to the squeeze of his son, he might choke. Pinocchio squeezed back, and was amused to find his own strength did not match that of his boy's.

"You've got it!" Pinocchio managed to wheeze out.

"What?" Albero asked.

"The papa hug!" Pinocchio answered.

Without letting go, Albero corrected him. "No. That's given to papas. This is the 'daddy hug,' and it's given to daddies."

And it is fair to say, my friends, that of all the titles ever bestowed on all the kings, presidents, generals, and executives ever since society first saw fit to grant them, none was ever more heartily won than the one acquired that morning by a simple man in a Virginia suburb. None would ever more proudly wear it either, for you see, my friends, all his life Pinocchio had wanted to be *somebody*. Now he finally was.

Pinocchio was a *daddy*.

"At last, Pinocchio was somebody!"

Epilogue

In the months that followed, Pinocchio remained, for a short time anyway, a topic of some conversation around the country—as fascinating to the scientists who sought to explain his existence as he was to the conspiracists who denied it.

Never one to turn down publicity, George took the opportunity to muscle his way onto any and every news program that would have him. Within a week, he had accepted what he called the "inevitability" of his fame and headed for Hollywood. For months afterward Pinocchio would get excited calls from the new thespian whose career was off to a slow, though George assured him, promising start. They would talk, and laugh, and reminisce about old times until George finally came right out and asked for some money. Of course,

Pinocchio never turned him down. His support paid off one day when, while watching a popular nurse-and-doctor drama, Pinocchio caught a glimpse of a bedridden patient with a familiar smirk—and a seven-foot pair of wings. George had finally made it as an actor, though it was a nonspeaking character, which made it the most challenging role the Englishman would ever play. It was a small step, but as Poppa was fond of saying, "A small step for a man is an insurmountable leap for an insect," and who are we, my friends, to judge the dreams of insects?

For his part, Poppa had accepted the queen's offer and returned to The Great Beyond to raise his family in the warmth of the tropics. Pinocchio had resigned himself to never seeing his dear friend again, so he was more than surprised one day when he received a phone call from the little roach. After all, The Great Beyond may be a mythical land reachable only in the infinite possibility of dreams, but it still got great reception. Pinocchio listened excitedly as Poppa talked about their new life and of the children, how many of whom were already married and raising families of their own. Poppa, it turned out, was now a *Grand-Poppa*! And little Squeak? Poppa told how he had sprouted in his adolescence, now towering over his father by a full eighth of an inch (though his voice change made the little bug's nickname perfectly prophetic). Though he was too busy to talk, as all teenagers—man and bug alike—seem to be, Poppa assured Pinocchio that young Squeak often asked about him, and also about George. It seems that of all the bonds formed on that strange journey so many years ago, the unlikeliest, yet still the strongest, was the one between the tiny insect who longed to fly, and the drunken Englishman who did.

Geppetto stayed with his son's family for a while, not knowing that Pinocchio had secretly purchased for his father a cozy three-room cottage at the foot of what passed for a mountain in Virginia. The surprise with which his son had presented his new home was overwhelming, but what waited inside was enough to move the old man to tears, for the garage had been stocked from floor to roof with all manner of chisels, saws, jigs, lathes, and sanders—each glistening new, and each of superb quality. It was a workshop suited to a master, far superior to any Geppetto had worked in before. But, as old fathers often do, Geppetto at first refused the gift as too opulent, before finally surrendering to Pinocchio's insistence. It would be a waste of space otherwise, Pinocchio argued, as neither one of them owned a car anymore.

As for The Kronos Group, though it would never again reach the heights of power it had known under Charles Stevens, for a while it remained a potent force in Washington, fighting often, but not always, in favor of just and righteous causes. Though Nancy preferred to keep her clientele exclusive, The Kronos Group remained a business with financial needs that more often than not precluded its idealistic ones. Before long, old clients began to leave, and new ones were becoming hard to find. Eventually, The Kronos Group stopped growing altogether, flickering and dying as its young talent moved to more important positions with more important corporations. When Nancy finally retired five years later, The Kronos Group shuttered its doors for good. Few in the media, and even fewer in the industry, noticed that the first—and last—of the great lobbyists had disappeared. K Street, like Madison Avenue, was but a symbol now—a sentimental monument to an idealism long since changed, evolved, and evermore confined to the realm of corporate myth.

After the firm closed, Cassandra married a handsome young attorney and left Washington so they could start their own practice. Though she would never tell anyone, in quiet moments she would reminisce about the young puppet she once loved and about the adventure they shared. She marveled at how her feelings for him came so quickly back to her heart—like a fire rekindled, though it faded back to embers the moment she heard the voices of her children in the next room. In these moments Cassandra knew she would never truly be "over" Pinocchio. He was, after all, most unique among men. He had changed her life so profoundly by doing so little, while many others had done much, yet changed nothing. She would always be thankful to him, and he to her, for in the end she recognized the importance of keeping distant, and thus they allowed their friendship to survive on legacy alone.

Yes, my friends, these fantastic events changed everyone who lived through them, but none more than Pinocchio himself—much more than physically, much more than financially. Gone was the boy who had lied without knowing consequence. Gone too was the adolescent who hid when the consequence became clear. Pinocchio was truly a man now, and as men are wont to do, Pinocchio had made many mistakes. But he vowed that he would never again hide from what he had done, never deny it, or spin it, or cover it up, for he had learned that to do so gives strength to the sin. Instead, as he had come to understand through bitter tears (and desperate prayers) during that terrifying journey across the ocean, the only way to take the power away from a wrong is to own it. In this way, that which man has broken, man can also mend.

And even after all it had put him through, Pinocchio never lost the taste for policymaking. After leaving The Kronos Group, he waded into the much more rewarding (by which, I mean lower-paying) world of nonprofits. There, he continued the fight for the cause to which he would forever after be linked—environmental rights. Gone were the cul-de-sac house, the German coupe, and the Swiss watch. The humble lobbyist now called a two-bedroom flat his home, a rickety old train his transportation, and for timekeeping he turned to the same rubber-coated digital watch given to him in college by his wife. It was a simple life, but one he wouldn't trade for the entire world.

And I know what you're thinking, my friends—this is all well and good, but what happened to the reporter? Well, as it turns out Max Wiggs had a Pulitzer-worthy story on his hands with his coverage of the Kronos Affair—or as the wags dubbed it, "Splintergate." But in a strange twist of fate, the paper ended up burying the story. The editors, it seems, had bought into the growing theory that these events as I have relayed them to you never actually happened. Yes, my friends, despite the millions of views on Internet clip sites, despite the fact of Pinocchio's testimony in the congressional record, despite all the evidence to the contrary, in the end, the people simply refused to believe such a fantastic tale. Men are quite fickle that way, and it is ultimately their curse that they forget.

But I won't let you forget, my friends, for I have seen these events with my own eyes, and I can tell you that they are true. Animals do indeed talk, fairies do indeed exist, and a puppet once changed the course of history, if even for a moment.

That's why I have laid these events down for you in this book you have just read. The paper may have buried my story, but it's still a wonderful tale (and nomination committee, take note), still Pulitzer-worthy.

And when all was said and done, Pinocchio's name finally left the world of history and returned to the world of fairy tale, for some say it is there that Pinocchio truly belongs. Perhaps no one believes that more than the man himself.

Not too far from the little flat the Pinocchios call home is a park, and in that park grows a small grove of maple trees. For the past nineteen months the trees watched as the strange little man, whom they all agreed looked quite familiar, had gone to and fro, busying himself with this business or that. Often they would lean in together and discuss this little man, agreeing that people were very odd indeed, for their lives were filled with such uncertainty, and such fear, and such excitement, and such adventure. Such a life is foolishness compared to the solid, predictable lives of trees, and as such they agreed to pay the little man no more mind, choosing to focus instead on things much more important, such as the rise of the sun and the fall of the rain.

But the decision was not quite unanimous. For one little branch on one little tree watched the little man and saw something else—he wasn't sure what it was, but he was intrigued by it. For you see, this little branch had always been a curious and inquisitive sort ...

"Greetings from Hollywood!"

ENJOYED THE BOOK?
PLEASE LEAVE A REVIEW

Reviews are the lifeblood of independent authors.

If *Splintered* entertained you—or even challenged you—would you consider leaving a brief review on Amazon?

It doesn't have to be long.
A sentence or two makes a difference.

Your review helps new readers discover the book and keeps independent satire alive.

Thank you for supporting original fiction.

—THOMAS LONDON

JOIN THE THOMAS LONDON INNER CIRCLE

If you've just finished *Splintered: A Political Fairy Tale*, thank you.

This story began as satire but soon became something sharper.

Pinocchio's struggle isn't about politics. It's about identity—the lies we tell ourselves long before we tell them to anyone else. I think that's something we all can relate to.

So if the story made you laugh, wince, or recognize something uncomfortably familiar—then as an author, I did my job, and I'd appreciate the chance to do so again.

Please join my private mailing list and you'll receive:

- Early access to new releases
- Exclusive short fiction
- Behind-the-scenes research notes
- Advance reader opportunities
- Occasional commentary I can't post anywhere else

Sign up at:

www.ThomasLondonBooks.com

No spam. No nonsense. Just stories worth your time.

MORE BOOKS
BY THOMAS LONDON

The Masada Option

A vanished CIA contractor.
A buried Cold War secret.
A city reduced to ash.

When disgraced historian Ethan Falk is pulled into a decades-old conspiracy, he uncovers a weapon designed to end nations—and a second device still waiting to detonate.

Hunted by intelligence agencies and terrorists alike, Falk must expose the truth before history repeats itself in nuclear fire.

Fast. Smart. Disturbingly plausible.

If you enjoy high-stakes geopolitical thrillers with moral tension and historical depth, *The Masada Option* is your next read.

Available now at Amazon.

ABOUT THE AUTHOR

Splintered: A Political Fairy Tale is the debut novel of playwright and award-winning screenwriter Thomas London.

A veteran of the Armed Services, Mr. London holds an M.A. in Entertainment Business and frequently writes about history, power, and the persistent illusion of control. His work reflects a belief that while circumstances may change, human behavior tends to remain stubbornly familiar. Mr. London currently resides in Los Angeles, where this theory is tested daily.

Mr. London's second novel, the pulse-pounding thriller *The Masada Option*, is available now.

www.ingramcontent.com/pod-product-compliance
Lightning Source LLC
LaVergne TN
LVHW100506110826
845146LV00002B/540

* 9 7 9 8 9 9 3 2 1 8 9 1 5 *